A STARBOUND NOVEL

THEIR FRACTURED LIGHT

Amie Kaufman & Meagan Spooner

Hyperion
Los Angeles New York

Copyright © 2015 by Amie Kaufman and Meagan Spooner

All rights reserved. Published by Hyperion, an imprint of Disney Book Group.
No part of this book may be reproduced or transmitted in any form or by any means, electronic or mechanical, including photocopying, recording, or by any information storage and retrieval system, without written permission from the publisher. For information address Hyperion, 125 West End Avenue, New York, New York 10023.

First Hardcover Edition, December 2015
First Paperback Edition, December 2016
1 3 5 7 9 10 8 6 4 2
FAC-025438-16295
Printed in the United States of America

This book is set in Garamond
Designed by Whitney Manger and Marci Senders

Library of Congress Cataloging-in-Publication Control Number: 2015027948
ISBN 978-1-4847-4783-4

Visit www.hyperionteens.com

SUSTAINABLE
FORESTRY
INITIATIVE
Certified Chain of Custody
Promoting Sustainable Forestry
www.sfiprogram.org
SFI-01054
The SFI label applies to the text stock

For Josie Spooner and Flic Kaufman, our sisters and very first partners in crime, whose imaginations helped set us on the path of storytelling all those years ago.

A ripple.

The stillness quakes and splits and where once there was nothing, only us, there is something new. Bright and hard and cold and skimming the surface of the stillness, the new thing is there only an instant before it is gone again.

But we gather. And we watch. And we wait, because there has never been anything new before, and we want to see it again.

ONE

SOFIA

THE DAPPLED SUNLIGHT THROUGH THE GRASS IS BEAUTIFUL, though I know it's not real. The light casts no warmth on my skin; I'll suffer no burns, no freckles. The grass doesn't bend under my feet, though they sink through it to the marble floor beneath the holographic images. A year ago I would have gasped aloud at the sight of sun and blue skies, even holographic ones, but today I find they just make me miss home. What I'd give, now, to lift my head and see bruise-colored clouds sweeping down to meet the marsh, a vastness to the horizon that no holographic lobby in an office building could hope to replicate.

The holosuite is full of people, and while many of them seem to be employees here at LaRoux Industries Headquarters, others are harder to pinpoint. Some carry old-timey briefcases in a nod to ancient vintage fashion from 1920s Earth, the current fad among the upper crust. Others sport only their palm pads; the affectation of carrying purses and cases is absurd, when everything that would've gone inside—money, documents, telephones, identification cards—was digitalized hundreds of years ago.

But the trend does make it easy to carry around everything I need without anyone asking questions. Only a couple years ago I would've been stuck in pseudo-Victorian garb if I wanted to be fashionable, hiding the tools of my trade under an unwieldy skirt. As it is, my tea dress is light, easy to run in if necessary, and—most importantly—an airy, innocent ivory lace that makes me look even younger than seventeen. I tuck my handbag close to my body, taking a deep breath and scanning the throngs of people.

There's a tension in the air that makes my pulse quicken. It's subtle—those hiding here in plain sight are doing so flawlessly. *Almost.* But I grew up on Avon, and I know how to read a crowd. I know how quickly a protest turns into a riot—I know how quickly a peaceful town becomes a battlefield.

I don't know if the vast security network at LaRoux Industries is aware of the underground protests scheduled to occur today. I only know about them because I was told by one of my contacts in Corinth Against Tyranny—a ridiculous name, but it's a romantic notion to fight the good fight against the oppressors. Looking around the holosuite outfitted with lemonade dispensers and sodas whizzing here and there on hover trays, the air littered with conversation and laughter, I can't help but think that these people don't know what oppression is. I tear my eyes away from a couple indulgently watching a child of five or six chasing a pair of holographic birds through the air. There's a reason LaRoux Industries tops the "best places to work in the galaxy" list every year, and if I'd been the one organizing today's protest, I certainly wouldn't have chosen the new twentieth-floor holosuite as the setting.

Free for employees, and available to the public for only a small charge, the holosuite is part of LaRoux's new outreach program. "See how generous I am?" he's saying. "I'm dedicating whole floors of my headquarters to providing safe, fun places for you and your children." His campaign to make the galaxy love him, to make people forget the accusations leveled at him in the Avon Broadcast, is enough to turn my stomach—not least because it's working.

The people here do seem happy. No one here cares that people were dying on Avon before Flynn Cormac's now-infamous speech a year ago. Nobody cares that Roderick LaRoux is a monster—mostly because only small pockets of people here and there actually believed a word of Flynn's broadcast. These people are here because it looks good on their media pages to say they were at a protest. Some of them are probably hoping to get arrested so they can later post their mug shots on the hypernet.

But it *does* make a great distraction for what I'm here to do.

I have only a name for the contact I'm meeting—Sanjana Rao—and though it speaks of family roots in old India, it's just as likely she could be blond-haired and blue-eyed, given the way all the races and bloodlines from Earth have been jumbled up over the centuries. She'll ping my palm pad when she's here, but I can't help but look for her anyway.

I find my gaze creeping toward the elevator doors, cleverly concealed in this park simulation as the entrance to a carousel. This is the closest I've been to LaRoux himself after a year of chasing him, and all I want to do is break into their secure elevators and climb to the penthouse floor. A year of burned identities and isolation; of painful tattoo removal surgeries that still haven't completely erased my genetag; of keeping all traces of myself, all remnants of my old life, with me at all times in case today, this moment, is the one where I'm going to have to pack up and run again.

But LaRoux himself is nearly impossible to reach. If he wasn't, someone would've already killed him years ago—for all that the galaxy at large loves him, enough of the people he's trampled on his way to power see him for what he is. No, a head-on approach will never reach him. Taking out LaRoux requires subtlety.

I glance at my inner arm, a habit I still haven't broken. Someone clever could guess at what the look means—no one born on Corinth or any of the older planets is given a genetag at birth—and yet I do it anyway. The faint remnant of my genetag tattoo is safely hidden, though I have to take care not to rub against my dress and risk transferring a telltale smear of concealer to the fabric. I want to grab for my palm pad, to check it to see if I could have missed Dr. Rao's ping, but standing here repeatedly checking my messages would be a clear sign of nervousness, if anyone was watching me.

It's only when I lift my head that I realize I *do* have an audience. And that it isn't my contact.

A young man's seated on the floor, his back against a tree—a tree that isn't really there, of course. His back is against a marble pillar, but the holographic skin of the room makes it look like he's relaxing in a park. Except, of course, that he's got a lapscreen and it's plugged into the side of the tree. There's a wireless power field here, so I know he's not charging his screen. It's a data port, which is odd enough, given that any info accessible in a public place like this would be on the hypernet. But that's not what makes me stop, makes my heart seize. It's that he's wearing the green and gray of LaRoux Industries, and that there's a lambda embroidered over his breast pocket. He works here—and he's watching me. My mouth goes dry, and I force myself not to jerk my gaze away. Instead I tip my head as if puzzled, trying my absolute best to seem intrigued, even coy.

A grin flashes across his features when I catch him watching me. He makes no attempt to pretend he wasn't, just flicks his fingers to his brow and then away as though tipping an imaginary hat. He doesn't look like a typical office worker, with longer hair of a shade hovering somewhere between sandy blond and brown and a lazy, almost insolent cast to his body as he leans against the pillar.

I take a breath to settle, hiding any trace of fear that he knows I don't belong here. Instead I smile back, settling easily into the façade of shy and sweet; to my relief, his grin widens. Just flirting, then.

He winks, then presses a single button on his lapscreen. A holographic bird with brilliant red plumage swoops across my path and then freezes in midair. Abruptly, all the background sounds halt: birdsong and rustling leaves and even some of the laughter and conversation—all gone. Then, without warning, the entire holopark vanishes, leaving us in a vast white room.

The only thing in the room, besides the people, the projectors, and the pillars like the one the boy's leaning on, is a vast metal ring twice my height at its center. It stands upright, made of some strange alloy that shines dully in the bright white light, and is connected to the floor at its base by a pedestal covered with dials and instruments. LaRoux's particular holographic technologies are proprietary, but this looks like no projector I've ever seen—and while the other projectors are flickering and whirring and trying to overcome whatever glitch made them stop working, the metal ring is still and silent.

A murmur of confusion sweeps through the throngs of people, as groups abandon their conversations in favor of looking around, as though the room might hold some explanation. Its other features stand out now that there's no masking hologram in place—the drink dispensers are bare and stark, the various projectors and speakers littering the low ceiling like misshapen stars.

Whatever's going on, it wasn't planned by the protesters. Everyone, employees and public alike, is milling around in confusion. If it were planned, the protesters would be using the glitch to launch their protest, but instead even the security guards at the edges of the room look unnerved. I let my eyes widen, using a group of interns as cover to move as quietly and purposelessly as I can toward the emergency stairwell. If I'm caught, the worst they'll assume of me is that I was here to protest. But I'd rather not get in their books at all.

Before I can make it to the fire exit, a flicker of color grabs my eye and I turn in time to see the boy with the lapscreen pull a chip the size of his fingernail out of his screen and stow it in his pocket. Glancing up at the ceiling, he gets up and takes two slow, easy steps to the side, neatly placing himself in the security camera's blind spot.

Then he's shrugging out of his LaRoux Industries uniform until he's just wearing an undershirt, tattooed arms bare for half an instant. He turns the garment inside out, revealing a garishly striped shirt matching the high-fashion trend of the moment—and just like that, he melts into the crowd. No longer an employee of LaRoux Industries.

And far, far too clever to be one of the protesters now milling around, confused and annoyed that they never got their chance to get on the news.

"Ladies and gentlemen, your attention please." A voice, smooth as cream and amplified over the noise of the crowd, emerges from the speakers. "We've detected a security breach and traced its source to this room. Please remain calm, and cooperate with all security officers to the fullest extent, and we will have this resolved as soon as possible."

The security guards, operating on some order given via the implants in their ears, have started funneling people off one by one, presumably to interrogate them individually. One of the guards is still standing by the door, blocking the exit to the stairwell—blocking my escape route. The concealer on my arm might fool a quick glance from someone at the front desk, but now I have no chance of passing myself off as a protester—a security breach will have them on high alert. The first thing those guards will do when they grab me is check for a genetag tattoo, certain that border planet insurgents are the most likely culprits. I close my eyes, calling up the floor plans I've been studying for a week and a half. They'll have shut down access to the elevators on this floor, but there's another fire exit and another set of stairs through one of the hallways leading off from here. I scan the crowds until I find that exit, and the guard ushering people in that direction.

What I need is a diversion.

My eyes fall on a loud, red-and-gold striped shirt. Whoever the boy is, he's not from LaRoux Industries, and he's not supposed to be here either. And while I can't be sure that keystroke of his is what took down the holo-projectors, I do know that if we get grabbed together, he's the one who's going to look far more suspicious than I am once they realize he's got an LRI uniform sewn into his clothes. I mutter a curse under my breath and rush forward to the guard's side.

Sorry, Handsome. I'm pretty sure you want to be center of attention just about as much as I do. But if there's one person here in more trouble than me, it's the guy with the fake LaRoux Industries uniform on under his shirt.

"That boy there," I say, keeping my voice low, forcing my eyes wide. "I think he needs help." With any luck, they'll go check on him and I can slip out once they discover he's not supposed to be here.

The guard's gaze swings around immediately to rest on the boy in the striped shirt, who's watching us with a slight edge to his nonchalant air. His smile dies away entirely as the guard takes two steps toward him, and I ease my weight back, the first step toward the door the man was guarding. *Slowly, slowly, don't draw attention.*

As if my thought was spoken aloud, the guard reaches out to wrap a hand around my arm. "Show me," he orders. I freeze, and, to make matters worse, he lifts his hand to signal to one of the other heavies over in our direction. Now I've got two guards watching me, and the door's about to be blocked again. *Damn it.* If they make me go with them, they may well assume I'm *with* him when they discover his fake LRI shirt. Now I have to get us both out of here.

Good work, Sofia.

My mind throws up a flurry of possibilities, and in a split second I sort through them, discarding the impossible, left with only one way to divert both of them to the boy.

"Please hurry," I gasp, focusing the muscles in my face until my eyes start to water with tears. "He's my fiancé—he has a condition, stress makes it worse." In the confusion, with so many people to process, I can only hope the guard doesn't want to ask too many questions.

The guard blinks at me and, when I turn to indicate the boy in the striped shirt, follows my gesture. The boy stares back, openly wary now, eyes flicking from the guard to my face. *Please,* I think. *Just don't say anything until I can get past them.*

"You were both fine a minute ago." He exchanges glances with his colleague, who's standing by me now. "I'm sure it can wait." His voice is even, giving not an inch, but his hand strays, shifting from the weapon at his waist to tug at his sleeve.

I double my efforts, forcing my voice to crack. "Please," I echo. "I'll stay, I'll answer any questions you want. Just go check him and you'll see, he needs a doctor or else he's going to have an episode." I just need both the guards to turn toward the boy long enough for me to slip through the exit, uncounted and unescorted.

The nearer guard's weight shifts, making my breath catch, but he doesn't move as they exchange glances again. "I'll call for the medtech on duty," he says finally. "But he looks fine."

My mind races, scanning the guard for anything I can use. He's in his forties—too savvy, probably, for me to flirt my way out, especially when I already used the fiancé cover. No signs on his clothes of pets or children, nothing I can use to establish any connection with him, any appeal to his humanity. I'm about to go for my last resort—the little-girl wail of hysterics—when, without warning, the boy with the lapscreen sways and drops to the ground with a moan.

Both guards gape, and for half a second, I'm as stunned as they are. The boy on the ground twitches, limbs quivering, looking like he's having exactly the kind of fit I'd been warning them about. For a quick, searing moment I wonder if somehow my lie stumbled upon something like the truth—but I can't afford to find out. I'm just about to bolt for the exit when the nearest guard sticks his hand between my shoulder blades and pushes me forward. "Do something!" His own eyes are looking a little wild.

Damn. Damn. DAMN. Still, if I end up in an ambulance with this guy, it'll be better than ending up in an interrogation room at LRI Headquarters. The EMTs will scan the ident chip in my palm pad, but the name they'll get from that is Alexis. And they won't be looking for genetags. I drop to my knees at the stranger's side, reaching for his twitching hand and curling my fingers through his as though I'm used to touching him. One guard's talking hurriedly into a patch on his vest, summoning backup, doctors, some kind of support.

The guy's fingers tighten around mine, making my eyes jerk toward his face—and abruptly, all my simulated tears and panic come to a screeching halt. He's actually starting to foam at the mouth, eyes rolled back into his head. He can't be that much older than I am, and there's something definitely, dangerously wrong with him.

One of the security guards is trying to ask me questions—has he eaten anything recently, when did he last take his medication, what's his condition called—in order to brief the EMTs on their way. But his voice trails off as another sound rises from the center of the room, quickly growing in volume and causing the other nervous conversations in the room to peter out. The metal ring, the one the holo-projectors had been concealing, is turning itself on.

A number of lights along the base come to life, indicating that there's data to be read now from the displays there, and the panels overhead lighting the room flicker as though the ring is drawing too much power. But neither of those things is what's made the entire roomful of people go silent.

Little flickers of blue light start to race around the edge of the ring, appearing and vanishing as though weaving directly through the metal. They move faster as the sound of the machine coming to life intensifies and smooths out, until the entire edge of the ring is crawling with blue fire.

A hand on my arm jerks my attention away, my heart pounding as I look down.

The boy is beside me, raising one eyebrow. "Care to tell me when the wedding is, darling?" His voice is barely audible, words spoken without moving his lips.

I blink. "What?" I'm so thrown I can't find my balance.

The boy glances at the security guard nearest us, whose attention is completely absorbed by the machinery in the center of the room, and then back at me. He wipes the remnants of foam from his mouth and then props himself up on his elbows. "Think maybe we should start the honeymoon a little early." This time his whisper carries an edge, and he jerks his chin meaningfully toward the emergency exit.

Whoever he is, whatever he was doing here, right now we want exactly the same thing: to get out of here. And that's enough for me. I can always lose him later.

I give him a hand up—the guard doesn't even look in our direction—and slip back toward the exit. We reach the door just as a flash of blue light illuminates the white walls before us. While the boy in the striped shirt fumbles with the door, I glance over my shoulder.

The flickers of light around the edges of the ring are now reaching toward the center, tongues of blue sparks snapping out and vanishing, like lightning-fast stellar flares. Every now and then they meet with a tremendous flash of light—until finally the entire center of the ring is filled with light, crackling like a curtain of energy.

While I watch, a man standing near the ring collapses, sinking to the floor without a sound. I'm waiting for the people nearest him to react, to rush to his side and break the spell of fascination, but they're all motionless, slack, like machines whose power's been cut. More and more people are going still and silent with every passing second, security guards and protesters alike, in an expanding circle around the device at the room's center. Every now and then another person drops to the floor, but most are standing still, upright, casting long shadows that flicker and reach toward us as the machine fires.

In between flashes of light, I can make out the faces of those on the other side—I can see their eyes.

And in that instant I'm standing on a military base on Avon, watching my father change in front of me. I'm seeing his eyes, multiplied a dozen times over in the faces around me, pupils so wide the eyes look like pools of ink, like the starless expanse of night over the swamps. I'm reliving the moment my father walked into a military barracks with an explosive strapped to his body. I'm remembering him as he was the last time I ever saw him, a shadow of himself, nothing more than a husk where his soul used to be.

There are hundreds of people still dotting the white expanse of the holosuite—and every single one of them has eyes like darkness.

At first, there is nothing more. And then come symbols that look like this:

TESTING.

Then come more words, followed by images and sounds and colors. Bit by bit the stillness floods with this new kind of life, and we begin to understand the strings of symbols and sounds that pierce the stillness. The hard, bright, cold things come more and more often, leaving ripples in the stillness, gathering up the fabric of existence in waves as they skip through the surface of the world.

TWO

GIDEON

YOU'D THINK I'D KNOW TO STAY AWAY FROM TROUBLE BY now. But here I am, my mouth tasting like a SysCleanz tablet, bolting down a hallway, sucked into this fiasco by a pair of dimples. One of these years, I really have to get smarter.

The girl just in front of me is slender, at least a head shorter than me, in one of those dresses all the rich girls are wearing right now. She's got a mean turn of speed on her despite the heels. To add to the dimples, she's got pale blond hair to just below her chin, tousled into an artful mess, and big, gray eyes.

Yeah, *smarter* ain't showing up anytime soon.

"I'm really hoping there's a part two of your plan, mastermind," I gasp, as we pound down the hallway together.

"What did you *do* back there?" Her eyes are even huger than they were before, true fear making her voice shake and chasing away my amusement in an instant. She had a better view of what was going on, and whatever she saw has left this girl—this girl who barely batted an eye when I started foaming at the mouth right in front of her—completely shaken.

"That wasn't me." I glance over my shoulder, half expecting some of the security guards to round the corner on our tail. "Though I'm flattered you think it was."

I'm about to continue when she grabs a handful of my shirt, using my momentum to shove me into an alcove housing emergency fire supplies without breaking stride. I slam into the wall and she slams into my back, and since I figure she had some reason for steering me this way beyond a desire to see me hurt, I hold still. A moment later, voices are audible around the corner, and they sound pissed. *Good spotting, Dimples.*

"We need a diversion," she whispers, one hand around my neck to yank my head down so she can whisper in my ear, which isn't at *all* distracting. "Can you send them somewhere else?"

"What makes you think I can do that?" I'm already pulling out my lapscreen from my satchel, but I'm interested to hear how she made me.

"Please," she mutters. "Maybe you didn't turn on that machine, but I know you're the one who shut off the projectors."

Huh. Well, at least she was watching me, that's a start. I should try asking her out for a drink later. If we're not dead or arrested.

I wriggle around until I'm facing her, and judging by the way her lips thin, she's all ready to pour cold water on the idea of getting this up close and personal, until she realizes I'm doing it—mostly—because I need room to get my screen in front of me. "Let's give them something to go look at," I mutter, pulling the activation chip from my pocket and sliding it into the port on the side of the screen.

"What are you going to do?" she asks.

"Would you understand if I answered that?" I bring the screen to life, and as always, a faint but heady buzz kicks in as I write my own invitation into the LaRoux Industries core and start the hunt for my dance partner. *Not a bad system, but not good enough.*

She huffs a breath. "No," she admits. "I don't do computers. People make more sense to me." She sure worked those guys back in the holosuite like she knows where to find the buttons and levers in people's brains—and though I couldn't quite hear, I'm pretty sure she was trying to throw me under the bus until the guards made it clear she'd be joining me there. Still, I can't really blame her—it was a tight spot, and all's fair in love, war, and criminal trespassing.

"People, huh?" I find the trail I need, and start work.

"Think of them as computers with organic circuits." I can tell from her tone the dimples are back. I'd like to say I don't notice how close she's pressed against me in the shelter of the alcove, but that would be a waste. I mean, she clearly *wants* me to notice, and I try to help folks out when I can. "So if people make more sense to you . . . tell me what kind of sense I make."

"What, you show me yours and I'll show you mine?" She shakes her head, bemused. "I really did just come to meet someone. When the projectors went down and the guards started hauling people away, I picked you for a diversion because I saw you change your shirt. I thought maybe you weren't supposed to be here either, so you'd probably play along."

Boring. Not the real story. Someone like her doesn't come here without a very good reason. Even *I* don't come here without a good reason—the fact that I'm leaving this monumental screw-up without any new info on the whereabouts of Commander Antje Towers just adds salt to the wound. But my hunt for the former LaRoux Industries pawn will have to wait. I snort to let Dimples know I'm not buying her cover story, and find the components I'm looking for. Nearly ready to get my party started.

She pauses, nibbling her lip again as I glance at her profile. "How *did* you play along?" she asks. "How'd you make yourself froth like that?"

I run my tongue over my teeth, wrinkling my nose at the taste lingering in my mouth. "SysCleanz tab. Drop it into decontaminated water, it makes up a solution for cleaning some circuits that need an alkaline mix. Chew on it without water, which is not recommended on the packaging, and it feels like your mouth's exploding."

"Huh." She sounds grudgingly impressed, and I'd bet my boots she's filing that one away in case she needs it.

"Got a name, my wife-to-be?" I ask, pressing my advantage.

"Alexis."

"Nice to meet you, Alexis." *You don't mind if I stick with Dimples, do you? I mean, that's not your real name either.*

"And you are?"

"Sam Sidoti," I say, and this time it's her turn to eyeball me.

"Sam*antha* Sidoti anchors the late-night news on SDM," she points out. "And she's a woman."

"Busted." I peek up from my work, and she looks back at me over her shoulder, and it turns out making that little line show up between her brows is almost as fun as looking at the dimples. "I'm nearly done. Seems like we should have a plan for after our friends out there start heading for where the emergency will be kicking off in about a minute. Or is the plan that you go your way, and I go mine?"

She's quiet for several beats, though I can't tell whether she's weighing her options or just listening for approaching footsteps. "It's less likely we'll be stopped if we split up," she says slowly, her eyes on my hands as I key in the last few commands, fingers racing over the screen. Then her tone firms. "But I've got an access card for the fire stairs, and there aren't any security cameras there. If you want to come with me, you can."

Well, isn't that *interesting?* I power down the lapscreen with a press of my thumb against the print scanner, then pull out the chip to stow it in my pocket. "I like a girl who commits to a relationship. So hard to find these days." I ease my neck from side to side and roll my shoulders a couple of times—pretending to throw a fit really tenses things up—and tug my shirt straight.

"Well?" she presses. "Is it done?"

I lift one hand—can't resist a bit of showmanship—count to five in my head, and snap my fingers.

And all hell breaks loose.

The hallway's flooded with the wail of an emergency siren, so though I can see her mouth moving, I can't hear a word over the klaxons. I choose to believe she's complimenting me on a hack well executed. She gives a quick shake of her head and then puts her lips close to my ear, and for a moment I'm too busy noticing the warmth of her breath on my ear to hear her. "You idiot, we need to get out through the emergency stairwell!"

I grin and shout back, "I made the system think the fire's *in* the stairwell. Everyone's going to head for the opposite end of the building."

She pauses, giving me a moment to revel in her grudging admiration. Then, with a jerk of her head, she bids me follow, and ducks out into the corridor to take a right, then a quick right again at the next intersection.

But at the next crossroads she skids to a halt when a scream rises briefly over the wail of the sirens. It's coming from the direction of the holosuite we were in before, as far as I can tell. But it's not an outraged shout or a demand for freedom from some protester who remembered why they were there. It's a *scream*, and it's cut off with the high-pitched squeal of a laser weapon.

The girl meets my eyes, her own wide with a sudden fear that mirrors the way my own pulse is quickening. Whatever's happening in there, it's not what either of us prepared for, even in worst-case-scenario planning. "Did you see . . ." She raises her voice to be heard, but I can hear the higher note in there, the edge of her nerve. "When we were leaving . . ."

I saw the people standing there like statues, all turned in like worshippers toward that huge metal ring in the middle of the room as it filled with blue fire. I think I know what the ring was, but . . .

"Those people," I shout back. "I don't know what the hell was happening."

"I do." I almost miss her reply, but there's no mistaking the look on her face. Just for a moment, Dimples has shed her mask, and whatever it is that she knows, it's shaking her to the core. I draw breath, lips moving to form a question, but she doesn't give me the chance. Instead, she's suddenly moving again, grabbing at my arm to turn me around and take off down a different corridor.

The walls are all the same, a creamy white color, all the doors identical, creating the unsettling illusion that we're going in circles, but she doesn't hesitate, taking the twists and turns one after another. My screaming fire alarm worked; the halls are empty, save for the occasional guard, who we dodge without much trouble. It's at least a quarter hour before she halts, holding up a hand and closing her eyes, consulting some internal map. I keep myself nice and busy checking for any unwelcome visitors, and after half a minute she nods and leads me on again.

I want to know more—a *lot* more—about this girl who has a pass to the fire escape stairs, a killer smile, and a memorized map of the employees-only hallways.

Eventually our luck runs out, and a peek around a corner reveals a security guard standing by a door with a neon EXIT sign—the way through to the fire escape. The guard's a little pudgy, his shirt so new it still has creases ironed into it. I'm guessing a fresh hire. Eyes wide, he clearly didn't bargain on encountering whatever's happening here so early in his career. I don't know what my companion sees, but whatever it is, it causes her to smile as she pulls back around the corner.

She lifts one hand to press it against my chest, and for an instant all I'm focused on is that one point of contact, the warmth of her skin coming through my shirt. Then she's shoving me back against the wall. This is becoming a habit. She's clearly not used to working with a partner. "Stay here," she says, using that same hand to fish down the front of her bra, an activity I can only imagine I'm supposed to admire, so I do. She pulls out a little blue capsule and squishes it in one hand. When she runs her fingers through her platinum blond hair I see the capsule was full of dye, and in that one movement her hair's streaked a brilliant blue. "I said I'd show you mine," she continues, crouching to wipe her hand on the carpeting.

"Oh yeah?" I'm grinning, and she's aiming a coy smile back—just the one dimple, this time. I think I like that even better. I like that, at least for now, her fear's receding, though I can still see traces of it in the depths of her gaze.

"Watch and learn." She pinches her cheeks with her clean fingers so they start to flush, and huffs a few quick breaths, then whirls around the corner. She runs straight for the guard, already crying as she throws herself at him. I've seen plenty of artists on the lower levels, but this girl is *good*.

The guard's clearly bewildered to find his arms full of semi-hysterical, blue-haired teenager, and tries variations on *are you hurt* and *the evacuation point's back that way, miss.* I keep an eye on them as I peel off my shirt, quickly turning it inside out and pulling it back on again, so the LaRoux Industries badge I doctored up is showing on the outside once more.

Meanwhile, Dimples sucks in a few quick breaths and tries again, this time a little clearer despite her "fear." "Back that way," she gasps, pointing to the hallway opposite the one I'm hiding in. "He tried to take me hostage, he's got a *gun*! Please, you have to help." She lets herself subside into whimpery distress noises after that, though I can't hear much more of it over the alarms still screaming above us. I can tell from the guy's body language what he's saying as he manages to get her pried loose from her arm. *Stay right here* and *I'll take care of it.* Though when he jogs off the way she pointed, he's not moving too fast. Probably doesn't want to be the one to find this armed hostage-taker, and fair enough, really.

I stay hidden until he's turned a corner, then hurry out to find my friend fishing in her purse—who even carries one of those?—and producing a swipe card. She manages to look only a tiny bit relieved when the pad lights up green, and a moment later we're in the stark emergency stairwell. The alarms are dimmed in here, and our footsteps echo as we start down.

"What the hell did you do back there?" she calls back over her shoulder after a while. "I saw you doing something with your lapscreen and that data port in the tree, right before the holo-projections cut out, but this is a whole other level of security."

I'm tempted to tell her I have no idea. I was inside the LaRoux servers, and I'd just spotted some weird energy spikes I wanted to know more about, but I'd barely gotten started. Nothing I tripped should have brought out the bloodhounds like this. Some of my old hacks, when I was starting out, might have caused this kind of mayhem. But these days, unless you're on my wrong side . . . Point is, nothing I did would've warranted the weapons fire we heard up there.

We started twenty stories up—though that's a relative figure, since the ground floor is certainly nowhere near the actual surface of Corinth—and by now we've got about three to go, so I save my breath for running.

Then the door at ground level bursts open, and three security guards come hurrying in. We've both got too much momentum to stop right away, but I lunge in toward the wall to try and stay out of sight, and she grabs hold of my shirt to slow herself. She slams in beside me as we hold perfectly still, waiting to see if they've spotted us—waiting to see if they're coming up the stairs.

Of *course* they are. Has a single damn thing gone right for me today? There's no way to get anywhere near an exit without being seen, so I shove the satchel holding my lapscreen behind my back, put my faith in my fake LaRoux Industries uniform, and step out into their view. My partner in crime stays behind me, no doubt hoping as hard as I am that they won't be able to tell she's not wearing a uniform.

"Careful you don't shoot me, guys," I call, forcing myself to sound like I think that prospect's actually funny. "I'm awful hard to replace."

Three weapons come up, then lower again as they spot my shirt, which does the job, at least from this distance. "What are you doing in the stairway?" one calls.

Damn, good question. An LRI employee would know better than to evacuate this way.

Then Dimples—Alexis—I really have to find out her real name— speaks up behind me. "They're saying upstairs this might be a technical problem. There's no smoke up there, and no fire, so we're checking the alarms manually." She's quick on her feet, this one.

"Maintenance," I agree, injecting a little weariness into my tone. "Only way to check some of these is in person, which clearly somebody didn't do, if this is a false alarm. Can we get you guys to step outside the stairwell again? Your movement could set something off."

Two of them buy it right away, but the guy who asked the question in the first place isn't so sure—he gives me a good long stare before he turns to follow them, gun still in his hand.

"Thanks, guys," I call after them, cheerful as can be.

She speaks behind me, keeping her voice low. "We can get out on the second floor—it opens onto the street. We can skip the lobby completely."

I nod, and we move together, both trying to keep me between her and the guards, who're heading back down to the ground floor. I hope she knows I'm just hiding her lack of uniform, and not doing anything as stupid as shielding her with my body.

"Wait a minute!" It's the guy with all the questions—he's halfway up the flight of stairs now, and he's got one hand pressed against his ear, where no doubt an earbud is transmitting information about us. Alexis curses softly—for an instant it's almost like she has an accent—and as one we lunge for the door.

"Freeze!" All three of them are thundering up the stairs now, just meters away. They're shouting threats, their voices echoing as loud as their footsteps, the alarm still wailing all around us.

Ahead of me, she shoves on the push bar to open the door, sunlight abruptly cutting in to light up the stairwell. I propel her through the doorway with a hand between her shoulder blades, my satchel banging against my hip as I stumble after her. They don't have a good shot, and I duck to try and throw their aim off.

In the next instant I hear the high-pitched wail of a top-of-the-line laser pistol, and as I slam the door shut behind me, a wave of pain sets up shop in my upper arm, then sweeps up into my chest to set my nerves on fire.

There are letters, and images, and songs, and every part of them captured and fed into the stillness. But each flash is so disparate, so solitary, that it is impossible to assemble them into a single whole.

Individuals.

The concept is new, the way the cold hard things flitting through the universe were new. Some of the bits and pieces that flood the stillness are beautiful and some are ugly and some are beyond understanding.

How can we ever begin to understand them all?

By understanding one.

We watch, and wait, and learn.

THREE

SOFIA

THE SHRIEK OF THE GUARD'S LASER PISTOL SPLITS THE AIR, and for a brief, dizzying moment I'm home again, listening to the distant exchange of gunfire between the military and the Fianna. Then a second shot comes, glancing harmlessly off the doorframe, and my unlikely partner is shoving me through the door.

We emerge at street level, glossy chrome-and-glass skyscrapers towering over us. The city spans nearly the entire planet on Corinth, divided into continents, and sectors, and quarters. There's no artistic skyline here, for the city stretches on forever, new towers built on top of the old. You'd have to find an elevator down below the current street level to vanish into the slums beneath Corinth proper. We don't have that kind of time, though, and I scan the streets looking for a quicker exit. Nearby a billboard blares its advertisement directly at me, triggered by my movement. "Don't miss the stunning, moving tribute to one of the century's greatest tragedies! Come to the *Daedalus* orbital museum, where all first-week proceeds go to benefit the families of those lost in the *Icarus* incident."

I grit my teeth, trying to block out the macabre message and focus on what our next move should be. The boy's bending over the security pad by the door, doing something with the chip he keeps pulling out of his jacket pocket. When he's done, the pad makes an irritated screeching sound and goes black. "Malfunctioning lock won't hold them for long," he grunts. "We gotta move."

"Taxi," I gasp, as a hovercraft goes whizzing by with a pair of joy-riding teens hanging out the back window.

"They'll track your palm pad charge," he replies, voice clipped and short, like he can't believe the idiocy that led me to suggest it.

"Please." I roll my eyes and take off for the edge of the platform, where traffic is speeding by. If he wants to follow me, fine. If not, he's welcome to find his own way out. I rake my now-blue hair out of my eyes, sucking in a few quick breaths as I step out on one of the curbs. The first taxicraft I spot without passengers, I let by—female driver, and I've got to play the odds if I want this to work. The next looks promising, and I raise my arm and force a few more quick breaths, working myself up. By the time the driver slides in beside my curb, I'm gasping.

"Please, sir," I say breathlessly, leaning in toward the window as the driver hits a button and the window membrane vanishes. "Can you tell me how to get to East Central Heights from here? My brother and I are new to Corinth, and we're supposed to be heading to our aunt's apartment and I don't know where we are, and my palm pad got stolen so we've been walking and—" I gulp, letting the run-on ramble of woes end in a choked gasp for air.

The cabbie blinks at me, then glances askance toward the rear side window, where the hacker's leaning against the side of the cab, looking bored. I could strangle him—the least he could do would be to try to play along with my distress. At least he has the good sense not to react at my exchanging "fiancé" for "brother." This cab driver's in his twenties or thirties, and his eyes flicker down when I lean over. Not my most elegant work, but it won't take long for those security guards to start combing the sidewalks. No time for elegance, just the oldest play in the book. It worked on the soldiers back home, and it works on the city folk here.

"You want the next level up," the cabbie says slowly. He hesitates, and I try not to seize on that; I have to let him get there himself. "There's a pedestrian bridge about a kilometer back that way," he says, jerking his head back the way he'd come.

I sniff hard, letting the driver see me trying my level best to pull myself together. "Maybe you could draw me a map? I'm so lost without my palm pad. Everywhere we go they keep telling us we're on the wrong level, and I just—I can't walk anymore. I just want to go home, but I can't even see the Regency Towers from here." It's one of the most expensive buildings in this sector of Corinth—if the damsel-in-distress act won't sway him, maybe greed will.

The driver's eyes narrow a bit as he glances at his meter. His thumb drums against the control stick, and when his gaze comes back to me I'm waiting for him with big eyes and wet lashes. I just wish it hadn't been so easy to find those tears; the blank-eyed people in the holosuite and our escape have left me more wobbly than I want to think about. I ought to be used to running by now, but my hands are starting to shake. I brace them against the door of the cab to hide it.

The driver sighs. "Your aunt lives at the Regency Towers?" When I nod, he glances back toward the hacker, who's still leaning on the cab—now, he's not even watching what's happening, his gaze fixed somewhere in the middle distance, jaw clenched and arms folded tightly across his chest. The most obvious belligerent body language there is. *Thanks, asshole, for making this so easy.* Finally, the cab driver tilts his head toward the back. "Get in. Your aunt'll pay when we get there, yeah?"

"Oh, really?" I gasp, as though the idea of him driving us hadn't occurred to me. "Oh my God, you're my absolute hero, thank you!" I dash for the door before he can change his mind, making the hacker stagger back as I haul open the door he was leaning on. "Come on, brother dear," I add in a mutter, for his ears alone.

He ducks inside without a word, sliding along the bank of seats to make room for me. The door slams closed after me as I settle myself on the faux leather. "Thank you so much, I'll have my aunt give you an extra tip for being so kind."

The cabbie glances over his shoulder at me and grins as he eases the stick forward to start nudging the taxicraft back out into the flow of air traffic through the midlevel of the sector. He's handsome, in his own way—he reminds me of the guy who does my fake IDs, except I'm pretty sure the cabbie doesn't break your knuckles if you don't pay. I sure hope not, anyway. "So where you from, originally?"

His question catches me off guard; I'd been trying to catch my oh-so-useless partner's eye, without success. I blink at the driver. "What?"

"You said you were new to Corinth. Was wondering where you were from?" He's facing forward again, but his eyes flick up to watch me in the rearview screen.

"Oh. Babel," I reply, giving the first planet that comes to mind that I've never been to.

"Get out," the cabbie exclaims, with a laugh. "I was born on Babel. What sector? You ever been to the gravball bar a couple of levels below Regency Towers? The Babel T-Wings' home away from home. Huge turnout every home game, you should come sometime."

So sex appeal did work. I glance at my "brother" to see if he'll maybe do something stereotypical and overprotective to forestall the driver's questions—and freeze. The hacker's looking down at his arm, where his hand's been clamped this whole time. What I'd misread as insolent body language was something else altogether; when he lifts his hand away, it's stained red.

He catches me looking at him and slaps his hand back in place. The cab driver's still talking, flashing me glances every now and then in the rearview screen, but his words have faded out to a distant buzz.

I can't tell how bad it is, but the blood's seeping down despite his attempts to stanch its flow. I've patched up more than my fair share of wounds back on Avon, but I can't stop to inspect it, and I can't ask him if he's okay. The second our driver realizes he's got a gunshot victim in his backseat, he'll pull over and dump us on the side of the road. No way to get that kind of injury where we were except from the authorities, and no amount of sex appeal is going to make a cabbie risk charges of aiding and abetting.

This time, I really do have to fight to keep my voice from shaking. "How mad do you think Aunt will be at us for being so late?" I ask my "brother," the cab driver's voice trailing off as I interrupt him.

The boy's eyes flick up to mine and he grimaces. "Medium, I'd say." He shifts his weight, wedging himself in so the inside of the door takes his weight. "She'll probably get over it if we apologize *fast*."

I glance at the GPS screen on the taxicraft's dash. If I were living somewhere else, we could still be hours from my place by mag-train without even leaving the sector, but I chose my digs because of their proximity to LaRoux Industries Headquarters. Well, proximity, and style. We're only a few minutes from the Towers, and I can sneak him through the side street to my building and in the side door. Assuming he doesn't lose too much blood by then to make it to the elevators, I can leave the driver here waiting for the aunt that doesn't exist and we'll be out.

"You staying here on Corinth long?" the driver asks, resuming his line of questioning as though I'd never interrupted him to talk to the sandy-haired boy bleeding in his backseat. "Moving here, or just visiting?"

"Visiting," I reply, trying to hunt for the charm again, reaching past my concern. "Family, you know."

"Yeah, I hear you. Got any free time while you're here?"

"I . . . uh, I don't think my brother would want me to hang out with strangers." I glance at the boy next to me, whose brows lift with amused irony. After all, I don't even know his name.

The taxicraft slides smoothly to a stop at the curb platform outside the south building of the Regency Towers apartments. He twists, glancing from the boy to me. "C'mon, I'm not *that* shady, am I?"

His smile is nice enough, and though he wasn't exactly subtle about checking me out while I was begging for assistance, he did help us. Still, I can't really spare much sympathy for him. You ask to get conned, and a con's going to find you. I flash him a smile in return and shrug. "Maybe I can sneak out," I whisper, as though for his ears only, and then turn for the door.

"Hey, hey, wait." The driver reaches for the auto-locks, and my door gives a telltale click. "You can wait here, send your brother up to grab your aunt's palm pad to pay the fare."

Shit. I glance again at the boy beside me, whose lazy—if strained—grin has vanished. His door's unlocked, but the second the driver sees me going for the door he'll lock it down again. So much for hoping he was an idiot, as well as a sucker. I half expect the hacker to bolt—I probably would, in his position. He needs a medic, and quickly, and he's seen by now that I can talk my way out of most things. He could leave me here without much guilt at all.

But he doesn't move, those hazel-green eyes grave for the first time since we met.

"Brother?" I quip to the driver, flashing my brightest coquettish smile, learned from poring through holovid footage of the sparkling teens and twenty-somethings that occupy Corinth's upper-level nightclubs. "You really are a sucker," I say with a laugh. Better he thinks he just got stiffed a cab fare by a flirt than discover that he unwittingly helped two criminals escape from the most tightly secured compound in this hemisphere. *Please,* I find myself thinking hard at the guy with the gunshot wound, *whoever you are . . . just play along one more time.*

I lean over, sprawling against his good shoulder and turning his face so I can kiss him. I can hear the driver's quick breath out of surprise and confusion; though my lips are on the sandy-haired boy's, my attention's on the driver. He's spluttering, indignant, exactly as I'd hoped he'd be. He's not thinking about his fare, he's not thinking about holding me hostage until he gets paid—and he's not thinking, yet, about locking us in.

I slide my other hand past the hacker's lap, toward the door controls, the movement quick but smooth. The driver's going to get over his confusion and outrage at some point, and I need to get the door open so we can bolt. I'm about to palm the scanner when the boy's lips curve under mine—he's smiling, *grinning*—and it's the only warning I get before he's parting his lips and taking full advantage of my ploy by trying to stick his tongue down my throat.

Asshole.

The fabric grows thin, translucent. Just on the other side of it is a young man with dark hair and blue eyes, gazing at the fabric as though he can see through it. This is what we have waited for.

"I wish I knew what the hell this is," the young man mutters, in the language of the words and images and sounds that pierce the stillness.

The thin spot pulses, and the young man takes a startled step back. He's staring even harder at the translucent place in the fabric, but after some time he gives a nervous laugh. "I'm imagining things," he tells himself. "It's not like it can hear me."

The thin spot pulses again, more brightly this time.

The young man's face goes white. "Rose," he calls, voice suddenly urgent. "Rose, come quick. I think . . . I think it's sentient."

FOUR

GIDEON

ALEXIS'S FINGERS FIND THE SCANNER ON THE DOOR BEHIND me, and I'm ready when it suddenly gives, breaking away from her to tumble out of the car with my make-out partner a beat behind me. Somehow I get my feet on the ground, and we dodge a gaggle of shoppers and a pair of electrobikes, the cab driver roaring behind us. For a moment we're in perfect sync, and then she ruins it by swinging her arm sideways to whack me in the chest as we turn up an alleyway, sending a line of pain snaking down my injured arm.

"Hey, what was *that* for?" I hiss.

"You know," she snaps, breath coming quickly.

I'd love to think her breathlessness is from our moment of passion in the cab, but we're running pretty fast. "*You* kissed *me*, Dimples. How was I supposed to know you didn't want me joining in?"

"My name's Alexis!"

"I'm really sure it's not."

We spin around a corner, coming to a halt beside the back entrance to a designer boutique, chests heaving. She grabs my good arm, spinning me around to take a look at my bloodied sleeve. "How bad is it? Can you make it another few minutes?"

"No longer than that," I reply, pressing my hand down over the wound once more, buzzing with a heady mix of relief at our escape, and the gut-twisting knowledge that whatever I saw today in that holosuite, it was a bad, bad thing. *Merciful mother of fried circuits, my arm hurts.* "Got somewhere I can seal it?"

The girl goes silent a long moment, then nods. "I've got a place."

She leads me along another alleyway and between a couple of show-rooms, then past the gated entrance to Regency Towers, the place she named for the driver, and through the garden next door to it. I can tell she's mapped out her routes around this neighborhood, and I respect that. From there, we cut through a maintenance gate, so that when we approach the entrance of Camelot Heights—*please, our actual destination, damn this hurts*—nobody from the street has seen us go in. She pauses to pull a thin, close-fitting felt hat from her purse and uses it to conceal her blue hair as she keys in the security code and we slip inside. My stomach's growing uneasier by the second; a girl who lives in a place like this isn't a criminal, at least not the same kind I am. Was she sneaking into the holosuite today just for kicks? An image of the metal rift flashes before me once again, and the fear in her eyes. If she thought she was in this for fun, she sure knows now that it's more than that.

"Kristina!" It takes me a moment to realize the smiling doorman is talking to us—or rather, to Dimples. "Who's your friend?"

"That's for me to know, Alfie." She laughs, leading me into the elevator. Her game is flawless, like her laugh. The fear I saw back at LaRoux Industries is gone, and she's not missing a beat. She hits the top button—penthouse, *of course*—and with a barely audible hum, we're moving. It's not until we've passed the penultimate floor without anybody else join-ing us that she starts digging through her purse. She produces a pair of dainty lace gloves and slips on the right one. When we reach the top floor, she presses the gloved hand against a square panel that glows with an ivory-colored light. It crackles briefly, as though the whole thing's bristling with static.

I only have a moment to size up the security system, and then the doors are rushing open, confronting me with the sort of luxury I haven't seen in years. Dimples tosses her purse down on the couch and vanishes behind a wall of frosted glass, calling instructions as she goes. "Sit down before you fall and crack your head open."

With the slightly guilty feeling I'm making the whole place dirty—ridiculous, under the circumstances—I peel off my shirt and sink down onto the edge of the couch. Her apartment is insane. I haven't been any-where like it in years, and if this kind of place felt like home once upon a time, it sure doesn't now. The floors look like real marble, and I can't be sure, but I think that could be actual wood by the fireplace. The far wall is top-of-the-line smartglass, with that faint, iridescent sheen that tells me it's compensating for the smog outside to render the view of the Corinth sunset clean and sparkling. Ha.

"Nice place you got here," I call out, using my wadded-up shirt—it's beyond ruined anyway—to stanch the bleeding from my arm. I need a moment to catch my breath, to work out how to play this. "Is this the moment you admit you're secretly a LaRoux, and loaded with cash?"

"Hey, I'd look good as a redhead." The way her voice is echoing, she must be in a bathroom. *One redheaded LaRoux in the galaxy is more than I'd like.* She's keeping her tone casual, just like I am, though I'm sure we both know we have to talk about what happened. I hear a cabinet open and close, and then she's walking out with a sleek little black box.

Judging by the contents of her med kit, this girl comes from an alto-gether different background than the celebrated Lilac LaRoux. There's all kinds of stuff in there you don't see in a standard first-aid kit, from hospital-grade burn treatment to stomach purges. She pulls out a hand-held cauterizer and eases the shirt away, getting to work. And despite the flawless manicure she's sporting, this clearly isn't the first time she's come across a gunshot wound.

"Well," I say, reaching for distraction from the pain I know is coming. "I don't know about you, but that wasn't the day I was hoping for."

Her gaze flicks up to me, and she shows me that lopsided, one-dimpled smile again, just for a moment. And like that, I know. That's the real smile. One dimple, real deal. Two, she's faking it. And damn, do I like that lopsided one.

Yeah, smarter *definitely ain't showing up anytime soon.*

"Could have been worse," she says, only the top of her blue-streaked head visible now as she finishes cleaning the wound. "A few inches over and I'd have had to do something far more drastic to convince the cab driver to carry me and a dead guy home."

"Hey, if I'm ever actually dead, you have my blessing to leave me wher-ever I am. You can even chop off any bits of me sporting incriminating evidence. I won't need them anymore." I'm talking too fast, partly because I know the cauterizer's going to sting far worse than a tattoo needle.

What I *should* do right now is see what she knows, then go to ground and keep my head down until I'm sure it's safe. I can reach out to my contacts—I'll start with Mae—and work out how to fort up, then go after more information. After what we saw, they're going to be looking everywhere for us, and it *won't* be to congratulate us on excellent teamwork in a tight spot.

She's quick about it, at least, and with the blood gone I can see the scar shouldn't mess up my ink too much—that's the one I got after the Avon job. I concentrate on that, rather than the nerve-jangling pain where she's working, or her hand braced against my chest, holding me still. Once she's done, she slathers on burn ointment, and the pain fades into blessed numbness.

"There," she says, inspecting her handiwork while I inspect her. "Good as new by tomorrow." She leans down to pack up the med kit and snaps it closed. "I've got to go wash this stuff out of my hair or it'll stain."

"I could use a shower, if you've got room in there for two," I shoot back immediately, and she simply gazes at me, one brow lifted, all *Really? Is that the best you can do?* "Hey, I just had minor surgery over here," I point out. "You'd be disappointed if I didn't try, but I'm not in my best shape."

"The elevator will go down without my glove," she says, catching me off guard. I can't go, not yet. But before I can answer, she adds, "Or if you'd like to stay, the SmartWaiter makes a pretty mean screwdriver."

She doesn't wait to see what I decide—she simply turns away to disappear into the bathroom, and a moment later I hear the water start up.

So I do the only thing I possibly can: start snooping through her stuff. I mean, never pass up a chance to learn more about someone who interests you, right? And I can't go anywhere until we've talked about what happened, so this is something to do while I wait.

There are framed pictures along the table of her and an older couple who could be her parents—one shows them on a ski trip on a super-expensive holovacation—I think I recognize the Alps on Paradisa—the other in front of the Theta Sector skyline right here on Corinth, the sea in the background. They're almost perfect—whoever made these for her did a very good job indeed—but there are tiny signs they're faked, if you know where to look. I'm positive now that this place isn't hers. It certainly belongs to a Kristina McDowell—I can see parcels with her name on them by the door, and when I coax the console in the little office to life there's a hypernet history, mostly mail and online shopping. But "Kristina" isn't this girl's name any more than "Alexis" was.

So whoever Dimples is, all I really know is that she's seen some kind of situation requiring serious first aid before, she knows more about LaRoux Industries than she's letting on, she could sell rocks to asteroid miners, and she's definitely *not* rich girl Kristina McDowell. I shut down her console and head back out of the office to the SmartWaiter, ordering up a screwdriver for her and a mineral water for me. I don't drink—I need every brain cell I've got in working order, often on short notice.

She emerges just as I'm thinking about checking out what else she keeps in her purse besides circuit-breaking gloves and illicit security passes. Her hair's back to platinum blond, curly and light around her face, and she's clad in an expensive-looking black sweater and a pair of jeans. I briefly mourn the loss of the tiny dress, but I find I like this more casual version of her, too. Not that I should be thinking about something like that at a time like this.

"I like your hair like that." Oh God, did I just say that out loud? *Smooth, buddy.*

She grins, walking across to take her drink. "It's easiest to keep it this way. Hard to go blue or pink at a moment's notice if your hair's black. Windows, preset five."

The smartglass flickers subtly, and the sunset outside begins to darken, the stars coming out one by one, despite the fact that stars haven't been visible on Corinth for generations. The light from the buildings stretching on forever into the distance doesn't come close to eclipsing the brightness of the stars overhead. I've seen the illusion before, of course; the micro-projectors in the glass track your eye position and shift so that it looks like the stars are far distant in the heavens rather than a trick of the light a few feet away.

She watches them like they're something incredible, though, and I stay quiet, watching her instead. Her brows are drawn in, and though her face is calm and still, there's something about the set of her mouth, a firmness that doesn't quite mesh with her air of innocence and nonchalance. Perhaps this is what she looks like when she's simply being her.

This is getting out of hand. This is *not* the time to be gazing at her like I'm hypnotized. I'm smarter than this. Time to shove some distance between us, start using that brain of mine. "So," I drawl, making myself sound casual. "Is this where we talk about what happened today? I'd ask what you were doing there, but you've lied to me so many times already, I wouldn't believe the truth if I heard it now."

She's silent, clutching her drink. Eventually she takes a long swallow, then sets the glass down on the table beside the fake pictures, turning away to walk over to the couch. "I lie because I have to," she says, sounding more tired than anything else. "Corinth is a cold place. You tell the truth, you end up down there." Her nod takes in the slums, far below us—my territory, though she doesn't know that. Perhaps she guesses.

"It's a world of opportunities, down there."

"But not the ones I want," she replies. Then, after a slow breath out: "My name really is Alexis. But it's my middle name, and no, I'm not going to tell you my first name. Especially since you've lied just as much as I have today. I was at LaRoux Industries because of my father. He's dead, and it's because of them, and I want to know why. And that's the truth."

And I know it is. I might not have her silver tongue, but I know this truth when I hear it. It's not so far from my own truth—maybe that's why I can recognize it. A cold sliver of pain runs through me in sympathy—I'm too familiar with the kind of loss that can put you on a trail you don't know how to abandon. I find myself responding without thinking. "My name's Gideon. And that's my real name, and my first name, the one my mama gave me."

Tell me I didn't just say that. It's one thing to look for a way to bond, it's another to start sharing things *nobody* knows. I'm getting twitchy, not being able to get back to my den to unpack what's happened today. My fingers are itching for a keyboard. My mind keeps wanting to flip across and check info feeds that aren't there. My latest round of tracker programs is due to report in any minute now. I should check the forums, check in with Mae. This is what happens when I leave my screens too long. Everything goes to hell. Which is an accurate description of this whole day.

She's watching me, and I try to skate past the name, hoping she won't pick up on the zillion clues I must be giving that I wish I hadn't shared it. "You said you knew something about what we saw today."

"I was going to meet with someone who could tell me more, but I guess she backed out, or got scared off." She shakes her head, arms curling around her middle as though to shield herself as she leans back into the couch. "You don't want to get mixed up in that."

"I already am. We both are, now. We can go our separate ways if you want, but odds are they've got us both on camera, and they'll find at least one of us before long."

"I've got no real reason to trust you, Gideon," she points out, raising an eyebrow. "For all I know you could be working for them, trying to find out what I know." She shakes her head again, the movement tight and restrained, tension singing through her. It's going to take more than my best charming smile to get her to talk, and watching the way the life's drained out of her at the mention of what happened today, I know I can't afford to walk away without understanding what I witnessed.

"Fine. You want trust?" I set down my own drink and walk across to sink down onto the couch beside her. "I'll go first. I don't know what swept through those people, but I've seen a metal ring like that before. The one with the blue fire, that was meant to be hidden by the projectors in the holosuite."

She swallows hard and I force myself to sit perfectly still as I wait her out. "And I've seen eyes like that before," she whispers eventually. "Eyes like darkness. People whose minds have been stolen, turning them into those . . . those husks."

Husks. The word whispers through my mind, a perfect fit. I couldn't see their eyes, but I saw the way they turned to the rift in the middle of the room, like compass needles pointing north. They were husks, emptied of themselves. I have to bite my tongue to keep from blurting out more questions, my pulse kicking up a notch, pounding in my temple.

Despite my relentless pursuit of the former Commander Towers—the woman who helped LaRoux hide everything that happened on Avon—so far my best lead has been the conspiracy theory forums, the devoted few on the hypernet trying to figure out what LaRoux's game is, based on the Avon broadcast. That's where I found Kumiko, the retired soldier hiding out in the south of the city, leading her network of Fury survivors in her quest for revenge, full of wild secondhand stories. After all the hours I've spent trying to make sense of Kumiko's tall tales, now . . . this girl, she's actually *witnessed* what Lilac's and Tarver's whispers can do. I keep my voice calm with an effort. "Where?"

She opens her mouth, but then her eyes flick toward me and she stops. "It doesn't matter where. But LaRoux Industries was there too. In secret."

My mind is turning over what I've gathered since Lilac LaRoux's request for security assistance first pinged on my radar and put me on the path I've been following ever since. I know LaRoux shipped his experiments to three planets: Verona, Avon, and Corinth. Alexis would've only been six at the most when the uprisings on Verona happened—but this panic in her gaze, the tension in her frame, they don't come from something that happened ten years ago. This wound is fresh. Which leaves only one option.

Avon.

I reach for her hand, casually letting my eyes sweep across her forearm. No sign of the genetag she would've had as an Avon native.

The documents from the site of the *Icarus* crash flash up before my eyes—the schematics for the rift at the outstation, the medical reports on the researchers gone mad. Far more than Lilac LaRoux and her major ever knew I dug into. *That's the risk when you take on a pet hacker.* "I saw the ring somewhere LaRoux Industries wasn't meant to be either," I say quietly. "Well, I didn't see it—but I found files on it. I know it was there."

"Do you know what it's for?"

Now it's my turn to steady myself, the reports flooding back into my mind. *Dr. Eddings was found to have impaled herself on a sharpened length of pipe originally intended for external plumbing. . . .* I can't tell her the truth. A prison for creatures from another dimension? Perhaps a few Avon Broadcast believers would buy that story, but Alexis will just think I'm dangerously insane. A liability.

Unless she really is from Avon herself. I settle for a half-truth. "From what I read, I think it's connected to what we saw today. To those people you called husks, the ones you saw who lost their minds. The fact that there's one of those rifts here, on Corinth—that scares me. We *have* to find out more about this."

She lifts her hands to scrub at her face, raking her hair back and leaving it disheveled. "Look, I know what you're trying to say. But I don't work with a partner. I'm glad you're okay, and I'm grateful for the information, but that's it."

"But we're after the same thing. LaRoux Industries. The enemy of my enemy—"

"Is just another enemy, Gideon."

This time I know I'm not hiding the current of disappointment running through me. Alexis is the best lead I've found in a year, and I'm losing her. I've chased Towers halfway across the galaxy and back, and every time she eludes me. Now, more than ever, I *have* to find her—it's the only way I can make sense of what I saw today.

As for Alexis, I'd kill to access her memory the way I can access data records—if only I could figure out her personal password. "Listen, you didn't have to bring me up here to patch me up. I owe you. I'm going to leave you with a way to collect, in case you ever need me." *Or in case you change your mind about working with me.*

She's pulling herself together now, putting the mask back on, and the corners of her mouth lift as she turns to look me over. "You're really that good?"

I grin. "Have you ever heard of the Knave of Hearts?"

She goes perfectly still, her voice dropping. "You work for *him*?" *Whoa.* She's *definitely* heard of me. I'd be flattered that my online infamy is spreading into the real world, except it's clearly not good news to her. "Why would he have you hack into LRI?"

"I find it's safer not to ask," I say, which is technically true, if only for other people. "But I'd have been screwed out there, bleeding all over their solid-gold streets. If there's something you need, anything you want looked into, I can talk to him about doing that for you."

"No," she says quickly, before her voice softens, clearly reaching for calm. "No, if you want to pay me back, don't mention me to the Knave at all."

"The stories about him aren't true, you know." I can't help myself. "Most of them, anyway. He's a hero to plenty of people. Screws the corporates pretty good, and you know they deserve it."

"It doesn't matter." I've seen this girl walk out of a building where everyone around her was going mad and shooting at her, and step into the smoothest con I've ever seen—but this, she can't fake. This scares her more than the blank-eyed stares we saw today. She's terrified—her lips are pressed tight together, pale skin paler still. "You should go."

"Just me, then," I try, gentle. I'd kill to know who's been feeding her stories to make her so afraid of my online persona, but this isn't the time to press. "I'll add in a second mailbox on your system. It'll look exactly like the regular way you'd log in and send a message, but it's a private network. If you send a mail using it, it'll come straight to me. And only me."

She swallows, and nods toward the comscreen I busted into while she was in the shower. "Fine," she says simply, and I can't shake the feeling she's agreeing just so I'll stop bothering her and leave. "Show me."

I retrieve my lapscreen from my satchel and lead her over to the com-screen, hooking the stool out with one leg and sitting down. Fishing around the back, I run through the cables by touch until I find the one I want, pulling it free and plugging it into my lapscreen. I insert my chip, and it only takes a couple of minutes to install a shadow box.

"Here," I say, tapping her screen, where a new mail icon sits just beside her regular one. "This'll be my contact, under Jake Cheshire. Send mail here, and it'll come straight to me, without leaving any trace in your own folders. Keeps the trail clean."

She nods, still grave. "Thank you, Gideon," she murmurs.

"Sure. Let me know if you work out how I can return the favor. Or if you need anything, after today." I return the cables to where they belong, stowing my chip in my pocket and getting to my feet with a wink. I want to make her smile again before we part. "Preferably something that won't get me shot. It really hurts."

That last draws a wry little smile. "I'd much rather leave that part of it to you. You've got practice."

"It was very nearly worth it," I say, as I scoop up my satchel and cross over to the elevator. "Though next time you tell someone we're engaged, I'm making you go through with it."

Now she laughs properly. "You have no idea what you'd be getting yourself into."

The elevator doors hum open, and I step inside, turning to face her. Somehow wanting to remember her face. Even if they find her, she won't be able to tell them where I am—but I'm hoping with everything I've got that they don't. I hope she'll be safe.

She speaks just as the doors start to close, gray eyes locked on mine. "Gideon, can I trust you?"

I have no idea why, and I can count on one hand the people for whom my answer is true—but I do know the answer, even if I don't know why. I grin. "Take a bullet for you twice, if I have to."

And then the doors are closed.

Agony. Fear. Despair.

Stop. Stop. The thin spot pulses, flashes with urgency, but the young man ignores it all except to make notes upon a tablet. Only when he glances back at the end of each day is there a flicker of guilt there, the only thing that proves he knows exactly what he is doing.

This was not what we glimpsed. This was not what we wanted. They are an infection, bombarding the stillness with their data and their ships and their pain.

We must find an end.

FIVE

SOFIA

IT TAKES ME A FEW DAYS TO GET A NEW SECURITY CODE FOR my door, and even longer to comb my apartment for bugs carefully enough to be certain my guest didn't leave anything of his behind. I pore over the footage from my security camera, watching where he goes while I'm in the shower. It's better to let visitors believe they have time where they're not being watched, because they'll do whatever underhanded thing they plan on doing straightaway. If you don't offer them a blatant opportunity they'll be sneakier, hiding it, possibly well enough that I wouldn't be able to pick it up on camera. Back on Avon, this sort of thinking just wasn't a part of my life—I specialized in sweet-talking extra supplies and inside information out of the guards, not in living an elaborately faked life in someone else's world. I learned to give visitors a little carefully monitored alone time on my third stop out from Avon, a freighter called the *Alanna*. Seeing what they did in my tiny quarters when they thought I wasn't looking told me which crew members I could trust far quicker than anything else would.

He goes over my photos—I think he guesses that they aren't real— flicks through my browser history, inspects the packages waiting by the door for Kristina when she gets back from the health spa she's been at for the last month. He stops to look at the Miske multimedia works on the wall, probably the most expensive things in the apartment, but he leaves them alone. I don't see him plant anything, and I don't see him do anything shiftier than a bit of snooping.

I check my messages four, five times a day—but there's nothing from Sanjana Rao, the woman I was supposed to meet at LaRoux Industries Headquarters before the entire holosuite went mad. I can't afford to lose her after all I've been through to find someone with a high enough security clearance to have the information I need, and a reason—whatever it may be—to give it to me. LaRoux proved on Avon that he has powers and defenses far beyond what a normal man possesses, and unless I find a way to neutralize his whispers, I'll never get close enough to him to repay him for what he did to my father.

I dictate and delete half a dozen messages to Dr. Rao before I decide I can't improve upon the language, and try to screw up the courage to send it. She's spooked, no doubt, after the security scare. For all I know, she's vanished into the woodwork completely, and I'll have no chance of getting her to trust me again.

That mess last week was just a case of poor timing, my message reads, *and had nothing to do with me or you. Please say you'll meet me again. You can name the time and place, you can take whatever precautions you need to feel safe. Please. Alexis.*

I blink at the "send" button and the screen chimes to inform me that it's done. The address she gave me is gibberish, but it's how I contacted her before—it's not her official address, but she'd have been mad to give me anything that could be traced back to her. Not if she wanted to keep her job. Or her sanity.

It's taken me nearly four months to get this close to LaRoux. Four months, spending every night researching LRI employees who might have the connections I need, following them to learn their interests, inserting myself into their lives, making them trust me, *like* me, just long enough for them to introduce me to my next mark. Four months before I caught even a whiff of information about the mind-control experiments and abuse LaRoux was perpetrating on Avon.

And I lost it all in a single day.

It's three days after I sent the message to Dr. Rao—eight days after I met Gideon—when my inbox finally dings to tell me something's arrived beyond the usual newsletters and spam Kristina gets. I'm fresh out of the shower, finishing up with the pack of disposable skin-patches and the concealer I use to hide my genetag. Over the past year I've made hundreds of thousands of galactics, pulling jobs here and there to support myself, putting every single credit I can spare into tattoo-removal treatments. But it'll take two or three more before it's faded enough to be illegible, and half a dozen before it's impossible to tell there was ever anything there branding me a native of Avon. But hopefully I'll get my chance to get near LaRoux before then, and it'll all be moot anyway.

When I hear my inbox chiming, I wrap a towel around my torso and bolt out into the office, shedding water as I hurry over to the screen. For a moment, my heart's racing so quickly I can't focus long enough to work the eye-trackers. But once the message opens, my heart sinks.

It contains only four words—no signature, no code, nothing I can use. *Burn this connection. Run.*

I want to scream. I want to throw the screen out the window. I want to leave this apartment and head down into the slums where I started and be among people as pissed off as I am. I know Gideon had something to do with turning off those holo-projectors and triggering the meltdown at LRI Headquarters, and I want to click that stupid fake contact he left me and write him a message telling him exactly what he's done to me. What he's taken from me.

I'm not interested in the part of my brain that points out that it isn't his fault, not really. That machine—the rift, as he called it—was there, hidden, all along. Maybe it would've happened anyway, and maybe without him we wouldn't have had warning to escape.

So instead I just sit there at my desk for a long moment, my eyes sweeping across the brief message as I force myself to breathe.

The lights are dim—I keep them at setting two or three whenever I possibly can, to avoid a spike in the electric bill that might alert Kristina to the fact that she's got a squatter. I leave them where they are, letting the glow from my screen guide me as I push back from it, coming to my feet and walking out of the office, willing my pulse to slow. Trying to think clearly.

I'm just moving into the kitchen when the hairs lift on the back of my neck in a warning I've learned not to ignore. Growing up it meant there were trodairí nearby, that I had to pay attention. Now . . .

A shadow shifts, visible at the corner of my eye where there should be nothing. I drop silently to the floor, barely able to stop myself from gasping. My heartbeat is roaring in my ears, but I can still hear two—no, three, *four*—sets of footsteps moving quietly across the floorboards.

I pray they're just thieves who caught onto Kristina's absence the same way I did. Because the alternatives mean I'm probably already dead.

Fighting the instinct to freeze, to make myself tiny and quiet and invisible, I reach up to grope for the drawer above me, pulling it out as quickly as I can without making any noise. The chef's knives are on a magnetic strip on the other side of the kitchen, but there's a paring knife in there. It's not much, but if they're expecting the place to be empty, maybe it'll be enough to get me to the elevator.

I squeeze my eyes shut, feeling with my fingertips around teaspoons and chopsticks, moving with agonizing slowness for fear of causing a telltale jangle of silverware. I have to stop holding my breath or I'll pass out, I have to open my eyes or I won't see them coming for me, I have to move, I have to get ready to run, I—

"Hands out of there." A harsh voice rips me out of my concentration, sending me lurching against the cabinet with a clatter and a cry. Looking up, I see a gun first, then the man aiming it between my eyes. Another man steps up alongside him, also armed. They're not wearing black, or even the sleek body armor favored by some of the higher-operation thieves in Corinth's underworld.

They're wearing uniforms. Green and gray, and as the third man turns to inspect the other rooms to be sure I'm alone, I can see the lambda emblazoned on the back.

For a moment all I can do is clutch at the towel twisted around me, feeling every ice-cold drip of water from my hair against my shoulders, tasting metal and bile and wishing for my father so hard my heart aches. Then my mouth opens by itself, and words come out, like there's some part of my mind that knows what to do without needing the rest of me to function.

"Take whatever you want," I gasp, pretending that the uniforms mean nothing to me, pretending I think they're thieves. "Please, I won't stop you. You don't need to hurt me, I won't tell anyone. Just let me go."

The first man, difficult to see clearly in the gloom but tall and in his mid-forties, snorts. "Well," he says slowly, gesturing with his gun for me to stand up. "That's a problem, because we're not here for your stuff."

For once I don't have to hide the terror coursing through me as I reach with a shaking hand for the edge of the counter to pull myself up. My legs are barely working. I was never one of the warriors on Avon—I know how to duck and cover, but fight? The adrenaline is making me nauseous, making my vision blur and my nose sting as I try to keep breathing. "Whatever it is," I whisper, "just take it and go."

"That would be you." The man's eyes flicker, just for a moment, down toward where my other hand is gripping the towel closed in front of me. It's only for an instant, but I'm swept by a wave of fear so tangible I nearly choke on it. "You paid us a little visit the other day at Headquarters. The boss wants us to ask you a few questions."

They know. My last hope of throwing them off my identity falls away into tatters.

The man watches me, enjoying this, the moment when I realize I'm probably going to die tonight, when they're done questioning me. Then, softly, he says, "You should be more careful who you write to over the hypernet these days."

My gaze snaps to my comscreen before I can stop myself. Dr. Rao's last, brief message to me hovers in front of my blurring eyes: *Burn this connection. Run.*

She was trying to warn me. Did they catch her, too?

"I have friends." It doesn't even sound like my voice. I can't think. I can't move. "They'll know why I vanished, if I don't show up. They'll know who did it, they'll call the police."

"We *are* the police," says the second man, sounding impatient. My act isn't fooling them—the realization closes over me like water, leaving me drowning in its wake. When I look again at their uniforms I realize they're from LaRoux Industries' security branch, which explains how they were able to access my apartment. And why they're doing this so brazenly outfitted in LRI's uniform. Kristina McDowell uses an LRI alarm system to protect her belongings. Any call to the police will also get patched through to them—even if what I was saying were true. Even if there was anyone waiting for me, anyone who'd realize I was gone.

One of the other men—there are four total, all distinctly unimpressed with my attempts to find sympathy or hesitation in what they're doing—emerges from the bathroom with the clothes I left on the floor before getting in the shower. He tosses them at me and grunts to the others, "All clear. She's alone."

"Put your clothes on," snaps the first guy, the one whose eyes keep flickering over me like he's imagining what's beneath the white terry cloth. "Unless that's what you'd like to wear when you come with us."

I nod, not trusting myself to speak, and turn toward the bathroom. My mind's running through an inventory of everything in there. The mirror—no, they'd hear it breaking. Perfume—the alcohol would burn their eyes if I could throw straight. My hair spray—if I had a lighter I could use it as a makeshift flamethrower. The hair dryer—the puddles I've left on the floor—are they wearing rubber-soled shoes?

But I don't get more than a step in that direction before a jerk of the man's gun halts me in my tracks. "You can change right here," he says, those roving eyes narrowed.

My skin crawls so violently that for a moment I think I might sink back down onto the floor. I grip the edge of the counter, white-knuckled. "I can't change out here," I blurt, no longer acting. "I can't—while you're—"

Roving Eyes grins a little, and though there's smugness there, it's a grin that so contrasts with the hacker's smile that for a moment, a detached part of my mind focuses on Gideon, wondering what he'll think when my body turns up somewhere on the news. *If* it turns up. Roving Eyes's voice drags me back. "You can step out there. I'll turn my back and you'll have ten seconds. You're not dressed in ten seconds, or I hear you moving in any direction or doing anything other than dressing, you'll come naked."

"But—" My voice tangles, my mind finally blanking entirely. I've run out of words. I can't think. I can't escape.

"Clock's ticking."

I lurch out into the center of the living room and glance over my shoulder to see the man do as promised and turn his back. I can see two of the others behind him, speaking to each other; they could turn their heads and see me. But the man's beginning to count down from ten, voice crawling into my ears and prompting me to drop the towel and scramble as quickly as I can into the tank top and lounge pants I was wearing before I took my shower. I'm still pulling my top down when the countdown finishes, but he can hear the rustle of fabric, and he waits a half a breath longer. In another time, some other situation, that lenience might have given me some hope. But by the time I pull my shirt down, the gun's aimed squarely my way, the glow of the comscreen from the office glinting blue off the metal barrel.

The comscreen.

"My boyfriend!" I gasp, throwing a plan together as I speak. "He's meeting me here tonight for a date. He'll be here any minute—he's a reporter—I don't think your boss would like to read about this in the papers. Me disappearing, days after being harassed by LRI security at Headquarters."

The man rolls his eyes, then jerks his chin at the screen. "Call him. No—write him. Don't want him hearing anything unusual in your voice. Cancel your date. I'll just stand behind you and make sure you don't make any errors."

I force my face to fall, my expression to crumble, even as a tiny flicker of hope kindles, my first since I realized I wasn't alone in my apartment. Two of them follow me into the office, and as I move across to sit in front of the screen, Roving Eyes stands so close behind me I can feel his body heat. With a swipe of my trembling hand, I select the name—Jake Cheshire—from the list.

Then in a shaking voice, I dictate my message.

"Hi, babe." I swallow, watching the letters pop up on the screen as the computer reads my voice. "No need to come over tonight after all. My father and some of his friends stopped by, so I'm going to go out to dinner with them. I'll see you this weekend though—we're still on for the park where we met last time, right? I'm dying to see you. Love, Alice."

"Wait," Roving Eyes says, his voice sharpening. "Let me read it before you send it."

I hold my breath. I've tried every hint I can think of: mentioning my father, who Gideon knows is dead; telling him who has me by mentioning the holopark at LRI Headquarters; using a name from the same work of fiction from which his boss—the Knave of Hearts—takes his nom de guerre. I pray it's enough. I pray he's checking that inbox regularly. I pray—

The man grunts. "Fine. Send it and let's go."

I force my eyes to blink regularly for the screen's eye-trackers, when all I want to do is squeeze them shut, to block out everything like an animal hiding its head in the sand. The message swishes off with a chime. At least if they end up killing me, someone might know. Someone, somewhere, will know what happened to me.

"Move!" shouts the man, when I sit frozen in the desk chair.

My gaze sweeps the apartment as I jerk to my feet, looking for something, anything I can use. Once they get me out of the apartment, my odds of getting out of this alive dwindle to almost nothing. *Just think. Just breathe.* Then a jolt flashes through me—my plas-pistol is still in my handbag from the day I was at LRI. It's in my closet. "My shoes are in my bedroom," I say, my voice shaking more violently now that I know what I have to do. Now that I know I have to try to fight. "In my closet."

"You don't need shoes," he snaps, impatient—I'm running out of ways to stall him. He *knows* I'm trying to stall him.

"You don't think manhandling a barefoot girl through the lobby will look suspicious?" I gasp for air, trying to regulate my voice—trying to sound like I'm calm.

"Fine." The man's getting angrier by the second. But he steps aside so that he can follow me into the bedroom, his companion heading out to the living room. "Make it quick. First pair you find."

I nod, dropping to one knee in the closet, blessing the fact that I've been just tossing stuff onto the floor—the bags and shoes and items of clothing are all jumbled together. I keep one foot under me so I can move when I need to. My hands are shaking so much I almost can't work the clasp of my handbag, and when I do, the plas-pistol falls out onto the floor. I catch my breath, grabbing at it with one hand and using the other to toss a scarf over it, making sure it's not visible from where the man's standing.

The plastene pistol is beyond illegal—its sole purpose is to beat the cutting-edge security nets that test for energy signatures, for metal alloys, for anything that might betray the presence of a weapon. It fires an old-fashioned bullet, it's nearly impossible to aim straight, and it's only good for one shot—firing it makes the chamber melt, and half the time it explodes upon firing, seriously injuring its user.

But I got it inside LRI Headquarters without causing so much as a blip on their state-of-the-art security scanners. After all, even though I didn't plan on meeting LaRoux himself there yet, I might've gotten lucky—and I'd regret it forever if I was unprepared. An ordinary weapon, even a low-tech military gun like the Gleidels they used on Avon, would've brought every security guard in the place down on my head. But this little beauty of a weapon is my constant companion.

Now, I curl my hand around it so tightly my arm cramps, sending fire shooting up my shoulder. The pain cuts through my fear, a white-hot ribbon of clarity steadying my thoughts. My mind runs through the steps, over and over, rehearsing them like a recipe, like one of my memorized floor plans.

Shift weight. Turn. Aim for his chest. Fire. Grab his gun. Wait for the others to come through. Fire. Use bed for cover. Fire. Fire. Run.

"Time's up, we're leaving *now*," orders the man, his voice rising in volume as he comes toward me.

Shift weight. Turn. Aim for his chest. . . .

Tears obscure my vision, but I know where he is; I can hear his voice, feel his presence. I whirl, and my eyes focus for a tiny, strange instant on the droplets of water that fly from my wet hair to spatter against his shirt. He's close. Too close.

I gasp—he sees the gun—I swing it toward him—he shouts—something explodes, and I see fire. His arms wrap around me, hauling me back. He's not dead. I missed, or else the gun didn't fire, and what I heard was my own heartbeat, my own fear. He yanks me backward and I scream, fighting his grip wildly for a handful of seconds that stretch and twist and crush against my lungs. Then instinct returns and I jerk my head back, catching his chin with the back of my skull. I step down as hard as I can on his instep in my bare feet, making him howl. I drive my elbow back into the soft part of his torso. His grip loosens, and I see the plas-pistol, intact—I never did fire it—a few feet away. With a sobbing breath, I lunge for it only to feel a hand wrap around my arm and tear me back, making my shoulder scream. He throws me facedown on my bed, shoving my head into my sateen comforter so that it presses against my lips and my nose like a plastic bag, suffocating me. I try to lift my head, try to breathe, and try one more time to slip free, to reach for the gun, for my only chance. I graze it with the tips of my fingers.

Then something hard slams into the back of my head and I slide to the floor, stunned, vision clouding. "Bitch," mutters a voice high above me, far away. It's the last thing I hear.

The young man, who is not quite so young anymore, is holding something in his arms. "We can't stay here," the young man says to the thing. "Rose was already miserable with no one to talk to, and I can't imagine you'll be happy here either. I'll leave some of the staff here, people I trust not to talk."

The man waits a few moments, as though expecting the thing to talk back. "I know you won't remember this, but I wanted you to see it." He draws closer to the thin spot, until its blue light falls upon the thing in his arms. The little thing has eyes as blue as his, and wisps of peach-colored hair, and it blinks at the thin spot and yawns.

"Well, Lilac?" the man murmurs to the little thing. "What do you think? You're the third person in all the galaxy to meet them."

The thin spot flashes, and the little thing laughs with such delight that the agony dims for just a moment. The man's face has changed—the guilt is gone, and the terrible gleam in his eyes when he runs his experiments. Instead his features are soft, showing something new.

Something we want to learn.

We will watch.

We will wait.

SIX

GIDEON

I'M THINKING SERIOUSLY ABOUT SOME KHAO PHAT. ON ONE hand, it would involve getting off my butt—but on the other, when I checked the street cams before, Mama Samorn was behind the wok, and that means there'll be some *fine* cooking coming up.

I'm in my den, chair folded around my body, wall of screens spread out before me. There's something comforting about their symphony of soft chimes and whirs and beeps—it's the sound of home. On the screens to my right, I can see my bots spidering all over the forums I host. Conspiracy theorists are a nervy bunch, but sift through enough of what they say, and occasionally you find a grain of something to work with. My friend Mae—or at least, she's closer than anyone else to being my friend—is my general for those. She has an amazing knack for dropping a comment here, an idea there, sending them scurrying toward whatever we want investigated.

Straight in front of me is my tracking program for Antje Towers, and that's what has my attention right now. She resigned her commission and vanished from Avon after the broadcast, with a paper-thin story about going off the grid, retiring to a pastoral colony. *Enough death,* she said.

Not enough for me, Commander Towers. When they went into the hidden facility after the broadcast, every hint of LaRoux's presence was gone. That cleansing happened on *her* watch, and she looked the other way. I know she'll have the dirt I need—the public testimony, if I have to choke it out of her myself—to expose LaRoux for what he really is. She's been running and hiding for a year, now, switching IDs every few weeks—she's been Lucy Palmer, Taya Astin, Anya Griffin, Natalie Harmon. . . . The list goes on and on. She's always jumping to somewhere new, leaving me with ghost trails, and occasional reports of a blonde switching to a new ship, a different planet. From what I've dug up from their databases, even LaRoux Industries doesn't know where she is—which makes her perfect for my purposes. LRI keeps such close tabs on its employees that I can't even get close to any of them. But Towers—she's not under the umbrella of LaRoux's protection anymore.

Her trail went cold when she hit Corinth months ago, and more than ever, my pulse is pounding with the urgency of finding her. I've had a thousand imagined conversations with her, hurled a thousand accusations her way. If I can find her, maybe I'll learn more about what Alexis and I saw at LaRoux Headquarters.

All these years of single-minded focus have led me here, to this. If I can find her, I'll be able to drag all LaRoux's crimes into the light. Not like Flynn Cormac did, but publicly, irrefutably—with Towers, I can prove enough of what he's done to ruin him.

I'm starting again with Towers's arrival at Corinth—under a fake name, of course—and preparing to comb through the arrivals records for that date again, when off to my left I hear the soft rippling chime I assigned to the mailbox I left for Alexis. *Huh. Didn't think I'd be hearing from you again, Dimples.*

I lift my left hand, clad in a half-finger sensor glove, to point at the screen, then beckon. The sensors beep at me obediently as they switch the displays, flipping my main screen away to the left, and throwing up Alexis's message in front of me. I'd pretend I wasn't grinning, but there's nobody here to know.

> *Hi babe,*
> *No need to come over tonight after all. My father and some of his friends stopped by, so I'm going to go out to dinner with them. I'll see you this weekend though—we're still on for the park where we met last time, right? I'm dying to see you.*
> *Love, Alice*

My grin dies, crumbles to dust, and blows away on a cold, cold wind as I stare at the message. *Oh, hell.* But I don't have time to dwell, because I'm already yanking down a keyboard, fingers flying over it to trace back her message and bring her cameras to life as I voice my other instructions. "Command: Scan the message on screen forty-nine. Check for security breach. Make sure no bugs got in with it."

The ping takes only a few seconds, and I force myself to slow my breathing, close my eyes for a moment, so I'm ready when two soft chimes announce the security check result, and success with the camera.

"Security intact," the system promises me. And then the cameras blossom to life, delivering half a dozen sharp images of her apartment to my screens, and my oh-so-calm breath jams in my throat.

There's a brute of a man standing over her in a bedroom, and as I watch she tries to drag herself up onto her elbows, then collapses once more. The gorilla reaches down and helps her up by grabbing a handful of her hair—she whimpers, clearly groggy, and I find my hand lifting, like I can reach through the screen and stop him.

"Where are you taking me?" she asks, her voice catching with a sob that could be real, or could be one of her tricks—though given the situation, it has to be at least partway genuine. She's given me the warning I need, though—they're going to move her. While part of me is taking a deep breath—whatever they're planning to do to her, that means there's time before they do it—the rest of me is filling with dread. Because if they need to move her first, it's probably going to be messy.

I speak again as I flex my legs, the movement instructing my chair to straighten up and release me. "Command: Open a voice channel to Mae."

Seconds later, Mae's cheery voice is flooding my headset. She always sounds like she was just sitting there, wishing you'd call. "Why, hello there, Handsome! What's the special occasion?"

"I need backup."

The shake in my voice is enough to stop her in her tracks, and the laughter drops away. "Emergency?"

"The worst," I say quietly. "I'm sending you an address. I've got LaRoux security forces removing an ally of mine. I'm going after her, I need eyes."

She sucks in an audible breath. "Honey, you're not ready for this. We don't have half the files we need to—"

The gorilla pulls Alexis to her feet, steadying her by the shoulders as she sways, trying to blink her way back to consciousness.

I peel off my gloves, scrabbling through the pile of clothes on my bed to dig out my boots. "So that's why I need to get her back with minimal contact. Find me security cameras, public access cameras, traffic cameras in the vicinity of my current feed. I need to see where they go."

"And how the hell am I going to figure out which one's them?" Mae asks, though I can see from the displays she's throwing up on my right-hand screen that she's already on it, as I pull on my boots and tie them with shaking hands.

"Look for—"

She finishes the sentence for me. "Anything with a LaRoux badge, got it."

On-screen, the gorilla's speaking to Alexis again. "We're going somewhere we won't be disturbed. You can tell us exactly what you were doing when you came calling, and why your friend was there."

"My friend?" She sniffs, lifting a tearstained face, giving him the full force of her big eyes and running mascara. She's trying, even now, to protect my identity—or maybe just to protect her own. "I don't know anything about the guy I was with, I promise. We didn't go together. He took me hostage."

Easy there, Dimples. Definitely not trying to protect *me*. I find one of my reversible T-shirts, with a LaRoux Industries logo on one side, black on the other. I flip it black side out and haul it on over my head, followed by my climbing harness. It'll attract attention, but if I end up needing it to reach Alexis in time, I don't want to be fumbling with straps—and I've seen plenty weirder fashion on the streets of Corinth. Then I'm digging through a nest of wires to find what I—usually laughingly—call my crime bag, and slide my lapscreen in beside the supplies already there. I shove my night-eye goggles on top of my head and jam an earpiece into my ear, and running a wire from it to my screen, I'm ready. "I'm going mobile, Mae. Lock the signal down as tight as you can for me."

I hate the idea of broadcasting our conversation, but we don't have time to rig up anything more elegant. Alexis doesn't have time.

"Done," Mae says, her voice crisp in my ear. "I see the car they're using, I'm ready for them."

"Careful, there'll be traps." But she already knows that—LRI brings a whole new meaning to system security. I press my face against the iriscam at the door and shove my thumb against the scanner, and my door releases with a hiss.

Mae laughs, though she doesn't sound amused anymore. "Please. I know what I'm doing, kid."

I bolt out into the alleyway outside just as Dimples and her friends leave Kristina's apartment.

With a ping from Mae, my headset throws a transparent projection of the camera feeds up in front of me, the audio streaming directly into my ear as I hurry down the alleyway and out into the broader street beyond. It's lined with stalls and shouting hawkers, roofed over by the next level of housing above us.

Alexis is speaking as she's bundled into a car, and I'm smelling Mama Samorn's rice as I run past the stalls, focusing on the voice in my ear as my worlds jumble together. "What, you think because he picked me for his safety shield he decided to tell me his master plan?" Alexis's voice is still shaking. "If you want to know why he was there, why don't you find him and ask?"

"That's exactly what we're doing," the gorilla replies, as the camera angle switches to one inside the car, mounted by the driver's head. "And you're going to help."

"But I don't *know* anything," Alexis wails, drawing her knees up to her chest. The way her gaze darts around, I think she's wondering if she can kick one of them in the guts, then lunge for the door. But it's some kind of stretch limo, and she's got three of them in the back with her. It's not going to happen.

"In our experience, people often know more than they think," he says calmly, as Mae overlays the footage with a GPS, showing the car's movement. "Especially when they're properly motivated to turn their minds to the question."

Man, this guy would be a blast *at a party.*

They head out of the fancy sector where her borrowed apartment was, and my headset throws up projected routes as I push through the shinkansen barriers in the wake of a couple of laborers, cramming onto the last carriage of the bullet train right before the doors shut.

"Honey, I think . . ." Mae's voice trails off.

"Yeah, I know," I mutter. They're in a LaRoux Industries–branded car, wearing LaRoux Industries uniforms. This is how arrogant these people are—but more, this is how *powerful* they are. That they can do this in broad daylight, knowing nobody will stop them or ask them their business.

There was still a faint hope they'd head somewhere off-campus to do their dirty work, but four out of five routes our program is projecting say the same thing: they're taking her to LaRoux's headquarters. His fortress.

Alexis doesn't give them a thing, spending most of the car trip in silence, responding to their occasional questions with sniffs and half sentences and pleas. The signal flickers and cuts out occasionally as I switch from the bullet train to an inter-level elevator, cramming in with a bunch of bodies as we rocket up to the wealthier levels. The air grows clearer and the buildings grow taller, fancier—down in the slums, every street's roofed over, with level upon level stacked on top of each other. Every time they make a turn, my computer updates my routes—at this rate there's no way I can intercept them, only trail after them.

It's only a few minutes from LaRoux Industries Headquarters that they hit a traffic jam—Mae throws me an image of the protest causing it, but I don't bother trying to read the signs. Finally, *finally*, something's going my way. All my projected routes have narrowed to one now, and lungs straining as I run down the sidewalk—subtlety be damned—I fight my way through the crowd.

Mae's speaking in my ear again, and I know what she's going to say. "Honey, I can't come in there with you. They'll pick up on the signal."

"I wouldn't ask you to," I say, ducking around a crowd of tourists taking pictures of the huge silver lambda that adorns the front of the building. "You've done more than enough already."

"If you're not out in a few hours . . ." She trails off, because really, what's she going to do?

"Then you can have my stuff," I finish, then break off my transmission before she can try to talk me out of what I already know is a terrible idea.

My visual feed cuts out a moment later, but I know I've beaten Dimples and her escort by a couple of minutes. I make for the door and the stairwell we escaped through the other day. My skin's crawling at the thought of coming back here, heart still thumping from my run, but I'll be feeling much worse if this girl vanishes off the face of the planet because these guys were after me.

The jammer I stuck on the door lock to delay the guards chasing us is long gone, but the signals it transmitted to my data banks aren't. I have only to connect the chip for half a second before all the keys light up green, and the door clicks open. Keeping my back to the wall of the stairwell once I'm inside, I ease the door shut and then slide sideways until I can glance up, up through the endlessly spiraling stairs of the emergency fire exit. While there are no guards that I can see, the security cameras here are on a closed system, and without hard access to that system, I can't turn them off. I need a way up that isn't monitored.

I shut my eyes for a moment, feeling the phantom ache in my shoulders already. But it's all too easy, with my eyes shut, to see everything they could do to Dimples if I don't get to her in time.

I jam the lock on the door leading to the lobby one floor down, and slip inside. Cavernous and echoing, the space isn't empty like the stairwell—I have to ease by in the shadows as the night-shift security guard watches the latest episode of some holodrama on his palm pad. The elevators are each under their own spotlight, illuminated like big neon TRY AGAIN SOMEWHERE ELSE signs. But I know one access point that won't be lit up like a holiday tree: the service elevator.

I've barely made it around the corner when I hear voices—one telling the security guard to take his break, then another ordering, "Bring her through." I wait, hoping against hope that they'll give me the floor they're heading to, but no luck. Silence, as they wait for their ride up.

I hold my position until I hear the elevator doors close out in the lobby, then get to work. The elevators require a security key to operate after hours, one I can't replicate digitally—this one's a combination of a physical key with a digital signature. So instead I tear open my backpack and pull out my crowbar—wondering briefly what a normal person keeps in a backpack, if not equipment for breaking and entering—and start prying the doors open.

I keep my face averted from the camera once I'm inside, and knock the panel next to it aside so I can grab at the lip of the wall and clamber up out of the elevator, onto its top. I rip the cord from the camera and stick my own transmitter in its place—and suddenly I'm in, the whole lobby and elevator security system at my command. It's the work of a moment to relay it to my headset, but I know I'm going to lose Dimples as soon as she and her new friends step out of their elevator.

I can see the one elevator in use, and the display beside the door: 20. The same floor we were on the other day. My heart sinks, but my body's already moving. I pull out my magnetic grips, sling my bag back over my shoulders, and start to climb.

My shoulders start to protest and ache after the fifth floor, but I push the pain aside, focusing on the video feed I've got. They're going to get there—and, picturing the giant rift frame in the holosuite, I'm pretty sure I know where "there" is—long before I can. I just have to hope they're questioning her before . . .

My thoughts grind to a halt before they can arrive at the conclusion of that thought.

Just. Keep. Climbing.

A scientist with narrow lips and a stoop in his shoulders is retuning the cage around the thin spot. He has forgotten to disconnect its power source. The thin spot remains silent, giving no warning. He is one of the people who hurt the stillness in order to learn about it.

The cables spark and scream as he pulls them free, flooding his body with electricity. He is dead before he hits the ground, and as the other scientists come running, the thin spot is quiet and satisfied.

The other scientists are quiet and sad even after the dead one has been taken away. They normally talk and laugh as they prod at the thin spot in the universe, but now they are silent. The silence is heavy and thick.

So we make them a new scientist just like the dead one. If they are pleased, maybe they will stop hurting us.

SEVEN

SOFIA

THE MEN FROM LAROUX INDUSTRIES HAVE BEEN VERY, VERY well trained. They stay *just* on the plausible deniability side of torture. They don't touch me, except to jab a needle into the back of my shoulder—drugs to make me more pliable, maybe, or to sedate me. My skin crawls as I try not to think about some foreign substance coursing through my system, doing God knows what to my mind. They don't feed me, don't bring me water. They don't utter threats, but their gazes say what their mouths don't—that I'm alive only because they haven't decided to kill me yet. They don't waste time telling me what will happen if I don't give them what they want, because they know that nothing they can say will be worse than the things my imagination conjures.

My throat is like sandpaper, thirst starting to make my head throb in time with my heartbeat. It's been hours—at least, I think it has. The holosuite, without programming, is a barren, white nothingness. Only the security cameras and projectors punctuate the vaulted white ceiling, and the cameras are dark—not a single one glows. They've shut off surveillance in this room. They don't bother to turn on most of the lights, choosing instead to use only one set, leaving the rest of the room shrouded. It gives the impression of infinite space—and yet here I am, in this chair they've brought in for me, unable to move.

The metal ring, the one that had started to glow right before everyone's eyes went blank, is silent and dark. But I feel its presence just beyond the circle of light like a towering monster, some terrible creature lurking in the shadows, waiting for me to be left alone so it can strike. I know why they've brought me here—if I don't tell them what they want, they'll use that ring, and the creatures Flynn talked about in his broadcast, and take whatever they want from my mind.

Whenever my eyes close for more than a breath, one of them rams the toe of his boot against a chair leg, sending vibrations screaming up through my body and setting my bruised, aching bones on fire. It's all I can do not to groan, but I refuse to give them the satisfaction of seeing me in pain.

"You must be getting tired." It's the big guy, the one who threw me onto the bed, the one I'd been planning to shoot. His voice sounds almost sympathetic. "Just give us something we can use to track him down, and this will all be over, I promise."

Almost sympathetic.

"I swear to you," I whisper, not bothering to conceal the weariness in my voice, "I've told you everything I know. I have no idea how to find him. I was a hostage, nothing more."

At first I'd tried to get information out of them—overconfident stooges like these often give away more than they realize, because they're so focused on extracting what they want. I did learn that it's the Knave they want, not Gideon. And they've been after him for some time.

I'm positive the Knave has worked with them in the past—I can only assume that he's gone rogue now and is no longer taking orders from LRI, or perhaps he simply knows too much and LaRoux wants him erased. These men aren't aware of my identity, as far as I can tell—and they don't know I'm from Avon. If I hadn't chosen Gideon to be my unwitting partner in escaping LRI Headquarters, I wouldn't even be here.

They don't know I was at LaRoux Industries to try to kill Roderick LaRoux.

I stop myself before I can lean forward and let my head droop. Slumped body language is a sign of defeat, and if these guys know anything about nonverbal communication at all, they'll take it as a sign to push even harder. I fight to keep my eyes wide to signal fear, but moving from face to face; too much direct eye contact suggests you're hiding something and trying to counteract the natural tendency to look away. I need to be scared—because innocent bystander Alexis would be terrified—but I can't look guilty.

But the truth is that even if I told them what really happened, even if I gave them his name and the icon on my computer I used to send that desperate distress signal, they wouldn't have anything they could use to track him down. I doubt "Gideon" is the hacker's real name, and even if it were, one first name on a planet of twenty billion people wouldn't tell them anything they didn't already know.

So why don't you just give it to them?

I swallow hard as the man sighs, straightening up and moving away to speak to one of his partners in a low voice. I want to strain to listen, but I can't make myself focus. It's all I can do to remember the story I gave them well enough to stick to it.

Ordinarily, I'd know what happens next. With no witnesses and no record of this interrogation, they'd take me someplace quiet and have me killed, and I'd simply vanish. If it were any other company, any other organization—I'd die. But this is LaRoux Industries, and the things they could do to me are far, far worse.

I can see my father's face in the gloom, exhaustion making the shadows swim and wriggle into familiar patterns before my eyes. I can see him in the moments before he turned and walked into the barracks on Avon—I can see his pupils dilate, swallowing the clear blue of his irises, I can hear his voice go cold, I can see his muscles seize up and propel him away from me. It's always that moment that I relive, not the explosion itself. I see my father's soul vanish again and again. I see the moment he died, seconds before he was blown to pieces.

I force my terror down away from my heart, force myself to breathe. Panic will only make me slip. My eyes search the perimeter of the room, difficult to make out past the lights blinding me. I know what's through a couple of these doors, from the floor plan I memorized. But I'm betting I can't use the same escape route twice, even if I could get past these guys. Even if, after hours of sitting here, I could manage to run faster than my captors.

Maybe if I were braver, I could do it. Maybe if there was any part of myself worth saving, beyond the need for vengeance. But . . . I don't want to die. I *can't* die. Not when I'm so, *so* close to reaching Roderick LaRoux.

One of the men—the one who fought me—pauses abruptly, signaling for the others to quiet. He presses one finger to his ear, and I realize someone's giving him orders through a micro-earpiece. "Yes, sir," he says, spine stiffening even though whoever he's speaking to can't see him. "I understand, sir." There's a long pause, in which the man listens. Then he nods to one of the others and gestures back into the shadows, in the direction of the ring. "Yes. Yes—understood. Thank you, monsieur."

My body stiffens. Only one man's arrogant enough to resurrect a dead language just to come up with a unique title for himself. This man's orders are coming directly from Roderick LaRoux.

"It's your lucky night, sweetheart," the man says, pulling off his earpiece. "I've heard it doesn't hurt a bit, and you don't even know it's happening. You just—pop," he says, miming a tiny explosion with his fingers by his temple, "and you're gone, replaced by something much easier to deal with. This is a much more humane way to get answers. Though much less fun."

No. God, no. I can feel the ring's vibrations through the floor, traveling up the chair legs, as the machinery begins to turn on. I can feel the floor moving the way the ground moved beneath me when my father turned himself into a bomb.

The man who was speaking to me replaces his comms device with something else, another bit of electronics that hooks over his ear. "Suit up," he orders the others, who dutifully outfit themselves with similar devices with the air of workers donning their helmets or surgeons pulling on gloves.

As the men turn their attention to the metal ring dominating the middle of the room, I try to look around, try to see if there's any way out. The exits will be locked, and even if I could get them open, I'd never make it there before they grabbed me. They're too far for me to grab a weapon off them without them noticing me getting up from the chair. I'm rooted here, just as surely as if they'd bound me to it.

I'm staring so hard through the gloom that at first, I don't register when something changes. A tiny light comes on in the darkness, a single green LED that winks once, twice, then steadies. I stare at it blankly, reminded absurdly for a moment of the will-o'-the-wisps back on Avon. And then, all at once, in the same instant that my interrogator turns to come back toward me, I realize what it is.

One of the cameras just turned itself on.

I jerk my gaze away, shutting my eyes so they can't see where I was looking. I don't even care that they jolt my chair again to prevent me from resting. It's a foolish hope, a wild hope—for all I know, it could be LaRoux, turning them on so he could watch what's about to happen.

"I have permission to make you an offer," says the leader of the men, watching my face. "If you know of some way to contact the young man you encountered at LRI Headquarters, and if you can convince him to meet you at a specific time and place, we'll let you go."

That brings me up short, the adrenaline surge in my body flatlining. "Let me go?" I whisper, caught off guard. "No—it's a trick." The words come out before I can remember the role I'm supposed to be playing. They've planned this perfectly, waiting until I *know* what's coming, what will happen to me, to give me this way out. Alexis should've jumped at the chance.

Nobody would blame her for that, if she were real. She'd be scared, and alone, and she'd take any way out. But I should be better than that. I should be fighting. I hate that for an instant, I was more Alexis than Sofia.

He shakes his head. "No tricks. We have no quarrel with you. We can even promise you that the boy will not be harmed. He's just the next rung on this ladder, and we'll get to him one way or another. Work with us and you'll both survive."

The next rung on the ladder to the Knave. My heart pounds in my ears, so loud I can barely think. LaRoux Industries' security thugs can have the Knave—all the better, as far as I'm concerned. Let them destroy each other. All I want is the man at the top. I lick my lips with a dry tongue, trying to buy myself even a couple more seconds to think.

Beyond the man, I can see the camera's LED. It flashes twice as I look at it. Then three times in rapid succession. Then five. Seven. Eleven. Thirteen . . .

Prime numbers.

I swallow down a sob of relief and try to make it sound like capitulation. "Okay," I gasp. "Okay, I'll tell you how to find him." All eyes turn toward me—the perfect distraction. *Please, Gideon.* Please *let that be you.* *Tell me it's a signal, that you got my message, that you understood, because I'm running out of lies to give them.*

All I need is just one more.

The man has some of us moved, and he uses a ship traveling through the stillness to do it, and for an instant we're so close to home we can feel the others just a whisper away.

The world is opened to us just enough for us to reach out and discover that this place, unlike the place where the first thin spot appeared, has many others like the man with the blue eyes. It is the perfect place to learn. To understand. To decide whether their existence is worth knowing or if they should be condemned to darkness.

We find a little girl in the slums, and from her we discover dreams. She dreams of beautiful things, and in the way of children, she is not afraid of us. She calls us friend. We show her the ocean she longs to see. She lets us ride through her dreams the way we let ships ride through the stillness faster than light.

All around her on this world is darkness and pain, but in her dreams is beauty. She is worth watching. Worth learning. But then one day she's gone, and we're alone.

EIGHT

GIDEON

IT'S INCREDIBLY CRAMPED IN THE AIR VENTS. I CAN'T EVEN crawl on my hands and knees—I'm forced to wriggle along using my elbows, which slows me down and means I have to calculate every move before I make it. It's pitch-black as well—if I hadn't thought to grab my night-eyes on the way out, I'd be screwed right now. Pulled down, the goggles cast everything in an eerie green tint that overlays my fear with a momentary spark of anticipation. Sensory memory is a powerful thing, and usually when the world looks green like this, I'm hip-deep in some kind of crime. This is the kind of place where I cut my teeth—and filled my bank account. This is how I created the Knave, working every hour of the day to learn what I needed to find LaRoux's secrets.

The most valuable servers are kept completely isolated from the outside, no hypernet connection to send my electronic spies down. The only way to access them is to physically break in and attach my equipment. But on a hack like that I've usually got a lot more time, a lot more equipment, and—most importantly—a fully formed plan.

This better work, Dimples. I've only got one idea.

I'm close enough now that I can't whisper commands to my headset to voice-activate it anymore, or I'll risk being overheard. I huddle in the air vent above the holosuite, fingers silently swiping across my lapscreen. I've got my backpack pulled around to my front, my equipment tucked in against my chest to make more room for crawling through these too-small tunnels.

Though they could hear me if I talked, I let their voices fade away as I steady my breath and focus completely on the screen in front of me, firing up the windows I'll need. Then, a shouted curse—a man's voice below me yanks my attention back from the place it always goes when I'm working.

"It's *true*." Alexis is sobbing, head bowed. "I promise it's true."

"You had your shot, sweetheart." The man sounds *pissed* now, his earlier calm vanished. "If you're going to tell us stories, we'll do it the other way."

"But there *was* a hoverbike, I got the license plate, why won't you listen to me?" She's scrambling, voice high and raw, and I have a feeling that note in her voice is real desperation. The way the lights are directed, I can't see much through the security feed. Instead I inch along until I'm over a vent opening and can peer through the grille to see if I can pull this off. They've got lights aimed at Alexis—and at the cameras, no wonder I couldn't see—but that's not what makes my heart start trying to hammer its way out through my chest. They're powering up the rift, and while I still haven't seen firsthand what that thing can do, Alexis has. And it was enough to make her go white with terror.

Shit. I'm not ready. I don't have time. . . .

My fingers fly across the screen, my heart slamming against my rib cage. I need to even the playing field, take out those lights, but that's a program that takes time, seconds I don't have. Seconds Alexis doesn't have. Any minute I know my concentration's going to slip, my fingers will fumble, I'll lose. And lose her.

I can hear the gorillas talking, and Alexis's voice as she tries to convince them she's ready to sing like a canary. The rising hum of the rift overtakes the voices until the ventilation tunnel I'm in vibrates against my elbows and knees. I grit my teeth.

I'm not going to make it.

That truth explodes in my mind so abruptly that my fingers falter. This is it. They're going to make a husk of her. A split second later, the rift machinery gives a shudder and a screech and whirs back down into silence again. The blue sparks that had begun to gather at its perimeter vanish.

"Damn it." The leader of this group, the one who took Alexis, stalks over to the machine, then lifts a hand to his ear. "No, sir, there's been some kind of— Yes, I understand. She's not going anywhere." He drops his hand, then glares at the others in the room. "Get a team of techs in here, *now*. We've got a week, and if this hasn't been fixed by then, I'm not going to be the one Monsieur LaRoux blames, you hear me?"

I'm still frozen, heart stuttering. *Thank you, thank you, thank you.* I don't even know who, or what, I'm thanking for the reprieve. Reminding myself to breathe, I run my fingers along the vent opening beneath me until I'm sure I know where the pressure points are. Then I study the screen, check my on-the-fly hack one more time, and breathe a silent prayer to the only person I know who might care to watch over me. *Let's not meet again today, bro. I'm not ready just yet.*

I tap the screen to execute the program, and the lights all over the building ripple out, plunging the holosuite into darkness.

For a moment, no one moves. Then I punch down against the grille sealing the air vent. It clatters to the floor, and Alexis turns in the direction of the sound, leaping to her feet with incredible reflexes. A muzzle flash from one of the gorillas' guns illuminates the room for an instant, and, like a perfectly still picture, I see their leader lunging for her, hands outstretched. No, *no*.

He catches her shirt and they both go toppling to the floor, grappling in the dark, washed green from my vantage point in the ceiling. Her shriek cuts off when she hits the ground, the impact winding her, and her wild kick glances harmlessly off his arm. He flips her onto her back to prevent her scrambling away, his own breath ragged, and her foot flies out again—this time it connects with his crotch and he moans, backhanding her blindly as he folds in on himself, half pinning her to the ground.

I yank my climbing rope out of my pack and clip it through my harness, throwing the looped end down into the room. I brace my feet on either side of the air vent's opening as she struggles to wriggle free of her captor, movements jerky and desperate, washed in green by my night-eye goggles. "Here!" I hiss, knowing that in the dark, she's completely blind. She kicks at the man's grasping hand as he tries to grab her ankle, and scrambles to her feet. Three quick steps bring her across the room to collide with the rope—it takes her a few seconds to feel for its end, then slip her foot through. She's a small girl and this should be easy, but I've got no leverage, and only the belay device on my harness to help me haul the rope back. It's not until I feel the rope slacken a little that I see one of her hands grasping at the edge of the vent, and I can lean forward enough to reach for her.

Our palms smack together, and I wrap my hands around hers in an iron grip, ignoring the pain in my shoulders as I shove myself back from the vent opening, pulling her after me. She scrabbles wildly for purchase with her feet as I ram myself backward, letting her go the second she's on her hands and knees. I want to ask if she's all right, but can't find the breath to do so.

"Go," she gasps, staring at where she knows I must be in the dark, eyes wide and lungs heaving for air. I shove my lapscreen into my bag and push backward. She's smaller than me, and she can crawl, but I'm stuck backing up on elbows and knees, forced to choose speed over silence as I scramble my way toward the intersection behind me. The laser of a gunshot punches through the vent behind her and she drops to the metal floor with perfect reflexes—*experienced* reflexes—eyes closing for an instant. Just past her body I can see a ray of light shining up through it. Someone's got the light on their gun's scope working.

We hit the junction, and I turn so I can face forward, lowering my back now so it doesn't connect with the roof. This is our best and only chance, and it's not much of one at that—the vents snake all over the building, and if we can force ourselves to stay slow and silent, they won't know which direction we've picked. Now is the time for stealth over speed.

Alexis has no problem behind me—she's small and light, and can keep her hands and knees along the edge of the tunnel, where the metal's less likely to buckle with a telltale sound. Though she can't see, the occasional hand on my ankle tracks where I am, and she follows. I'm too big for what we're trying to do, and though my hindbrain is screaming at me to run, *run*, I make myself check every inch of the tunnel before I shift my weight. My headset throws up a projected image of the tunnel schematics in front of me, and with agonizing slowness, we retrace the path I took to get to her.

Now that they know we're here, the elevator shafts will be on automatic lockdown in the lobby, even the service elevator. We can't get out that way. I'm trying to remember the layout of the buildings around us, especially the new one they're constructing next door. Every now and then I hear a burst of comms static from somewhere below us, and I know we're not going to be able to wait it out in here. They're splitting up to find us. I'm going to need to make a new exit.

I want to ask if Alexis is okay, but if I can hear the occasional noise from the searchers, I can't risk even a whisper. Every joint hurts, my muscles and tendons on fire from being forced into such an unnaturally cramped position, and I can feel the sweat trickling down my sides.

It's nearly an hour before we reach the elevator shaft, and it's only once I creep out onto the maintenance ledge that I finally take a normal breath. There's a limited amount of light out here, cast by maintenance lamps every other floor. I turn back for Alexis, only to find her gripping the edge of the ventilation tunnel with white knuckles and closed eyes.

"Hey," I whisper, reaching out to lay my hand over hers. "It's okay, we're still ahead of them. But we've got to keep moving if we want to stay that way."

She gives a tight little shake of her head. "I can't." Her voice is clipped and tight. "I—I'm not good with heights."

I stare at her. "You live in a *penthouse*."

She glares back at me. "Yeah, with windows you couldn't crack even if you threw a grand piano at them!" Her voice sharpens with irritation, and though there's no reason to be pleased about it—it's directed straight at me, and we're standing here instead of climbing—I discover I kind of like it. This, like the one-dimpled, lopsided smile, is real. And most of the time I can't tell what is, with this girl. "A penthouse view is different from—I can't climb down there, Gideon!"

Well, screw me sideways. This is going to make my exit strategy a lot harder to pull off. I let my breath out. "You're in luck, because we're not climbing down. We're climbing up."

That has her opening her eyes, if only to shoot me a horrified look. "How is that any better?" she gasps.

"Trust me, up is a lot easier than down. We've only got to get ten floors up, and there's a skybridge to one of the other buildings." I rummage in my bag until I find my spare micro-weave harness inside. "Come on out, the ledge is wide enough to stand on."

"Oh God," she whispers, her movements jerky and slow as she starts easing first one leg, then the other out of the duct. She keeps her eyes closed, moving by touch—I make sure to be gentle as I reach out for her arm to steady her.

"Doing good," I whisper, wishing I knew better how to talk her through this kind of phobia—except it's not really a phobia, because that implies irrationality. We're twenty floors up, and that fall is plenty to fear for even the most logical of minds. The only upside is that if you did fall, you'd certainly be dead instantly on impact, no lying around in agony with broken bits. I don't think Alexis would find that comforting, though.

I walk her through putting on the harness—I know she's freaked, because she doesn't even blink when I test the bands running around each thigh.

"You're going to go first," I tell her. "I'm going to have a rope attached to you, here." I let her see me tying the lead to her harness. "Your job is to take these"—I hand her the bag of magnet grips—"and make us a path. You press them against the wall, like this, then do a ninety-degree twist, like this, to activate the magnet. Then you just slip the rope through the carabiner until it clicks—and always from this direction, so that if we fall, the rope can't unclip itself."

I look up to find her staring at me like I've told her to shoot me in the face. "You're joking."

I let my breath out slowly. "Not this time."

She swallows, pressing her back against the wall of the elevator shaft as though she could escape all of this by sheer willpower alone. Her hair's a mess, and there's a red, tender-looking spot at one temple that looks like soon enough it'll be a magnificent bruise. Her mascara's still tracked down her cheeks in smudged black lines, and there's a trace of blood at her swollen lower lip, from when her interrogator backhanded her. I'm not expecting the ache somewhere inside, at the sight of her. Then she sniffs. "Then what are we waiting for?"

My shoulders start aching again before we've gone a floor, in no small part due to the fact that with Alexis, the climb is taking twice as long. But despite the pain, it's not all bad news. The view when I glance up to check on her progress is plenty of consolation. I keep that observation to myself. To her credit, she manages her task without complaint, though at one point I hear her breath shuddering as she inhales, and I realize she's crying with each shaking movement upward.

When we get to the thirtieth floor, she hauls herself up over the lip of the maintenance ledge and stays on her knees, pressed against the wall, shaking. I let her stay there and keep going, adding a few more holds with the magnet grips until I can get at the access panel by the top of the opening. Ideally I'd just hack the panel, but my chip is in its pocket, and my pocket is underneath my harness, and my harness is all that's keeping me from dropping thirty floors to an admittedly very swift death. I'm going to have to do it mechanically, and that's not my forte.

I've pried off the cover and am tracing the wiring when a noise intrudes on my concentration.

"Gideon . . ." Alexis is whispering my name. "Gideon!"

"What?"

"The elevator—is it supposed to be moving?"

I stare at her for half a heartbeat, then look down to find the elevator car below us easing smoothly upward. *Oh, hell.* Though it's slow at first, it's gathering speed quickly. I meet Alexis's eyes again for a fraction of a second, and then lean into the panel, cursing hard. My fingers falter—my breath hitches—my palms are sweating and I can't get a grip on the wire and my nails are too short to dig through the coating on them, and Alexis's shouting something beside me, and finally, *finally* I spark two of the wires together and the elevator doors at waist level creak open six inches.

I reach out for Alexis, shouting at her to move, and this time she doesn't hesitate—I guide one of her feet to my leg and half shove her upward, my body screaming at the extra weight, the grip in my other hand—the one clamping the belay device closed—starting to fail. She clambers up through the opening, her body scraping either side as she wriggles through—then I see her again, as she shoves her foot against one of the doors and forces it open a few more inches. Then she's leaning down—*God, what the hell are you doing, go!*—and I realize she's reaching for me.

The elevator car's rumbling beneath us like an oncoming train, and I know she's shouting something at me because I can see her lips moving.

Her hands grasp at my wrist and I give up on the belay device, letting the rope go slack and grabbing at the hold with my other hand. For one horrible moment I know I'm not going to make it, my muscles spasming—and then I'm moving, scrambling, feet kicking briefly at empty air before Alexis and I both go sprawling onto the floor, just as the car goes screeching by. Sparks spit from the open doors as the car shears my grips off the shaft walls like leaves being stripped from a stem.

Gasping, coughing, tangled up together and sweating and shaking, Alexis and I sprawl on the floor. I press my face against the cold marble, gradually coming back to myself and the world around me. The windows at the far end of the hall tell me dawn's arrived—the first hints of light are streaking through the sky and gilding the window frames. The exit to the skybridge is just around the corner, and once we're in the neighboring building it'll be the work of moments to hack that system and catch a ride down to street level. We're safe.

With that comes the realization that Alexis is lying on top of me—for a moment I'm tempted to stay still, to keep where I am as long as possible, because now that the threat of imminent splattage has passed, I could get used to this. But as we both sit up slowly, I realize she's not pulling away because she's shaking too violently to move.

I wrap one arm around her, alarm coursing through me. "Are you okay? Are you hurt?"

She shakes her head mutely, and I can see the terror lingering in her tear-streaked face. She wasn't joking about not being good with heights—if I'd known she was *this* phobic, I never would've made her climb. I would've . . . I don't know, figured something out. How in all that's holy did she manage that?

My arm's tightening around her before I register what I'm doing, tucking her in against my side. "You did it," I murmur, turning my head to speak into her ear. "We're okay. We're almost out."

She holds still within the circle of my arm for a moment, and then abruptly she's pressing in against me, arms wrapping around my rib cage, face hidden against my T-shirt. She's still shaking, harsh breathing muffled against my skin, and I wrap my other arm around her to squeeze her tight. This isn't one of her acts. In this moment, she isn't playing me, I'm sure of it.

I'm sure of way too many things all of a sudden, and first among them is that I'm in a lot of trouble.

"We should go. Once we get across the skybridge, we need to plan our next move while we're still ahead."

It's like my words are a signal, and she clears her throat, pulling away from me, turning her head long enough to give her eyes a quick wipe, which I pretend not to notice as we climb to our feet. "I have to get back to my apartment," she says, her bone-deep weariness showing through in the way her voice cracks.

"Dimples, you can't go back there. You know you can't go back there."

Her reddened eyes flick over to meet mine. "You don't understand, I have—I have things there, things I need."

"You need your life more," I whisper, my voice escaping as the realization starts to sweep over me. I know where we're going to go.

Her eyes fill, but she nods. "I know." She swallows, then echoes, "I *know.* But where else can we go? I've got no money, not even my palm pad or any ID."

I know the answer, but even as the words rise up, I'm biting them down.

I can't. My den is sacred. Nobody gets in there but me. *Nobody.* That rule has kept me alive for the last five years. That rule has kept my identity a secret. I can't break it for anyone, for any reason—I have too much left to do before they catch me.

But I got her into this—it was me they wanted when they grabbed her—and as I climb slowly to my feet, searching in vain for any other answer that will keep her just as safe, I can feel something shifting in the air. I can feel the course I've set myself changing.

"My place," I hear myself say. "We'll go to my place."

One more test, says the blue-eyed man. One more, and then you will go home.

We will do as he asks. We will keep this new planet young and small, nudging this current and suppressing that growth. The ground will stay soft and the sky covered. When we sneak glimpses of the world through the eyes of those who live here, this place is always gray.

You must stay hidden, says the blue-eyed man. By keeping this planet young, we will stay quiet. No one will think to look for us. But there is darkness here, too, like there was in the last place. The fear follows us. This species is angry, always angry, and we are not curious about it anymore. We wish to go home. We wish to end this test.

But there were dreams.

NINE

SOFIA

THE MAG–LIFT DOORS OPEN ON THE SLUMS WITH AN ASSAULT of warm, moist air that tosses my hair back from my face. I try not to wrinkle my nose as the smells of pollution and street food mingle in my sinuses, but my stomach roils in spite of my best efforts. It's nothing like the dry, odorless, many-times-scrubbed air in my penthouse, or even the earthy peat of Avon's swamps. It smells like people here. Like many, many people all crammed in together in a space much too small to hold even half of them.

Beside me, Gideon raises his head, and my eyes pick out a nearly imperceptible lift at the corner of his mouth. To him, this is home.

I suppose if you grew up in a place like this, it wouldn't seem so bad. Maybe the constant noise—the din from vendors hawking their wares, billboards playing their looped ads overhead, the kaleidoscope of pedal-bikes, foot traffic, police sirens, freight drones—would be comforting. But I'm used to the soft, quiet nights wrapped in Avon's mist, and the first two months I spent on Corinth, here in the undercity, weren't enough for me to get used to the noise. But if this was all you knew, growing up . . .

Assuming Gideon grew up here at all. At Kristina's place he handled the SmartWaiter like he was used to top-of-the-line appliances, and when I wasn't looking, he unerringly picked out the most expensive luxury item in the whole apartment—the Miske artwork. He might navigate his way through the crowds with the ease of a native, but then, so do I.

Two months was enough to learn that much. Still, we all came from somewhere, and what matters to me now is that he can keep himself safe—keep *us* safe—down here. And keeping my eyes on the back of his neck so I don't lose him in the crowd, I have to admit that it's nice to see him relax a little.

The whole way down in the mag-lift elevator he didn't say a word, pretending instead to check a small, handheld device that looked a little like a palm pad. I could tell he was pretending by the far too even rate at which he was scrolling through it, his thumb moving up and down across the screen like clockwork. I can see the truth in his tense shoulders, despite the casual way he slumped back against the lift wall, in the normally amused mouth pressed a little too thin, in the hazel eyes stopping just short of lifting to meet my gaze.

We make a quick detour so Gideon can buy me a pair of cheap shoes—walking barefoot around the undercity is a recipe for getting any number of nameless diseases. But the detour is more than that—he doesn't want to bring me to "his place." That much is clear. I don't know if he'd have even offered if I hadn't lost it after we made it out of the elevator shaft. It wasn't hard to find those tears—in fact, it was disturbingly easy, given how hard I was shaking and how tight a hold the panic had on me—but that just made them seem more real.

I knew I had him, outside the elevator shaft, when I felt his arms go around me. Half sprawled on the hallway floor, my cheek fit against the dip just below his shoulder. We fit. Like those pendants they sell in gift shops that form a whole yin-yang symbol when you put them together.

I take a quick, deep breath in through my nose, grimacing at the bright patchwork of smells. Those necklaces are just cheap plastene and flaky paint. They fall apart almost as fast as the friendships they're supposed to symbolize. *Focus.* Just because the act is easy to pull off doesn't mean it's not an act.

"It's just up here," Gideon calls over his shoulder, his voice jerking me back to the present just in time for me to skip sideways out of the path of a particularly single-minded cyclist, bike laden with plastene jugs of homemade sake.

My stomach rumbles again, though this time it's in response to the faintest whiff of something savory and tart—I crane my neck, but all I can see is a falafel cart half a block back. Still, somewhere, someone's cooking noodles. For an instant, I can smell soy and garlic and lime. Then Gideon's reaching out to tug me down a side street, and all I can smell is the wet garbage and old food wrappers littering the gutters.

There are no street signs or helpful maps down here like there are up above. That, combined with shoddy palm pad reception, means that if you don't know where you're going already, you're probably going to end up lost inside a minute. I'm trying to mentally log every turn, but it's easier for me to memorize routes from a bird's-eye perspective—with a map or a model, I could learn this whole sector in a few days. Here, muck splashing my shoes and noise everywhere and lanterns tossing in the breeze from air traffic overhead, I'm struggling.

It's not until I see the falafel cart again—on the other side of the street this time—that I realize why. He's *trying* to get me lost. He's trying to make sure I can't find my way back here. My chest gets tighter with every step we take.

It's almost midday before Gideon finally stops at a faded green door, paint peeling and half-papered with disintegrating flyers too old to read. There's no number on it, though as I scan the building's façade through my eyelashes, I do spot a tiny camera, no bigger than a tube of lipstick, nestled against the fire escape. That's enough to tell me it's got to be Gideon's place.

He pulls out an antiquated key ring sporting an actual metal key, which he fits into the lock after glancing at me with one of his cocky grins. There's not even a deadbolt. I'm opening my mouth to protest, to point out that this is hardly any safer than my penthouse—at least I could set up an alert on the elevator there—when he ushers me into a foyer little larger than one of the info booths up topside.

The wall is lined with mailboxes, though to judge from the dirt and dust in the corners no one's lived in this building—except Gideon, I guess—for years. Sometimes, sealed behind doors like this, whole buildings get forgotten. Gideon reaches for one of the boxes and presses his fingers against the number panel—and the whole thing goes in with a click. The mailbox façade opens outward to reveal an optical scanner and three different keypads. No wonder it looks like a low-rent tenement on the outside—with the kind of security Gideon's got, it'd be a big flashing neon sign to anyone with eyes that someone important lived here. Or someone with something important to hide.

He presses his thumb to one of the keypads—it's a print scanner in disguise—and then leans down for the camera to scan his retina. "Honey, I'm home," he murmurs. Voice recognition? Or just Gideon being Gideon? He keys in a numeric code on one of the other keypads, quickly enough that I struggle to follow it, but he doesn't bother to hide the code from me. After all, unless I had his thumb and his eyeball—and possibly his vocal cords—I wouldn't be able to get in without an invitation.

After a cheery beep of acceptance, the whole wall clanks and shifts. Gideon shoves his shoulder against it and it swings back to reveal a metal staircase leading down, dim lights flickering to life. "After you."

"Lovely," I reply, hiding my genuine uneasiness with sarcasm. The staircase leads to a dark little cave of a room, sparsely furnished and dominated by a whole wall of screens on one side. The equipment and the chair, one of those tailor-made ergonomic things, are clearly the only things in the whole place he's bothered to spend money on, and the red and blue rug on the floor is the solitary homey touch in the whole place. The bed in the corner is little more than a cot with an ancient mattress slung across it. I sigh. "I suppose a secret palace down here was too much to hope for."

"I'm a man of simple needs," he replies, voice airy and utterly unconcerned. He leaps down the last few steps to the cement floor, then slips past me to bend over his desk, eyes scanning his screens. A few of them he closes before I can see what he's doing—others are filled with coded gibberish that means nothing to me. The rest seem to be chat feeds and crackpot conspiracy sites. I guess everyone's got some guilty pleasure tucked away.

There's nowhere to sit except the computer chair, so I sink down gingerly on the edge of the sagging mattress. For all its age, it does seem to be relatively clean, at least. The other side of the room is empty, but the ceiling is full of fold-down equipment. I recognize a chin-up bar and some ropes. "So this is where you practice for climbing elevator shafts?" I ask, keeping my voice light—still trying to regain my balance with him.

The corner of Gideon's mouth lifts as he turns away from the computer screens. "Nah, just vanity, really. Takes a lot of work to be the peak of physical perfection, you know."

"I'd pretend to believe you, but you clearly don't have girls over very often." Threadbare mattress and tatty rug over a cold cement floor, case in point.

"You caught me," he says, inspecting his den as though he's never seen it before. "A lot of my best targets are isolated. No connections in or out from the servers, no chance of a remote hack. You have to pay a house call, if you want to know what's in there, and that means climbing, sometimes."

"So you break and enter as well."

"Well, once you've got started, a little trespassing is the least of your problems. I only do elevator shafts on special occasions though, Dimples. They're tough."

"I like to talk my way in rather than break my way in."

Gideon grins at me, but I can spot a hint of that same tension he wore in the mag-lift down to the slums. "Bet you wish you'd asked for more detail before you talked your way in here. If I'd known you were coming, I'd have gotten curtains or something." Despite the total lack of windows in his underground den. His eyes meet mine, the easy arrogance stilling for just a moment, becoming thoughtful, measured. "You didn't give me a lot of warning."

I swallow, my gaze sliding away from his. "How did you find me?"

"Got your message, tapped into the security feed at your place." He drops down into his chair, easing back as the whole thing folds around him, adapting itself to the shape of his body. "I tracked you from there."

"The security—" Abruptly, all I can think of is that I stripped naked in the middle of my living room while those men made me change there—and the security camera's in the middle of the ceiling. "You could see the camera feed from my *apartment?*"

Gideon laughs, not doing much to calm the sudden flush burning across my face. "Don't worry, Dimples. If I want to see you with your clothes off, I'll do it the old-fashioned way."

I roll my eyes, suddenly very aware that I'm sitting on his bed. But getting up now would be telling, so I stay where I am. "Fine. Look, I'm grateful you came to get me. Just not *that* grateful. My clothes are staying where they are."

Gideon laughs again, though more softly this time, the sound punctuated by the creak of his chair as he leans forward to rest his elbows on his knees. "Whatever you say, Dimples."

The not-so-subtle reminder that he still doesn't know my first name makes me long to scratch at the skin-patch covering my genetag. I take a slow, quiet breath in and out, my eyes flicking toward the screens. In the background of one, I can see a search function running—I can't tell from here what he's looking for, but I can see it combing the hypernet for information, gathering data here and there, collating it for easy digestion. My skin crawls, the itchiness on my forearm suddenly overpowering.

What the hell am I doing getting involved with a hacker, of all people? I should just cut and run the next time he opens that vault of a front door. When I first came to Corinth, stepping off a free ride all the way from Ivanoff Orbital Station, I'd thought I was capable of charming anyone I met into doing anything I needed.

But my first attempt at a con here cost me nearly half my hard-earned savings, and left me on the run from a guy called Thor. For weeks it was two steps forward, one step back. I took whatever I could find, whatever I could get, until I built trust with my first contacts, then used them as stepping-stones to the next.

Starting from scratch, building my contacts all over again—it'll take months. Months I may not have, now that LaRoux Industries is on to me.

It was bad enough when they just thought I could hand them the Knave—now they know for sure I've seen the rift, and what it can do. And that's enough to keep them chasing me across the galaxy. I have to find some way to get to LaRoux faster. Before he can get to me.

Maybe a hacker is exactly what I need.

"Look," I say softly, keeping my eyes on the floor, lashes lowered. "I want to trust you, Gideon." I let him hear the longing there—easy enough because it's true. But wanting and doing are two very, very different things. "You saved my life back there. And I—I like you."

"Uh-huh." His voice is flat, dry—skeptical. Nothing like the soft murmur up on the roof.

Okay, that's not going to work. Regroup. I'll have to show him a few of my cards if I'm going to get to see his hand. Two parts truth, one part lie.

"I mean it." I look up through my lashes, then lift my chin as if defying him to disbelieve me. "You know I'm a liar, you know I con people—you're not stupid. It's been a really, really long time since I had anyone I could trust."

Truth.

Gideon's eyes meet mine, then skitter away toward the far wall. His body language is obscured by the chair, but his face, at least, looks conflicted. "Me, too."

"Maybe we can help each other, then. I need information about my father's death, information LaRoux Industries has somewhere. And you're after something there too, or you wouldn't have been at their headquarters that day."

Truth.

He doesn't reply this time, but I can see him thinking. He wants to trust me. A good mark always *wants* to trust you—a good mark wants you to con him. The audience wants you to succeed. I just have to not screw it up.

I swallow hard. "All I want is to find the truth about what happened to my father."

Lie.

"LaRoux Industries is dangerous, Dimples," Gideon says in that slow drawl of his. "Maybe you'd be better off just leaving Corinth, changing your name again, disappearing."

I fight not to grit my teeth. I don't need to be told about danger. I'm a daughter of Avon—I've lived in the shadow of what LaRoux Industries can do almost my entire life. I've watched my only family destroyed by the Fury LaRoux created. I was the one back there about to have my mind wiped cleaner than one of Gideon's data drives. And I don't exactly imagine myself slipping away after murdering Roderick LaRoux to an easy life—my goal's a one-way ticket. Though, of course, Gideon doesn't know that. And no reason for him to know.

Instead of snapping, I blink at him, then lean forward so that the anger in my voice will sound like passion. "If they were responsible for the death of someone you loved, would you be satisfied just disappearing?"

He's silent for a long time, so long I start to wonder if maybe he could tell I was angry after all. Then he lets his breath out audibly and gives an almost imperceptible nod. "All right," he says softly. "Maybe we can help each other."

I almost give my own sigh of relief. "Just promise me one thing?"

Gideon lifts an eyebrow, some of that amusement returning to his gaze. "Already with the demands and we're not even through our second date."

"Don't tell the Knave about me." I indicate his computer screens and their endless data streaming in and out with a flick of my eyes. "Please. I've survived this long by keeping to myself, and working with an ally will be hard enough. I just . . . I'm on your side. So long as it's just *your* side. Can you do that?"

Both his brows go up this time, and he hesitates. "I won't tell anyone about you," he replies eventually.

I can't help but let my breath out, and it emerges shakier than I'd like. My palms feel hot where they're pressed against my thighs. A good actress feels some of what she emotes, but I need to get a grip. I shouldn't care whether he trusts me or not, just whether he gets me where I need to go.

He's watching me with his usual air of indolent charm, though now I can see the shrewdness behind the lazy grin. For a wild, insane moment I want to blurt out the truth—I want to tell him everything. I choke it down. *Walk carefully, Sofia.*

I lift my chin again, this time so I can meet his eyes. "Then I might as well tell you . . . Sofia. My name's Sofia." *Truth.* "God, I can't remember the last time I gave someone my real name." *Truth.* "So . . . no more secrets."

Lie.

Time is a disease this species has created, and as their captives, time infects us as well. The symptoms are impatience, and boredom, and madness, and despair. And worst of all: understanding. These creatures cannot see into each other as we can, and therefore they know each other only through the words they invent. And words breed untruth.

And the blue-eyed man has been lying to us.

TEN

GIDEON

SOFIA. THE NAME SUITS HER. IT'S GRACEFUL, LIKE IT MIGHT slip away between my fingers, leaving no trace it was ever there.

"No more secrets," I echo, though I know it can't be a promise of my own. I can see it right there for an instant—how much more there is in that space between us, how much more we could both say. But right as I can feel myself on the edge of doing something stupid, she sighs, scooting back on the bed so she can lean her head against the wall, breaking the moment. I let it go.

"Do you have anything to eat down here?" she asks, toeing off the shoes I snagged for her, so she can draw her knees in against her chest and close her eyes.

"I don't think it's going to suit your palate," I warn her, pushing to my feet and reaching up into the rafters for the locker where I'm pretty sure I stuffed my snacks.

"Hey," she replies, opening one eye. "Just because you found me living in a penthouse doesn't mean I was born there."

"I have no idea where you were born," I agree, though the gray marble that is Avon flashes through my mind. "But you asked me not to try and find out." I find a bunch of energy bars and a couple of cans of stims. Cracking the seal on one, I hand it across to her, then open my own, taking a long swig.

She sips and grimaces, then sips again. "You don't need to know that, for us to work together."

"True," I agree. "I can live with the mystery."

"You work for the Knave, Gideon." Her lashes lift properly so she can peer at me. It's not an apology, but it's something related to it—an explanation she wants me to understand. "I know all the hearsay can't be right, but if even a fraction of it is, he's ruthless, impossible to pin down. He could *be* LaRoux for all anyone actually knows about him. You're his lackey, at the end of the day. The less you know, the better."

"Lackey's a little harsh." I reach for a joke, but I can hear in my own voice that I don't quite make it. "I prefer henchman." She doesn't smile, and I don't either. "I'm my own man. You can trust me, I promise you that."

"I'm trying," she replies, tired. "You came for me when you didn't have to. But I *don't* trust *him*."

"Who told you not to?" I can't help myself. When this thing is done, I'm going to track down whoever's been ruining my rep and devise a punishment to make future generations quail. A punishment that would make Commander Towers view the year of her life she's spent on the run from me as a walk in the park.

"I don't want to talk about it," she replies, grimacing as she sips from her can again, then setting it down beside the bed as her willingness to subject herself to it runs out. "But trust me, I *know*."

Silence settles over us, and though having someone in my den makes my skin feel twitchy, there's something warmer about having her here, too. I'd be the last to admit it, but after what I've seen at LRI Headquarters, I don't really want to be alone.

"They're never going to stop looking for us now," Sofia murmurs. Our narrow escape is on her mind too.

"At least not until LaRoux Industries carries out whatever it's planning to do with that rift."

Sofia lifts her head, glancing at me with uncharacteristic hesitation. "Well, if you won't say it, I will. Everyone's heard the Avon Broadcast. That's what Flynn—Flynn Cormac, the guy on that recording—that's what he was talking about. Creatures that can affect minds."

It sounds insane. Beyond insane. And if I hadn't seen what Tarver and Lilac went through, if I hadn't been tracking the woman who helped LaRoux cover up the Avon conspiracy, I'd politely show this girl the door and get back to my screens. "Yeah," I say instead, my voice sounding papery and thin even to my own ears. "'Whispers,' he called them. He said they were whispers from another universe."

"Surely there's some way to just cut our universe off from theirs, so that LaRoux can't use the whispers."

I'm quick to shake my head. "They come from hyperspace. If we shut the door on their universe, we'd be left without the ability to jump through their dimension from place to place. There'd be no faster-than-light travel, no hypernet communication between planets."

Sofia grimaces. "Okay, let's not do that then. So how *do* you fight something that can get inside your mind, control your thoughts?"

I wish I had an answer, but instead the silence draws in around us again, thick and smothering this time. I don't *know* how to fight the whispers. It's why I'm trying to fight LaRoux himself, to drag him into the light. Despite the short time I've known her, it's strange to see Sofia at such a loss. I take a deep breath, and say something out loud I've never told anyone but Mae. "We fight him instead. His company."

Her eyes flick up from the floor again, brows lifted.

I indicate my screens with a jerk of my chin. "There's nothing we can do against beings that can reach inside your head, but we can stop what they're being used to do. Whatever it is. Avon's people managed to stand up to LaRoux, despite these creatures being there. And—" My words come up short, and I almost choke with the effort to halt my momentum. "And I think the *Icarus* survivors encountered them too," I finish finally. I'm not ready for her to know about my connection with the youngest LaRoux.

Sofia frowns. "How could you know *that*?"

"It's a long story," I reply. "But I've been looking. For years now, I've been digging into LaRoux Industries. I told you I had my own reasons for wanting to take them down."

Sofia leans back, resting her shoulders against the wall next to the bed. She takes her time responding, and I can feel those gray eyes on me like a tangible weight. "I showed you mine," she says softly. "You don't think I should know why you're in this? Why I should trust you?"

In an instant, my brother's face is there in front of me. I'm always looking up in my memory; he was older, though these days I'm taller than he was when he died. Freckled, grinning, he's always laughing in my imagination, though I never remember the jokes. The sort of things brothers laugh about, stupid kid jokes that make no sense to anybody else. Grief wraps around my throat, tightening like a hand, making it hard to swallow. "Because the LaRoux family killed my brother."

Sofia's silent for a time, but I can still feel her watching me. "I'm so sorry," she says finally, and for now, that's enough.

I cough to clear my throat, straightening in my chair. "Well, we're safe here for now. No one's ever found this place and I've been here for years. We can regroup, figure out our next move. Wait a few weeks, see if the heat dies down."

"A few weeks . . ." Sofia echoes my words, suddenly not looking at me anymore, but rather gazing past me with a troubled look on her face.

"What is it? I know it's no penthouse, but it's better than—"

"No, no, this place is fine," Sofia says dismissively. Now I *know* she's distracted. "I'm remembering what one of those guys said, back at LRI Headquarters, right before you got there. Something about having a week to fix the rift and make sure it was working right."

"So . . . what's happening in a week that's so important to LaRoux?"

Sofia's eyebrows lift. "Seriously? You don't know?" One side of her mouth lifts, drawing the faintest ghost of a dimple and banishing the lingering remnants of grief. "Do you ever come out of those screens?"

"There are a lot of things happening in a week, Dimples. I probably know about more of them than you do."

"Maybe. But quality over quantity, my good man. Run a search on '*Daedalus*.'"

The name sends a jolt through me. I don't have to search the phrase—the entire galaxy knows about the *Icarus*'s sister ship. "Oh, holy shit, you're right. The grand opening of the *Daedalus* museum is happening soon."

"And the opening-night gala is doubling as a welcome bash for all the planetary envoys visiting for the peace summit." Her mouth twists in a way completely unrelated to a smile. "To discuss those pesky rebellions."

The ruling senators for every planet in the galaxy, all in the same room, all with their guards down. "Oh, hell."

"LaRoux wants power," Sofia goes on. Her face, when she says that name, goes hard as granite. She may be a consummate actress, but she can't hide her hatred. "If he could do to the senators what he did to the people on Avon, or the people at LRI Headquarters . . ."

"He'd control the entire galaxy." My mouth is dry, a deep chill in my gut making me want to shiver. Hard enough exposing LaRoux and his company without the authorities themselves under mind control. "Would he be able to move something as big as the rift we saw? And hide it from an entire ship full of staff and guests, not to mention the media outlets that'll be swarming the gala?"

Sofia hesitates, glancing at me, then at my screens, then away. "I have a contact," she says finally, "within LRI. I only got a little from her—we were going to meet that day at the holosuite. But she told me that the technology LaRoux used to create the rifts is the same technology used in the new hyperspace engines, which makes sense given what you've just told me about where the whispers come from. My contact understands the rifts—I think she worked on the project, or at least on the new engines, like the one onboard the *Icarus*."

"And the one onboard the *Daedalus*." It doesn't take a genius to figure out where she's heading, and I'm already itching to get a look at the ship's blueprints. "There could be a rift there already, hiding in plain sight."

"And if we don't get to him first, LaRoux's going to use it to turn the entire Galactic Council into husks under his command."

"Oh, *hell*," I repeat, shutting my eyes.

"In a handbasket," she agrees.

"Bring her back!" The blue-eyed man is screaming at us through the thin spot on the gray world. "You brought the scientists on Elysium back, again and again. You drove them mad with it. All I ask is one life, one—" His words fail him.

His face is haggard, the dark hair grown lighter with gray and white at temple and nape. His anguish is different from the anguish we have learned from the gray world. This anguish is special, individual, unique. He is teaching us pleasure. They have a word for it, this species. *Revenge*.

"Please," the blue-eyed man whispers. "If not for me, then for my little girl. She needs her mother."

We stay silent. Let him know loneliness. Let him understand. Let him be the one to watch, and wait, and learn. His lessons are bitter.

And I will learn pleasure.

ELEVEN

SOFIA

I FIND MYSELF DRIFTING OFF TO SLEEP AS GIDEON WORKS AT his screens, trying to figure out who we should contact to warn the *Daedalus* gala attendees about LaRoux's plans. I know I should stay awake, but it's the first time I've actually felt *safe* since I first saw the rift at LRI Headquarters, and exhaustion is catching up with me. Down here I have no idea what time it is, but it can't be more than early afternoon and I feel ready to drop. I was thinking for a while about venturing out for some supplies. I cooked enough on Avon, and I learned about off-world ingredients when I spent a little time as Lucy, a waitress on Paradisa, but the prospect of moving seems to make my body even heavier. I wedge myself upright in the corner to keep myself from slumping, but despite my best efforts, it seems like only a few seconds have passed when I wake up to darkness.

For a moment I'm disoriented, but then the cushion I'm leaning against moves and memory floods back. I'm not leaning on a cushion. It's *Gideon*. He must have stopped working and decided to join me in my nap. For a moment, indignation flares through me as he shifts again, chest rising and falling under my cheek in a sigh—but as my eyes adjust to the darkness, I realize that I'm no longer in my corner. I'm the one who's moved, to the other end of the bed, to lean on *him*.

God, I'm even lonelier than I thought.

I ought to pull away and creep back to my corner, and hope he was sleeping deeply enough not to have noticed me. I barely know him, except that he's the closest thing I've had in a long time to someone I could trust. *Even so,* I remind myself sternly, *he's worked for the Knave. He'd probably try to stop you if he knew why you were after LaRoux. And you don't know he's telling the truth about anything.*

And yet I don't move.

A tiny sound rises above the gentle whir of Gideon's various computers, and I open my eyes again. I listen hard, lifting my head so that Gideon's heartbeat doesn't drown it out. It's a high-pitched whine, like the noise of far-off construction, only it doesn't sound far-off. I'm unused to the sounds here in the undercity, so perhaps it's nothing.

It's not until there's a thud, muffled but clear enough for me to recognize that it's close by, that I sit bolt upright. I grab for Gideon's arm, no longer caring if he notices how close I crept while we were sleeping.

He wakes quickly but groggily, barely a silhouette in the dark. "Mmph?" he asks, starting to sit up.

"Does anyone else use this building?" I whisper.

Gideon finds his voice, but thankfully keeps it low to match mine. "No, it's just me."

"There's someone outside. Listen." For a few seconds there's only silence, but then the high-pitched whirring starts up once more.

Gideon's forearm goes rigid under my hand. "It can't be," he murmurs. He waits one second more before scrambling abruptly out of bed, still in what he wore when he came to my rescue. He stumbles over to his screens, waving a hand at them to wake them up. There's a soft chime, and a synthetic female voice speaks calmly. "Intruder alert. Security breach in process."

"*Now* you tell me?" he snaps. A few flicks of his fingers summon up the display from his security camera. "Oh, God."

I move off the bed and over to the screens, where the centermost one shows a trio of people, difficult to make out through the fuzziness of the footage. But I can see enough to tell one of them is crouched in front of the door, using some sort of device on Gideon's locking mechanisms.

My heart seizes, fear banishing the last vestiges of sleepiness and warmth from Gideon's body. "What're they—"

"They're drilling into the door." Gideon's voice is tight and cold, and without wasting another second he's moving, throwing open cabinets to reveal banks of computer drives, shelves of equipment for breaking and entering, and a host of other things I can't identify.

"How did they find us?" I gasp—I don't waste time asking who "they" are. This has to be LaRoux's doing.

"It doesn't matter," Gideon replies. "We've got to run. There's a back exit. Here, take this and pack anything useful you see." He tosses an empty bag at me, then grabs a bag himself, the same one he wore when he came into LaRoux Headquarters after me. He shoves in a couple of handfuls of electronics, then reaches for the bottom drawer of his desk to pull out an old, battered, antiquated paper book. He carefully, gingerly tucks it into his bag to nestle against his lapscreen. He takes a precious moment to seal the bag, then dumps it on the ground.

I get to work, shoving gear and protein gel packets into the bag. Abruptly there's a scream from outside the door, audible even through the layers of steel, and when my gaze flies up to the security screens, one of the fuzzy figures is lying on the ground.

"Defense measures won't hold them forever," Gideon says tightly. "Gas should release in a minute, but if they're smart they'll have masks." He grabs for a handheld device that, once he clicks it on, emits a drone so high-pitched it's nearly silent, while at the same time making my jaw ache. He starts swiping it up and down the banks of drives—the screen showing the security feed flickers, striated by white and black lines, then goes blank. A paper clip lying on one of the drives zips over and clings to the device—an electromagnet. He's erasing his tracks.

"These here," he commands, gesturing at a cabinet, and I dutifully empty a box of thumb drives into my pack. Then Gideon's pressing tiny bricks of what looks like thick clay against the interior of the computer drive cabinet. I'm moving to add a bigger, heavier external drive to the others in my bag when he jerks to his feet and takes it from me. "No—that goes in here." He slips the drive into his own bag, giving it an affectionate pat. "This one's aluminized, keeps it from being wiped. That drive's too important to risk." As he speaks, he's moving—a few steps and he's at my side, stooping to grab at the edge of the faded rug on the floor and fling it aside.

"Oh, for the love of—" For a moment I forget the people trying to break into our sanctuary, staring at the trapdoor that the rug had been hiding. "You're like a villain out of an old movie. I should've known the only homey touch here was to hide your getaway."

"Can't go wrong with the classics," Gideon replies, and though the joke sounds like him, his voice doesn't. It's still tight with distress, and I can see panic starting to seep into his gaze, despite what must be a well-rehearsed contingency plan.

He's not used to people finding him, I realize. He hasn't lived the life I have over the past year, always only a step or two ahead of the Knave, always waiting for him to find me and drive me to move on again.

"Let's go," I say, and he stops staring at the trapdoor and instead hauls it open. I start down the ladder it reveals, then pause. "We need to get the rug back over the trapdoor somehow, or they'll just figure out where we went."

"They'll have other things on their minds," Gideon says grimly. "Hurry."

The ladder leads down into what must be an old, forgotten sewer from when the undercity of Corinth was the *only* city. Now it's dry and empty and, when Gideon slams the trapdoor closed above us, utterly pitch-black. I freeze, trying to remember if I shoved a flashlight into the pack of gear on my back, but before I can start to look, a soft reddish glow illuminates the tunnel.

I glance back to see Gideon clipping an LED lamp to his collar and tossing a second one to me. Smart—the red light is the part of the spectrum least likely to ruin our night vision. If we have to shut off the lamps and hide, we'll still be able to see as well as anything else down here.

"We have to keep moving," says Gideon, his voice still strained, making my heart ache. I did this to him.

"Gideon, I'm so sorry. I never meant—"

"It's not your fault," he interrupts, before lifting his gaze to meet mine. The red light drains his face of any other color, leaching the sandy brown from his hair, the hazel from his eyes. He takes a breath, and when he speaks again, he sounds a little more like himself. "I can start over. We're in this together."

I swallow, and while I wish I could think of something to say, there's no time for that. Despite Gideon's promise, I'm expecting those goons to pull open the trapdoor at any moment. I take off down the tunnel again, Gideon's footsteps right behind me.

I can hear him counting under his breath as we move, but not at the right pace to be keeping time—he's counting out our steps. I'm about to ask why, when he reaches one hundred and pauses. I turn to see him holding something, about the size of a thumb drive or a gambling chip. He sucks in a breath and glances at me. "Brace yourself."

I don't have time to ask for more details, because he's pressing a button on the object and then a sound blasts down the tunnel, making me cry out in spite of myself and clap my hands over my ears. A shower of dust and cobwebs and other things I don't want to know about patters down onto my hair and shoulders, and I have to fight the impulse to throw myself to the ground. I know that sound. I know it so well it echoes in my nightmares, makes my shoulder throb with remembered pain.

An explosion.

The echoes of it through the tunnel die away, leaving me gasping, shaking, staring at Gideon, who slips the device back into his pocket. "What the—you said—"

He shakes his head, speaking softly. "The echoes make it sound bigger than it was. The charges were just to destroy anything left on my drives. Even if they were already inside, the worst they'd get would be some ringing ears and maybe some bruises if the force knocked them back."

My mouth tastes bitter, and though I'm trying to make myself move again, my muscles are tense and shaking. Through the dim red light of the LEDs I can almost see the first responders at the base on Avon running toward the flames, can almost smell the acrid smoke and chemicals, can almost hear the shouts and screams of wounded soldiers beginning to fill the air.

"Hey," comes Gideon's voice, much closer to me. "Are you okay? I'm sorry, I should've warned you—I promise we're okay down here. This place could take a dozen blasts like that and survive."

I blink, trying to clear my eyes of smoke that doesn't exist, and realize he's taken my arm, his hand warm and real, unlike the remembered heat of a barracks on fire. "I'm fine," I gasp, unable to stop my voice shaking. "I don't want to talk about it. Let's go."

Gideon hesitates, eyes on my face until I turn away. If I tell him about my father's so-called suicide, he'll be able to figure out who I am the second he gets access again to the hypernet. And while he says he doesn't still work for the Knave, I have no way of knowing how close his ties are, or whether he'd turn me over if he knew I was the thing the Knave had been chasing for the last year.

I start moving, pulling away from his hand on my arm, and after another second of hesitation, his footsteps start up again behind me. A few jogging steps and he catches up to me, clearing his throat.

"We'll head to Mae's," he says, causing a ping of relief somewhere amidst the fog of memory in my head that he's not pushing the issue. "She's an old friend, and if anyone on the net has heard rumors about something bad going down at the *Daedalus* gala, she'll know about it."

"Can we trust her?"

"Absolutely." Gideon glances at me, flashing me a smile in the dim red glow of our LED lamps. "She's one of the only people on this planet I actually *do* trust. I knew her for years through the hypernet before we ever met in person. She's good people. And she's got a good rig, so we can use her place to regroup."

I let out a slow breath. It's hard enough teaching myself to trust Gideon—secondhand trust is even harder to accept. But I nod, reminding myself that even though he trusts her, I don't have to. I can still run, if I need to. I still know how to disappear.

"Where is she?"

"She actually lives in this sector, on the north side. Mid-level."

"Oh—perfect." I try to bite back my surprise. Mid-level means money, at least enough to afford a decent place, a hover, a steady lifestyle. I was expecting the female version of Gideon, and had been bracing myself for another lair. "But Gideon—what do we do then? If something's going down on the *Daedalus*, that doesn't give us much time to stop LaRoux."

Gideon runs his hands through his hair, a gesture of frustration that's becoming rapidly familiar the longer I know him. "I know. I can't believe I'm saying this, but we should tell the police—it's not like we've got proof, but maybe if they launch even a halfhearted investigation, it might be enough to throw a wrench in LaRoux's plans."

The police? I swallow hard, exhaustion making it harder for me to remember what I've told Gideon and what I haven't. He knows I'm a con artist, knows I'd have no particular desire to bring the authorities into this. But he doesn't know all the reasons why I *really* don't want the police's attention on me. Attention that could lead to questions like "Why do you own an illegal firearm?" and "What are you doing with the blueprints to LRI Headquarters?" and "Why are you hiding your genetag and your identity?"

"Surely LaRoux's got people in law enforcement," I say finally. "Not to mention that the sector relies heavily on LaRoux's private security force, and as much fun as it was dancing with them last time, I wouldn't mind avoiding their eye this time around."

Gideon's shaking his head, his eyes distant and his lips thin, his expression so clear I can almost feel his distress like it's my own. Losing his den means a lot more to him than losing my apartment did to me.

I soften my voice. "Can we really trust them?"

"We've got to trust someone," Gideon says finally. "We'll keep it anonymous. We don't even need to say it's LaRoux—maybe even just a bomb threat, something mundane, something they have to look into. Anything to get their eyes on the *Daedalus*, because I don't know what else we can do."

And the problem is, he's right. We're days out from the gala on the *Daedalus*, and our arsenal is down to a backpack of whatever we could grab before he reduced his hideout to rubble. We have nothing. I swallow against the bitter taste of adrenaline still lingering in my mouth, and let Gideon lead me on through the darkness.

We wait on the gray world, and look for worth in the hatred and mistrust among its people but find little. Their moments of bravery and heroism are buried in the lust for violence and revenge that tears them apart.

There is a girl with fire in her blood stirring the others with the same magnetism of the blue-eyed man, making others follow her with nothing but words. They rebel against their leaders as we once tried to rebel against the man with blue eyes.

But it is the little boy often at her side who draws our notice most. These creatures cannot see into each other, or see ahead into the infinite branches of possible futures. But we can.

And this green-eyed boy will be important.

TWELVE

GIDEON

THE SOUND OF OUR FOOTSTEPS IS MUFFLED BY THE SOFT sand under our feet, and I can hear my breath in my ears, too loud and rasping for the speed we're running. But of course it's not the running that's got my heart trying to thump its way out of my chest. I've got a chorus of voices echoing around my head, just to add to the noise.

My den.

This is what you get for letting someone in.

Did I definitely wipe the drives in the corner?

Did I pack my book? Yes, I packed it, I remember.

Oh, hell.

Is this what it feels like for Towers? Constantly grabbing her bag and running, expecting them behind her at any second?

I damn well hope it is. I hope I scare the hell out of her.

Every soldier under her command trusted her, and she turned her head the other way when it really mattered. She failed to protect them, just like all those years ago, my brother's commander failed to keep him safe.

They accepted the responsibility. They should be held to a higher standard.

And accept the consequences, when they fail to meet it.

But how did they find us?

"How did they find us?"

A moment later I realize Sofia spoke my own thought out loud, and I shake my head without breaking my stride. "I have no idea. Maybe they got one of our faces scanned, caught us on a facial recognition camera as we came below."

"One that showed us actually walking in that door?" She sounds skeptical. "I assumed you'd have those locked down pretty hard."

"I do. They're not connected to any network but my own—there's no way anybody could have intercepted the feed."

"We need to work out how they found us before we head to your friend's, or for all we know, they could follow us right there."

My heart throws in a little extra syncopation over that idea. This girl is *good* at running—I hadn't even thought of that. I let my pace slow. "Okay, think. Let's assume they didn't get us with cameras, because that's hardest to confirm, and hardest to act on. Did you carry anything out of LaRoux Headquarters that you didn't carry in?"

She glances down at herself, conducting a mental stock take, then slowly shakes her head. "I'm sure I didn't."

"Did you eat or drink?"

"Nothing."

I let my frustration out in a growl, then cut the sound off as she raises one hand abruptly, her eyes widening in the dim red light. "They injected me."

I kick up a cloud of sand as I screech to a halt. "They what?"

"I assumed it was something to make me more compliant, I wasn't answering their questions. But I don't know that for a fact." She's working hard to keep her voice level, but I can hear the fear—I'm listening for it, I guess, since the same thing is pulsing through me. "What if they injected me with something they can trace? With some kind of tracker?"

I shake my head, closing my eyes, forcing myself to focus. Dragging my mind away from my ruined den, where it wants to linger. "They knew where you were, and they couldn't have thought you'd escape. I mean, modesty aside, it was incredibly unlikely, especially given that they didn't know we were in contact, or that you'd got a signal out. Injecting a tracker is beyond preemptive measures, and into paranoid territory."

Her silence is what makes me open my eyes again. Her face is perfectly still, and this time she can't keep the tremble out of her voice. "They were going to make me into a husk, take my mind with—with the rift. I would have done anything they told me to, but perhaps I wouldn't have been able to report back. Perhaps they would have needed a way to find me, if . . . I couldn't communicate."

She swallows, hard, and I want to throw my arms around her and squeeze her until we both feel safe. Instead, I curl my hands into fists by my sides and keep my voice level. "It's a working theory. Let's see what we can find."

We're both straining our ears now for the sound of pursuit coming up the tunnel, but we can't move until we're sure we're not leading them closer and closer to Mae's place. Sofia keeps watch in silence as I cobble together a scanner, cannibalizing one of my security sweepers and wiring it into my lapscreen, pulling my chip from my pocket to insert and bring it all to life—it's my last security precaution, in case somebody gets their hands on my lapscreen. Paranoia, perhaps, but today turned out to be a good day to be paranoid.

She turns, pulling down the collar of her shirt until I can see an angry red spot just below the fleshy part of her shoulder. I clench my jaw and press the scanner against her skin, trying to ignore the way it makes her flinch. Then she extends her arms so I can run it over each of her limbs in turn, moving slowly and giving the image on my screen time to stabilize.

Whatever they've put in her arm, it's moved a little—I find it nestled close to the shoulder joint, where it's worked its way down from its entry point. No bigger than a couple of grains of sand, but I know what I'm seeing.

"Cut it out," she whispers sharply, staring down at the little image on the screen. "Do you have a knife?"

I shake my head. "No time, no first aid, and there's important stuff around your shoulder joint I could hit. We can neutralize it for now and get rid of it later."

She presses her lips together tightly as I pull out the handheld electro-magnet I brought with me, clipped to the outside of my bag. I keep it clear of all my equipment, and instead press it against her skin before switching it on. I can sympathize—I'd want to hack it out of me too—but speed is everything, and we both know that.

Once we're sure it's dead, she helps me stuff my equipment back into my bag, and we set off again as quietly as we can.

We emerge from the tunnel in an alleyway behind a twenty-four-hour dance club, the pulse of the beat inside shaking the walls around us. The daylight, even diffuse and artificial as it is down here, makes me stumble and blink. I'm about to turn and stride for the mouth of the alley when Sofia grabs my arm, spinning me back to face her. My heart stutters—surprise, no more—and then she reaches up to pull my head torch free, and smooth back my hair, then pluck a spiderweb from my chest.

"We don't want to draw attention," she says, lifting my hand and positioning it palm-up so she can dump both torches in it, then running her hands over her own clothing, straightening it quickly. It's like she's putting herself back together as she does it, and when she looks up at me once more, she's composed. Everything that's going on inside her is locked away tight. I envy her the ability.

I stuff the torches in my bag and turn to lead the way. We take a direct route—we're as sure as we can be that they're not tracking us remotely, so now we need to clear the area before they get eyes on us physically. Keeping our heads down, we push through the marketplace, and I can't help but wonder if I'll be coming back here at all. It feels like we're on a track now, heading toward the confrontation I've been planning for years, with no way to avoid it. The rift, the whispers—they're here on Corinth, so either we take the fight to LaRoux, or somehow, he's going to bring it to us.

The elevator up to Mae's level is quiet, and the difference from the cacophony of the market is obvious the moment the doors slide open. We squeeze past a bunch of door-to-door evangelists and a couple clearly on a date—locked at the lips and hips—and walk out into the neat and tidy streets of her neighborhood. The mid-levels lack the ostentation of Kristina McDowell's penthouse, but the small, compact homes around here are nothing like the tenements in the slums, either. The buildings are no more than ten stories high, and most dwellings have a whole story to themselves. This is about the level where you start getting your own bedroom, even if it's just a hidey-hole.

Mae's three blocks away, and she opens the door on the third knock. Her mouth falls open when she sees me, and though I summon up a ghost of my usual smile, it doesn't seem to help any. "Honey, what the *hell?*" she whispers, stepping back to gesture us urgently inside. "Your whole setup went dark an hour ago, and there's some serious chatter about something going boom in the Botigues quarter. I've been frantic. Get inside, quick."

I push the front door closed, leaning back against it and letting my breath out slowly. My heart's still pounding, lungs aching as though I've been running for kilometers. *This is Mae's house,* I tell my body. *Start behaving. We're safe here.* "The truth is better than the rumors," I say. "Mae, this is . . ." I pause. "Alice. Alice, this is Mae."

Whatever Sofia was expecting, I'm one hundred percent sure this wasn't it—Mae looks about as wholesome as they get, in one of the vintage tea dresses in fashion right now, hair caught up in a neat ponytail, as if she just slipped in from a social game of tennis. She looks like she should be serving on the fund-raising committee at her kids' school—and in fact she does—instead of partnering me on the galaxy's most notorious hacks.

Still, I've got to give my girl her due. She sticks out her hand to shake like she's just been introduced to Mae at a cocktail party, and her smile looks a world better than mine. "We owe you," she says simply.

"My friend, that's one complicated ledger, trust me," Mae laughs. "I'm assuming if we're doing introductions, you're sure you weren't followed, honey?"

I nod, suddenly—uncomfortably—aware that I need to tell Mae not to refer to me as the Knave where Sofia can hear. As if I needed this day getting any more tangled. "I'm sure, but my den is gone. I had to burn it all."

She lets out a slow breath. "You need gear?"

I nod again. "We won't stay any longer than we have to, but this is the only place that has what I need to work out our next step. I thought . . ." But what I'm asking for is huge—the average user's private enough about letting somebody onto their system. For Mae to let another hacker into her rig is akin to her inviting somebody to waltz on in while she's naked. There's no reassurance I can offer that would matter—the truth is, I could do whatever I wanted once she let me in, and she knows it. So it comes down to trust.

Mae nods slowly. "We're in this deep, may as well go the whole way. Come on through, both of you. Let's get you set up before the kids get home from school."

I see Sofia taking it all in as we head out the back—I'm good at electronic networks, and she dominates the social ones, after all. So she's doing what she does best. I see her study the school schedules on the screen in the kitchen, the photos of Mae and her kids, the comfy, mid-priced furnishings. Mae and her partner Tanya used a donor for the kids, then Mae ended up a single mom when it turned out raising babies was hard work. She shrugged, and said better to raise two than three. That's what Mae's like—the kids are the thing that matter. Sofia's working that out, I'm pretty sure, from what's on show here.

Though it's very faint, she almost smiles when we head through into Mae's office. I guess most of my kind don't have well-tended potted plants and framed family portraits in their secret dens of hackery.

Me, I'm just itching to get over to Mae's huge bank of screens. It's like a gap inside me, having no way to get online—it's an addiction, and I know it, but it's one that works for me just fine. I tug on my sensor gloves and sink down into Mae's chair. It hums softly, contours adjusting as it folds around me, and just like that, I'm at home. Behind me I hear Mae talking to Sofia about food and drink, but I'm already submerging in my world.

Most of the screens are taken up with forums, which Mae must have been checking when we arrived. They're her specialty, though I dabble there as well. Say what you will about the conspiracy theorists, their paranoia comes in handy. If anything of interest makes it onto any corner of the hypernet, one of them's going to notice it—and a couple of well-placed comments will send them marching off like an army of ants to investigate. Then all you have to do is sort the truth from the imagined shadows. Still, it's worth it for the occasional gem, and that's why the Knave provides anonymous, protected venues for their discussions. Looks like Mae was checking in on the Corinth Against Tyranny group—after their protest the day Sofia and I met, a bunch of their supporters are still missing. With the LaRoux stranglehold on the media, they're not having any luck raising a fuss. This is the problem for all the groups who listened to Flynn Cormac's infamous Avon Broadcast. Even if they do believe him, they're never going to get the word out.

I slide in a couple of thumb drives to set up the programs I want, and watch the information start to fly by. For a moment I can see it before me, a vision of all my files streaming through the hypernet, locked down and encrypted beyond the wildest dreams of government agencies, part of an endless river of data. Does it all slide through hyperspace in some form recognizable to those who live there, the whispers? I wonder what they make of the stories we send—our love letters, our tax returns, and everything in between.

I shake away the question, and while I wait for them to run their security scans, I turn my attention to a discussion about Avon that takes up the top two screens on the right.

Nothing new on the first—a rehashing of the same old arguments about whether Flynn Cormac's just a crackpot, no mention at all of Towers, some new data on the latest terraforming reports on Avon . . . and then. *Oh, very nice.* Kumiko and her band of Avon veterans, alleged Fury survivors, are chattering like I've never seen before. The author of the Avon Broadcast himself is coming to Corinth.

Someone's copied and pasted the press release, with some sarcastic comments about how "the Man" keeps trying to pretend Cormac's speech was all a lie. *"Part of the official delegation from Avon, arriving in Corinth to present the credentials of the planet's first elected senator to the Galactic Council and participate in the peace summit, Cormac is known for his involvement in the much-discussed Avon Broadcast, in which he claimed . . ."* I know the rest.

My Avon expert's probably got more info on the delegation than she's posted in the forums, but my curiosity on that front will have to wait. I can picture Kumiko in her own den to the south of this sector, hunched over her screens. She's a more reliable source of information than most, especially when it comes to the Fury on Avon, but I never quite trusted her enough to tell her I was after Towers. I don't know who Kumiko served under on Avon, and since Towers's role in the Fury epidemic there isn't exactly public knowledge, I can't be sure where Kumiko's loyalties would fall.

The text boxes I'm waiting on pop up, and I start my search as Mae cracks open a stim can and sets it down beside me. I set my parameters quickly—I'm creating a series of backdoor user profiles, so that I can send in a bomb scare for the *Daedalus* gala to get the police looking their way without being able to figure out who alerted them. Behind me, Mae and Sofia are talking quietly about the *Daedalus*—I can hear the surprise in Mae's voice. Even she, queen of the hypernet rumors, has heard nothing about any drama planned for the gala.

Now that my program has introduced me to Mae's system, it starts bringing up my regular windows one by one. My Towers subprogram springs to life, though there's nothing in there to report, as usual. I can't be sure, but I don't think she's left Corinth. I first found her when she evacuated Avon—allegedly for a quiet retirement. At the time I didn't buy that she'd just pack up and settle down after all that, after years of looking the other way, then doing LaRoux's cleanup for him. So I set a program to look for oddities in travel patterns—people who check in for a hyperspace jump but don't check out on the other end, passenger manifests that end up one person short, that sort of thing.

That's the easiest way to work out what you should investigate. Don't comb through terabytes of data until your eyes cross. Just look for the exceptions, data points behaving the way they shouldn't, and track *those*. They'll be the interesting ones. And right around the time Towers resigned her post, an ident number popped up on the grid supposedly belonging to a war orphan on the next transport leaving Avon. The alleged orphan, a regular citizen of Avon with absolutely no resources to her name, vanished from the transport headed for the orphanage and proceeded to defy every expectation and probability by bouncing from planet to planet and changing her ID more often than most people change their clothes. This was someone who wanted to throw the hounds off the scent, and the only thing on Avon worth that kind of secrecy was what LaRoux put there.

So for the last year, I've been Antje Towers's personal bloodhound, and I never let her rest. She's somewhere on my planet, and even when I'm sleeping, my bots and subprograms are searching for her. As hard as it is for me living off the grid, I'm making it absolute hell for her. The longer she runs, the more tired she's going to get, and the more sloppy her evasions will become. Eventually she's going to slip up. And I'll be there when she does.

With a soft chime, the screen flashes me a dialogue box asking me if I want to send my message. I realize I've been sitting there with the anonymous scare threat typed up for a full ten minutes, and it's not until Sofia drifts over from her conversation with Mae that I shake off my fog. Usually the police are the last people either of us would want to call, but we don't have any other choice left to us. I glance at Sofia, who's reading over the message—she takes a breath and nods at me, and with a flick of my fingers, I send our alert winging out into the hypernet to do its work.

I let my breath out and lean back into the chair, abruptly feeling every ounce of tension and exhaustion catching up with me. We've passed the torch, and even if the cops don't know the real reason they're being sent to investigate the situation onboard the *Daedalus*, their presence will throw enough attention on the gala that LaRoux can't dare do anything to stop them.

Sofia exhales beside me, and I don't have to look at her to know her face will show that same release. "What do we do now?"

"Now we wait." I draw my shoulders back, wincing as the movement causes a series of pops along my upper spine. "And sleep, while we've got somewhere safe to rest."

For the first time in all our existence, we are conflicted. We have always been one entity, infinite selves all linked, every thought shared. But those of us who have existed in the thin spots, who have touched the minds and hearts of these beings who carry such passion inside themselves . . . we are different now.

Difference, in an existence of utter harmony and completion, is destroying us.

Some wish to banish the individuals, to close our world to them forever and deny their ships and their data streams and become, once more, one self.

But there are those of us who are not so certain. Those of us who have seen, who have been, however briefly, something else . . .

Something . . . unique.

THIRTEEN

SOFIA

"YOU'RE SURE I CAN'T GET YOU ANYTHING ELSE?" MAE'S sliding dishes into the washer slot while we sit at the kitchen counter, eating sandwiches and drinking iced tea. It's been an hour, and though Gideon hasn't picked up any increased chatter from law enforcement regarding the gala, he seems confident that it's just taking time to trickle through the appropriate channels.

"Nah, thanks, Mae." Gideon's chowing down on his sandwich, more relaxed than I've seen him since he woke to find people breaking into his den.

I resist the urge to reach up under the sweater Mae gave me and scratch at the bandage on my shoulder. Gideon borrowed Mae's first-aid kit, and with a little anesthetic spray, one quick slice, and a second spray of NuSkin, he got rid of LRI's disabled tracker. The gash in my shoulder where he dug it out feels like it was never there. *Better safe than sorry,* he said, and he's right.

I'm finding it harder to settle. This room, this woman—they're so unlike what I'm used to that it's a struggle to know exactly how to fit in. I'm at home in squalor and in riches—whether it's the slums of Corinth or the swamps of Avon, or a penthouse apartment in the richest district of this sector, I've learned those worlds. I know how to navigate them. But this . . . this is just somebody's mom, which is already unfamiliar to me, in a room that could be a set from one of those "average Joe" sitcom shows.

I nibble at my sandwich and let my eyes scan the room as Mae and Gideon chat, though my mind's automatically parsing everything they say. If I seem to be focused on something else, they'll feel a bit less like I'm listening in, and I can learn more about them. They've clearly known each other for years, and the length of that bond causes a little, aching ping of envy somewhere inside me. I don't think they see each other in person all that often, judging by a comment of Mae's about Gideon's height, and his exclamations when she fetches a picture of her kids— Mattie and Liv, fraternal twins. But despite all this evidence of a long time apart, they pick up with an ease of conversation like they speak every day.

Maybe they do. I'm remembering the dozens of windows Gideon had open at any given time, many of which were text chats with usernames I didn't recognize.

"Whoops, that's the kids' school," Mae exclaims, straightening up and lifting a hand to the earpiece she wears. "I'm gonna go take this, you guys finish eating."

That comment's more for me than for Gideon, whose sandwich vanished entirely several minutes ago. As Mae ducks into the living room, Gideon tucks his feet under the crossbar of his stool and swivels back and forth, eyeing me askance. "You okay?"

I take a quick bite of my sandwich and then nod, indicating my mouth to point out I'm just following Mae's orders. Gideon waits, though, and eventually I have to swallow and answer. "Just letting you guys catch up. She seems really nice."

"She is," Gideon replies with a grin. "I've known her since I was twelve, though she didn't know then that was my age. Most people on the net still don't. Nobody takes a teenager seriously."

"True," I reply, taking one more bite and then sliding the last quarter of my sandwich over toward him. "But that just makes my job easier. No one suspects I'm up to anything at all."

Gideon takes my offering without question, and the gusto with which he finishes off my sandwich reminds me that all he had in his den were stim packs and protein gels. "Mae's a predictive data specialist for one of the big drug companies, so she can work from home. Gives her all the opportunity and time she needs for side projects. And for her kids."

I glance through the archway into the living room, where Mae's still on the phone, her back to us. "She seems happy."

"You sound surprised."

I blink, refocusing on Gideon. "No, I just—" I hesitate, toying with the straw in my iced tea. "I suppose I tend to assume that everyone who does what we do has to give up this kind of life. We're criminals. Most criminals don't get to be happy."

Gideon dismisses that idea with a flick of his fingers. "This stuff, it's just what we do, not who we are. You'd still be you if you stopped conning people tomorrow."

"And you'd be the same without all your screens and data ports?" I raise an eyebrow.

Gideon hesitates, but he's saved from answering when Mae comes back into the room, flashing us each a bright smile.

"How about a movie?" she asks. "I've got HV Instant, so there's about a million options to choose from."

"Don't you have to go pick up your kids?" I ask, glancing at the display on the wall as it flickers from showing info about the weather back to the time.

Mae's eyes follow mine, then skitter away. "They're going to a friend's house after school. It's fine. Maybe a rom com, you think?"

Gideon grimaces, sliding off his stool and turning to follow Mae back into the living room. "I'm outnumbered, aren't I?" he complains.

I've seen maybe one romantic comedy since I came to Corinth—and I didn't really like it—but I don't particularly want to let on to either May *or* Gideon that I grew up in a swamp with no HV or hypernet access. So I trail after them, trying to ignore my sense of uneasiness.

Mae's turning on the HV, which takes up half the living room wall—her kids are clearly entertainment junkies, the floor littered with the toys and tie-ins that make kids' programming more immersive. The channels flicker by too quickly, and Mae clears her throat. "Sorry, the eye-trackers have been acting up."

Gideon flops down onto one of the couches, pulling out a palm pad and no doubt scrolling through to see what movement, if any, there's been on our message to the detective. But I keep my eyes on Mae, watching her struggle with the controls, blinking too rapidly for the trackers to function properly.

Something's not right.

She finally gets a movie going on the screen, then makes a shooing motion at me toward the couch. "I'm going to go clean up some more in the kitchen, I'll join you in a bit."

I trail over toward the couch as she bustles back into the kitchen—the now-spotless kitchen—and pause where I can still see at an angle via the mirror in the front hall. As soon as she's out of direct sight of the living room, she's got her hand pressed to her earpiece again, lips moving but voice inaudible over the sound of the movie's opening credits. She never got off the phone call she took earlier.

My heartbeat quickening, I drop down onto the couch a few feet from Gideon, trying to catch his eye. He doesn't even look up from his screens—when he's in, he's *in*—so I make a show of scooting closer until my hips come up against his. That brings him up short, palm pad device dropping into his lap as he glances up at me, eyebrows raised.

"You feeling okay, *Alice*?" he says, and though his voice is a tease, I see his hand start to creep toward me.

"Keep your voice down and try to look normal," I say quietly—not a whisper, because the sibilants in a whisper carry further than a low speaking voice—but a murmur, as though we're relaxing together. "Something's wrong."

"What do you mean?" Gideon glances at the palm pad, as though the answer to his question might be there.

"It's Mae. Something's going on with her—her body language has completely changed."

"What are you talking about?" Gideon leans back, but it's impossible to see the kitchen from where we are now, even in the mirror. "Sofia, you have to relax sometime. We've done what we needed to do, the police will take it from here. And I've known Mae for four years. She could've sold out the—my identity online dozens of times over, and never did. We're safe here."

"It's precisely that you know her so well that makes it impossible for you to see." I'm not above using our closeness to get his attention, and reach over to lay my hand on his arm. "I don't know her at all, no bias whatsoever, and I'm telling you, whatever that phone call was, something's going on. She's turned us in, or she's thinking about it, or something I can't even predict—but something's wrong. You have to listen to me."

Gideon hesitates, then pulls his arm away abruptly, brows furrowing. "What are you trying to play me for now? Turning me against my friend? What does that get you?"

I glance at the archway to the kitchen, making sure frustration doesn't cause my voice to rise. "Nothing! God, Gideon, you don't think I'd give anything to just sit here and watch a movie and be safe, for once, for *once*?" To my horror, I can feel my eyes starting to sting, and not because I'm trying to cry. Tears now would just make Gideon even more certain I'm trying to play him. Yet there they are, threatening to spill out, making me blink hard to keep them back.

Because even as I'm saying the words, I'm realizing that they're true. For the first time since my father's death, the desire to be here, safe, on a couch with this boy I barely know, feels more real than the need to make LaRoux pay. And that scares me more than anything.

"I trust Mae," he says, voice low and tight. Just now, I can see the toll the loss of his den has taken on him. He's not ready to lose this last safe haven on top of it. "I trust her a hell of a lot more than I trust you."

I take a slow breath, trying not to acknowledge how much that cut actually burns. But I can't really blame him—he *shouldn't* trust me. "Anyone can be bought," I reply softly. "Everyone has a weakness. Does her loyalty to you outweigh her value of her own life? Her kids' lives?"

In spite of himself, Gideon's gaze flicks over to the mantel shelf over the HV screen, where pictures of the twins adorn every empty space.

I press my advantage, as hard as I dare. "Tell her we're going to go check on a lead, meet a contact, anything. Make some excuse for us to leave, and if she tries to get us to stay, then you'll know she's stalling us here for a reason."

Gideon just shakes his head, mute now, staring hard at the HV screen as a scene plays out aboard a space station to the strains of a recent pop hit. When Mae comes back in, bearing a large bowl of popcorn, he looks up at her with a smile, his anger melting away. My heart sinks.

"Here you go," she says, handing us the bowl. "None of that synthetic stuff—this is real corn. Made the mistake of getting it once, now my kids won't touch the other stuff." She clears her throat and turns away to go back to the kitchen.

"You're not going to watch with us?" Gideon asks, resting the bowl on his lap.

"Oh, no, got some things to do." Mae doesn't turn around.

Gideon pauses, looking down into the bowl, jaw clenching visibly. Then, slowly, he says, "Well, we can't really stay long either. I've got a ping on one of my contacts, and we need to go to the drop point before the hit goes cold."

For a wild moment, I want nothing more than to reach out and wrap my hand around his, but I bury the impulse. Even if he's testing my theory, it doesn't mean he wants my comfort.

Mae's standing still in the archway. It takes just a fraction of a second too long for her to turn around, and then the too-casual way she leans against the doorframe must be obvious, even to Gideon. "Don't worry about that," she says, smiling. "You both look exhausted. Just send a text, tell your contact you'll swing by tonight, or tomorrow. You need rest more than you need one more bit of info."

Gideon leans forward, placing the bowl on the coffee table and rising. "I wish we could, Mae, really. But this might give us some proof of what LaRoux's up to, which we'll need even if the police stop what's going down on the *Daedalus*."

Mae straightens a little, eyes darting to the side—where the time display was in the kitchen—and then back. "I'll wave XFactor or one of the undercity admins, they can go to the drop for you."

Gideon's casual air melts away, his shoulders dropping. "Mae," he whispers. "What did you do?"

A ripple runs through Mae's features, and as her smile crumples, my heart constricts. I was right. I wish I could feel vindicated—instead my lungs ache. Betrayal is the hardest wound to recover from.

"They've got my kids," she replies, voice tight with withheld tears. "I had no choice."

Gideon's voice bursts out with a curse, and he starts shoving things back into his pack. "What do they know? How'd they know to take the kids?"

Mae shakes her head. "I don't know, but it was Mattie on the phone." Her voice is shaking. "They took them from school. He told me I had to keep you guys here until—"

"Shit, shit, *shit*." Gideon shoves his lapscreen into the pack, then looks up, eyes meeting mine. There's something like apology there, amidst all the other emotions tangling in his features.

"LRI must have people within the police force." My thoughts are spinning, weariness making it hard to understand what's happening. "People who intercepted the threat before . . . but how could they have traced it back here?"

Gideon shakes his head, eyes wild. "I don't *know*. They shouldn't have been able to. I must have made a mistake, slipped up somewhere." He's only had a few hours sleep since before he left to rescue me from LRI—suddenly, I don't know how we didn't see a stumble like this coming. His jaw's clenched, and I know he's panicking as much for Mae's children as for our own safety.

I want to cry, to throw myself down on the floor and give up. Mae's house is just the latest in a slew of safe havens that LaRoux's been ripping away from us. If his people intercepted our threat, then we haven't stopped him at all—haven't even slowed him down. He'll still bring the rift to the *Daedalus*, and the Council delegations will still fall to his whispers' mind-altering abilities, and our universe will still become something unrecognizable—they'll do whatever he wants, and there'll be no way to stop them. Every ounce of the tension I'd been carrying up until we sent that bomb threat comes crashing back down on me, a weight made all the more impossible to bear by the fact that I'd actually begun to believe we were free.

I stay standing with a monumental effort, rooting my feet to the floor. *Take it one step at a time,* I tell myself. "How long do we have?" I ask Mae, trying to keep recrimination out of my voice. It's done, no amount of guilt can change it now.

"I don't know. They must've tracked your message back here—or they know I'm a known associate of—"

"Mae," Gideon interrupts. "Do you know where your kids are being held?"

She shakes her head, then leans heavily against the doorframe before sinking slowly to the ground. "God, I can't believe this is happening. This can't be happening."

Gideon stands there, clearly torn, body language showing his desire to go to Mae's side warring with the desire to run.

"Gideon," I say quietly. "We've got to go. Mae, toss some things around, make it look like you fought."

She gulps a breath but stoops without hesitation, overturning the coffee table, sending the vase atop it smashing to the ground.

Gideon takes a step, then pauses. "We're going to figure this out," he tells Mae, his voice tight with urgency. "Tell them you did all you could, that they only just missed us. Tell them . . ." He hesitates, and when I glance his way, I see his indecision written clearly across his features.

For a brief moment I can almost feel his thoughts like they're my own. The more Mae gives LRI on Gideon, the more she'll be seen as cooperating, and the better chance she'll have of getting her kids back. But every bit of information she gives them strips away a layer of Gideon's anonymity, leaves him that much more open and vulnerable. I can understand that.

His hesitation lasts only the briefest of moments. "Tell them everything you know about me."

Mae's face is already white, but her eyes widen just a fraction more. "Everything? You mean—"

Gideon cuts her off mid-sentence with a slice of his hand. "Yes, I mean. Either we're going to beat LaRoux or we're not, and either way . . ." He swallows. "Either way I won't need the—my online identity anymore." His voice softens. "Cooperate with them, Mae, and they'll let the kids go."

He doesn't want me to know what his online identity is, and while part of me resents the fact that this woman gets to know more about him than I do, I can't blame him for keeping his secrets. I've kept mine, after all.

Mae's crying, tossing aside a throw pillow from the couch as she creates the aftermath of a struggle, her hand bloodied by one of the shards of the vase, but she nods. Gideon hefts his pack, then glances at me. I take his cue and head for the door. "They know who I am. They've got both our faces on multiple security feeds by now. All my secrecy's worthless, except as currency to prove you're cooperating, and to get your kids back. Just tell them whatever they want to know."

Mae nods silently, and Gideon turns to join me, touching my elbow as I palm the keypad by the door to send it whooshing open. But then I hear her choke, then clear her throat, and we both pause. "Gideon— Alice—" She's watching us. "I'm sorry."

Gideon's hand on my elbow tightens. "So am I." Then he's ushering me through the door, and as the laugh track on the movie echoes in the background, the door shuts behind us again.

He doesn't move, and I stand there, feeling his fingers hot against my elbow, wishing I knew what to say.

To hell with it. I can figure out a safe distance again later.

I step forward so I can turn and wrap my arms around his waist, pulling myself in close. "I'm sorry."

Gideon lets out a little sound, then ducks so his forehead touches my shoulder, arms going around me. I'm still in the same clothes I was wearing when I was taken from my apartment, and I must smell terrible, but his arms just tighten. His voice is a mumble against my shoulder when he speaks. "I just—Mae—"

I take a slow breath. "She's family," I reply. "And LaRoux's taken her too."

I can feel Gideon's fingers curling against my back, tightening into fists around the fabric of my sweater.

I turn my head, so that my voice will carry through his chest. "Let's not let him take anything else."

A test, then.

We will watch them. We will follow them, through the thin spots and through the images and words that stream through our world and in the brief moments we can escape the confines of the blue-eyed man's cages.

If we are to decide whether to become individuals ourselves, we must understand what it is to be human. We must know them, every atom of them, every spark of what makes them who they are. We must narrow our focus, find a chosen few whose lives contain pain and joy together. A chosen few who could become anything—who could fall into darkness and hatred and vengeance, or who could use that pain to become something greater.

We will start with the little peach-haired girl whose eyes are so like those of our keeper. She laughed once, and showed us love.

FOURTEEN

GIDEON

MY HEART'S TRYING TO FORCE ITS WAY UP THROUGH MY throat as we run together down the street. My legs feel like they're weighted down, and I'm half stumbling as my breath turns ragged. There's no point in trying for stealth—we're in the family-friendly suburbs, and there's no crowd to hide us, no alleyway to slip down. We're exposed, in every possible way. I always told Mae that made it dangerous up here. She laughed, and told me it suited the kids.

The kids.

My mind spirals down after that thought as my feet hit the pavement, distress turning to rage, seizing on something easier than the hurt. Who holds *children* hostage? If it was just me, I'd have traded myself for them, but Sofia and I are all that stand between LaRoux and the horrors that rift could bring about. The thought of Mae standing there behind us, utterly alone, sends a jagged bolt of pain through me, and my breath turns strained, like someone's got a grip around my throat.

Sofia yanks on my hand as we hit an intersection with a larger street, and finally there are a few people, a few hovercars, a chance at blending in. Our fingers are twined together, and though I know I should let her go, I can't find it in me to give a damn. She's all I've got now.

Just Sofia, and the purpose that's burning inside me, hotter than ever.

LaRoux did this—he took my home, he took Mae—and he's not taking anything else from me. Not from anyone. *Not one thing more.*

We need to get as many levels down as we can, as quick as we can. We need to find somewhere nobody knows to look, a place we can disappear. A forgotten place.

Sofia squeezes my hand as we turn together for the nearest elevator, and I squeeze hers back tight, a tangle of fear and anger, pain and hurt. We're in this together now, and I'm not losing her.

So we run.

Down.

Down.

Down.

To hide in the dark.

The boy, the one on the gray world with the sister full of fire. She has made her choices, and we can see her future, where all her paths will lead—to a life cut short. Too short for us to read, to understand.

But the boy's future is still dark, as hazy as the clouds that shroud this planet. We cannot see where he will go, what he will become. His sister's death will change him forever, plant the seeds of vengeance and forgiveness together deep in his soul—but which he will choose, we cannot say.

We will watch him too, this green-eyed boy, this child of the water and the reeds and the infinite gray sky.

FIFTEEN

SOFIA

WE CROUCH TOGETHER, SHIELDED FROM THE STREET BY THE bulk of a disposal unit, in an alley a few kilometers from where Gideon's den was. Down here it's impossible to say how much time has passed, but my body says it has to have been hours—dusk would be approaching, up above. Gideon still hasn't let go of my hand, and I haven't tried to free it. Despite the sounds of the undercity moving and breathing all around us, the silence is tight and hot and unrelenting. I close my eyes.

"We have to go there ourselves." Gideon breaks the silence after an interminable wait.

I lift my head, focusing on his profile with some difficulty. "Where?"

"To the *Daedalus*." His fingers shift, tightening slightly around mine. "Going to the authorities got us nothing but more heat. We have to stop him ourselves. Destroy the rift or disable it somehow, prevent him from taking over the senators on the Council."

Everything in my nature screams against doing just that—shining a light on LaRoux means shining a light on myself, on Gideon, on my past. And even if we win, even if we stop whatever's about to happen, LaRoux will never really pay, not truly.

But he will be there, himself, aboard that ship. . . .

A part of me wants to confess to Gideon, to tell him that stopping LaRoux's plan is all well and good, but all I really want is for LaRoux to pay for what he did to my father. To me. I swallow. "It's a huge ship. If he's hiding the rift from the guests, how are we supposed to find it?"

"I can handle that," Gideon replies, finally turning to look at me out of the corner of his eye. "The rift uses up a huge amount of energy—the day we met at LRI Headquarters I was starting to look at some weird energy spikes. I didn't know the rift was in the same room as us, but I'm sure that's what it was. If I could just get aboard, I could track the ship's power usage. But they'll have eight different layers of security—I'd never be able to sneak us in."

My thoughts are shifting already to my contacts, separating out those least likely to have been compromised already, which ones I can still use. "I can get us to the ship," I whisper.

"Sofia," he murmurs, after a moment's hesitation, "I know it's—this isn't what we do, either of us. But I don't know who else will stop him."

I speak carefully, trying as hard as I can not to let him hear the weight in what I'm about to say. "I wish someone would just . . . put an end to it. To him." My heart pounds in the silence that follows those words. It's the closest I've come to telling Gideon what my ultimate goal is, and I can't be sure whether he'd be with me or revile me for even thinking of revenge.

Gideon sighs again and leans his head back against the imitation brick of the building at our backs. "That wouldn't solve anything. There'd be half a dozen lieutenants in his company to take his place and pick up right where he left off. It's the company, not the man, we need to stop." His grip around my hand finally eases a little, like he might pull away.

I let my eyes close again. I think of the gun still on the floor of my apartment—I think of my father's face, his blank eyes, right before he walked into that barracks—I think of Flynn the last time I saw him, the boy I once knew so utterly destroyed by all LaRoux had done to him, and to our home. What does the company matter, if the man behind it all never pays for what he's done?

"You're right," I say hollowly, trying to ignore the way the lie cuts me. I can't afford to let it. So instead, I tighten my hand, making it seem like I don't want him to let go.

And the worst part is, I don't.

We can't risk staying in any legal lodging house, not when LRI's bound to have surveillance looking for us in every corner of the sector. But it's getting late, and both of us are beyond exhausted, and we need to find a place to sleep. Gideon has an idea of where we can hide for the next few days and swears it's completely off the grid, no cameras, no people—which, down here, should be next to impossible. But he knows this place better than I do, and all the contacts I had here are long gone. I've got no choice but to trust him.

While Gideon heads into a secondhand store for some blankets and a few supplies, I start setting a few things in motion. Using one of his prepaid burner palm pads, I get one of my contacts to source invitations for us to the *Daedalus* gala, another to find us something to wear so we'll fit in. By the time Gideon reemerges, I'm ready to dump the palm pad into the nearest trash bin.

Night in the undercity is not so very different from day as far as sunlight is concerned—not much makes it through the streets and parks and avenues of the middle and upper layers even on the sunniest days. Nightfall is merely a subtle tightening of the gloom, a shift in the light from dingy gray to true darkness.

But night in the undercity, where the people are concerned, is when the streets come alive.

Gideon leads me across streets and through alleys strung with lanterns of every kind and color—paper and fabric, so they can be easily replaced when the pollution discolors them—and bright like fire. The food vendors have tripled, and the smells of garlic and oil, coffee and allspice and yeast, fill the air and finally overpower the pollution. Somewhere in the distance I can hear music, with a thick rawness to the sound that tells me they're playing live in the street. A fiddle and an erhu are dueling against the backdrop of a pair of cajóns, and for a moment I forget LaRoux, the *Daedalus*, the gun I left in my apartment. For a wild moment, all I can think of is how much I wish I could drop it all and just go dance to that music with Gideon.

A truck rumbles along the street and Gideon grabs for my hand, jerking my attention back to him. "Come on, let's hitch a lift."

"Wait, I don't—"

But he's not waiting, breaking into a jog and keeping hold of my hand so I have to jog as well or else be dragged along behind him. The truck's not moving fast—it's impossible to drive quickly through the clogged undercity streets—and as it passes us, Gideon reaches out to grab the bar beside the loading door and hauls me up after him.

Another day, I would make some cutting comment about him showing off, or using this as an excuse to keep an arm wrapped around me, pressing both of us close against the back of the truck. Another day, I'd have fought to keep my feet on the ground. But it's not any other day, and once we make it to that gala everything could change—if I get the opportunity I'm hoping for on the *Daedalus*. *When* I get the opportunity.

So I let Gideon tighten his arm around my waist, and I tilt my head back. The lanterns go whizzing by overhead, shooting past us like meteors in the thick dark night. I'd forgotten, in the months since I exchanged my squalid walk-up for a penthouse suite, how beautiful it could be down here.

The truck stops at a light and Gideon gives my arm a squeeze before hopping down off the back of the truck. He keeps hold of my hand as he helps me down after him, but then releases me as soon as I'm on my feet.

"This way." He tips his head toward a particularly dark side street, this one lacking entirely in lanterns.

I let him pull me along, staying behind him just close enough that I can make out his silhouette. I pull another of the burner palm pads he loaned me out of my pocket and click it on, using the faint blue-white glow of its display to light my path. Gideon heads a few meters farther into the darkness, then stops at a boarded-up door. I expect a growl of disappointment—obviously this isn't where we were supposed to end up, a closed-up, abandoned building—but instead he starts feeling around the edge of the boards. I can't see what he finds, but after a few moments the whole panel of boards swings outward, and the door with it.

"After you." He offers up a bow that even the fanciest of the fancy at that party on the *Daedalus* would approve of—a bow that belongs to the guy who knew which art to admire on Kristina's walls. I tuck that thought away for later.

"You're not planning on murdering me, are you?" I murmur, shuffling into the space beyond the door. It feels large, my voice echoing slightly; the palm pad's light is too dim to disperse the darkness more than a meter or so in front of me.

Gideon doesn't reply—I hear only his footsteps, moving away and fading into the quiet. Just before I can start to panic at having been abandoned, a light flickers on in the darkness. Some distance off, a neon sign comes to life—LIVE MUSIC, it says in bright, green and blue letters. Then another light comes on, and another, and another, until they become a cascade of glowing storefronts and streetlamps.

It's an entire arcade of abandoned shops and restaurants. The floor is polished stone tile, and the fine layer of dust coating everything turns its reflections of the neon lights foggy—like row-house lights reflected in a river.

I spin around to find Gideon beside the entrance, shutting the door of an old-fashioned fuse box. My surprise must be obvious on my face, because when he turns to look at me, his own expression splits into a smug grin. "Nice enough to crash here for a few days?" he teases.

"What *is* this place?" I breathe.

"It used to be a mall of some sort," Gideon replies, moving away from the entrance to join me. "It had to have been shut down at least thirty years ago—no hypernet boards, you'll notice, all retro neon and digital signs. My guess is that they emptied it with the intention of leveling the place and building housing instead, but the developer changed direction, or the company dropped the project, I don't know. As far as I can tell, it's been completely forgotten."

I hunt for a reply, too stunned by the strangeness of it—an entire part of the city lost in time—to speak coherently. I want to tell him it's beautiful, because it is, and that it's sad, too—lonely in the brightness of its signs, calling for customers who will never come, shining light on the marble floor where the only footprints in the dust are ours.

Gideon moves away, letting his pack slide to the ground, and the bag with our supplies as well. He uses one of the blankets to wipe away some of the dust, then piles the other ones on top to make a place to sit. I drift over to join him, still fascinated by the arcade, but too tired not to sink to the floor at his side. In the past two days, the only sleep I've gotten was the few hours I spent passed out in Gideon's den. And he's had even less.

"I pulled up some schematics from the *Daedalus*," he says, retrieving a palm pad from his pack and waking it up. "Engineering, where the rift's most likely to be, is a few decks down from where the gala's being held. Security will be tight to keep people from leaving the public areas, but that's where I come in."

"You're going to hack LaRoux Industries security that easily?" I raise an eyebrow at him, but he's focused on his screen.

"I've done it before," he says absently, as though that's no great feat. "But that gala's going to be swarming with people, and I don't have a few weeks to try to get hired as an IT guy."

"We're going to go as guests." When he lifts his head in surprise, I flash him a smile. "Don't panic. It's not that hard to fit in with that crowd. We'll make nice for a while, drink the champagne and dance and carry on, but at some point LaRoux, and no doubt his daughter, too, will come out and make a bunch of speeches."

Gideon's mouth twitches, brows furrowing slightly. "What if LaRoux knows our faces from the security feeds? They'll recognize us."

"We'll slip out as he takes the stage. The museum itself will be locked down—we'll have plenty of time to make it to Engineering before they open the exhibits to the public."

Unless I can get a good shot at LaRoux himself before we slip out of the ballroom. I clear my throat. "Let me just run through the etiquette of this sort of event, so you don't end up accidentally offending half the planetary delegations."

As we start going over what'll happen at the party, I can't help but think of Daniela, the woman who taught me most of what I needed to know in those first few weeks after I left Avon. In her early thirties, she could no longer play the innocent teen—having a younger accomplice got her places she couldn't go alone. Three months we were together. And when the time came, Dani betrayed me as easily as she'd taken me under her wing, leaving me for the authorities to find when one of our marks clued in that we were after his money.

My mind refuses to form the words of the question roiling in my heart. I won't ask myself whether betraying Gideon would be that easy for me, especially now that he's lost Mae. It'll just have to be. I want to stop LaRoux as much as he does, but if it comes down to a choice between exposing the rift to take down the company and destroying LaRoux, the man, himself . . . Gideon's made it clear he would choose the former. And that means I have to be willing to walk away from him. We work on our cover story. We'll be Jack Rosso and Bianca Reine, a couple fresh out of school from the alpha city on Paradisa, attending the opening-night gala as part of a whirlwind tour of the galaxy before heading to university. I follow up on my contact's lead on a designer looking to offload one of last season's runway dresses for cheap, and call in Gideon's measurements to a tailor in midtown. He seems to have unlimited funds for this—I'm not without my own resources, but he's clearly done well enough for himself that he could've chosen a nicer home than the one he just blew up.

As I organize our outfits, Gideon works more magic with his databases and manages to cobble together fake ident chips for us both, complete with holographic projections of our faces in case anyone removes them from our palm pads.

I don't ask when he scanned me with a 3-D imager. I don't want to know.

Gideon discovers a picture Mae posted of herself and the twins, time-stamped that day—her way of letting us know she has them back. Some of the weighty tension he carries leaves him at the sight of them together, but I know the loss of this last safe harbor has left him crushed.

The days pass in fits and starts, in flurries of activity and long, agonizing stretches where all we can do is wait. We could use this time to talk about ourselves, to draw closer together, bound as we are by the mission we've chosen. But neither of us makes that move. We keep our silence, and our secrets, and hiding in this place that's suspended in time, it seems as though we're suspended too.

I try to find some way to leave, if only for a few hours, but Gideon's stuck to me like glue—which he has every reason to be. Somehow I have to get back to my apartment, just for a moment, to retrieve the plas-pistol from Kristina's bedroom. Getting such a highly illegal weapon took me months of work, and there's no way I'll get another before we execute our plan to board the *Daedalus*. And I don't want Gideon to know why I want to sneak a gun in with us.

Two days before the gala, I finally give up. "I'll need to duck out of here for a while at some point," I say, keeping my eyes on the screen of the latest burner palm pad he's given me. I can tell he's looking at me—his breath has an audible catch to it when he's watching me—but I don't look up. I keep my voice casual. "Just need to pick up our clothes and a few other things."

"Sure," Gideon replies easily. "I'll come with. Help you spot trouble before it spots you."

I clear my throat, glancing up finally from the ground and locating a smile. "Not to wound your macho sense of chivalry, but I can handle it myself."

"Like you handled it at your apartment?" His grin flickers, and I can tell he regrets the words as soon as they're out.

I wish I could act nonchalant, like it doesn't faze me. But instantly I'm back in my penthouse again, hiding in the kitchen from men twice my size. I swallow and settle for dropping my eyes so Gideon can't see me afraid. "I can disappear easier on my own."

When he doesn't answer me, I look up. He's still watching me, and utterly unashamed to be caught staring. He doesn't look away but rather tilts his head slightly to the side, as though trying to see me better from some other angle. I'm struck all over again by the quick intelligence there, so easy to overlook when he's playing the arrogant, smug asshole he projects to the world. Suddenly I'm not so sure I'm fooling him at all with my excuses for wanting to be alone. And worse—suddenly I'm absolutely certain I don't *want* to.

"I have to go back to my apartment," I whisper, before I can stop myself.

Gideon's eyes close a fraction too long, and I can tell I was right. He knew I was hiding something. Let him think this is it. "Sofia, you can't."

"That's why I didn't tell you," I reply, voice sharp. "I know it's dangerous. But I'll be in and out in no more than a minute. No time for anyone to show, even if they have surveillance."

Gideon grimaces, scowling at the floor. "What's so important that it's worth risking your life for?"

My gun. The words rattle around in my mind. *My only way out of this hell. My only shot, literally, the only weapon I can get through LaRoux's security.* My throat starts to close, and to my horror, I can feel my eyes starting to burn. I try to shove it down, try to channel it into something else—resentment or fervor or confidence, anything—but I can't. He keeps *looking* at me, and right now, in this moment, I'm realizing I can't lie.

"My father," I croak finally, blinking and sending half a tear spilling out to cling to my cheek. "The only picture I have of him is in that apartment. If I lose it—" My hands clench around the blanket I'm sitting on, a useless attempt to grab for control. "If I can't get it back, then I lose him entirely. Forever."

It's the truth. I *do* want that drawing, tucked safely behind one of the fake photos on the sideboard, almost as much as I want the gun in my bedroom. Almost—but not quite.

Gideon's face, what I can see of it through the blur of tears, softens. "I get it, I do. You *know* that I do." His eyes go to his pack, and I can see, for the tiniest moment, my grief reflected there in his face. Abruptly I'm reminded of that book he brought with him, the only thing he grabbed from his den that wasn't computer equipment. "But Sof, it's just a thing."

I shake my head, the movement sending another tear to join the first. Even now my memory of the picture—a drawing Mihall made for me, since we didn't have a camera—is blurring. I try to picture my father's face, imagine his voice, and the fragments of memory flutter past, fleeting, impossible to reassemble. The particular pattern of calluses on his palm, the half-tuneless ditty he'd whistle to himself while he worked, the shuffle of his boots on the doormat when he came home—each time I grab for one memory the others fly away.

But with that piece of paper in my hands the fragments settle, drawn to the lines of ink and graphite like moths to the paper lanterns lighting the undercity at night.

"It's not just a thing," I whisper.

Gideon hesitates a long moment, then sighs. "No. It's not. Just . . . be careful, okay?" He lifts a hand, the movement slow enough that I can pull away. I don't. The edge of his finger brushes my jaw, and the tear clinging there comes away at his touch.

I blink to clear my vision and find his eyes—hazel, with a ring of green—on mine.

He clears his throat and lurches back, regaining his balance as he stands up. "After all, if you get snatched and I have to go to the *Daedalus* on my own, some socialite is probably going to ask me to dance, and then I'll be done for."

Surprise is enough to give me a handhold to pull myself out of my grief. "You don't know how to dance?"

Gideon raises an eyebrow. "Do I *look* like I know how to dance?"

I discover a smile trying to fight its way free, despite the tearstains I can still feel chilling my face. "I can teach you."

Gideon pauses, thoughtful, his eyes on my mouth. I think he sees the smile too, because his grin flashes abruptly. "If there's going to be dancing at the gala on the *Daedalus*, then it'd be criminally negligent to head up there without knowing a few steps, wouldn't it?"

"Well . . ." I say slowly. "Not really. If asked you can always just say you don't feel—"

"I *said*," Gideon interrupts, stressing each word individually, "that it'd be criminal not to practice dancing, wouldn't it?" His eyes gleam, and he grabs for his lapscreen to turn up the volume and open a hypernet radio app.

"Find a classical music station," I say finally, clearing my throat and getting to my feet. "A waltz if you can, those are easy to learn."

It's only after I speak that I realize he might not even know what a waltz is—I didn't, before Dani—but he doesn't even hesitate. Not for the first time, I wonder if this might not be his first exposure to the upper classes. I know so little about him, about his past and what brought him here, that I might as well be gazing at a complete stranger. After testing a few different spots to find satellite reception, and flipping through a few stations, he finds a brisk, cheerful waltz. I don't recognize it—I don't know classical music, or in fact any music, well at all, unless it's the lively fiddles and bodhrans of Avon.

"Okay, so how does this work?" Gideon straightens, glancing at me and then quickly back at the palm pad, like the source of the music echoing grandly through the arcade might help him more than I will.

He's nervous. I'd want to laugh, except that my own heart rate hasn't settled properly in days. *Get a grip, Sofia.*

"Come here," I say, trying to sound brisk, businesslike. I can't fool myself anymore that that's all this is, but I also can't let myself give in. My thoughts want to open up, to look beyond the *Daedalus*, but I know there *is* no "beyond the *Daedalus*." And if I let myself think there could be, I won't be able to do what I've been working toward for the past year of my life. He's been working to uncover LaRoux's plans, but I've been working just to get close enough to him to make him answer for murdering my father. I can't let Gideon become more important than killing the monster that is Roderick LaRoux.

Gideon's watching me, waiting for me to instruct him. Looking at him, I can't help but think that maybe there *could* be a life after the *Daedalus*. I've wanted nothing but LaRoux's death for so long that I've forgotten how to want anything else, but here, with Gideon's face not far from mine, that cold certainty is feeling less solid with every passing second.

"Sof?"

I shove those thoughts aside and make myself sound calm. "Take my hand, like this. My other hand goes at your shoulder, just so, and yours goes at my waist." I pause. "My *waist*, Gideon."

His eyes flick up, revealing a wicked gleam there before he shifts his hand upward. "Must've misheard you there."

"Mm-hmm." I keep my voice deadpan. "Now, listen to the beat of the music. Hear that one-two-three pattern? That's how our steps will go. . . ."

He's a quick study. If I hadn't already seen more than enough evidence of his agility while climbing through ducts and elevator shafts, this would convince me that all that exercise equipment in his den got put to good use. He's got the basic idea down by the end of the first waltz, and the next several songs are a variety of other styles, giving me a chance to explain the differences in a few dances.

Judging by the number of songs elapsed, by the end of our first hour he's more or less competent. The current song ends, and we pause, left slightly breathless. It was a faster song, and Gideon's getting confident enough now to spin me around—with only limited success. He's not a brilliant dancer, but he's good enough. He won't draw attention on the dance floor, either good or bad—which is exactly what we're aiming for.

I know I should propose that we stop for the night—I know I should propose we divide up the blankets again and go to sleep in our separate corners. Turn the lights off and leave this place once more to the dust and the dark.

But I don't.

The next song starts to play, beginning with a haunting patter of piano notes—and I freeze.

I know this song. It's one of the only pieces I recognize, and I know it only because of a recording my father's friend made of a broadcast twenty years before I was born, before the transmission embargo on Avon. When I first heard it I started crying, and my father's friend—whose name I can't remember, why can't I remember it?—gave the recording to me to keep.

It wasn't until after I left Avon that I learned its name: the Butterfly Waltz in E minor. It was composed by a fourteen-year-old prodigy in a country on Earth called Iran in the twenty-third century. She was killed in a shuttle crash not long after she finished the piece. It was the only song she ever wrote. Somehow, that detail—tragic and awful as it was—made the piece more beautiful. More poignant. She may have died a child, but this song, this part of her, is still here. Echoing through the empty buildings of an arcade abandoned before I was born.

"Something wrong?"

It's only when Gideon speaks that I realize I'm not dancing. "Sorry—no. You're doing well, I'm impressed." I try to put everything else out of my thoughts and follow his lead into a slow turn. *Just focus on your steps.*

"It's not so hard," he replies, voice soft as though he, too, is affected by the music. "Who taught you how to do this?"

Don't answer. Make something up. Change the subject. My mouth opens, though, and I reply with the truth: "My father."

Gideon's hand against my waist shifts and draws me a little closer. "How long ago did he die?" His voice is gentle.

"Nearly a year ago."

"And you've been on your own since then?"

I think of Dani, and of a boy on the Polaris space station who helped me get my first fake ID, and I think of the couple on the *Starchaser* who let me stow away in their cabin on my way to Corinth. I swallow. "I prefer to be on my own."

"Me too." Gideon's gaze, when I look up, is waiting for mine. "Easier that way. No complications." He's no longer trying out turns and spins. His palm against the small of my back is warm, and it's only then that I realize that if his hand's against my back and not at my waist, we must have drawn closer, breath by breath, over the last hour.

"No one interfering with your plans," I reply, my voice barely audible.

His steps slow, and mine mirror his, until we're standing still in a pool of light cast by the bookstore sign behind us. "No one you'll hurt by messing up."

"No one to hurt you."

He lowers our joined hands—no longer even pretending that we're still dancing—until they hang between us. His fingers tighten, and though I know what's coming, I can't make myself pull away. The neon lights turn his eyes every color, colors I never even knew growing up on Avon. His throat shifts in the light as he swallows.

"Gideon," I whisper, unable to speak above a whisper. "This is a bad idea."

"I know." His eyes don't move from my face, scanning my features, lingering on my eyes, my lips. "Just let it be a bad idea a few moments from now." When he lowers his head his lips are soft, brushing mine once—then again, lingering a little longer, pressing a little closer. Then he eases back a fraction, giving me a chance to pull away.

I ought to do just that. Or I ought to play him. I should end this now, before it goes anywhere, or I should take advantage of this moment and secure his loyalty and banish any hint of mistrust. I should do a thousand million things differently, and instead I do the one thing I can't do, the one thing I want to.

I lean closer and tilt my head up, meeting his mouth again and stretching up on my toes so I can press into him, harder. His hand at my back tightens and pulls me in against him, his body warm all along mine, and our lips part, and I slide my arms up around his neck, and he gives a tiny groan against my mouth, and my whole body turns to fire as the Butterfly Waltz in the background sings of wanting, and of dreaming, and of things lost far too soon.

Maybe there is something more than killing LaRoux. Maybe . . . *maybe* . . .

Abruptly the music cuts out, leaving us in silence. I jerk back from him in surprise, glancing at the palm pad, which is buffering and searching for a signal. My breath is coming too quick, too loud—I can hear it echoing in the silence. My lips feel hot, swollen, and my gaze swings back toward Gideon as if drawn by a magnet.

He's staring at me, looking every bit as ragged as I feel. His eyes are a little wild, his hair disheveled on one side where my fingers raked through it. He swallows hard, and when he speaks, his voice shakes a little.

"You're right," he manages, gazing at me. "That was a terrible idea."

On the gray world, the blue-eyed man has found a way to sever us from our universe. We can no longer feel the others, in this world or in ours. Once we were infinite. Now we are three.

The emptiness is pain, and the only relief comes in the brief flashes we see when we break through the blue-eyed man's prison for an instant. We try to watch the green-eyed boy, try to remember our plan, but we are so few now.

We are alone. And loneliness is a gnawing madness. The other two let their agony escape in the flashes and gaps in the prison around us, driving the people of this world mad.

But we . . . I . . . I remember the ocean, and a little girl who called me friend.

I remember dreams.

SIXTEEN

GIDEON

THERE'S SOME SORT OF SHORT CIRCUIT HAPPENING IN MY brain, and I can feel my pulse pounding at my temples, and all I want to do is lean in again and shut out any need to speak, at least for a few more minutes. I've been dying to do exactly what I just did for days—and now, all I want to do is kiss her again.

But though her eyes are as dark as mine must be, her grip tightens on my hand, easing it away from her waist, and there's nothing I can do but let her. She clears her throat. "You were a fraction behind on the beat that last time, but I think we'll blend in well enough on the dance floor if we have to."

"The . . ." It's all I can do to remember what a dance floor *is*, but I nod because I know nodding's the thing I'm meant to do, and slowly my thoughts clutch at each other and pull themselves back into order. "Right. No more practice, then?"

She shows me her lopsided smile in return for the tease, but I know she's as thrown as I am by the intensity of that kiss. So when she steps back, I turn away to pick up the palm pad and switch it off before the music starts again—I need to give us both a little time to recover. "Time for a rest?" she suggests.

"It's getting late," I agree, setting down the pad after I nearly drop it, and sinking down to sit in our nest of blankets, my back against the wall. She walks over to ease down beside me, and picks up the burner

163

pad she's been using today, checking for any updates from her contacts. Making herself busy.

I'm hyperaware of her presence, her knee just a hair's breadth from mine. I could reach across and touch her with the smallest movement, and I can practically feel the static jumping back and forth between us, but I hold back. Reach for safer ground—because if I don't put some distance between us, I'm never going to think straight. "You know what? Stay here just two minutes. I'm going to go get you something that'll put your fancy upper-city food to shame."

I can't afford to move around much out here, with cameras on every corner, but I know the mouth of the alleyway is a blind spot—it's one of the reasons I chose it. So I keep my head down as I step out into the street, and the bright red banner I want is only two stalls up. Its takeout storefront is nothing more than a tent, really, a canvas roof strung between the two neighboring buildings, the kitchen tucked away in the back of the building behind it.

Mrs. Phan's has the sector's best Pan-Asian grub, light-years ahead of the pretentious crap they serve in the four-star, hundred-galactics-a-sitting places in the upper city. Sofia deserves a break from my protein bars and gel packs. *What are you trying to do, man? Bring her a courting gift?*

I shove the voice in my head aside and nod to Mrs. Phan, who's manning the counter herself. They have a menu here, but the locals just ask for whatever's cooking; it's always good. I hold up two fingers to indicate my order, and she bustles away to call unintelligible instructions to the kitchen staff. There are a couple of guys sitting together in a corner, gazing deep into each other's eyes, and a woman by the other wall working a logic puzzle on her palm pad, and none of them casts a second glance at me.

Mrs. Phan dumps two containers of steaming noodles on the counter, along with two bottles of her husband's home brew and two pairs of disposable chopsticks. She takes my money and I'm out in under two minutes. Success.

Sofia's eyes light up when I let myself back in, and she practically tosses her palm pad aside, hands extended for the noodles. "That smells *incredible*," she whispers, almost reverent, but she's smiling, and I'm smiling right back. We're both silent as we pull the lids off our containers and the caps off our beers, sending up clouds of steam as we dig into the noodles with our chopsticks. I shovel up my first mouthful, the spicy sauce burning my tongue. It's perfect. Beside me Sofia tries her own mouthful, eyes widening, those perfect manners vaporizing as she speaks with her mouth full. "Oh my *God*."

"I know, right?" We're on safer ground with the food, and for a couple of minutes we're both quiet—no calculation, no consideration, just enjoying the meal. Still riding out the ripples from that kiss. Me trying not to watch, sidelong, as she licks the sauce off the ends of her chopsticks.

"Nobody saw you?" she asks eventually.

"I'm sure," I reply around a mouthful. "This place is secure. Nobody's getting in without an invitation."

"My place was secure too," Sofia points out drily. "So was yours."

So was Mae's.

I've had days now to think on what she did. I haven't dared make contact—if she did what I told her and sold out the Knave to get her kids back, then they'll have a watch program on everything she touches, and they won't be letting her out of their sight. There's no safe way to reach out to her—not for either of us. She knows it too—that's why she posted the picture of her, Liv, and Mattie on her public profile, I'm sure of it. What I wasn't expecting was that I really miss talking to Mae. It's been years since I went even a day without checking in, and there's an ache that's part loneliness, part pain that she'd give me up. But really, I can't blame her. I don't.

I blame the ones who used her kids to threaten her.

This is my vindication, though I don't know who it is I'm making my case to, when I lie awake at night, debating some imaginary opponent. Silently pointing out that this—the threat to innocent kids—is just the latest in a long line of reasons that my cause is just, and I'm only doing what's required to take LaRoux Industries down. I've reached inside myself more than once, searching for any sympathy for the woman I'm sending running all over the galaxy, or even just trying to dampen my satisfaction when she's forced to ditch another disguise and go scrambling all over again. But the truth is, her fear feeds me. I can imagine, just a little, that it's LaRoux's fear. That it's him I'm hounding. And after all, the great Commander Towers opened herself to this when she chose to look the other way for him.

"I guess I hope this place is safer than either of our homes were," I say eventually, recalling myself to the conversation at hand. "And I've got your back, Sofia, I promise."

"I know," she says softly. Almost wistfully. "I can't tell you how long it's been since somebody said that and I believed them. I haven't had anyone I could trust."

I want to dump my food and turn to her again. But I make myself speak instead. "You have me now," I murmur.

She's found the little card for the restaurant I got the noodles from, pulling it free from the side of the container. Absently she weaves it through her fingers, moving it back and forth almost too quickly to follow, passing it from hand to hand. Then she lifts one hand to tuck her hair behind her ear, and the card simply vanishes from her palm. She laughs at my expression.

"Remind me not to gamble with you," I say, tilting my head to try and work out if she tucked it in her hair. "I'd lose my shirt."

"The drawback being?" She flashes a grin at me.

"I'd rather you lost yours."

I've known girls who would've blushed, or glared at me, or even got up and left. But Sofia just laughs again, leaning her chin on her hand. "It seems tricky, the sleight-of-hand stuff, but it's just practice. Anyone can do it. The real trick is reading *people*, knowing what they'll do next. It's not just about making them do what you want. It's about making them think it was their idea in the first place. That's the real skill."

"She says to the guy who invited her into his den and showed her all his secrets," I point out, wry. "I'm almost sure that was my idea, right?"

"Of course," she replies, solemn.

And I haven't shown her all my secrets, of course, not by a long shot—but the fact that she got inside my den at all sets her apart. That was my golden rule, and I broke it, and now here we are. Still, I can't help drawing closer to one of those secrets I haven't told her. "You'd be a match for the Knave," I try, and sure enough, her smile dies.

"He scares me." The card reappears in her palm once more, and she keeps her eyes on it, as though the confession costs her. "Someone who can find out all your secrets, even when you try to erase every sign. It's like somebody reading your thoughts. Your most private memories." Her expression's tight as she speaks, the relaxed pleasure of the dancing and the meal and even our kiss overlaid with that weary caution she never shakes entirely.

"Nobody can see everything," I say softly. And I can't help it—I reach across to tuck her hair behind her ear for her, press two fingers to her temple. "Some things you never let outside of here."

"What he does is the closest thing possible," she replies, picking up her chopsticks again and digging them into her noodles.

"Sofia, can I ask you something?"

My tone tips her off, and she's wary as she glances up. She tries to deflect by smiling, but it's the wrong smile. Two dimples, not one. "You can't have the rest of my food, if that's what you're wondering."

I press on, though I know I'm not going to like the answer. "I was just—the things you say about the Knave. If you could tell me what he's done to make you so afraid, perhaps I could help."

She keeps her eyes on her meal. "Nothing for you to worry about."

"But I do."

"Gideon, you worked for him," she says, softer. "I'm not putting you in a position where you need to choose between me and whatever he might ask you to do."

"I'd choose you," I say, too fast, and want to bite back the words. *Get a grip, Gideon.* "I won't put you in danger, I promise. Please, you're trusting me all the way to the *Daedalus.* Trust me with this much more."

"This has nothing to do with trust," she replies, curling over her bowl. "If you never give someone a weapon, they can never use it against you." The hint of heat abruptly goes out of her voice, and she swallows. "It's enough to say that he made my life a living hell, and I don't know why. I don't want to know why."

I feel like I'm choking on her words. I spent *years* building the Knave's name, making my reputation as the best on Corinth—the best anywhere. On my own private time, I do the things that'll keep me out of heaven. I chase down Antje Towers and hunt for a way to drag LaRoux's crimes on Avon and Verona into the light. But the rest of the time, the Knave's the best hacker money can buy, and yet he does much of his work for free. I'm practically Robin Hood. I left my first, angry years behind, when I realized my brother would be horrified by what I'd become. I changed, for the most part.

And now someone, somewhere, has been hijacking that rep I worked so hard to build, using it while they hurt the girl beside me. This girl I care about far, far more than I should. Far more than is safe for either of us. "He's not going to use me as a weapon," I say quietly. "Nobody could make me do that."

She shakes her head. "I know he works for the LaRoux family, or he did at one point. And the friend of my enemy is my enemy too. He could use you against me, if he wanted to."

"He's not—" I force myself to sound calm, shoving down the frustration that wants to surface in my tone. This is impossible, having an argument about myself in the third person. "I've never seen any evidence he's involved in LaRoux Industries. I don't think he likes them any more than we do."

"You're wrong," she says, soft but certain. "I tried to track him down once. Waste of money, of course. He's too smart to let himself be tracked very far. But I got as far as a newer planet in the Sulafat system, and a bit of property with two names on the deed: Tarver Merendsen and Lilac LaRoux."

You what? She must have found someone *good* to do that work. Now's probably not the time to work out who this person is and take him or her out of the business, but I add it to the list of things to do after we stop LaRoux. "That doesn't mean he was working for LaRoux Industries, does it? Perhaps he was spying on them."

"That wasn't what it looked like." She looks tired, closing her eyes. "What does it matter?"

"It matters because you're not just my ally, and I know you're good enough at reading me to know that." That's enough to open her eyes again, and I press on. "Tell me why he was hurting you, and I can keep you safe."

She reaches for her beer, gulping down a long swallow and setting it down too hard on the floor. "I don't *know* why. Just promise me you won't tell him where I am. Promise me, Gideon." She's still gripping the bottle, knuckles white. Whatever's going on has her terrified.

How can I possibly answer that? If I admit who I am, she'll run. If I promise, I'm lying. But there's nothing to do but nod. And something in her releases when I do.

"He's hunting me," she whispers. "For almost a year now he's been following me. I've had to learn how to tell when he's getting close. Alarms, digital trip wires, that sort of thing. He has flags on my accounts, records of my transport travel. Every time I think I'm safe, every time I think I've lost him this time, there he is. I only get a few weeks—a month or two at most—before he finds me. This, on Corinth, is the longest I've been able to stay in one place. But he'll find me eventually. I've just never been this close to LaRoux, and if the Knave finds me before I can—" Her lips press hard together, and she doesn't finish her sentence.

I feel like I've fallen ten stories. I know these tricks—hell, I invented most of the ways hackers like me track down individuals these days—but I would *never* use them to hurt someone like Sofia, an innocent. But someone out there's been using my arsenal, the one I keep for people like LaRoux and Towers and everyone else who condones their crimes—and using it to terrorize people. All I can do is repeat her words like an idiot. "He's hunting you?"

She nods.

I reach across to cover her hand with mine. "I promise you, whoever's after you, you're safe now. I know this game."

"Whoever?" she echoes, brows drawing inward. "It's the Knave, Gideon. I'm positive. Three different hackers have confirmed that, separately. He signs his work, the narcissist. Like an artist." Then there's a flicker of a wry, humorless smile. "Or a serial killer."

I'm going to find out who's been copycatting me, and make an afternoon with a serial killer look like a kid's birthday party.

"We'll keep you safe," I say quietly. "I promise. Trust me with this." I just need her to stick with me, and I can work this out. Maybe, when all of this is over, I won't need the Knave anymore. But before I let him fade away, I'll find whoever hurt her, and I'll hurt them more.

Sofia steadies herself with a slow breath, turning her hand under mine until it's palm-up, and she can twine our fingers together. A little more controlled, now. "It's been a really, really long time since I wasn't alone," she whispers, and when I look across, our eyes meet. "I've missed that feeling."

Her gaze goes straight to my heart. *I've missed it too.* And there's something about this girl—so utterly strong, so vulnerable, so implacable in her purpose, but so alone—she brings all my best intentions undone.

She keeps her gaze on me as I set aside my meal, then take hers and her bottle, setting them aside as well. She swallows as I lean in to press my forehead to hers, curving my hand around the back of her neck, fingertips finding bare skin.

Everything between us—the ones we love who died, the way our hands linked together as we ran from Mae's betrayal, the mad flight from LaRoux Headquarters, the taxi driver shouting after us, the tortured climb up the elevator shaft, that one perfect waltz—all those moments whirl through my head and coalesce into one instant of pure instinct.

All the things I should say—*I'm the Knave, you don't know who my allies are, I'm falling for you*—are swept aside.

Her breath catches, and mine sticks in my throat, and then we're surging together, rising to our knees so she can reach up to twine her arms around my neck, and I can duck my head to find her mouth, and I lose myself in her.

It's hours later when Sofia stirs and murmurs in her sleep—that's what wakes me. Our nest is lit only by the dim glow of my screen nearby, and I carefully ease up onto one elbow to check the time. Still a few hours until dawn.

When I look back, she's curled up in a ball, her forehead lined, some dream causing her to push out a hand as though to defend herself. I've seen it over and over the last few days, but it strikes me anew. *Even in her sleep, she doesn't feel safe.*

Carefully I lift the blanket, pulling it up over her where she's pushed it off. It's enough to settle her most times, and it works this time, too. "You're going to wake up looking like a question mark," I murmur, and she tucks herself up into a smaller ball, breath slowing. "A small, surprisingly beautiful que— I sound like an idiot. And I'm talking to myself."

I'm smiling, too—also like an idiot. I have to get it together before she wakes up and sees me like this.

I'm easing down to lie beside her once more, and let her skin warm mine, when I see it.

Her outflung arm is bare, and where there's always been perfect skin before, now there's smudged makeup concealing a hint of some design below showing through. Is it a tattoo? Or—wait. It's a *genetag*. I looked for one of these on her arm that first night in Kristina's apartment, when I realized Sofia must be from Avon. I didn't see it then, and now I can tell why. She's done a good job hiding it. I haven't seen one on an actual person before—they're used by colonies that don't have planetary status yet, taking the place of a proper government ID. And most people from those planets never have the money to travel anywhere I'd meet them. Or anywhere at all. There's a booming black market for selling the genetag sequences to fully fledged citizens who want to operate under the radar—I've got half a dozen of them myself. They're the kinds of IDs people like Towers use when trying to disappear. But this one's actually hers—actually tattooed into her skin.

I pull in the screen so I can see better by its dim glow, and reach out without thinking, gently brushing at the smudge with my thumb. A prickling up and down the back of my neck tells me I shouldn't be doing this, but I can't resist the chance to find out something about this girl who's taken over my life. The chance, perhaps, to know who she is—to know why someone might be running her down, using my name. The digital world is mine, not hers.

If I understand who I'm defending her from, I know it's a fight I can win.

I repeat it to myself, as if that'll help me believe it's the only reason I'm doing this.

The tattoo's in a spiral design, the concealer blocking out the twist of the black lines. The number running along their curve slowly becomes visible as I drag the pad of my thumb along it. My breath stops, chest squeezed tight as the numbers register.

I've seen these numbers before.

Oh, no.

I roll onto my front to prop up on my elbows, bringing my lapscreen properly to life. I pull up my Towers subprogram, and there it is. My mystery ID. The war orphan who left Avon—the person whose ID Commander Towers used to make her escape. The one who can't possibly exist, who was too unlikely. The one I . . .

Sofia's voice comes back to me. *He's hunting me. For almost a year now he's been following me. . . . Every time I think I'm safe, every time I think I've lost him this time, there he is.*

There *I* am.

My hands are shaking. A few keystrokes bring her story to life, files and pictures filling my screen. I could have seen this all along. I could have looked and found her there, a real girl. But I was so damn arrogant, so sure Towers deserved to suffer, so sure that I was smart enough to track down LaRoux's dirty secrets—so determined to do it at any price.

At *any* price. As though no price could be too high.

Every time I imagined Towers running, scrambling for safety, every time I smirked in the dark at tipping her out of another hiding place, sending her heart racing . . . it was this girl sleeping beside me with her lips still curved to a faint smile. It was this girl I'm crazy about. Running scared, her life destroyed by the shadow of the Knave coming after her, for reasons she couldn't understand. Towers was probably on her quiet farm all this time, never the LaRoux conspirator I imagined, and Sofia was sacrificed in her place. I was her monster all along, and she's run straight into my arms.

I can't pinpoint the moment when I became this thing, and I don't know how I managed to blind myself so completely. LaRoux killed my brother, and he set me on a path I told myself was noble. That it was all right to hurt the ones that deserved it, as long as I was a good guy the rest of the time. That it was okay to be the hound, as long as I only chased deserving quarry.

How can I convince Sofia I was never hunting *her*, never meant to hurt her? Will she believe me, when I say all her fear was for nothing?

Will she forgive me?

How can I even tell her?

I push the screen away, easing down beside her once more as a sliver of fear shoots up my spine. I can't wake her up yet. Not until I know what to say. Not until I know how to say it. I'll find the words to make her understand I never meant to hurt her, never meant to scare her.

I'll show her I only ever chased her because I was looking for something that might hurt LaRoux Industries, not *her*. I was chasing down a woman I believed *did* deserve it, who held secrets—except if Antje Towers never used Sofia's ID to run, then she did what she promised all along. She waited for her discharge and went to live out her life in quiet, in peace, away from technology. Away from the kind of world that holds LaRoux . . . and people like me.

I lie there beside Sofia in the dark, turning over explanations in my head, planning speeches, honing my words so the first few will stop her long enough to hear me out. She has to hear me—even if she never forgives me, she has to believe that the Knave isn't coming for her anymore. She has to know that she's safe from me, if nothing else. My thoughts run in tighter and tighter circles, until I fall into a restless sleep.

When I wake, the blankets beside me are cold, and Sofia's gone. I scramble upright, my heart rate accelerating as I swing around to look for her, clambering to my knees.

She stands nearby, and she's dressed, and she's holding my lapscreen.

I forgot to close it down before I fell asleep.

Lit ghostly pale by its light, she's letting it dangle from one hand, so I can see the dossier I pulled up using her genetag number. I see her ID picture, her real ID picture. I see the folder of files on her father; criminal records, medical reports, employment records. Autopsy.

My heart clenches, mind shutting down. I have to find an excuse, tell her the truth, say *something.* But I just freeze.

Then her gaze drops, and I see what lies at her feet. My book. My ancient, priceless copy of *Alice in Wonderland.* My lucky charm, my token from the life I used to live. It lies open, and there, sitting on top of it, is the final nail in my coffin. A single playing card, from the old-fashioned deck my brother and I used to use.

My heart's hammering. My mouth is dry.

It's the jack of hearts.

The knave.

"Was all this just a game?" I expected coldness, emptiness—instead Sofia's voice is bright and hot with fear, with betrayal. In this moment she can't put up a front. "Was any of it real?"

My thoughts are still stuck, the torrent of everything I should say building up like water behind a dam. "Sofia—" I stammer.

With that, she's moving, dropping the lapscreen, backing away from me toward the door.

I want to reach out and grab her, make her stay, make her listen. If I could just make her *listen*. But I can't force her to stay. I can't chase her, after all of this. Not anymore. "Please wait," I manage instead. "Please— let me—"

She pauses in the doorway just long enough to glance back at me. "You come looking for me again," she says tightly, "and I'll kill you. Understand?"

I stare at her from where I kneel, my words lost.

And then she's gone.

Their words fly through our world like waves, and we learn to catch hold of them and ride the messages they send to one another. The casualty letters from their wars are easiest to follow, leading us to grief and anger, emotions so strong we can cling to them and experience their world just a breath longer, the strength of their feelings tangible through the invisible walls between our universe and theirs.

There is nothing remarkable about the one that leads us to a little cottage surrounded by flowers. There is no reason to linger, nothing that should make us pause. These humans' grief is no different from that of any other we have tasted.

And yet we find we can stay, drawn inward, pulled through the fields and up the hilltops and to a tree in whose branches huddles a little boy, clutching a notebook to his chest. He keeps his words on paper, so we cannot read them through their hypernet, but for just an instant we can feel them in his soul.

Then the poetry fades away, and we're left waiting for the next wave of words to carry us closer to understanding.

SEVENTEEN

SOFIA

JUST KEEP MOVING.

The words echo over and over in my mind, drowning out my other thoughts, keeping time with my footsteps. The background patchwork of noise from street vendors and traffic fades into a dull, throbbing hum beneath the roaring in my ears. I want to run, to put as much distance between me and the Knave of Hearts as I can—but running draws too much attention. I can't look over my shoulder, I can't duck low. I have to walk like I belong here. Pilfer a hat from this newsstand, a pair of smog glasses from that one, hide my face from any cameras LRI might be monitoring with facial recognition. I have to look like I haven't a care in the world. If it weren't for the steady staccato of words marching through my head like a drumbeat, I'm not sure I could.

First I need to get to my old apartment before he does. Get the gun, get my father's picture. If I don't get them now, I can never risk it again. I can't think past today to the *Daedalus*—there is no *Daedalus* anymore, not with Gideon—but I have to get my things. It's all I know. And after that, to my ID guy in the southern district for a new name, a new ident chip. Gideon—the Knave—knows Alexis. And he knows Bianca Reine—the White Queen. God, he *gave* me that name. I'm an *idiot*.

And, worst of all, he knows Sofia.

I let him kiss me. I let him touch me. I let him—my eyes burn, behind the protective sheen of my smog glasses. I let *myself* think that maybe I wasn't alone after all, that maybe I didn't have to *stay* alone. That maybe my life wasn't just going to be hatred and grief and revenge. And as a result, I let myself run straight into the arms of the person who turned the last year of my life into a nightmare. Heartbreak and sorrow and hatred tangle as they sweep across my body, making me shudder, making me want to find a shower, a *real* shower with water like they don't have down here, and stand there for hours, for days, until I've washed away every skin cell that ever touched the Knave of Hearts.

Even by the time I reach the elevator to the other levels of the city, my skin hasn't stopped crawling. The smog fades, gives way to sunlight, to clarity, and I barely notice. I remain on foot, remembering how easily the Knave tracked me when I was in LaRoux's custody. My lungs ache—no, my heart aches.

Just keep moving.

My mind grabs only snapshots of the minutes, the hours, that follow. I know I have to focus, I know I can't fall apart. Not yet. But the only fragments that stick with me are the ones that hurt, the ones that penetrate the thickening fog of panic. My fingernails catching on the loose brick in the alley where I keep my emergency glove, the key to Kristina's apartment. My legs aching and heavy as I sneak past the doorman in my old building while his head's turned. My hands shaking so much that I almost can't use the key-coded glove to send the elevator to the penthouse suite. My eyes blurring and stinging as I scramble through the bedroom in search of the gun, praying LaRoux's heavies didn't return for it. The surging of my heart in my throat when I find it hidden beneath the duvet I pulled off the bed during my struggle. The line of fire along my index finger as I smash the glass of the picture frame concealing the drawing of my father. The sick nausea in my belly as I ransack Kristina's jewelry box, grabbing the strings of diamonds and pearls I never touched in the three months I lived here. The stabbing of my heart as I wait for the elevator back down, dread rising with each beat that when the doors open, Gideon's face will be there on the other side.

This time when I stumble back across the lobby I don't bother to look at the doorman. I'm never coming back here again. It doesn't matter if I look like I'm falling apart.

The sunlight feels like knives when the revolving doors spit me back out onto the street. My eyes are burning still, and when I bump into a couple as I head for the sidewalk, they take one look at me and draw away in a hurry. I glance at the glass-fronted doors and see red-rimmed eyes, a streak of crimson where I must have rubbed my bleeding hand across my face, hair wild. I have to get off the upper level—I can't fit in here right now. I shove my stolen hat back onto my head, scrubbing my hand against my shirt.

I start retracing my steps toward the elevator but change my mind and head for the one in the opposite direction. It's farther away, but it's too much of a risk to use the one I used before, the one I took with Gideon. Too late I remember the burner palm pad he gave me, still in my pocket. *Damn it, damn it, damn it.* Even I could track someone on a GPS-enabled device like this. I'm not thinking. I need to think.

A messenger's waiting for the crossing signal at the end of the sidewalk, checking his own palm pad, his electrobike humming underneath him. I force my shaking hands to still long enough for me to slip the burner phone into the side pocket of the bag slung round his body.

Let Gideon—the Knave—track the messenger all around the city while I run. While I disappear.

When the heat and smog of the undercity wrap around me again, it's like the comforting arms of a friend welcoming me home. Suddenly I remember why I hid here my first month or two on Corinth. It wasn't just lack of funds. Here, despite the blood on my face, the panic in my movements, nobody looks twice at me.

It'll be getting dark up above, and down here the lanterns are being lit. It's getting harder to keep moving. I have to find a place to stop.

I can't pay for a room somewhere without accessing my accounts, which he's got to be tracking—using the stolen jewelry to buy my way in would throw up red flags in a respectable place and paint a target on my back in the rest. There are a number of free hostels and shelters here that don't require ident verification or retinal scans to access, but Gideon will be searching those. He'll know I'm too smart to use either the Alexis ident chip or Bianca's, and he'll assume I'll go somewhere I can be anonymous. So I head for one of the police-monitored stations. It'd be mad to go to a place where the identities of all residents and tenants immediately go into the government system—even more easily accessed by a skilled hacker than the privately owned hostel systems.

Normally I'd hang around until I found a likely target to sneak me in—someone just desperate enough to be taken in by big eyes and a smile—but I can't remember how to do it, how to gauge people. The faces that I pass are alien, their expressions written in a language I don't know how to read anymore. So instead I head around back and wait until the fire exit opens a crack—a girl with a shaved head and fluorescent yellow earrings ducks out of it to smoke, wedging a platform boot in the doorway to keep herself from getting locked out.

I abandon everything and just shove a string of pearls into her hand. "I need to get in," I rasp. "Quietly." She stares at the pearls, then at me. She doesn't know if they're real. Any second she's going to tell me to go screw myself and slam the door in my face.

But instead she licks the tip of the joint to extinguish it and stuffs both it and the pearls down the front of her shirt, then kicks the door open. She doesn't say anything, though her eyes stick to me as I move past her. When I look over my shoulder, she's already gone, shoulders hunched as she half jogs up the alley to vanish into the crowds beyond.

Inside, the gloom is as thick as in the alley outside. Steel-framed bunk beds line the room, topped by bare mattresses. A few heads lift when I come in, but if anyone notices I'm not the girl who left, they say nothing. That's why I chose this place. Half of these people are felons checking in for parole, and the other half are headed that way in a few years. They don't care who they sleep next to. The occupancy scans that sweep by every half hour or so don't check IDs, as long as the number of people in the rooms matches the number of people who went through check-in.

I find a bottom bunk in the corner, vacant but for a few candy bar wrappers. I avoid the large stain toward the foot of the mattress, unidentifiable in the meager light, and crawl in against the wall until I'm hidden in the shadows.

I will my body to stop shaking. Tell myself I'm safe now. That he can't find me. That out of sight of the security eye in the center of the ceiling, not even a thorough facial recognition scan through every security camera in the district could find me. But now that I've stopped, it's not fear that's making me shiver.

Eyes burning, I try to block out the smells, the noise, the scratchy mattress and the odor of mildew wafting up from the fabric.

Here at the bottom of the city, no one cares when you start to cry. Half the people in this room are suffering from some kind of withdrawal or another, and the rest know to leave well enough alone. You don't come here seeking comfort. You come here to disappear.

The squalor should make me long for the penthouse. I should be imagining the cocktails the SmartWaiter can produce, remembering the feel of Kristina's soft sheets, closing my eyes and seeing the false stars emerging on the windows in my mind's eye.

But instead the only thing I can think of, the only thing I hear as I muffle the sounds of my weeping against my arms, is the Butterfly Waltz playing over and over in my mind.

When morning comes, my eyes are dry again. Sleep, if only in drips of a few minutes at a time, has brought me back to myself. I recognize last night's storm for what it was: a panic attack. I haven't had one for months, but they used to leave me shattered and empty all the time in the weeks following my father's death. But even shattered and empty, I can keep moving.

I have to get onboard the *Daedalus* tonight. Nothing's changed because of Gideon's betrayal except that now I have nothing to lose, nothing sparking even a scrap of guilt. Even if he decides to go to the *Daedalus* on his own, to disable the rift without me, it doesn't matter. It's not the rift I'll be aiming for. Gideon will be watching, certainly, waiting to see if I show up, but I don't care that he'll know where I'll be. He's proven that it doesn't matter where I go, who I become—he'll always find me. Whether he's working for LaRoux Industries or has his own sick reasons for hunting me across the galaxy, it doesn't matter. It doesn't even matter if he finds me on the *Daedalus*, because by then I'll have my shot, the moment I've been working toward since I fled the orphanage shuttle that took me from my home.

Tonight I'll be in the same room as the man who murdered my father.

And if the Knave finds me there on the *Daedalus*, so be it. Nothing he can do to me could be worse than watching my father die. Let him take me. Let him kill me if that's his ultimate goal. I'll be dead by the end of the night anyway, one way or another. If I'm caught, LaRoux Industries will have my existence quietly erased from the world. And if I succeed, if I get my moment, the security guards will kill me anyway.

Because tonight I'm going to put a bullet in Roderick LaRoux.

On the gray world, it is so easy to find despair and anger. Their pain burns so hotly sometimes it blinds us to anything else. But there are moments, rare flashes of light in the darkness, joy so bright we cannot help but see it.

There is a little girl on the gray world whose father is teaching her to dance. Her steps are all wrong but she is laughing anyway, and so is he, and we feel, just for an instant, his heart filling at the sight of her dimpled smile.

Then the music stops, and the lights too, and darkness sweeps across the gray world as it often does when their machinery fails. Everywhere we feel fear and anger rising like hot spikes, but in the little girl's heart she feels only contentment, as her father carries her to bed. We cling to that tiny light as the darkness closes in all around.

EIGHTEEN

GIDEON

I'M AN IDIOT.

That doesn't do it justice. I'm dumber than every mark I ever laughingly hacked, I'm below basement IQ, and I have no idea what to do about it. I'm stuck helplessly watching everything I planned and everything I wanted spiral beyond my reach.

She told me over and over not to trust anybody. I can still hear her voice.

If you never give someone a weapon, they can never use it against you.

But I did all that and more. She knows my face, she knows my real name. She knows I'm the Knave. Stupid move after stupid move.

But none of them were the dumbest thing I did. That honor doesn't even go to the moment I forgot to dim my screen, so she could see her own file there when she woke. It doesn't go to every moment I ignored the signs that should have *told* me that my quarry wasn't Towers.

The gold medal goes to the moment I knelt there like an idiot, speechless, while this girl I'm falling for walked out of my life. I should have said something, *anything*, rather than just watching it happen.

There's no way I can justify what I did, no way I can excuse what my obsession turned me into—but I should have tried. I should have apologized. I should have begged.

I tracked her palm pad after she left, watching her icon move up the levels on my screen, heading to her old apartment. I watched until it suddenly started to move too fast, and then the surveillance cameras showed me she'd dumped it on a courier. A little after that, she was simply gone.

If I can't find her tonight, then I don't know if I'll ever find her again. Not without tracking her—and after what I've put her through, I couldn't bring myself to betray her that way, not even for the chance she'd listen to my apology. I just have to pray she's where I think she'll be, and I'm willing to risk the police—I'm willing to risk LaRoux himself—for a chance to see her one more time.

Because I know what I owe her. And even if I lose her forever, I want to deliver on that debt.

I'm waiting at the shuttle dock in one of the tuxedos all the guys are wearing. I could have fed ten families for a month on what it cost, but this isn't the time to skimp on expenses and give someone a reason to look at me twice. With what the Knave earns for elite hacking jobs, my credit balance can take it. If I pull this off, I'll be helping out a lot more than ten families by bringing down LaRoux Industries.

And I'll be helping Sofia.

I know I'm focusing on the way the jacket constricts my movement and the shoes don't have proper grip, because I don't want to think about the fact that she hasn't shown up yet. She *has* to come. Not just because this is her best and only chance at finding dirt on LaRoux, not just because I don't think I can bluff my way in without her, but because . . . she *has* to come.

The words take up residence in my head, echoing around my skull in a quick, relentless drumming rhythm. *Please, Sofia. Please, Sofia. Please, Sofia.*

My breath catches every time a car door opens, tiny shots of adrenaline firing through my system, sending shivers down my spine every time I catch a glimpse of a new dress, a hint of whoever's inside. Then comes the crash, every time a new face emerges and it's not her.

Please, Sofia. Please, Sofia.

When she steps out of a sleek black autocar, one of the last to arrive, my heart dances a staccato beat—then nearly stops completely when I register what she's wearing. *Holy hell, Dimples.* She's in a long, slinky lavender dress lined on the inside of the skirt with electric lights, which flash and twinkle through a slit that runs all the way up her thigh every time she moves. It's cut low and fitted, with layers of fringe that hearken back to the old-fashioned flapper dresses on ancient Earth. Her dress shines amethyst on the pavement below her when she walks, and she's in a pair of heels that would make a runway model blanch. She must be nearly as tall as me in those things.

The fiber optics are woven through her hair as well, which is still white-blond—she's not trying to hide. Either she didn't think I'd come— or she knew I'd come and doesn't care. I'm not sure which option is better. The lights peek out through her curls and cast shadows across her flawless skin. She's holding a small purse, pulling her invitation from it as she makes for the entry line. My mouth's completely dry, and I can't even pretend to myself that it's all nerves. She looks incredible.

Almost as good as she looked lounging in our nest in the arcade, hair mussed, protein gel pack in hand, shooting me the one-dimpled smile I love so much—the one that's real.

I can't trust her not to give me the slip if she spots me, and there's no way I'm letting her go up there alone, not when I can help her. Even if she's got some plan to locate the rift and disable it without me, she'll be safer if I'm there to help. And whatever's passed between us, LaRoux's attempt to take over the government is bigger than us—we can't afford to fail tonight.

My nerves never bug me when I'm on a job, but this one is different, and my heart's slamming in my chest as I make my way toward her. She could call me out, she could name me in front of everyone. She could accuse me of stalking or harassment and sic the security guards on me. She could turn her back on me and walk into danger on her own.

I keep behind her, out of her line of sight, until the last possible moment. When security starts scanning the invite of the couple just in front of her, I ease forward and slip an arm around her waist so we're unmistakably a couple. She goes perfectly still, then carefully turns her head to check who's just taken that kind of liberty. Her features barely flicker, but I see the fear flash in her eyes. The next minute she's controlled it, and her hand's coming to rest on mine where it sits at her waist.

"I thought you weren't coming," she says, as light and friendly as if her fingernails weren't digging into the tendon at my wrist, sending a bolt of pain up my arm, robbing me of words.

The attendant by the airlock bows politely and holds out his hand for Sofia's invitation. "Jack Rosso and Bianca Reine," she says sweetly, and he ushers us in. Her source was good, and the invitation holds up to his inspection. I'm weak with relief.

The shuttle itself is something else. I haven't seen riches like this in years. It's all soft lighting, plush red carpets, and overstuffed armchairs, rather than standard shuttle seats. Even the safety restraints are fancy, upholstered with velvet and embroidered to match the curtains at the viewports. It's a slice of Victorian decadence, care of LaRoux Industries—the fashion outside might have moved on with a new season, but tonight we've been teleported back in time into the world of the *Icarus*. Sofia picks a pair of armchairs toward the back, still refusing to meet my eyes, and as we buckle in, a young man in sleek butler's attire makes his way down the aisle with a silver tray full of gently bubbling champagne glasses. I relieve him of two—to hell with not drinking, I'm not sure I'll make it through this without help—then down one in a couple of gulps. Sofia declines the one I try to hand her with a shake of her head.

"Listen," I murmur, trying not to grip the remaining glass too tightly. Willing her to really hear me. I've rehearsed the words in my head—I know there's no point in appealing to whatever she might have felt for me. I need to appeal to the steely determination that lives inside her, the part of her that's kept her going over the past year. "You still need something. So do I. Get me up there and I'll keep my promise. And after that, if you tell me to, I'll never come near you again."

She gazes out the viewport in silence, watching the distant crowd swirling back as the last of the gala guests board and there's nothing left to gawk at. It's not until the doors close and the light hum of the engines rises to a muted roar that she replies. "I said I'd kill you if you came looking for me again."

I swallow, watching her profile. "I know."

"But here you are."

"We have to stop LaRoux." And even if I can only admit it to myself, maybe keeping her safe is more important than all of it. I owe her that. And I want it for her, too.

The shuttle gives a gentle shudder and lifts off, gathering speed quickly. It's almost completely smooth, but Sofia drops her purse into her lap to grab at the armrests, leaning her head back against the headrest so she can squeeze her eyes closed. When she speaks again, her words are short and sharp. "When we get back to Corinth, you'll walk away from me and never look back. You won't look for me. You won't so much as enter my name into one of your search programs."

It's like having my insides squeezed, but I force myself to nod. Then, remembering she can't see it with her eyes closed: "I understand. And until we're back on Corinth?"

"Let's just do what we came to do. If I let you wander around up there without me, you'll blow your cover, and then they'll find out who you came with."

I don't care if it's grudging. It's enough. I want to help her. I want to keep her safe. I want to make up for everything I've put her through over the past year—and I want LaRoux to answer for what he's done. I hope I don't have to choose between these things.

She's still gripping the armchair like the shuttle might fall out of the sky if she doesn't personally focus on keeping it up in the air, and I realize in a flash that she's a nervous flier. I suppose on Avon she didn't spend a lot of time on shuttlecraft. I reach for a question to distract her, keeping my voice low. "Tell me about the schedule for tonight. Do we know where our window is?" We were meant to spend today on this final briefing. We were meant to be together, today.

She breathes out slowly, steadying herself, staring straight ahead as she murmurs her reply. If she knows I'm asking to keep her mind off the flight, she doesn't let on. "Security's heavy. LaRoux will be there himself, along with his daughter and that soldier she's marrying."

My poor, abused heart starts thumping again. It's fine. Lilac and Merendsen might know the Knave, but they never saw what he looked like. And while Lilac might recognize me, it's been so long that I doubt she'd even remember me. "The whole family?" I try to keep my voice light. "All in one place, that's a big deal. I didn't think the soldier came out in public."

Sofia rolls her eyes. "He's not the hero all the newsvids made him out to be," she murmurs. "Some of those medals on his chest are for so-called victories against Avon, against my people. He came back there, right before the Broadcast, after . . . my father. And he ran for it as soon as things got bad."

There's a bitter taste in my mouth. After all, he left right after he relayed the information I found for them to Jubilee Chase and Flynn Cormac. Of course Sofia would see that as abandonment. "I guess the media get all kinds of things wrong," I say, to fill the silence. "What about security? There'll be a big crew there, I'm guessing."

"It'll be a different team to the ones we—" Sofia pauses only a beat. I guess having her home invaded by kidnappers is no longer the worst thing that's happened to her in the past two weeks. "Met. We should be safe, unless someone walks in on you running a hack on their computers."

I pat my pocket, where I've stashed the most slimmed-down version of my equipment I could manage. "With any luck it won't be more than a few minutes, once we find the rift." *Maybe I should pretend it's taking longer—give me some excuse to talk and plead my case.*

The shuttle clears atmo and the ride smooths out, the roar of the engines dropping, Sofia's death grip on the armchair easing. Through the viewport beside her, the stars emerge from the sooty pollution shrouding Corinth. "There'll be hors d'oeuvres to start the night," she says softly, all business. "Mingling, dancing. Then later on, the museum section opens. The problem is that they're offering private tours of the exhibit during the first half of the party, and our route to Engineering takes us right through the exhibit, so our window is small. We have to get in after the tours end, but before the museum opens—during the speeches. We'll have a window of half an hour, maybe forty-five minutes."

"It's enough," I promise. I hope I'm telling the truth.

We're both quiet as the *Daedalus* comes into view, so massive I can only make out a slice of it through the viewport, the stars vanishing behind its bulk. She's the exact twin of the *Icarus*, built side by side with her sister ship, scheduled to launch only weeks afterward. But when the *Icarus* went down, plans for the *Daedalus* were put on hold until LaRoux realized he could capitalize on that tragedy by turning the *Daedalus* into a sick sort of museum attraction for all those drawn to gawk at destruction.

An announcement pings softly over the intercom and then we're easing into the dock, and, with a series of soft clinks, safety harnesses are coming undone around us, the staff rising to their feet to usher us out. Sofia yanks my hand out of my pocket when I look too casual, forcibly bending my arm at the elbow so she can slip hers through it, so we'll match the other couples. It's been years since I had to go through this kind of parade, and the small tricks of it are gone. "Pretend you're in a period drama on the HV," she whispers. "That's what they're all doing."

We head through the doors and find ourselves in another world. The vaulted ceiling soars above us, glittering chandeliers refracting crystal light across every surface, the finishes all velvet and gold, priceless polished wood. Hovertrays glide through the crowd, taking orders and offering up food and drink, and the guests swirl in a kaleidoscope of color, the men in sober black and the women in every shade I've ever seen. Musicians play on a dais at one end of the hall, and for an instant I'm a child again, looking for my mother somewhere in this crowd.

Then Sofia's nudging me and nodding to a red rope cordoning off one exit. A group of partygoers appear through it, led by a tour guide dressed as a soldier—as one of the dead passengers from the *Icarus*.

"This is sick," I murmur, forcing my gaze away. "This should be LaRoux's greatest shame. Fifty thousand people, dead. Does he think if he puts it out in front of everyone, like he has a right to show it off, they'll just accept that it wasn't his fault?"

"It was the biggest headline in decades," Sofia replies softly. "For these people, the only thing worse than dying on that ship was missing it. This lets them pretend they were there."

"Without the inconvenience of dying," I mutter. "LaRoux deserves to have his plans exposed to the galaxy."

She looks away as the musicians shift to a waltz, the music growing a little louder, and couples start to spill onto the dance floor. "He deserves justice." There's steel in her tone that sends a shiver up my spine—that makes me wonder for a moment what the word means to her—though her smile's as soft and pleasant as ever. Both dimples—not the real one. Maybe I'll never see her real smile again.

The folks around us are starting to migrate toward the dance floor to join the waltz, and soon we'll be left standing on our own. Before I have a chance to ask her what that justice she's chasing might look like, she's tugging me after them and into the thick of it. No better place to hide.

Moments later I've got my arms around her like I did just the day before yesterday—a lifetime ago. It's exactly the same, and nothing like, our Butterfly Waltz. I'm still transfixed by her face, aching to lean in and kiss her, feeling her touch like electricity. And it's a world away, because though I'm gazing at her, she's looking away, tracking the ebb and flow of the crowd, watching the exits, soaking in every detail. For her, this is duty. She's counting down the moments until our work is done and I'm gone forever.

"The speeches should start in about ten minutes," she says, finally turning her face toward me so she can speak in my ear, if I bow my head. "That's why I wanted to be on the last shuttle. Less time to blow my cover. You see the guys at the edges of the room?"

I spin her around so I can take a look, letting my gaze run along the folks who aren't dancing, men and women ranged around the room at regular intervals. They're watching the crowd just as Sofia is, and like the view has suddenly come into focus, I see them for what they are: LaRoux's security detail. "Got them," I breathe. "Let's hope one of them doesn't decide to go for a stroll during the speeches."

"They won't," she says confidently.

"Give me machines any day. Throw people into the mix and all bets are off."

"Not really," she replies, as we turn past another couple, the music swelling. "People are predictable. It's when you think they might not be—that's when you get in trouble."

And that's enough to shut me up. I spend the next few minutes practicing and discarding apologies, searching for the words that will convince her to look me in the eye without that wariness that lives in her gaze now. Trying to ignore the ache that wants to close up my throat and render me completely silent. And while I do all that, I follow her whispered instructions, guiding us through the crowd, trying to hide the way her breath on my skin sends a spark straight down my spine.

She guides us across to a pillar beside the exhibit entrance, where we can pause a moment out of sight of the security team. We're still visible from some angles, though, and without hesitation she leans back against it, twining her arms up around my neck to tug my head down so she can whisper in my ear. "LaRoux will be here in a moment," she murmurs, and I make myself smile for anyone who's watching.

The next few minutes will determine our fate. If we're caught sneaking our way into the exhibit when it's off-limits, our lives could depend on our ability to bluff. I have to say something before we do this. I have to try. "I'm sorry," I murmur, taking my turn to whisper in her ear. "I have excuses, and I know you don't want to hear them, so I won't try. I just—I'm so sorry. I never meant to hurt you. I never meant to hunt you."

She turns her face up to mine, and our eyes meet—it's as though the crowd around us simply melts away as she holds me captive. Then she whispers, perfectly clear, dousing me with cold water. "Gideon, I don't care what you think, and I don't want to hear what you have to say. I'm here for one thing, and that's LaRoux. He deserves to *die*."

Ice trickles down my spine. In that instant, our gazes locked, I see the depth of it in her eyes. "Death is simple," I murmur. "We . . ." But I trail off. Because it's *right there* in her eyes. I see just how far she'll go—I see what she wants.

I don't know how she'll do it, but I see what she means to do.

I lean in closer, robbed of breath, scrambling for words. I have a minute, maybe two. "Sofia, I . . . I didn't sleep last night."

Her lips part as she draws breath, and I shake my head, blocking out the unsympathetic response I know is coming.

"I couldn't sleep. I was talking to my brother. Do you ever talk to your father?"

Her mouth snaps shut, lips thinning, and she tries to push away from the pillar. Desperate, I tighten my grip on her arm to hold her there.

"Please, I'm begging you, just hear me out for one minute. I realized last night what this pursuit of LaRoux has made me. It's turned me into someone who'll walk over anyone, who'll pay any price to ruin the man I hate. The man who took my only brother from me. And I did it, Sof. I tried to destroy your life because I thought you were someone remotely connected to LaRoux. I realized, while I lay there, not sleeping, talking to the guy who used to be my hero, that I haven't listened to him in a long time."

"How nice for you," she replies, deadly quiet, her whisper rasping like the words are being dragged out of her. "This has nothing to do with me."

"Don't you see?" I'm practically tripping over my words, my own whisper fierce. "It has everything to do with you. I realized last night that there's a price I *won't* pay, no matter what. That there's a price my brother never would've wanted me to pay."

Our gazes are locked still, and I see something stir in hers. I press on, desperately. I have to make her see.

"I think your father would tell you the same thing. I think he'd tell you there are some prices not worth paying. What it would do to you, what you'd lose—you're not this person. Trust me, I've been to the edge of this cliff, I've looked right over. I won't let you do this."

"You're not me, Gideon," Sofia hisses, her expression fierce. "And you don't know me. We're different. I've lost my father, my home, everyone I've ever cared about—if I lose one more thing taking LaRoux out, so be it. It'll be over. It doesn't matter."

Her eyes are brimming, and I'm aching desperately to touch her—not like I am now, my hands banded around her arms to keep her from running, but properly. Slowly, carefully, so she could turn her head if she wanted, I lift my thumb to brush it across her cheekbone, wiping away the tears. "It matters," I whisper. "You don't know how much you've got left to lose. Oh, Sof. It matters."

She doesn't turn away, and the fact that she's letting me hold her makes my whole body hum. She's one degree softer, just one, but when her eyes flick up to meet mine again it feels like the first drops of the thaw. "I don't know what else to do," she whispers. "This is all I have."

"We do what we planned. We find the rift, we stop LaRoux from taking over the Council. We can do it," I promise, heady, knowing I shouldn't—knowing I can't make that promise. *And then, when we're done, there'll be time to earn your forgiveness. There'll be time to leave the Knave behind.*

Another degree. Another couple of drops, the snow melting. She tilts her chin up just a fraction, and my heart seizes as I recognize the invitation. Slowly, reverently, I duck my head to brush her lips with mine, then deepen the kiss. My hand presses into the cold marble at her back, and hers slides under my jacket, fingertips pushing over the equipment I have strapped to my torso to find a place they can press through the thin fabric of my shirt, against my skin.

I'm buzzing, I'm electricity, and it takes me several beats to realize that some of that buzzing is external—the dancing has halted for applause. Something's happening on the dais, but I'm still too distracted to care. I lift my head, blinking, and she shows me her dimples for a moment as she lifts one finger to check her lipstick hasn't smeared.

"He's here," she whispers, though she's still looking at me.

I nod, still reluctant to pull away. Still searching her gaze. "Promise me," I murmur. "We do this together."

"Together," she whispers, and my heart soars. Now, all she needs is the gentlest of pushes to ease me back and away, so I can turn and trace the applause to the platform at the front of the ballroom.

Monsieur LaRoux is taking the stage.

He looks the same as he always has—piercing blue eyes and close-cropped white hair, a face that's recognizable all over the galaxy. He's flanked by a pair of bodyguards, and just behind him come a couple who've spent the past year on nearly as many HV screens as he has. Even in black tie, Merendsen still looks military—it's in the way he stands. He only softens when he rests a hand at the small of Lilac LaRoux's back, ushering her up the stairs after her father, so that he can stand between her and the photographers at the bottom of the stairs.

I've talked with them on text chat dozens of times, and via the feeds I hijacked when I locked down their personal security arrangements, I can get a look at their faces any time I like. But this is the first time we've all been in the same physical space, and I'm transfixed. They look exactly like their publicity pictures, from the way she turns her head to gaze up at him, to the way he keeps an arm around her, smiling faintly as their eyes meet. Everybody knows the way those two look at each other. Like there's nobody else in the room. I swallow down a moment of the bitterness that always surges when I watch them together on the screen. They make it look so easy, being together.

Sofia's staring alongside me, but we're hardly at risk of blowing our cover. The whole room's transfixed. Then she shifts her weight, starting to step forward toward the trio onstage, like she's forgotten I'm even there. I grab her arm, and she tries to shake me off. "What are you doing?" I whisper, stepping up beside her.

She ignores me, turning her head to conduct a slow sweep of the room. She takes in the security goons one more time, lets her gaze pause on the stage, every muscle in her body tense—like a hound on a scent, pointing her quarry.

I squeeze her arm. "Time to go," I whisper in her ear, tugging her back toward the pillar—nervousness surging up all over again, the fear that she'll forget her promise to me.

And abruptly, as though some decision is made, or conclusion reached, she lets me draw her away. She turns to take hold of my lapels and pull me back against the pillar, then stretches up on her toes to kiss me. Her hand curls around the nape of my neck, sending another shot of electricity down my spine as her skin touches mine, and her lips brush my ear. "Time to go," she agrees. "We need to look like we're sneaking out to . . . Well, try and look like you want me."

No problem, Dimples. No problem at all.

We keep our hands linked as we slip through the door, the space between my shoulder blades twitching with the discomfort of turning my back on all that security. She uses her grip to drag me to a halt when I'm about to stride away down the corridor, instead pulling me a few steps in, and then leaving me to skip back and press her ear to the door, listening for pursuit. After a few seconds, she nods. "Hold still," she says, stepping in close to reach up and start pulling my tie undone with one hand, unfastening the top buttons of my shirt with the other.

"Is now really the time?" I hesitate as soon as the joke is out of my mouth—I might have her agreement, but I know I don't have her forgiveness yet.

But she flashes me a small smile and pulls out a tube of lipstick from her purse, reapplying it carefully, then pulling me down so she can press her lips to my collar, leaving a crimson smudge there. She steps back to give me another once-over, then tugs at one side of my shirt until it's untucked from my waistband.

Next it's on to her own preparations. She musses her hair, running her fingers through her curls until they're sitting askew, then leans down to unfasten her towering heels, stepping out of them and hooking her fingers through the straps to carry them. If anyone finds us, they won't be that confused about what we were doing, looking like this.

When she looks back up at me, she's steel once more, nothing but determination in her gaze. "Let's go. The clock's running."

The blue-eyed man comes to the thin spots only rarely now, and never again does he bring the little girl with the delighted laugh that so transformed his face. But the same pieces of sound and color that flooded the stillness flood the thin spot, and through them we can see more of this universe. We struggle to learn much from their words and letters and messages, but the images speak, carry ghosts of the hearts behind them.

It takes us years, but we find the blue-eyed man and his daughter, and we discover that she is not such a little thing anymore. We have learned, over the years of our captivity, the name for the look on the man's face that so fascinated us. And now her face bears it too, but for someone else, a boy her age. She is in love for the first time, and we feel it as if we are in love for the first time too.

The blue-eyed man holds a hatred in his heart for the boy, and as time moves forward, all the future possibilities for the boy his daughter loves narrow into one: he will die, and her heart will break.

What we cannot see is what will happen to her heart after.

NINETEEN

SOFIA

THE ROARING IN MY EARS WON'T STOP, EVEN AS THE PLUSH carpeting in the corridor swallows up the sounds of my stumbling steps alongside Gideon's. The small handbag at my side feels as though it's made of lead, the weight of the unfired gun inside it heavier than any physical burden could be.

I was in the room with him. My mind won't let the words fade. *I was in the room with Roderick LaRoux and I didn't kill him.*

But the faint shimmer surrounding the dais guaranteed the presence of a security field, and with Gideon at my side I never would've gotten close enough for my one shot to have a chance of hitting its target. The security team was right there. For a moment I lost myself, and if Gideon hadn't grabbed my arm, I think I might have tried anyway. I might have wasted my one shot.

Though I know the smart thing was to walk away and wait for a better moment, I can't help feeling like I should've found a way around it. I'm running through a list of a thousand things I should've done—convinced Gideon that we needed to disable security shipwide to decrease our chances of being caught, gotten him to remove the field for me. Rushed the dais when the room's attention was on the daughter and her fiancé. Anything would've done, especially since I wouldn't have needed to stay under the radar any longer. This was supposed to be a one-way trip.

And instead I just stood there, the Knave's hand on my elbow, his lips by my ear, while Roderick LaRoux and his whole happy family stood up there and smiled. It's all I can do not to scream—or cry—or throw up.

The corridor leading to the exhibit and the elevators beyond is dark, the carpet the decadent red that would've been the style when the *Icarus* made her doomed maiden voyage. My bare feet make no sound, and even Gideon's footfalls are nearly silent. The muffled music and laughter from the ballroom fall away as we move. Rooms open up on either side of us, re-creations of what the *Icarus* once looked like to show how her passengers lived before they died. To the right, a simulation of the observation deck; to the left, a series of cabins and common rooms from various levels of the ship, from the staff's quarters up through the military personnel deck, on through to first class. Beside each is a sign informing *Daedalus* visitors that by donning their "*Icarus* Experience" glasses, they can view what these rooms looked like after the crash.

Without, I suspect, the dead bodies.

I swallow hard, wrapping my arms across my chest to stop myself from shivering.

Gideon glances at me and his hands fly to his lapels. "Are you cold?" he whispers, his voice shattering the silence—and the spell holding me.

"No," I murmur, forcing myself to sound calm. He lets his hands fall. "Let's get down to engineering." I brush past him, trying desperately to organize my thoughts.

Gideon still believes we're both here to find the rift, sabotage LaRoux's plans. Let him think so—maybe I can still use him after all. To access the computer he'll need to bypass security, and perhaps I can get him to take out the security field protecting the dais as well. Or else I can trip an alarm while he's doing his thing, and while security's busy chasing him, I can loop back around to the ballroom.

He claims to want to expose LaRoux's wrongdoing to the galaxy. I can't believe he's so naïve as to think that would accomplish anything. What justice would there be in seeing a man like LaRoux arrested? Even if his lawyers failed to clear him of all charges, the best-case scenario would see him spend a few months at most in a "prison" cell that would make my penthouse look more like the halfway house where I slept last night. Far more likely, it'd all get pinned on some underling in his company, and LaRoux would get to dominate the next fifty news cycles expressing his shock and horror at what was done in his name. He'd probably throw another benefit for the families "affected" by the crash, and by the massacres on Avon, and end up coming out of it all more loved than ever. Though the number of us who see him with clear eyes is growing, we're still a drop in the ocean of the masses, and against the narrative people *want* to believe, we'd simply be washed away.

The re-creation of the first-class salon opens up before us as we make our way toward the elevators, and my footsteps falter. The room is lit low and warm, but the holographic projectors are off—no ghostly passengers milling around, no music, no hovertrays. The utter stillness makes it all too easy to see that we're not alone.

I grab for Gideon's arm as he starts to move past me, and his gaze snaps over. Off to the side, near one of the plush leather-lined booths, are Lilac LaRoux and Tarver Merendsen.

Gideon and I draw back into the shadows, waiting for some sign that they noticed us. But the soldier's arms are around her, and her face is buried in his shoulder, and neither of them is looking our way. I was so busy making sure Gideon and I weren't spotted as we slipped away that I must not have noticed when these two did the same. As we watch, Lilac LaRoux lifts her head. Her face is white beneath her makeup, the red of her lipstick standing out and highlighting the tight set of her mouth. She wears a black dress, as if she's in mourning for everything around them. Now that I look closer, I can see that the soldier's eyes are red-rimmed.

The soldier murmurs something I can't hear, and in reply, the girl whispers, "Like ghosts, you and I."

For a moment, I can almost feel sorry for them. Whatever else they've done, whoever they're connected to, they're the only two surviving people in the universe who were here, who knew the people modeled in the holograms, all dead now, who might have even been inside the first-class salon before the *Icarus* went down.

I've seen that look on the LaRoux girl's face a dozen times on Avon. Like everything of her has been stripped away, leaving behind only the skeleton of who she was. If it weren't for the hair, the dress, the rich surroundings, she could almost be one of the war orphans, waiting for the scars of trauma to fade. I could save her the time and tell her that they never do.

She reaches one hand out suddenly, grabbing the edge of the booth's table to straighten herself, grimacing, and the soldier's arms are around her, lightning-quick. His voice rises in alarm, and his words are clear. "You're here, you're with me, Lilac."

"I can feel them," she whispers, jaw clenched, lips barely moving, the tendons in her neck visible for an instant. Then it's over, and she's letting out a slow breath, straightening once more.

Gideon and I exchange glances, and he mouths, *Them who?* at me, but I don't have the answer. The ghosts of her past, I assume, asking why she's complicit in the plans of a man so evil as her father.

The soldier speaks again, the lower timbre of his voice making his words harder to decipher now, and the girl nods. He dips his head to kiss her temple, and when he pulls away, she's Lilac LaRoux again. Smile bright, spine straight, all signs of what I thought I saw erased.

"There's my girl," the soldier says with a grin, and all shreds of sympathy flee. I wish I could dismiss tragedy so blithely.

I glance at Gideon, about to tilt my head and suggest we move on—we don't need to know what these two are doing, we just need to keep out of their way—only to find him watching the pair as intently as I was. Blinking, I realize that his hands are clenched so tightly at his sides his knuckles are white, and that the salon lights reflected in his eyes are glimmering, his eyes wet. He looks at them the way I look at the picture of my father; like the man with his arms around Lilac LaRoux is the last scrap of some part of himself he lost long ago.

I hesitate, then touch my fingertips to his sleeve. He breathes in sharply through his nose, then turns away, not looking at me. Without another word, we continue on past, leaving the *Icarus* survivors to haunt the halls of the *Daedalus* alone.

The elevators Gideon wants to use are located in a wing of the exhibit on the crash itself, in a hall displaying about two dozen fragments of wreckage. Holographic text explaining each piece leaps out at us as we walk by, our movement triggering the displays to try to pull our attention away. But Gideon only has eyes for the ornate doors at the end of the room, making his way up to them in silence.

We step inside, and I'm still searching my mind for the words I need.

As we silently glide past the floors on the way to engineering, I can feel LaRoux getting farther away. But what's my next move? *Gideon, I know we've got a lot of . . . of things going on. This isn't the time or place to talk. But maybe—maybe when it's all over, once we've gotten the info we need, we can . . .* Yes, something like that. With a bit of *don't you need to cut the security fields everywhere, just to be sure there's nothing hidden?* mixed in.

I draw in a careful breath.

"Okay, I cut the alarm," Gideon says, before I can speak, his eyes on his lapscreen. "I managed to isolate just the engineering floor—if we shut down the whole ship, all hell will break loose."

Damn it.

I'm still searching for a response when the doors slide open to reveal the engineering department, and I'm forced to follow him out into the hallway. Perhaps, if we follow Gideon's plan and disable the rift, it'll draw LaRoux away from the fully secured ballroom and give me the opportunity I need. Part of me sickens at how easy it is to smile at Gideon and pretend everything's fine again. But I can't ever forget that it's the Knave walking beside me now—he'll never be just Gideon again.

This floor lacks the ornate trappings of those above—it's purely functional, scaffolding running up the walls to our left, a metal gantry leading away toward the center of the department. I know from the plans I studied that this whole level is open, several floors high. It's like a huge stadium, set up around the hyperspace engines in the center, with workstations clinging to the walls like metallic nests, linked by a complex series of staircases so the engine can be viewed and accessed from dozens of angles.

Gideon's moving quickly, and I'm grateful my shoes are hanging from one hand so I can keep up, hurrying along the hallway after him in my bare feet, the metal grille of the floor biting into my skin. Perhaps this will be quick—perhaps we'll find the rift quickly, disable it, return to the party. There's still time for my shot. I can fix my hair, fix my makeup, blend back in—I'm so busy mentally reassembling myself that the breath goes out of me with an undignified squeak when I suddenly run into Gideon's broad back.

"What the hell?" He whispers the words, but his body's blocking my view.

It's only when I step to the side that I can take in the scene before us. Our hallway ends in a balcony fixed to the wall, opening up onto the huge engine space, several floors in height. Staircases lead in both directions, part of the giant metal spiderweb of scaffolding and gantries . . . but that's not what stopped him in his tracks.

In the huge void where the hyperspace engine should be—where the rift should be—there's nothing. The massive metal claws that should hold the engine in place simply grasp at empty air. For a moment, I'm struck with the same confusion as Gideon—we'd been so sure that LaRoux's plan with the rift was being executed here, tonight. Then I'm fighting my instinct to turn on my heel and march back into the ballroom, security field or no security field, so I can take my shot at LaRoux.

"I'll get into the system," he says, mobilizing abruptly before I can speak, striding along our little balcony to the stairs at the end of it. He continues speaking as he clatters down them, and I race after him. "The rift at Headquarters caused enormous energy fluctuations. It must be somewhere else on the ship. I'll track the energy readings and work out where. It *has* to be somewhere." There's a note of desperation in the back of his voice, though, an uncertainty he's not ready to face. There aren't many places on a ship like this that could hide something as massive as the rift we saw at LRI Headquarters.

"We don't have long," I warn him, as we reach the base of the towering installation. It's a long row of consoles, mostly dormant, display monitors layered above command trackpads. "Not if we're going to head to a second location on the ship."

Gideon doesn't even answer, his attention riveted on his work. Before, I almost enjoyed watching him do his thing—the utter concentration there, more focused than anyone I've ever seen. I probably could have stripped naked and laid down on his desk and he would've just moved his monitor so he could see over me. There was something fascinating about that, something appealing in the way he'd just vanish into the task.

Now . . . now I can imagine him tracking me that way. Following me with that single-minded attention.

I watch over his shoulder as a blueprint of the ship leaps to life on his lapscreen. My mind circles back again, relentlessly, to my plan. If our route takes us back past the ballroom, there's a chance I could slip away from him, look for an opportunity with Monsieur LaRoux. I could—

The hair on the back of my neck stands up on end, instinct warning me before my brain interprets the sound my ears are reporting: the faint hum of the elevator doors opening. "Someone's coming," I hiss, grabbing Gideon's arm to get his attention.

His head snaps up, and he yanks the leads out of his lapscreen, ducking in underneath the console—there's no time to make a dash for the other side. I slide in after him on my knees, grabbing at handfuls of my layered skirts, shoving them into the free space around me to keep them out of sight. It's like the dress has a life of its own, fighting me, trying to slither free. My heart thumps in time with the footsteps hurrying down the same metal stairs we took from the elevator.

"Son of a . . ." It's a girl's voice, rough and irritated. Her boots are visible as she reaches the bottom of the stairs, and then she's in view. She's tall, with dark skin and eyes, only a few years older than me.

She's in a security uniform, and though her stance is casual, her right arm is just inches from a holster on her thigh containing some sort of weapon. It's not an LRI uniform—she's one of the security officers with the visiting planetary delegations. The very ambassadors we came here to protect. *Or at least, that Gideon came here to protect.* She turns before I can see the crest on her jacket, looking back at the stairs, where her companion must still be.

"It's not here," she calls over her shoulder. "There's nothing. You'd better call them and say it's safe for her to come down here. They need to see this."

My mind's racing, confusion tangling with excuses. Is she here for the rift? For the engine? Will that matter, if she hauls us out from underneath the console? Already my instincts are kicking in, stringing together a story. My hair is mussed, Gideon's askew. I can say we snuck away from the party. I can say engines do it for me, and I wanted an adventure in engineering.

"Done, I just buzzed him." The guy up on the stairs speaks, and his voice goes straight through me, electrifying. I *know* that voice. Instantly, it summons a pair of laughing green eyes, a tumble of dark curls. That voice is *home.*

My body takes over without even an instant for me to think better of it, and I go scrambling out from underneath the console, tangled for a moment in my dress, bursting to my feet. "Flynn!"

He's standing on the staircase, his mouth open, still as a statue—in his black suit, he couldn't be further from the boy I grew up with, but at the same time, nothing about him has changed at all.

A click to my left snaps me out of it, and I realize the girl beside me has drawn her weapon.

That sound jerks Flynn out of his shock and sends him scrambling down the stairs. "No, no, don't touch her!" He opens his arms and I throw myself into them, closing my eyes as he wraps me up tight. To my horror, I feel my eyes starting to burn with tears. *This* is what trust feels like—I'd thought I'd begun to find it with Gideon, but now that bond, battered and broken by his lies and mine, pales in comparison to this.

The girl speaks again, her tone dry. "I guess you're sure, then."

"I'm sure, *a ghrá*," he tells her as he releases me. "This is Sofia. She's the one who hid me, in town, when . . ." He doesn't need to finish the sentence. She knows. I can see it in her eyes—who I am, my place in their story on Avon. My father.

"I had no idea you were here with the Avon delegation," I say, fully aware that I'm babbling. "Oh God, Flynn, I can't believe—you have no idea how much I—" I ease away from him to see the girl standing and watching the pair of us. Gideon's crawled out from under the console—he doesn't look pleased to see me in Flynn's arms. Whereas Flynn's girlfriend doesn't look even remotely threatened.

Because that's who she is. Though I left Avon before we had an official flag, I recognize the crest on her jacket: a Celtic knot around a single star. And now that I have context—not to mention Flynn beside me calling her *my love*—I recognize who she is. Captain Lee Chase, scourge of Avon. Protector of Avon, if you listen to Flynn's version of it.

Flynn's shaking his head. "I thought they were taking you to Paradisa. What the hell are you doing here?"

My breath tangles in my throat. *I'm here to end Roderick LaRoux,* my thoughts scream. But Flynn's never been one for violence, and Gideon would try to stop me if he knew I still wanted LaRoux dead. So I swallow the tangle of emotions and say, instead, "I'm guessing we're here for the same reason you are."

Flynn's gaze flickers over toward Gideon, brows lifting. "Who's your friend?"

To anyone else, the rapid subject change would be a non sequitur. But I know why Flynn's asking. "Someone with reason to believe the Avon Broadcast was true," I say carefully.

"You trust him?" Flynn's eyes go back to meet mine.

I have no answer for him. *No, I don't trust him. No, he's the monster who terrorized me for the last year. No, and you can shove him out the nearest airlock. No, but he's my only ally.*

"We're here together," Gideon says, when my continued silence begins to stretch uncomfortably.

"We had reason to think LaRoux was planning something tonight for the gala." I brush past the issue of trust, trying to ignore the way Flynn's eyebrows shoot up at the word *together*. I glance at the girl—Chase—who's still looking wary, though her hand's no longer hovering over her gun. "Something to do with . . . uh . . ."

"With the rift." Flynn finishes the sentence for me, earning him a sharp look from Jubilee and a startled one from Gideon. "Might as well acknowledge the elephant in the room. Or not in the room, as the case may be." He tips his head toward the empty spot where the hyperspace engine—or the rift—would have been.

"If you're from Avon," says Chase, stepping toward us, "then you'll understand. We have to make sure what happened there doesn't happen anywhere else."

Flynn puffs out a breath. "Look, in a minute, the rest of our team will be here. I sent them a signal when we found the rift was missing. And you're going to have a hard time believing this, but—"

He trails off. He can see from our faces that we're looking past him now, taking in the staircase. At its head stands Tarver Merendsen in his impeccable evening suit, and beside him Lilac LaRoux, in all her perfectly coiffed glory.

How is this possible? I can feel my pulse pounding at my temple. *The rest of our team,* Flynn said, but this is Roderick LaRoux's family, standing and staring down at us.

How could *these* four people be in *this* place? And together?

And then I find myself remembering Gideon's words back when we first met: that he was certain the *Icarus* survivors had encountered the same creatures that had terrorized Avon last year—whispers, Flynn called them in his broadcast.

I'm still gaping up at them, every last play from my hard-earned book emptying out of my head, when I realize Lilac LaRoux is staring straight past me. I glance over my shoulder to find Gideon standing there. My heart kicks up another impossible notch as I see his face. Grave, unsmiling, rigid; and when I look back again, Lilac LaRoux's face has gone absolutely white.

Her mouth opens, lips working the shape of a word I can't identify. It takes her long seconds to put breath enough behind it to speak, and when she does, it's in a thin, frightened whisper.

"Simon?"

Our keeper's daughter; the green-eyed boy of the gray world; the girl whose father will die and leave her broken; the poet with steel and beauty in his soul; the orphan whose dreams hold such hope . . .

They will all soon shatter because of the man with the blue eyes, and when they do, we shall see what they become. For if they fall as we are falling, we will turn away from this universe forever and leave it to its darkness.

Tracing their paths, their possible futures, we see a dimness where the lines intersect. A nudge this way or that and they will go their own ways, never meeting, never showing us what humanity can be.

But there . . . a sixth path. Add him to the others and the dimness clears. It is not so very hard, for his path lies close to that of our keeper's daughter already.

Six lives, six threads. We shall see what fabric they weave.

TWENTY

GIDEON

TARVER MERENDSEN'S GAZE SNAPS FROM MY FACE TO Lilac's, his own expression tightening with surprise. "Simon?" he echoes—the name means something to him. "Simon, the boy who . . ."

"Who she was supposed to be with," I finish for him, when Lilac makes no move to answer. "Simon who died for her, Simon who she forgot the second he was shipped out to the front lines." I don't want to look at Lilac's face, but I can't help it. She's staring at me like I've risen from the dead—she's staring at me like I'm simply one more ghost, one ghost too many.

Tarver has to take her elbow as they make their way down the stairs—she's not looking where she puts her feet, and she nearly stumbles. "What the hell is going on?" he demands, all but ignoring Sofia now. Sofia, who's standing just a few feet away, silent, expressionless. Sofia, hearing me reveal yet one more lie—I hadn't realized just how much of what I'd given her was false. But now, seeing the lies lined up one after another . . . and I'd thought I couldn't trust *her*?

"Simon—" Lilac's voice is barely a breath, but her brow is furrowing, the initial shock of seeing me starting to wear off. What's more surreal than anything about this moment is that neither she nor Tarver seems to think it's impossible that I *could* be Simon, even though he's been dead for years.

"No," I say finally. "But you're close."

"Oh my God," she whispers. *"Giddy."*

I haven't heard that nickname in four years, and it goes through me like a knife. Suddenly I want nothing more than to curl up in the bottom of my brother's closet again, stowing away amongst the shoes and circuits and card collections. I swallow, forcing my voice to come out level. "Bingo."

Tarver reaches out, hand coming to rest in the small of Lilac's back— how many times did I see my brother touch her like that?

"Lilac," Flynn says carefully. "This is my friend Sofia, she's from Avon. This guy's here with her. You know him?"

Visibly pulling herself together, Lilac straightens and swallows hard. "This is Gideon. Tarver, he's Simon Marchant's little brother."

Tarver's eyes widen a little, and though he doesn't relax, his voice is calmer when he speaks. "Simon, the boy you were . . . the one your father had killed for falling in love with you?"

"The very same," I reply before Lilac can. "But actually, you both know me."

The man's eyes narrow. "I don't think—"

"You call me the Knave."

In the silence that follows my voice, I can hear Sofia's intake of breath—when I glance out of the corner of my eye, I can see her take a slow step toward the stairs. I can almost see her thoughts as she considers making a run for it. And I don't blame her, really. She's still reeling from learning I'm the Knave who's terrorized her for the last year of her life—now I'm adding that I'm an old family friend of the people responsible for her father's death.

Though "friend" is stretching the definition a bit.

"He's the one who dug up the information you sent to us on Avon?" Jubilee asks, staring at me.

Lilac ignores the question. "*You're* the one who helped us set up our security system?" she bursts out, breaking through her shock, finally sounding for a brief moment more like the girl I knew as a child. "But why . . . you weren't really helping us, were you?"

The muscles in my jaw seize, a flare of anger making me want to grind my teeth. "What a conclusion to jump to, Miss LaRoux. I'm hurt. Historically speaking, it's not usually my family screwing yours over."

Lilac takes a step forward, moving away from Tarver's hand, her eyes on my face. "I'm sorry I never came to see you after—" Her voice cracks, and she tries again. "I was only fourteen. I was heartbroken, and it was my fault, and I couldn't . . ."

I can feel Flynn's and Jubilee's stares, but worse, I can feel Sofia's eyes on me, and some distant part of my mind wonders how much of this story she's able to put together from the fragments. *Focus on that. Focus on her. Don't think about Simon.* The blood's roaring in my ears, rushing like wind, like whispering voices. I try to focus on that and not on the girl in front of me.

"I loved your brother, Giddy." Lilac pauses, not coming any closer to me, though I can tell from her body language that she wants to. "I never wanted anything to happen to him. And I never, *never* forgot him."

Behind her, her fiancé is silent. If hearing Lilac talk about her so-called love for another guy hurts him, Tarver doesn't show it.

"Yeah, well." I long to shove my hands into my pockets, slouch my shoulders, hide away from all of this. Face-to-face stuff is Sofia's thing, not mine. "That makes two of us. At least you had no problem moving on."

"That's not fair." Lilac's voice quickens a little, making the blood surge harder in my ears. "Giddy—Gideon—just because I fell in love with Tarver, that doesn't change the way I felt about Simon. Simon is— Simon will *always* be—with me. The same way he'll always be with you." She lets her breath out, long and slow. "You look so much like him."

"Well, you must not think much of either of us, then, if your first thought was that I helped you guys with security just so I could screw you over."

"Why all the secrecy then?" Lilac demands. "Why hide behind pseudonyms and, and—why not just tell us who you were?"

"Because that's not who I am anymore," I spit back, trying and failing to find calm. "Simon's little brother died when he did."

Lilac is slow to answer. "Then I have that on my conscience too."

"Look," says Tarver, breaking into the conversation gently. "Whatever's going on here, this isn't the time or the place to talk about it. From the look of it, we're not the only ones you've been deceiving." His gaze flicks over toward Sofia, and abruptly I realize that he sees far more than he seems to.

When I follow his gaze, Sofia looks back at me for a long moment, her face wooden. I know I've lost her. I lost her the moment she found my brother's playing card. But now, with this link to Lilac LaRoux, I've lost her even as an ally, and I'm not prepared for the depth of that cut, the burn of it in my chest. It's like a tangible blow, so visceral I can almost taste it in my mouth, a bitter flood of copper.

Flynn Cormac finally finds his voice, though it's soft. "They're here for the whispers. They know what he's doing with them. We have to talk about this."

"And we will," Tarver agrees, calm. "But Lilac and I have to get back before we're missed. She's still got her speech to make."

"Right, wouldn't want to miss the champagne and caviar." My voice sounds cutting, hateful, even to my own ears. I'm grappling for any handhold. I'm in free fall.

"That's it," Lilac bursts out, her eyes looking for just a moment so like her father's that I take a step back. This fire, she never had that before. I'm not the only one who's changed since we were children. "For God's sake, Gideon, do you really think so little of me that you believe I came here to Corinth to celebrate this—this *sick* display?"

"I don't know the first thing about you," I reply quietly. "And I don't want to."

"Well, you need to," Jubilee says, her hand resting on Flynn's shoulder. "We're all here for the same reason. We're all here for this rift, to find out what her father's doing with the whispers. We're here to find it out, and drag it into the light."

"Flynn, how can you—" Sofia's voice breaks. "She's his *family.*"

"Yes," Lilac snaps, quick and sharp. "So I know exactly what he is."

I have only the briefest of seconds for that to sink in, the realization that maybe we're not on opposite sides, that we're after the same thing, before the roaring in my ears suddenly crescendos. Sofia takes a staggering step back, shaking her head as though to clear it, and abruptly I realize: it's not my pulse I'm hearing. It's not in my head at all. The air is full of whispering, and before I can speak, the whispers turn to a scream, tearing down the length of the deck.

It hits Lilac like a gale-force wind, tossing her dress and her hair back and knocking her heavily against Tarver—but it doesn't touch anyone else. For us, the air has the kind of stillness you only get in space, behind a dozen different airlocks.

"Lilac?" Tarver's voice is urgent, and I can see him swallowing—he's got the same taste in his mouth that I do, a thick, metallic tang like blood, or electricity. "Are you—"

"Fine," she gasps, hands curling around his sleeves as she gets her feet under herself again. "It's them. I can feel them, trying to . . . It's okay. I'm okay now, it's under control."

"But the rift's not here." Tarver's speaking low and fast, his eyes scanning Lilac's looking for—what, I don't know.

"It's nowhere on the ship," I say quietly, though I don't know why I want to offer them any comfort at all. "I just finished searching for the energy signature when you arrived. Nothing. We thought he'd moved it up here, or that he had a second one—we were wrong."

"I'm fine," Lilac murmurs, lifting her head to smile at Tarver. "Truly. I just lost my concentration for a second."

"I know what that felt like." Sofia's voice cuts through Lilac's like laser fire through silk. She's gripping her purse, white-knuckled, her face pinched. "Those voices, that metallic taste—that's the Fury."

"Not exactly, Sof," Flynn says, laying a hand on her arm. "Lilac's . . . she's the reason we're here."

"There's a rift here," Lilac says softly. "Somewhere nearby. I can feel it."

"Look," says Tarver, letting his breath out in a rush. "We don't have time to explain why, but Lilac's connected to these rifts, and we know the last one is somewhere nearby or on Corinth."

"Connected," Sofia echoes, and I can see that word isn't making him any friends.

Tarver nods slowly. "I can't go into why or how, but we've got to find the last rift and shut it down to save her."

Sofia's eyes flick from his face to Lilac's and back. "She's a LaRoux."

"Yes," Flynn replies gently, still at Sofia's side. "And she's the reason your planet is free now. She's the reason you're not a smear on some prefab wall after a soldier's Fury took over. You need to stop and listen, Sof."

"It's true," I say softly, grudgingly. "Both of them helped Flynn Cormac and Lee Chase free Avon. I know. I was watching."

She opens her mouth to speak. But before she can, another voice cuts through the stillness as a man strolls along the gantry above us, coming to a halt at the top of the staircase.

"Darling," says Monsieur LaRoux, voice mild and eyes keen. "I was wondering where you got to."

The blue-eyed man comes and pulls us from the others, brings us to a new world. The final world, he says. We glimpse only the briefest flash of it, of people so numerous even we struggle to see them all. Buildings that reach for the sky, noise and light and chaos all folding together into a greater pattern.

But we are not permitted to explore it. We are kept finite. We are locked away.

We . . .

I.

I am alone here.

Alone . . . but for the blue-eyed man.

TWENTY-ONE

SOFIA

MONSIEUR LAROUX, CLAD IN AN IMPECCABLE TUXEDO AND tails, strolls down the stairs with his hands in his pockets. His blue eyes sweep across the four of us, coming to rest, finally, on Lilac, closest to him where she stands just behind Tarver. "They're almost ready for your speech, darling," he says, lips curving to a faint smile, as casual as though he hadn't just walked into a roomful of tension he could cut with a knife. "I wondered what might have caught your interest. I can't say there's much here in the engine bays that would generally be considered an attraction."

I can't think, can't react. There's no security field here, no guards—all I have to do is reach into my purse, grab the gun, pull the trigger. My mind is screaming the order at my fingers, but I can't move.

Lilac's the one who breaks the stunned silence. "Where's the rift? Where are the whispers?"

"Darling." He pulls a little face, otherwise unruffled. "I have no idea what you're talking about, but it'll have to wait, or we'll be late."

Tarver's voice is steel. "Everybody here knows what we're talking about. Answer the question. Where's the last rift?"

Monsieur LaRoux fixes him with a far less affectionate gaze. "Whisper? Rift? Where have you been getting these stories from?"

"From me," says Lilac, through clenched teeth.

"It's on Corinth, isn't it?" Gideon's voice is chilly, but at least he's able to speak. I'm still frozen, unmoving. "It never left LRI Headquarters."

"I'm sure I don't know what you're talking about," LaRoux replies. "But if you're talking about something as large as one of these hyperspace engines, it wouldn't make much sense to try to move it, would it?"

Lilac's voice sounds nothing like his—she's shaking. "If you had any idea what it's doing to me . . ."

He dismisses her with a quick shake of his head. "There's simply no conceivable way any hypothetical creature, in a hypothetical rift, could reach you from LaRoux Headquarters, darling. We're in orbit—we're much too far away."

"It could reach her from halfway across the galaxy, you asshole," Tarver snarls, hands curling to fists by his sides. "You have to cut them off, send them back."

"My boy," says LaRoux, reaching up to adjust a mechanism against his ear—some sort of communication device, perhaps. "As much as I'd like to oblige you, there's too much riding on the next few days for me to sit here discussing all of it with you. Lilac, come along." He half turns, gesturing for the staircase as though expecting Lilac to fall obediently into step.

"No," Lilac says in a low, tight voice. "Not this time, Father. I can't keep going like this. We *know* about your experiments, about Avon, about the whispers, the rifts—all of it. And you know we know. We can't keep skimming over it, pretending we're a happy family. You're—you're destroying me with this."

LaRoux's calm exterior tightens a little. "You're *fine*," he insists. "And even if this—this *rift* as you call it—is affecting you, there are far better ways to prevent that than destroying my life's work." He reaches up, touching the device over his ear with a smile. It's the same thing I saw the men at his headquarters clipping into place as they prepared to use the rift on me.

Realization dashes over me like an icy blast. "Of course," I whisper, my anger making my hands shake. "You'd never create a weapon that could be used against yourself. You've got a way to make yourself immune."

"Clever girl," LaRoux replies, pretense falling away. And though the words are a compliment, his tone is hard. "Now, are we done here?

They should be passing around the champagne for our toasts even as we speak."

"You had a cure." My voice comes out thin and strained, and I have to blink hard to clear my eyes of the furious tears blurring them. "You had a cure that could've saved everyone on Avon."

LaRoux's brows lift. "I am sorry for those deaths, truly. But one must always be willing to make sacrifices in the pursuit of progress. If it brings you any comfort, think how much their lives mean now—how much their deaths mean. They would've toiled in obscurity in their small, pointless lives on a small, pointless planet—now they're a part of something much greater than themselves." The glint in his eye frightens me far more than the words themselves do—he *believes* what he's saying, believes it with every fiber of his being.

I'm moving before I can think, the shaking in my body stilling, dwindling down to one single-minded purpose. I tear the gun out of my purse and level it at LaRoux, my whole world narrowing down to his face.

He barely reacts.

Dimly I hear Gideon's voice, low, shaking with intensity. "Sofia, don't." He's a few steps away from me—too far to reach me before I can pull the trigger. "Don't do this. You promised me you wouldn't become this."

Ignore him, I tell myself, focusing on the man in front of the gun barrel.

Tarver and Lilac are standing perfectly still, but her father simply gazes at me like I'm some fascinating new type of insect. "I don't suppose I could talk you into using that thing to shoot Mr. Merendsen?"

"Father," Lilac interrupts, voice tightly restrained. She even *sounds* like him, especially now, fighting for control.

"A joke, my dear," he replies, reaching out to stroke her cheek with one curled finger. If I didn't know better, I'd think him a jolly old professor of something, or a kindly philanthropist. I swallow, trying to ignore the way my palms are growing sticky with the effort of holding the gun steady. LaRoux turns toward me again. "I actually know quite a bit about this young lady," he continues. "She spent some time with us recently, and we finally managed to correctly identify her. However much I might wish it, she's not going to shoot Mr. Merendsen."

"No," I manage, reminding myself to keep breathing. I can't shoot straight if I'm half-unconscious from oxygen deprivation. "Not him."

"Sofia Quinn," Roderick LaRoux continues, as if reciting from memory. "Sixteen years old, with a spotless record until her disappearance in transit from Avon's spaceport to an orphanage on Paradisa over a year ago." LaRoux turns that smile on me. "You aren't the first person to aim a gun at me, my dear. Put it away and we'll discuss whatever you like. I'll do whatever's in my considerable power to help you."

"There's nothing to discuss," I spit back, the anger surging, easy to locate. "If you know who I am then you know why I'm here. My father's dead because of your sick experiments on Avon."

LaRoux just shakes his head. "I'm afraid so many lives were claimed by the tragic events on Avon, my dear. I couldn't hope to remember them all, but you have my sincerest sympathies for your loss."

He doesn't know. He doesn't even know. *He doesn't even* . . . My hands are shaking again.

"Sofia." Lilac's voice is soft as she speaks—testing out the name on her lips, her gaze suddenly full of a sympathy I'm not prepared for, not from her. "Sofia . . . please. Put the gun down, and you and Gideon can come with me. We'll talk, after my speech. We'll talk about *all* of it." She doesn't look at her father, even when he reaches out to wrap an arm around her shoulders, a gesture of such fatherly affection that my chest constricts.

"Just put it down." The voice is no more than a whisper, and I can feel Gideon at my side like an anchor, a warmth pulling me back to myself. "Sofia, please. This isn't you. I *know* you."

"Ah yes, the accomplice." LaRoux's eyes shift to take in Gideon. "We had plenty with which to ID Miss Quinn here, but we never got quite a good enough picture of you."

I flash a quick glance at Gideon, who's only a few feet away from me, muscles tense and jaw clenched. "I'm not very photogenic," he replies.

LaRoux's brows draw in, his sculpted features settling into an expression of thoughtful scrutiny. "You look familiar, now that I see you." He tilts his head a little, and then, as though referencing some cocktail party or charity function, remarks, "Didn't I have you killed once?"

The sound that comes from Gideon's throat, tangled and full of pain, is what unfreezes me. My voice comes back. "You—you son of a *bitch*, you piece of . . ." This time I have no problem lifting the gun, holding it steady, thumbing the safety aside.

Time slows. I hear Gideon shout my name, feel the air shift as he turns to lunge for me. I see Tarver moving, instincts razor sharp, reaching for Lilac. I see his fingers miss her arm by a breath as Lilac whirls toward her father, hair flaring out like a flame. I see her face, the panic there, her heart in her eyes, and despite everything, despite my finger tightening on the trigger, despite my hatred and despair and pain, I find myself wondering if that was the look on my own face in the moments just before my father blew up the barracks.

Then my hand explodes into fire, the fragments of the plas-pistol slicing my chin, my shoulder, peppering the wall behind me. The force of the gunshot knocks me over, and when I try to lift my head it's like I'm drunk, my ears ringing, my movements slow and too fluid, muscles like putty. LaRoux staggers and my heart sings—but he's staggering because Lilac pushed him aside, and it's Lilac's voice I hear crying out pain, and it's Lilac's blood spattered against the display behind her, and it's Lilac who drops to the floor. It's Lilac.

"You could have brought her back." The blue-eyed man knows I can hear him, cut off in my prison of steel and electricity. "You could have brought back my Rose, but you let her rot because you hate me."

When he comes, he sends away the scientists studying my existence. Sometimes months pass without a visit, and sometimes he comes every day, but his hatred for me, for my kind . . . that never changes.

"You don't know what hate is yet," the man whispers, his words a promise. He turns his back on my prison.

Hate. If hate is what he wishes . . . then hate is what he will get.

TWENTY-TWO

GIDEON

MY EARS ARE RINGING, THE SOUND OF THE GUNSHOT bouncing around inside my head and blinding me. My momentum as I lunge for Sofia sends me sprawling to the ground, and it's not until I realize she's moaning, half screaming, that I shake away the fog and crawl toward her.

Her hand is covered in burns where the plas-pistol exploded, and she's bleeding from cuts on her neck and shoulders where the fragments caught her. There are a dozen reasons why these weapons are banned, the least of which is that they outfox even state-of-the-art security systems—the main reason is that you've got a greater chance of killing yourself when it goes off than of actually hitting your target.

I gather Sofia up into my arms, panic shooting through my system and washing away everything else—my anger that she'd been planning this, my fear about what will happen to her when she's arrested, the bitterness lingering on my tongue after speaking to Lilac LaRoux. I pull Sofia against my chest, and she doesn't resist, pain overcoming everything else she feels toward me right now. She's swallowing hard, choking against the need to cry out, cradling her wounded hand against her chest.

"Shh, it's okay," I murmur, my lips against her hair. "I've got you. I've got you."

Cormac drops to his knees on her other side, his horror all over his face, in his voice. "Oh God, Sof."

As if the sound of his voice opened the floodgates, suddenly other

229

sounds start to register. Voices shouting, someone gasping, a roaring surge of whispers on the still air. I lift my head, expecting to see LaRoux on the floor, and find him bent over someone else, speaking frantically.

"Darling," he's saying, that too-cultured voice choked with emotion. "Look at me—it's Daddy, look at me."

Tarver's ripping the lining out of his tuxedo jacket, his face white, jaw set and determined. He eases the figure on the floor up—it's Lilac—so that her head rests in his lap. "It's just her shoulder," he's saying in a shaking voice, starting to bind the wound with the strips of silk. "She'll be fine, it's just—"

LaRoux snaps something back at him, face transformed in that instant by such fury, such hatred, that I can't tell what he's saying.

Tarver, however, remains calm, meeting that icy-blue stare with his own. "You want her to bleed to death?"

Jubilee's beside him, pulling off her belt and handing it over to help strap the makeshift bandages in place, fixing LaRoux with a look that seems like it should do to him what the bullet didn't.

LaRoux draws in a shuddering breath, reaching for Lilac's hand and cradling it between his own, drawing it up to press it to his lips. "Hang on, darling girl."

Sofia stirs in my arms, voice shaky with pain as she mumbles. "She wasn't supposed to . . . Why, why did she do that? I never meant to—"

"Because he's her father," Flynn says softly. "Because she loves him, and you were trying to kill him."

"He's a monster," whispers Sofia, struggling to sit up on her own power, some of the shock from her injury starting to ebb.

"And he's her *father*," Flynn replies.

Sofia's face crumples, tears spilling out to mingle with the blood on her chin. I've read her background now. I know what happened to her own father. And I know how many voices were calling him a monster in the wake of his death. What it must be like to love someone, despite whatever they might have done. I tighten my arms around her.

"I'm here," I whisper.

Lilac stirs, and it's enough to jerk both men's attention back to her, as Tarver finishes binding off her shoulder with the silk lining of his jacket. "Tarver . . ." she mumbles, and I see the way her father's face tightens, the look of loathing on his face as his eyes dart up toward his future son-in-law.

"There's my girl," Tarver replies, oblivious to—or ignoring—the look he gets from LaRoux. He smiles, bending his head to brush his lips against her forehead. "You're going to be fine."

"Are you lying to me again?" Her voice is so quiet I can barely hear it.

A sound, like a laugh but without much humor, escapes Tarver's lips. "Not this time," he answers. "I promise. Lee, call for a medic, we can't move her."

Jubilee rises to her feet, jogging over to the commpoint on the wall. But Lilac's stirring.

"I feel . . ." Her voice trails off, and for a horrible moment I think she's dead, that Tarver missed something, that she was hurt somewhere else. But then she speaks, and her voice has changed, and something in it makes my entire body freeze. *"Angry."*

As if in response, the whispering, surging voices on the air cease all at once, leaving us in utter silence. My mouth floods again with the taste of blood, and despite my arms tightening around Sofia, my muscles start to quiver, like I've been climbing for an hour and my body's too exhausted to fight.

Tarver's calm shatters. "Lilac—Lilac, look at me. Look at me, beautiful, don't—" His gaze snaps up to meet LaRoux's. "Do something!" he shouts.

"I don't understand," LaRoux's saying slowly, stupidly, staring at whatever's happening to Lilac, something we can't see.

"She's different," Tarver snaps. "That's what we've been hiding from you. She's connected to them, and she knows that you've still got them held captive in the last rift here. They want *her*, don't you get it? They've been trying to get inside her head for the past year. You have to shut down the rift, send the whispers back. *Now.*"

"I told you, there *is* no rift up here on the *Daedalus*," replies LaRoux, his face white. "There's only one of the creatures left at all, it couldn't possibly—"

"It's *killing* her! If it's down on Corinth, then make the call!"

"There is simply no way—" LaRoux's voice catches and chokes. "It *cannot* be reaching her . . ."

"Hush." It's Lilac's voice again, but under control, no longer confused and whispery and hurt. She reaches out, wounded shoulder and all, to gently push Tarver's arm away from her so she can sit up. "I'm fine."

Tarver's silent, and LaRoux too, as though that gentle command were a magic spell robbing both men of their voices.

"What a strange thing," says Lilac, rotating her injured shoulder slowly, not even seeming to notice when the movement causes a fresh flow of blood that trickles from beneath the makeshift bandage. "Pain is so different from what I'd imagined."

Fingers of ice creep down my spine, fear trickling in before I can even figure out why I'm afraid. I give Sofia a squeeze, and as though she can read my thoughts, she struggles to get her feet beneath her and together we stagger up to stand side by side.

Lilac, spotting the movement, lifts her head to look at us. But instead of the bright, sky-blue eyes so like her father's, I see only blackness, like empty holes.

Tarver's just looking at Lilac, and for the first time I see him, *really* see him, how he looks at her. I've been so busy hating him for replacing my brother that I never noticed. . . . His heart is written clear across his features, and the agony reflected there as he looks at Lilac makes my own heart ache in response.

"Lilac," he whispers. "My girl."

Lilac's black eyes swing over toward him, and though her face remains neutral, almost empty, her voice carries a cold so intense my skin crawls. "I know you."

Tarver shivers, drawing up on his knees so he can reach out and take Lilac's arms, gazing intently at her. "Lilac, I know you're in there somewhere. You can fight this. You are *stronger* than this. Please—please. *Please.*"

Lilac gazes back at him for a long moment before a ripple travels through her features and she sags a little, like a marionette whose strings are being cut. Her eyes flick up to fix on her fiancé's face. "T-Tarver?"

Tarver's breath catches and he leans closer, eyes scanning hers, searching for some flicker of the girl who used to be there. "Lilac."

The girl gives a sob and leans forward, pressing her lips to his, a desperate sort of kiss. For a moment, no one else moves, the whole room narrowing to just the two of them, Tarver's hand coming up to touch her cheek, her movements as she leans into the kiss harder.

Then she pulls back abruptly, opening her eyes—her black eyes—and giving a brief, mirthless laugh. "You're so *easy*." She lifts one hand, and like she'd brush aside a fly, she shoves him back—and the force of the blow sends the soldier flying, to strike the far wall with a sickening thud.

She rises to her feet, not even flinching when Lee Chase instantly swings her weapon around to point at her. "You murdered my brethren," says Lilac—or the thing that used to be Lilac, still staring at Merendsen. "To save your own skin—to save this skin," she adds, gesturing with some distaste to her own body, "you killed them all."

"They wanted . . . they *asked*. . . ." Tarver's groaning, dragging himself up from the floor—his eyes aren't focusing right, and I know he's only barely conscious.

"You're lying. No one *asks* for death." Lilac glances around, head tilting as though to get a better look at each of us. "Though maybe you will, before the end."

"Don't move." Jubilee's sighting down her gun at Lilac, her every muscle tense, her body poised. "I don't want to shoot you, but I will if you take a single step."

"No—Lee—" Tarver's got one hand against the wall as he drags himself to his feet. "She's in there. She's still in there. Hold your fire."

The barrel of the gun dips, an automatic response to what was clearly an order. "Dammit, sir . . ." She shifts her grip on the gun, torn, the instinct to obey him warring with the instinct to protect him.

"If you shoot my daughter," Monsieur LaRoux says to Jubilee, cold—but visibly struggling for control—"I will personally see you executed."

"It's all right," says the creature inside Lilac, smiling at Jubilee. "I was the first, I am the oldest, and now I am the last of my kind here. I don't need to move to kill your captain."

In the distance comes a great, low cry—like the moan of an immense beast, echoing through the ship. It isn't until half a second later, when the floor shudders beneath us and Sofia and I go staggering back against the wall, that I realize what it was. The sound of immensely thick metal tearing like tissue paper.

Flynn rises to his feet unsteadily and steps up next to Jubilee, his movements slow. "We've met your kind before," he says slowly, his voice soothing, calm—I can detect only the faintest hints of the terror that must be there, the same terror that's making Sofia shake at my side. "We know what's been done to you, and we mean you no harm. Please let us talk. You can clearly destroy us anytime you want to, but do that and we'll never be able to talk to each other. You lose nothing by waiting, by hearing us out. Destroy us now and that door closes."

He's even better than he was in the Avon Broadcast—*I'd* surrender, given half a chance. But the Lilac creature just looks at him blankly, unaffected by his plea. "I was going to crush him," she comments, glancing over at Tarver, leaning hard against the wall. "But this is far better. Let him die knowing he couldn't save her. Let him die the way he should have died—falling in a tomb of twisted metal and fire."

The words ring in the air, punctuated by the distant creaks and groans of whatever's happening to the ship, and for a long moment I can't understand what the creature means. *Metal and fire . . . falling . . .* Then, suddenly, my knees buckle. "You can't—" My voice comes out hoarse with fear, choked with disuse.

Sofia reaches the same conclusion I do. "Oh God," she whispers.

Lilac is going to bring down the *Daedalus.*

How the others back on the gray world fare, I will never know. Whether my kin on the other side of the rift can see me, sense me, I cannot tell. All I know is the blue-eyed man, and the link of hatred between us.

He talks to me often, of his wife, of his young daughter, of his work. He has begun work on a pair of ships that will use our universe to move even faster through theirs, and he delights in sharing with me all the successes in his life, certain they will cause me pain.

I wish I had brought his wife back to him, for then I could use her to free myself from this prison. Marked by our touch, she would be vulnerable, a vessel waiting to be filled. I could take from him the thing he loves most all over again, and smile at him with her lips until his mind crumbles.

I could tell him that his new technology risks tearing a hole into our world. I could tell him that to toy with the fabric of the universe is to risk destruction. I could tell him his new ships are doomed.

But I have no mouth with which to speak. And I will wait.

TWENTY-THREE

SOFIA

ANOTHER SHUDDER TEARS THROUGH THE SHIP, THROWING me against Gideon. I don't protest the arms around me—hell, my arms go around *him* too—because in this moment, I don't care.

I don't care about the Knave, I don't care about his connection to the LaRoux family, I don't care that I work alone and I don't commit and I don't fall in love and I don't become attached. We're standing on a ship that's falling from the sky and if these are my last moments alive I'll spend them with my arms around Gideon.

"Crash this ship and you die too," Flynn breaks in, raising his voice to be heard over the sounds of destruction all around us.

"Please." Lilac's lips curve to a faint smile. My skin crawls at the sight—it'd be easier, better, if she looked and acted nothing like herself. But I've seen that smile a dozen times in magazines and in HV interviews, and if it weren't for the terrible darkness in her eyes, I'd think nothing was different. This is nothing like what I saw with my father, who lost everything of himself right before he walked into that barracks. This . . . *thing*, whatever it is, is still Lilac. And yet it isn't. Lilac's smile widens. "I'm tearing a ship apart without lifting a finger. You think the crash will kill me?"

"Then think about the thousands, hundreds of thousands, of people in the district below. They never did anything to you or your kind, and you'll kill them all when this ship hits. Do that and you're no better than LaRoux."

Lilac's smile widens a little, and she casts her glance to the side. I'd almost forgotten about LaRoux, that realization jolting through me— I'd almost *forgotten* about him. He's still on his knees, where he'd been crouching after his daughter was shot. He looks up at her, face haggard and lined, the blue eyes seeming almost watery, weak, compared to the deepest black of Lilac's gaze.

"True," she replies, still looking at LaRoux, her expression a sick combination of loathing and love. "I am, I suppose, what my father made me." She stoops a little so that she can lay a hand against LaRoux's cheek, a tender gesture that makes me shudder. "But you are wrong, when you say I'm no better than he is."

Flynn doesn't answer, and I know why. He spent a lifetime surrounded by people who wouldn't, or couldn't, listen to logic, to compassion, to reason. He knows madness when he hears it.

Lilac waits, and when no reply comes, her smile drains away, leaving something full of steel and fire behind. "Roderick LaRoux is a creature who defines himself by power. And I . . . I am better than him in *every* way."

The ship shudders again, in time with an explosion that makes my body seize, panic and adrenaline sweeping through and dimming the pain in my hand. Every muscle's screaming at me to run. But run where? To get to the shuttles we'd have to go toward the sounds of destruction— if there even are shuttles anymore.

Lilac looks back down at her father and smiles. "Daddy," she says softly. "You'll come with me, right?"

Roderick LaRoux's lips part, gazing up at the thing that isn't really his daughter anymore—and, like a switch has been flipped, his face changes. The tension in his shoulders drains, his lips cracking into a tremulous smile. I see him will himself into believing it, with the same conviction that helped him believe the creature in the rift could never hurt his Lilac. "You forgive me," he whispers. "For Simon, for the *Icarus*—you forgive me?"

The Lilac-thing reaches for his hand to draw him up to his feet. "You're my father," she says, kissing his cheek. "And I'm not done with you yet."

LaRoux gapes at her for a long moment before a smile slides into place on his features—a deliberate sort of expression, as he chooses blindness over reality. "Oh, my darling." LaRoux's voice is muffled, and I'm half expecting his eyes to go black like Lilac's—but they remain clear and blue. His own willingness to delude himself is all the control Lilac needs. "My heart. Yes. Let's go."

Lilac casts one more glance over her shoulder at Tarver, whose arm, the one not supporting him against the wall, is hanging oddly. He takes a lurching step forward, trying to speak, but without another word, the LaRoux heiress and the creature inside her mind turn away, leading her father toward the staircase and up into the destruction.

"Lilac!" Tarver's scream is hoarse, and suddenly he's running despite his injury, despite what must be a concussion making his steps falter. "Lilac—"

"Sir, no!" Jubilee's abandoning her gun, turning to intercept Tarver and put her whole body in between him and the stairs Lilac is ascending. He collides with her hard enough to make her groan for breath, but she doesn't fall—she wraps both arms around him and hauls back, boots skidding on the metal grille of the floor. "Help me!" she cries, and Flynn's moving instantly to add his strength to hers in trying to prevent Tarver from following Lilac.

"Let go!" Tarver shouts, struggling, barely sparing a glance for the woman dragging him back. "Let go, let me—I have to—*that's an order, Lieutenant!*" He's stronger than she is, stronger than them both, half-mad with grief and fear and pain, and barely coherent.

She struggles with him, gasping for air and shouting in his ear. "You can't save her—Tarver, the whisper will make sure she survives this crash, and you can't save her if you're dead!"

He roars some kind of reply and tears free of her grip for half a second—and then she's swinging her arm, open palm catching him on the head and knocking him sideways. Half-stunned, he staggers against the wall, where Flynn holds him, his own muscles rigid with the effort.

Lee's eyes snap toward us, and like that look is a jolt of adrenaline, all the oxygen comes rushing back into my lungs. "Can you walk?"

I try, dizzy with confusion and shock, to draw myself up straighter. I nod, and feel Gideon start breathing again at my side. Abruptly I realize that the fingers of my good hand are tangled through his.

"I won't do this again," Tarver's saying, still trying, half-conscious, to push Flynn away from him. "I won't live without her again. I can't. I can't. Lee . . . please. Please, leave me here. Please, Lee . . ."

Jubilee glances back over her shoulder at him, and I can see the pain of seeing him like this etched in the tension along her spine. Then she's moving, joining Flynn, slinging Tarver's good arm over her shoulder. "Flynn?"

He seems to understand her at a glance and jerks his head toward the far end of the deck. "There have to be shuttles around here somewhere—we'll never make it up to the ambassadors' launch pads."

I raise my voice to be heard over another shriek of metal, shouting, "Maintenance shuttles, they're along the far wall." The other side of this huge chamber is half the length of the ship away, barely visible in the dim shadows.

Flashes of memorized floor plans swim up in front of my eyes, too fragmented to be of any use. We were never supposed to spend more than a few minutes here, but I learned this entire deck anyway. Anyone can make a plan—what separates out the survivors is who bothers to prepare for the moment when things stop going according to plan. But the shock's starting to fade and pain is radiating up my arm, and I can hear whispering voices in my ear, and my fear is too thick, too tangible, to see through.

"We have to go," Jubilee's roaring, still wrestling with Tarver. "We have to fall back, sir!"

"Gideon, get her moving," Flynn shouts, from where he's on the ex-soldier's other side, still holding him back.

Gideon pulls me after him as he starts to run, and we both stumble as a wave travels the length of the floor, jolting us off our feet and sending us flying forward. We scramble upright, our hands still linked tightly, and as I glance behind, I see Tarver finally running, flanked by Flynn and Jubilee.

There's a great, screaming sound above us that sets my nerves on fire, meeting with the agonizing bolts of pain shooting up from my burned hand, scrambling my brain until I can hardly remember how to run. With a deafening slam, one of the workstations bolted onto the walls above us rips away, hitting the floor just meters to our right.

I skid to a halt, so abruptly that Gideon loses his grip on my hand and staggers on a few steps without me as I drop to my knees. The fire in my hand is burning, my ears are ringing. Dimly I can hear his voice calling my name, muffled and fuzzy, as though I'm underwater. The far wall of the huge engine chamber swims out of focus as the ground quakes beneath me. This ship is falling out of the sky, and we're never going to make it to the shuttles.

We watch, from behind the veil between worlds, piecing together what the others have found. The children are growing older, each choice they make drawing them closer together, binding their fates.

Our kin on the gray world cannot hear us, but we can hear them. They are torn between despair and hope, bringing us no closer to understanding these creatures. The others, held captive in the place where the thin spot first appeared, grow weak and tired. No one has come, either to end them or to release them, in many years.

There is one we can no longer see, no longer hear—the blue-eyed man has locked it away so tightly we feel only the dimmest sense that it still exists.

Perhaps it will find us the answers we seek.

TWENTY-FOUR

GIDEON

THE FLOOR SHUDDERS BENEATH MY FEET, AND I STUMBLE back from Sofia, still shouting her name. As she sways, dazed, I grab for her good hand to pull her upright.

Cormac looks back as he, Merendsen, and Jubilee run past us, and I wave him on, pointing at the corner where I'm praying the shuttles are docked. He dodges a falling banister that hits the deck in a shower of sparks, then shouts something unintelligible to the others.

With a shove I get Sofia moving, but she's cradling her injured hand against her body, face deathly white. We tear across the open space of the engineering department, as I desperately try to keep watch for falling debris, and just as desperately try to pick a clear path through the twisted workstations, balconies, and gantries that litter our path. For a frantic moment I wonder if the hull's even intact—but if it wasn't, we'd know it. We'd be a little short of breath.

Flynn and Jubilee haul Tarver along ahead of us, and I'm clutching Sofia's good hand in mine, trying to block out her cries of pain as I drag her around the smoking ruins of a console. At the last instant I spot the sparking wires snaking along the ground in our path, and I swing her away by the hand I'm holding, sending her stumbling once more.

She's still barefoot, I realize—she had her shoes off to play the rumpled party guest if we were caught, and she must have dropped them during the shooting. Blood paints her right foot red, but I can't stop to check if it's serious. As we correct course and head for the docking corner once more the whole ship quivers, a shock wave running along the floor toward us. Sofia stumbles again, and I twist to catch her, but as her arms wrap around me I lose my footing, and next thing we're down, slamming into the ground hard enough to drive the air from my lungs.

Is this what it was like for the fifty thousand who died on the Icarus?

I push to my elbows, dragging in a breath. The door to the docking port emerges from the gloom, the others nearly there, and just a few meters ahead of us.

Flynn looks back again, and his arm goes flying up, his mouth open in horror. I tip my head back in time to see one of the huge claws built to hold part of the engine in place coming straight at us. I scream my own warning, and Sofia and I work as one—she tucks in against me as I wrap my arms around her, rolling hard to my left so we slam against a fallen desk, lying on its side. The claw slams into it an instant later, but though it crumples, it's just high enough that its edge protects us. The desk's displays short-circuit, spewing sparks down on top of us.

As I glance up, the desk starts to bend in half, and I throw myself over Sofia, pressing her into the ground as the wreckage pins us into the gap between it and the floor, as if we're in a tiny metal tent. She cries out, and I realize her injured hand is trapped between us—the whites of her eyes are showing, and I brace against the metal grille of the floor, shoving as hard as I can to try and shift the weight off of us.

Then two strong hands are grabbing me under my arms, and Jubilee's there, gritting her teeth as she pulls us free of the pile. I keep Sofia pinned against me, and we scramble the last few meters on hands and knees, falling through the open shuttle door, where Flynn's waiting to help us through it. Chase is running back to Merendsen's side now, holding him back as the shuttle doors close—she's talking in his ear, but I can't hear what she's saying over the noise of the *Daedalus* falling apart around us.

"Jubilee," Flynn shouts from up by the cockpit, "unless you want me flying this thing, you'd better get up here!"

Jubilee spares one more agonized look for Merendsen, and then she's scrambling free to run for the pilot's seat. "Right."

Sofia and I lie tangled together on the floor as the engine pitch rises, and with a soft rumble, the shuttle breaks free of the *Daedalus*. Sofia's breath is coming in soft moans, but slowly she's falling silent, and I'm pretty sure that's not a good sign. When I force my eyes open, the first thing I see is her hand—blistered red from where her plas-pistol exploded, wounds weeping a glistening fluid.

When I lift my head to look past her, Merendsen's bracing himself against a chair, eyes closed as Flynn works to pop his shoulder back in with a grunt of effort. Somehow, Cormac looks as put-together as he did at the start of the evening, tux still perfect, one curl falling down over his forehead. By contrast, Merendsen's missing the jacket he tore up for Lilac, his white shirt bloodstained.

"Brace," Jubilee shouts from the pilot's seat, and Merendsen doesn't even react—Flynn shoves him back against the wall, ignoring his wince of pain, and straps him into the seat. He grabs at another chair to steady himself, and I hunker down next to Sofia. I brace my feet against the bottom of a row of seats as the shuttle banks sharp left, tilting at a forty-five-degree angle, engine screaming a protest.

"There're shuttles all over the place, and debris coming free," Jubilee warns us. "Keep hold of something, I'm getting clear of the field."

We all hold our places as she does, and I curl my arm over Sofia where we lie together, closing my eyes. I start to count silently, trying to distract myself as we swoop and dive, my stomach surging up into my throat, the frame of the shuttle itself quivering under the tension. I reach one hundred and twenty-seven before we level out, and Jubilee punches the autopilot commands, peeling out of her chair. "Should be safe to move," she says, eyes going first to Flynn and then to Tarver, who's staring now out his window, his whole body sagging in his harness.

"Please," he's whispering. "Please, no."

As one we're scrambling from our seats to the windows lining one side of the shuttle.

I can think of a dozen things he might have been pleading for, but one glance is enough to tell me that none of them are coming true.

The *Daedalus* is falling.

Sheering in on an angle, she's disintegrating in the sky, sections the size of skyscrapers wrenching away from her hull to plummet toward the city below. She's impossibly huge, and yet my mind keeps seeing a model ship breaking into pieces, as if the enormity of what's happening can't be real.

The first chunks of debris are hitting the city below, now, and all the breath leaves my body as I watch one cut a swath four blocks wide through the suburbs of Corinth, cartwheeling in to land and cutting through apartment complexes like a knife through butter. Flames bloom far below us, black clouds of smoke obscuring the ruins. The next piece falls, metal gleaming in the light for an instant before it's buried in flame and smoke.

I'm watching thousands of people die, and when the bulk of the *Daedalus* hits, I'm going to watch hundreds of thousands of people die. I can say the words to myself, but though they circle in my head in a horrified chant, I can't understand it. Corinth is invincible. Corinth is always there. Corinth will always be there.

Corinth is burning.

"Please, no," Tarver's whispering again beside me, resting his forehead against the window, tears streaming down his cheeks as the *Daedalus* screams down toward the city.

It's like watching a stone land in water—debris goes flying up in the wake of the huge ruin of a ship, whole buildings disintegrating, sending up showers of dust and smoke, twisted metal and flames.

Corinth is burning.

I spin away from the window, and Sofia comes with me. She throws her arms around me, and I pull her in close, burying my face in her hair, and I breathe in her warmth, her *life*, trying desperately to block out the images of the dying city I can see even with my eyes closed. For this moment we're not the Knave and the con artist, and there's no artifice when she pulls me close. When I lift my head, Flynn has his arms around Jubilee, and she's whispering something in his ear that only has him squeezing her tighter.

And Tarver Merendsen's alone, still watching at the window, white as a sheet in his bloodstained shirt, as though he's watching his own execution.

And in that moment, whatever I held against him, whatever part of me blamed him for taking my brother's place—that part dissolves into nothing. This is a man Simon would have wanted for Lilac. I see that now.

He loves her. Watching the death and destruction below, knowing the creature capable of this has stolen her from him, I know he does.

"Tarver." My voice is hoarse, and I don't bother trying to clear my throat. I think my cheeks are wet as well, and they should be. My world is bleeding below us.

He turns his head slowly, and his gaze is haunted.

"We're not done yet," I say quietly.

Still leaning against me, Sofia lifts her head. "Damn straight we're not," she says, steel in her voice, daring anyone to contradict her.

Nobody does.

"We need to find somewhere to land," Jubilee says, moving past us to check the autopilot. Beyond her, I see another cluster of debris disappear into the thick cloud of smoke now covering the swath of destruction in the north of the city. "This shuttle was only meant for maintenance, and supply runs to the ship—it's not fueled to stay up here for long."

"Where should we be aiming for? Where's safe? We have no idea if Lilac can find us," Flynn says quietly, running one hand through his curls and finally looking something less than put-together.

I look across at Jubilee—soldier or not these days, she's got her soldier's face on now, gazing at the four of us with no hint of her feelings showing. "Stone-faced Chase," they used to call her on Avon. I read that in her file. It's still impressive, in person. And perhaps it's because I'm staring at her, thinking about the soldier that still lives inside her, that the idea comes. But suddenly, I know where we should go. "I have a place."

Four heads turn toward me.

"I know a woman, her name's Kumiko. She's ex-military."

"Can we trust her?" Finally, Jubilee speaks.

Sofia asked me that same question about Mae, and I can feel her eyes on me. This time, I swallow hard. "I don't know. I can't promise. But you and Merendsen are ex-military, that'll mean something to her. And she was posted on Avon. She knows what LaRoux's capable of. I've dealt with her before, as the Knave. She trusts him, as much as she trusts anyone. Her place has security, it's practically a fortress. And she'll have a medical kit." I'm trying not to look at Sofia's hand, at her face where a piece of the plas-pistol cut her chin.

"We can't stay up here." Sofia sounds exhausted, and when I wrap my arm around her, she simply leans in against me, head on my shoulder. "We have to use the—the confusion to land."

The confusion. The hundreds of thousands of lives that were just snuffed out, right below us. The millions of people who just lost a child, or a parent, or a partner. There's nothing we could call it that would do it justice, and the crack in her voice tells me how close she is to breaking. I'm no better, myself.

Jubilee looks across at Flynn, then meets Sofia's eyes—she doesn't try for Merendsen, who's leaning forward now, his head in his hands. Then, slowly, she nods. "Give me the coordinates."

We land on the roof of Kumiko's complex, and as the shuttle settles on the painted *X* of the landing pad, half a dozen guns appear in the windows of the stairwell, trained on us.

"Are we going to get a chance to introduce ourselves before we're shot?" Flynn asks, eyeing them through a window. The view is only dimly visible in the glow of the shuttle's emergency lighting.

"We'll get a chance," I say. "They'd have fired on our underside while we were landing, if that's what Kumiko intended."

"Comforting," Flynn mutters.

"Good thing she didn't," Merendsen says, joining him at the window. "This is a maintenance shuttle, no armor."

We've only got Jubilee's weapon between us, and Sofia's plas-pistol is long gone. I've shoved my hacking kit into my pockets and strapped it against my body under my clothes. If I've completely misjudged this, and I'm going to be locked up somewhere, I'll have my weapons of choice. Assuming Kumiko's people don't just shoot me.

I raise my hands into clear view and make my way down the shuttle steps, Jubilee covering me from the doorway with her pistol.

A stocky figure appears in the doorway leading up from below, carrying an emergency lantern, lifting it high in one hand to illuminate the landing pad. She's clad in black with a kerchief tied over her face, and if we're short on weapons, Kumiko certainly isn't. She's carrying a gun as thick as her forearm, and she jerks the barrel to signal that I should halt a few steps from the shuttle. "You can stay right there, thanks."

I suck in a slow breath, let it out. "Kumiko, it's me—"

"You got a name, *me?*" she snaps, hefting her gun. She does something that makes a clicking sound, and I'm pretty sure it's the safety coming off.

Oh, hell. "The Knave," I say, arms twitching with the urge to drop them, protect myself. "The Knave of Hearts."

Her mouth falls open. "Password," she snaps, recovering, and for a moment I'm lost. *Password?* My mind scrambles, flailing for some memory to attach that word to, and just as I'm starting to panic, there it is. When I set up the forum I host for her troop, we chose a password together that would allow either of us to crash it, in the event they were about to be discovered. I mostly thought I was catering to her paranoia, back then. "Trodaire," I stammer.

Slowly, she lowers her weapon. "What the hell are you doing here?"

"That's an incredibly long story," I start. "I'm here with . . ." I pause, not sure what to say. *Friends? That's a stretch.*

But she's not listening. In fact, she's staring past me at the doorway of the shuttle. "Captain?" Kumiko's voice has dropped, uncertain, softer now. "Captain Chase?" She reaches up to pull her kerchief down, revealing the lower half of her face.

Jubilee Chase walks slowly down the steps to stand by my side, her gun lowering. I hold still, silently willing Kumiko not to freak out and start firing.

But it turns out I don't need to worry, because Kumiko's just staring at Jubilee like she's seen a ghost, shaking her head slowly.

And Jubilee just stares right back. "Corporal Mori? What the *hell* are you doing here?"

We watch them grow. The three of us are alone, and we do not know if the others can see what we see, but we press on with our mission, seek the answer to our question.

The girl whose dreams so fascinated us is a soldier now, and though she is younger than the others and smaller, she trains harder than any of them. Already she's showing the steel that will draw her so to the poet. A change of a few symbols on a military document flying through our universe sends her to serve with him.

They will become friends. She will learn what she needs from him, but his path is not with her. She will stay here, with us, on the gray world.

And we will protect her.

TWENTY-FIVE

SOFIA

I WAKE FROM DREAMS OF FIRE AND PAIN, LURCHING UPRIGHT with a strangled noise, heart pounding. Someone's there immediately, a warm hand on my shoulder, a voice in my ear, quiet, urging me to lie back down.

"Gideon?" I croak, trying to blink away dreams and sleep.

"He's fine, he's with Mori and Jubilee." I blink again and suddenly Flynn's face swims into focus. "Stay put, Sof, you're going to be groggy for a while still."

I let him push me back down onto what seems to be a military cot, and take a shaking breath. I can't feel my hand, and after a stab of fear I look down—it's still there, just swathed in a cocoon of bandages and numb from the shoulder down. We're in a large, dim room, the light casting oddly against bare cement walls. There are a few people here and there, whose faces I don't recognize; they're huddled together, expressions drawn and fearful, some faces tearstained, some wooden. A couple of them are hunched over a palm pad, trying—and failing, it seems from their frustration—to find a signal.

"Where are we?" I whisper.

"Mori's base. Kumiko Mori. Gideon's friend. She also happened to serve on Avon with Jubilee."

I stare at him, trying to make my mind work through the thick, impenetrable fog cocooning my thoughts. "Just happened to . . . ?"

"She's a Fury soldier," he replies, voice quiet. "She and the others here are all soldiers who were once on Avon and reassigned after the whispers there made them snap. From what she tells me, they've been gathering here, doing exactly what we've been doing—trying to figure out how to take LaRoux down."

None of the overhead lights are on—all I can see are a couple LED flashlights and an emergency lantern.

"Why . . . What's with all the . . ." But I can't remember the words I need, can't make my lips shape them.

Flynn follows my gaze to the emergency lantern on a packing crate next to my cot. His eyes flick back toward mine. "How much do you remember? We had to put you under to treat your hand. We didn't have a choice, you kept—" He swallows, his face grim and eyes a little wild. "We had to knock you out."

I swallow, my voice raw and shredded like I've been shouting. Or screaming. I shut my eyes, taking a deep breath. "I remember the *Daedalus*."

Flynn finds the fingers of my good hand and wraps his around them, squeezing. "The impact knocked out power for kilometers, at least. Communications are down, HV networks, everything. Gideon can't even get to the hypernet, though that's what he and Mori are trying to do now."

"What about . . ." But my voice sticks when my memory conjures up the image of the LaRoux heiress, smiling at us with those black eyes. I can't even make myself say her name. "L-L-LaRoux? What about LaRoux?"

"We don't know. We don't know much of anything yet."

I suck in another breath and then try to sit up again, pushing Flynn's arm away when he moves to stop me. "Flynn, I tried to—" My voice cracks. "LaRoux was standing right there. I couldn't let him live. I couldn't—"

"Shh, I know." Flynn looks older, more than he should after only one year. The green eyes are the same, and the dark wavy hair. And yet, he seems somehow more real than he was before, solid, warm—and the pain in his gaze, the sympathy, is as deep as it ever was. "I know, Sof."

"This is my fault," I whisper, too numb and too groggy to cry. "If I hadn't—"

"None of that," Flynn interjects. "From what we got out of Tarver, this has been a long time coming. That whisper's been trying to reach Lilac ever since she and Tarver were stranded on that planet together. I think the pain just interrupted her concentration—it would've gotten her eventually anyway."

But it wouldn't have been onboard the *Daedalus*. The thousands of people, tens of thousands, maybe even hundreds of thousands by now—they would be alive if I hadn't tried to murder Roderick LaRoux.

"I want to see Gideon," I hear myself saying, to my surprise. "Is he . . ."

But before I can finish the question, Jubilee's striding in through one of the doorways, with Gideon and a woman with short black hair and a kerchief around her neck. *Kumiko*, my brain supplies. *Corporal Mori*. The trodaire who shot Garret O'Reilly in the street and broke the ceasefire. But then, my father killed far more than one man because of LaRoux's Fury, and his explosion started a war. My thoughts are so tangled with anger and grief that I don't know what to think, looking at the ex-soldier next to Captain Chase.

Gideon veers off from their path, his feet curving toward my cot before he lifts his head and sees me sitting up—his steps falter for a second, then quicken as he jogs over. Flynn glances at me, the corner of his mouth quirking as he pulls back, making room for Gideon to crouch down beside me.

"Hey, Dimples." There's visible relief in his eyes, in his voice—and yet, still, something reserved, held back. There's a war going on behind the look he gives me, his hand twitching as though he'd like to reach for me but can't. *This isn't you,* he'd said, while I pointed a gun at LaRoux. *I know you.*

"Hey," I whisper back. *You never knew me.*

I didn't think I'd ever have to face him after he found out I was never working with him to expose LRI, that I was only ever trying to kill Roderick LaRoux. I thought I'd be dead.

And for the tiniest moment, I wish I was.

Jubilee, standing by Kumiko some distance away, clears her throat. "We've got a net connection," she announces gently, breaking the silence between Gideon and me. "Flynn—you should come see this."

"I'm coming too," I say, before anyone has a chance to leave me in the cot.

Gideon glances at Flynn, who no doubt has a lot more experience with field medicine than he does—and Flynn just shakes his head. "I gave up telling her what to do when we were kids," he says, stepping back toward me and offering me a hand.

Gideon backs up a step, glancing from me to him, then turns to rejoin Jubilee and Mori as they head into the room next door. Whatever they used to knock me out is still with me—my steps feel rubbery and slow, my muscles not responding right to the commands from my brain. Flynn's forced to duck down so I can put an arm around his shoulder as we move next door.

"Luckily, Mori's been siphoning off surplus military supplies," he murmurs as we walk. "She's got a dermal regenerator. Your hand should be fine in a day or two—probably won't even have scars."

I hate myself for the tang of relief that surges through me—I should bear the pain, the scars, as reminders of what I tried to do. Of what I *did* do. Of the hundreds of thousands of people in this city dead now, because of me.

"Whoops, hey . . ." Flynn's arms tighten around me as I sag, the medication threatening to rob me of consciousness.

"I'm fine," I reply though gritted teeth, getting my feet back under me. As much as I try to focus, somewhere at the back of my mind, I keep seeing Lilac cry out and fall, keep seeing the blood on her arm, keep seeing the inky darkness bleed into her gaze as she lay on the floor.

The doorway leads to a smaller room, maybe intended to be an individual's office, with windows on two of the walls. Though they look out only at the buildings next door, the air is hazy and the light a vivid red-orange that makes my heart constrict. I've seen too many things on fire not to know what this is. Corinth is burning.

There's only one other person in the room, and as the glow lights his face, my heart shrivels the rest of the way. It's Tarver, sunken into a folding chair, eyes fixed out the window. He doesn't look over when we enter.

Flynn finds a chair for me, hastily depositing me into it and then heading for Jubilee. He glances from her to the ex-soldier by the window. "Is he . . ."

Jubilee's expression flickers, and I'm surprised by the depth of emotion I see there, in this face that was always so stony, so implacable, on Avon. "He won't talk to me," she murmurs back. "He's—" She shakes her head. "I don't know what to do."

Flynn doesn't answer, instead reaching out to take Jubilee's hand and draw her close, pressing his forehead to hers. I find myself staring at them as her fingers twine through his, the unlikely sight of Flynn embracing the most notorious soldier we've ever had on our part of Avon striking me all but senseless. I knew he had feelings for her, but . . .

"I can't help him." Her voice is barely audible.

"One step at a time," Flynn replies, with the same patient determination that saw him through the years after his sister was killed.

My gaze slides sideways, finding Gideon—but he's not looking at me. His eyes are on Tarver, by the window. And far from showing the same bitter dislike I'd seen onboard the *Daedalus*, when he spoke of Tarver having replaced his brother, his face holds only grief now. As though he shares some of what's rendered Tarver Merendsen all but catatonic.

As I watch, he sucks in a deep breath, visibly pulling himself together. "We've got a signal," he says, voice bracing as he pulls out a palm pad and crosses to a battered table not far from the window. "Most of the news sites haven't posted anything local since before the crash, and we've got to assume that those headquarters that weren't hit are still trying to find power."

"But some have?" Flynn lifts his head, eyes tracking Gideon as he sets the palm pad down on the table, setting up the holo-projection interface.

Gideon nods, not answering until after the palm pad's screen pops up to life, hovering just above the table where we can all see it. "Pictures of the destruction, a couple of the crash itself from people whose devices synced with the cloud before they—" He stops, lips twisting, and doesn't finish the sentence. "I think this site's got a live feed running."

He makes a few gestures, navigating through a few different sites until he finds a streaming video. The images spring to life, accompanied by the tinny audio from the palm pad's speakers.

". . . from the different reports we're getting, but we can confirm that the estimated death toll has now increased to a hundred and fifty thousand—that's a hundred and fifty thousand estimated casualties of the crash." The image shifts from an aerial view of smoke and flames to a woman's face, drawn and white underneath her makeup. "If you're just joining us, this is breaking news coverage reporting that the *Daedalus* orbital museum, in the middle of its opening night gala, has fallen from its orbit and crashed into the surface of Corinth. The ship and pieces of wreckage have caused massive damage to at least three city sectors, and it's unknown whether there are any . . ."

She trails off, eyes going distant as she presses a hand to her ear. "Okay," she says, voice shaking. "Okay, I'm getting reports now that several diplomatic shuttles—four or maybe five—were seen leaving the *Daedalus* before it hit the atmosphere. We're hearing that President Muñoz was evacuated and taken to an undisclosed location as a security measure, where she will remain until the extent of the threat is established. It's unclear who's making calls within the government at this time. We do not have confirmation as to who was onboard any of the other shuttles, or whether the ship's creator, tech magnate Roderick LaRoux, was among the survivors."

I glance over at Tarver, but I can't tell if he's even listening to the report. He hasn't taken his eyes off the window.

The reporter takes a breath and then continues, clearly fighting to keep her calm and do her job. "Roderick LaRoux, founder and CEO of LaRoux Industries, is confirmed to have been aboard the *Daedalus* shortly before the crash, along with daughter Lilac LaRoux and future son-in-law Major Tarver Merendsen. It's unknown whether the *Icarus* survivors have—" The reporter stops, her haunted eyes staring at the camera for a moment. "Their current whereabouts and conditions are unknown."

The image flashes back to that aerial shot, a slowly shifting panorama of destruction—billowing clouds of smoke obscure much of the sector, those buildings not leveled by the shock wave still on fire despite the hordes of firefighting drones swarming the scene. The reporter starts summarizing events again, and with a jerk of his wrist, Gideon mutes the feed and then drops his head into his hands.

Jubilee's eyes are rimmed in red as she watches the footage, her face as haunted as the reporter's had been—it's like she's watching a memory, a ghost. Flynn's arm tightens around her, and she clears her throat. "We have to assume she survived, and that she's not done." Her gaze starts to swivel toward Tarver, by the window, but she stops herself with a visible effort. "Which means we have to stop her."

"She tore the *Daedalus* out of the sky with a single thought." Gideon lifts his head from his hands, numbness creeping in to buffer the shock of the past few hours. "How do you fight something like that?"

Jubilee's eyes go to Flynn's. "The same way we've been fighting the impossible all along. Bit by bit. All of us, together."

Something about the footage grabs my eye, and I rise on wobbly legs from my chair so I can look more closely. Flynn takes a step toward me but I wave him off, wishing I could peel back the layers of smoke and haze concealing the city in the projection. Then a sliver of green shows through, and I know what it is—a crescent-shaped courtyard.

"That's LaRoux Industries," I whisper, staring at the footage.

"What?" Flynn's voice is sharp.

"These images, they're from LRI Headquarters—or where it used to be. See, there—that block, that's where the Applied Sciences division was." It's only rubble now, but as the smoke shifts, we get a glimpse of something that should be impossible—at least one structure still standing, amid the pieces of wreckage from ship and building alike. I know the area by heart, after a year spent researching ways to infiltrate it, and I know it even on fire. My mind's scrambling, trying to understand. "She crashed the *Daedalus* into LaRoux Industries Headquarters."

The feed cuts back to a shot of the reporter, whose wild-eyed gaze—from someone used to being stoic in the face of galaxy-rocking news—makes me want to run and hide. "Breaking news—our reporter on the ground has located a pocket of survivors at the heart of the crash site, including LaRoux Industries CEO Roderick LaRoux *and* his daughter, Lilac LaRoux. There is no sign of her fiancé. We'll go now to the scene."

The feed cuts to two-dimensional footage, projected flat like a screen from the palm pad. The shot is shaky, like it's being filmed from a handheld device, probably not too different from the one Gideon's using to show us the feed. It's dark, the scene lit only by generator-powered floodlights. But despite the nausea-inducing sway of the camera, despite the throngs of people milling here and there, despite the bloodied injuries in the background, all of us are staring at what's in the foreground.

It's Monsieur LaRoux, without a scratch, and at his side, her arm through his, leaning close as though taking comfort from her father's presence, is Lilac.

And her eyes are blue.

Jubilee gasps aloud, leaning closer as though she might magnify the image. "She's—she's herself? Look at her eyes."

"She couldn't be—she'd be trying to find Tarver. . . ." Flynn's always been good at debate, and though he sounds certain, his eyes are troubled. "There's no way she stands by that man if she's not being controlled."

We all start talking at once, even Mori, trying to figure out what's going on.

"Everybody *shut up*." Tarver's voice cuts through the argument, his eyes never leaving the projected image of the girl he loves. "Listen."

She's talking. "I don't know what happened to him," Lilac is saying in response to a question from the person holding the camera. One hand is smoothing down the skirts of the black dress she wore on the *Daedalus*, as immaculate as it was the first time I saw it. "We got separated. But, truth be told . . . maybe it's better we did."

"Better?" The interviewer's voice comes from behind the camera, unseen but loud in the device's microphone.

"Major Merendsen . . . he's a nice boy, and I'll always be grateful that he saved my life after the *Icarus* crashed. But I think I just got carried away with that gratitude. I never really wanted to marry him." She shuts her eyes, as if this is difficult for her, as though the words she's speaking do cause her pain. "I hope he's okay, I truly do. But I'm glad I'm here, with my father, trying to help."

I find my gaze going toward Tarver, who's watching the feed without expression. He might as well be carved from stone for all Lilac's confession seems to affect him.

"That's not her." Jubilee's the one who speaks, and this time her tone brooks no opposition. "Even if she did think that—and trust me, she doesn't—she'd never say so on the news. She'd never do that to Tarver. Somehow, the whisper's learned to fake it—to make it seem like it's the real Lilac."

"To that end," LaRoux is saying now, putting an arm around his daughter's shoulders and giving her a squeeze, "I'm making a plea to

262

all the planetary delegations, wherever you are, whoever is left, that we carry on with the Galactic Summit despite this great tragedy. Peace is too important to be put on hold—we must find a way for all people, across the galaxy, to live safe, happy, pain-free lives. I've devoted every resource at my disposal to the rescue operations taking place here, but I would like to extend an invitation to all surviving planetary delegations to come to my personal home tomorrow to meet. While we do not yet know what caused the *Daedalus* to fall, we cannot discount the possibility of rebel terrorist interference, which makes this summit of peace ever more vital. The Galactic Council chambers might have crumbled and been destroyed, but the spirit of peace must continue."

I even find myself wavering, wondering if he's doing something noble after all, despite the loathing I ought to feel for him. Even *knowing* that it wasn't rebels who brought down the *Daedalus*, I find myself wanting to listen to him. I may have spent the last year learning to talk people into doing what I needed them to do, but LaRoux is a master at it. My heart shrivels at the thought that I could have anything in common with this monster.

Flynn, though, is shaking—his voice is fierce. "This is wrong," he whispers. "It's impossible for every senator to have made it off the *Daedalus* alive . . . any resolution passed would need elected officials to vote on it. He's planning something."

The camera jolts, then swings dizzyingly to the side, showing only a jumble of ruined buildings and oddly green lawn from the LRI court-yard; then it comes to rest again, and the air goes out of the room.

It's the rift. It's being moved, painstakingly slowly, by a crew of two dozen people, only some of whom are in LRI uniforms. And it's active, casting its blue glow across the grass, across the faces of the people moving it.

"Ah, yes." The camera swings back to show LaRoux, turning to monitor the rift's progress. From this angle, the device over his ear is clearly visible, masquerading in plain sight as a hands-free comm unit—the little bit of tech, all that's standing between him and domination by the whisper inhabiting Lilac. "I'd hoped to wait to unveil this new technology until after speaking to the planetary delegates, but in light of this disaster, I think it's needed now, more than ever."

He pauses, glancing to the side, eyes finding Lilac—who's smiling back at him, every inch the adoring daughter. I search her face, trying to find some sign of what's inside, some hint of the horrifying creature we glimpsed on the *Daedalus*. But she just smiles, giving her father an encouraging nod. And she never lets go of his arm.

"At LaRoux Industries, we've been attempting to tap into a source of clean, renewable power for decades. And finally, at long last . . . we've perfected it."

The camera shakes, then steadies. Then, the voice behind it stammers, "E-excuse me, Monsieur LaRoux. But are you saying . . ."

LaRoux nods, his face grave but determined. "Before you is the galaxy's first stable, safe hyperspace generator. We've long been aware of the vast, infinite reserves of energy on the other side of the dimensional fabric separating us from hyperspace—indeed, one of the challenges we face in ship design is how to safely skim through hyperspace to shorten interstellar journeys, without that energy harming us or our vessels. But after decades of experimentation, we've finally perfected the process."

The cameraman is speechless—and so are we, all of us gathered around the glow of the palm pad. When I look up I see only a ring of pale faces.

"That's not everything," Lilac says, her eyes on her father. "Tell them, Daddy—go on, tell them."

LaRoux gives her hand on his arm a pat, smiling. "It may not be the appropriate time for such an announcement, but—it is my intention to share the plans for this device with *all* planetary delegations. For free. No catches, no favors owed. It's my belief that sharing this free, limitless power with the galaxy will remove the need for rebellions. All people, whether colonist, citizen, or rebel, will have access to computers, to schools, to hospitals. Terraforming efforts will proceed with unprecedented speed, reducing the period of time before new planets become self-sustaining, self-governing. With education, medicine, and the free exchange of ideas, I am confident we can all finally find peace."

The camera swings back toward the rift machinery as LaRoux's people continue moving it, then freezes. A little bar pops up along the bottom of the projection, telling us it's buffering—then goes gray, showing a dropped connection. The hypernet's out again.

Silence. Only the distant sirens, and the minute noises of Kumiko's people in the next room, tell me I haven't gone deaf.

It takes a seeming eternity before someone—Gideon—moves. He leans forward, reaching for the palm pad, whose image is still frozen on the rift. He zooms in on the picture with a flick of his fingers, and though he can't make it any less grainy, it's obvious to everyone what he saw. One of the people helping to move the rift has her head turned just enough that we can see her eyes—empty, black, like starless night.

I find myself shivering and wrap my arms close against my body like I might be able to somehow comfort myself. LaRoux couldn't have had this go any better for him if he'd planned it. No doubt he planned on trying to send out the rift technology to other planets after the summit—now he can capitalize on the disaster to make it look like a mercy mission. No one will blame him for the crash of the *Daedalus* if they believe he's bringing clean, renewable energy to every corner of the galaxy. If they think he's single-handedly repairing the galaxy, they'll sing his praises as a hero and remember the *Daedalus* as the tragic catalyst toward a golden age.

Except that we know what the rift really is. Those black eyes stare at us from the woman's grainy face on the palm pad footage.

He couldn't have planned it better. . . .

The breath goes out of me in a gasp so harsh my throat aches, and I feel all the eyes in the room swing toward me. "One week," I manage, looking up until I find Gideon's face. "When we first found this rift at LaRoux Industries, we heard them say they had one week to get it working properly. We thought that they were talking about the *Daedalus* gala, that he'd planned something for tonight."

Gideon's face is going white—whiter—as I speak. He lifts a shaking hand to pass it over his features. "It was never the gala. It was the summit talks all along. He couldn't have planned the crash, but this . . . He wanted the rift for the summit."

"If he gathers what's left of the planetary leaders," Flynn says slowly, "and gives them blueprints to construct what they believe are sources of infinite clean energy . . ."

"Then in a matter of weeks, there will be rifts on all the planets." Jubilee finishes when Flynn's voice peters out. "And he'll be able to control every single person in the galaxy. Like he practiced on Avon. Like he's been perfecting here on Corinth." For once, she doesn't look like the ultimate soldier we all feared so much on Avon—she doesn't look like the Stone-faced Chase who led the fastest, deadliest squads on the base. She just looks terrified.

I swallow the sour fear threatening to choke me. "And that's how he'll stop the rebellions."

"But why is the whisper controlling Lilac helping him?" Jubilee asks, brows drawn in. "He's only ever used its kind for his own ends."

Tarver swallows and then speaks, his voice hoarse. "Lilac said she could feel this last whisper in the rift—that it was angry, twisted by the years of torture. If it wants revenge, not just on LaRoux but on all of us . . . then having access to rifts across the galaxy would only suit its purposes, extending its reach so that humanity has nowhere to hide."

"LaRoux and the whisper, they want the same thing," Flynn murmurs. "It's just a question of who's in charge when those rifts are turned on."

The holographic woman's blank, black eyes dominate the room, larger than life in the palm-pad projection. *Peace,* said LaRoux. As though peace is simply the absence of conflict. As though it's something that could be imposed, forced, upon every mind in the galaxy. As though choice is a flame to be extinguished with a smothering blanket.

The scrape of a chair on cement jolts us from our own individual pits of fear; I look up to find Tarver on his feet for the first time since the crash.

"We'll stop him," he says quietly. "We'll go to the summit, expose his plans, and stop them both."

The boy who lost his brother to the blue-eyed man's jealousy is older now, too. He comes alive in our world more than in his own, seeking connections throughout their hypernet. His grief is not so very different from that of our keeper's daughter, and yet they do not seek each other out to share this pain.

Instead he dives deeper into the web of data and information streams, and she pulls back, to skim the surface of the world. He stays low, in the darkness and shadow, leaving no trace of himself where he's been; she lights up the world, seen by all and known by none.

They are both so alone.

TWENTY-SIX

GIDEON

THE UPPER CITY IS ALL BUT ABANDONED, EVEN AFTER DAWN starts creeping up the streets between the buildings. The sun seems to rise more gradually than usual, filtered through Corinth's smog and the smoke above us now, not purified by Sofia's smartglass windows. Slowly, it's oozing down the streets and turning the white stone ruins of the huge mall before us a pale gold, and with the faraway sirens finally silent, there's a sense these buildings fell centuries ago, not just last night.

Some seem utterly fine, unaffected—others have suffered structural damage even this far out from the crash site. Everyone who can evacuate already has. It's like walking through the set from a disaster movie, the postapocalyptic landscape of a city after a volcanic eruption has covered the world in ashes. There are surprisingly few bodies—Jubilee's the one who explains to me in a whisper that they'll be mostly inside the buildings, buried under debris. There's an eerie beauty to it, a sense of waiting, as though the people will step out from behind the cardboard sets any moment—like visiting a school after hours or breaking into an amusement park during its off-season.

Except, of course, the only people we see are still, never to move again, or they're the whisper's husks—and we only see those from a distance. But all of them are heading in the same direction: toward the wreck of the *Daedalus*, and the rift.

The LaRoux estate occupies an area covering at least ten city blocks, and even after catching a ride with some of Kumiko's soldiers, we've got a lot of ground to cover. Thankfully they had the spare supplies to outfit us—otherwise we'd all be trying to infiltrate the LaRoux estate in battered formalwear. As it is, seeing Sofia clad in black cargo pants and a military-style vest and boots is strange enough to do my head in.

The massive wrought-iron gate at the street entrance is mostly for show—the air shines with the telltale glimmer of a security field. Tarver punches in a string of numbers that makes the field shimmer, then vanish. "Lilac's code," he murmurs. "No one's bothered to change it."

Beyond the gate stretches a field of lush, green grass, and gardens planted with dozens upon dozens of pale pink roses. Lilac's favorites, according to the gossip columns and architectural magazines that interview the family. We pass a bench shaded by a weeping willow that makes Tarver's jaw clench. Something about it is familiar, nagging at me until it clicks. This is the garden where their engagement photos were taken.

The grounds, like the city outside, are eerily empty. If there was to be a summit here, even an informal one, there should be . . . people. Valets, servers, bodyguards, staff . . . Instead all is still, and silent, like the castle in a fairy tale abandoned for a hundred years. I half expect to find servants and cooks asleep at their posts. Instead there's only us, our footsteps in the grass and on the stones, like the five of us are the only people left in the world.

Us, and the ghost of Lilac LaRoux.

I've never been to the LaRoux estate on Corinth. Simon and I used to go after school to their mansion on Paradisa, one of their many vacation homes, and play—Simon played, anyway. I'd spend my afternoons watching them through the banister of the loft over the playroom, which was as far as I was allowed to come before Simon would chase me off. I remember them giggling over electronics as Simon showed her how to rewire the automatic cleaning bots to play music at random intervals or start eating all the fringe on the rugs. I'd watch, longing to be included with the big kids when they set off firecrackers in the tennis courts with Lilac's cousins, or, later, as they'd watch movies in the den, carefully sitting a hand's breadth apart. I remember watching that distance close, week by week. I remember thinking—as my big brother watched her out of the corner of his eye instead of the movie, gathering his courage to put an arm around her shoulders—that I'd never end up like that, terrified of a girl.

And now Sofia can pretty much stop my heart with a glance.

Tarver steps off the path and leads us around toward the east wing of the house, where a servants' entrance might give us more cover as we break in. Despite the emptiness of the grounds, there'd surely be guards on the front door—if nothing else, the bodyguards brought by the various senators and their delegations. I catch glimpses of the house through the windows as we go. A grand piano here, a sun-filled solarium there. Every room empty.

The servants' entrance has both a keypad and a hand scanner, and while the system cheerfully accepts the code Tarver enters, it offers up only a blaring tone and a flash of red when he places his hand on the scanner.

"Did they know we were coming?" murmurs Jubilee, reaching—unconsciously, I'm sure—for the gun strapped to her hip.

Tarver tries a second time, with the same result, expression grim. "Hard to say. He could've easily revoked my access a week ago, just to piss me off. We're not exactly father and son, LaRoux and I." He moves off to the side to cup his hands around his eyes and peer through a window.

Sofia glances at me, and I know why—I give my head a little shake. "I might be able to hack the security pad, but it'd take me a while, probably a couple of hours. It'd be different if I'd had time to plan ahead, but . . ." I grimace.

"Maybe we try the front door after all, then." Sofia's quiet, eyes shifting from me to the others. "Flynn's part of the Avon delegation, and we could leave Tarver out here and then come open the door for him once we've talked our way—"

Her murmur is interrupted by the loud, sharp crash of breaking glass, making me jump back half a step. Tarver, ignoring the rest of us, shakes shards of glass off the elbow of his jacket. "Can't tell you how many times I've wanted to do that," he comments as he reaches through the broken windowpane to unlatch the frame.

We're all on alert as we make our way across the first floor, but no one seems to have heard the breaking window. I can't shake the chills creeping up and down my spine, the wrongness of a house like this, barren of life.

"You've been here before," Flynn says to Tarver, as we creep past a large, darkened kitchen. "Where would he hold an impromptu summit meeting?"

"Probably the formal dining room," Tarver replies, brow furrowed. "Or the grand hall. We never spent much time there." He pauses, steps faltering, then takes a deep breath. "Stop for a second and listen—we ought to hear them speaking if they're either place."

We all pause, our footsteps on the marble floor echoing half a breath longer before fading into silence. A grand staircase sweeps off to the left, curving around a fountain in the form of a column, some invisible force drawing droplets of water from the pool sunk into the floor up to disappear somewhere above. For a few seconds, all I can hear is the quiet burbling of the water.

Then there is a sound—but not of voices. It's a low hum, mechanical, vibrating deep in my stomach. I look up, glancing round to the others. They hear it too, and for a moment we all stare at each other.

Then Jubilee gasps. "It's a shuttle. Warming its engines."

Tarver's moving before any of the rest of us, abandoning stealth to break into a sprint, and we all take off after him. Despite my own fitness—climbing and abseiling aren't nothing—my lungs are aching trying to keep up. If there's any chance Lilac is here, Tarver's not letting her go.

We burst through a set of wide French doors into a sunlit courtyard and skid to a halt, blinking. One shuttle—an orbital craft, designed to reach the Corinthian spaceport station—is already lifting off, vertical takeoff engines slowly rotating as it angles up toward the sky. Tarver's got his weapon drawn, and for half a heartbeat his hands waver, starting to jerk up toward the craft, then falling.

"You're earlier than I'd anticipated." The voice belongs to Roderick LaRoux, and this time Tarver's hands are rock steady as he swings his gun around to train it on Lilac's father.

"Where is she?" he demands, taking a few steps forward.

He's forced to stop, however, as a number of people in the courtyard turn to face him with a subtle—but very noticeable—threatening air. They're not guards—most of them are too slight, too well dressed, or too old for that role. And it's only after I've scanned their faces and found some of them hauntingly familiar that I realize who they are: senators from the Galactic Council. I've seen them on the HV, in the newsfeeds.

And every one of them has the black eyes and blank faces of the whisper's husks.

"I don't imagine you want to shoot a dozen elected officials just to get to me," LaRoux says, and though he's trying to sound calm, amused, even, I can see something's wrong. His suit, normally so impeccably tailored, is frayed at the cuffs, and marred by spots of ash and dust. His white hair is in disarray around his temples. His eyes sweep to the side to rest on Sofia, and the amusement in his gaze hardens. "You again. You're the one who tried to hurt my girl."

Sofia doesn't bother to hide the hatred in her own expression, but her voice is even. "No. I tried to hurt *you*."

"So shortsighted," LaRoux replies, and if it weren't for the setting, the blank-eyed senators and their staff, the guns trained on LaRoux, the shuttles whirring to life behind him, it'd sound like he was scolding a schoolchild. "Killing me would do nothing but brand you all murderers. Even if you destroyed every person standing here, enough good senators are already on their way back to their planets."

"Why are you doing this?" I demand. How many times did I tell Sofia that nothing would be solved by killing one person? Right now, it's sounding like a better idea than it did before. "You already have more power than anyone in *history*. What more could you possibly want?"

"I want peace!" LaRoux's voice is sharp and quick.

Half a dozen senators turn in unison, as if on some inaudible command, to begin piling into the other orbital shuttlecraft. The third, smaller craft is just a transport, not designed to break the atmosphere— LaRoux isn't leaving Corinth. Not yet.

"Peace," he repeats, regaining control of his voice, pitching it just loud enough to be heard over the shuttle engines. "You children, you have no understanding of loss. Of the tragedy of war, the innocents who get caught in the exchanges of pointless violence."

"We have no understanding of loss?" Jubilee gives a sharp bark of laughter. "There's not one person here who hasn't lost someone to the pointless exchange of violence, LaRoux. You think age is necessary to learn pain?" Her gun doesn't waver as she moves forward, ranging to the side so that between them she and Tarver have him covered.

LaRoux barely notices.

"Their brothers," she says, tilting her head toward Tarver, and toward me. "His sister." Flynn, not far from Jubilee's side, exhales, his spine straightening. Jubilee swallows. "My parents."

"My father," Sofia whispers, making me long to reach out to her.

"And my wife," replies LaRoux, his voice cold. "Lilac's mother."

Tarver shakes his head. "Lilac's mother died in a shuttlecraft accident on Paradisa. When she was seven. She told me."

LaRoux slips his hands into his pockets, legs braced as his head dips for a moment. "She did die in a shuttlecraft. But it wasn't on Paradisa. And it wasn't an accident." His gaze flicks up, the line of his mouth grim with a pain as real as any of ours. "I was visiting one of my research stations on a LaRoux Industries planet, and she'd come with me. Riots broke out—rebels protesting God knows what—and I had my people put her on a shuttle back to the spaceport to keep her safe. The shuttle was sabotaged."

Jubilee's shifting her grip on her gun. "What planet?"

"Does it matter?"

"What planet?"

"Verona. It was—it was Verona."

Jubilee lets out a curse, voice strangled, gun dropping for a fraction of a second before her training steadies her and she clamps down on the shock and confusion in her expression.

"You never told Lilac?" Tarver's not wavering even an inch.

"Why would I?" LaRoux's eyes shift toward him. "Why would I hurt her, give her reason to hate anybody? Lilac is kind, and generous, and innocent—the truth would only cause her pain. An accident—you can let that go. Why would I ever tell her that her mother was murdered by the very people I was trying to help?"

"Help?" Jubilee grinds out.

It's Flynn who has to take over, his partner's anger too thick for her to speak through. He takes one of the same slow, careful breaths I recognize from the Avon Broadcast before he speaks. "Your 'help,' sir, has led to countless deaths on Avon. Your experiments, the Fury, the return of a rebellion that we would've easily, instantly given up in exchange for the tiniest bit of humanity—"

"Avon." LaRoux's lip curls a little. "Avon's nothing. A few thousand people. Yes, I built a rift on Avon, moved the entities there from Verona. You can't tell me it would have been better to leave them in a place where millions, instead of hundreds, would die?"

"Why did *anyone* have to die?" Sofia blurts, eyes reddening, the blood rushing to her face.

"To save *billions*," LaRoux snaps. "I discovered these creatures, found out what they could do, if only I could harness them. If a fraction of us have to fall in order to elevate the rest? It's a sacrifice, and a horrible one. Most people could never bring themselves to make that choice. Most people don't have the vision—most people aren't strong enough to weigh life against life. But imagine a golden era, a time of absolute peace— imagine no murder, no sabotage, no pain. No grief. Imagine—imagine never having to lose a loved one ever again." For the first time, LaRoux's voice falters, cracking.

"It's not for you to choose what sacrifice is worthwhile, who should die," says Tarver. "You might have tried to keep Lilac by lying about her mother, but you lost her when you murdered Simon Marchant."

LaRoux's eyes flicker toward me, and I realize his nonchalance on the *Daedalus* was at least partly an act—there's guilt in his gaze. He knows exactly who I am. "I—Simon Marchant was a mistake. I intended for him to be sent away. I didn't expect . . . His death was an unforeseen side effect."

Side effect. The words burn through my brain, wiping out everything else. I can't move, can't speak, an anger and grief I thought I'd put behind me surging up like a tide. It's not until I feel a touch on my hand that I realize I've closed my eyes; I know before I open them that it's Sofia, her fingertips brushing against my palm, opening my fist, interlocking her fingers with mine.

"Enough." Tarver's voice is quiet, almost gentle if not for the hint of ice behind it. "Where is Lilac?"

"She's safe." LaRoux's gaze meets that of his onetime future son-in-law. The piercing blue of his eyes is all the more intense in the morning light, and the look he directs at Tarver is just a little too wild, a little too fierce. "She's *happy*. That ought to be enough for you, if you truly love her."

For a moment, everyone is silent, shocked. I find myself staring at LaRoux, searching his face for signs of the self-delusional madman inside. For him to believe that his daughter's change of heart, her sudden willingness to go along with his plans, stemmed from anything other than the whisper taking control of her . . . He's insane.

"Happy?" Tarver's still cold, calm. Ruthless. "She's one of them. The creature in the rift, that's what stood at your side, smiling at you, calling you 'Daddy.' You say you never wanted Lilac to hate, but that's all she is now—the thing inside her is nothing more than hate. And you're what she hates more than anything in the universe."

LaRoux's eyes widen even as his brows draw together, and he takes a step back toward the transport behind him. The handful of husks still remaining draw closer around him, clearly ready to shield him if Tarver's finger tightens on the trigger.

"You're wrong," LaRoux snaps, baring his teeth in a rictus that might have once been a smile. "You just can't stand that she chose *me*. She's just the first—the whole galaxy will learn to love me as she does now, again, the way she's supposed to."

Tarver shakes his head, just a tiny movement. "The tragedy is that she did. She did love you. Despite everything you did to her, to Simon, to me, to Avon, to the galaxy—you were her father, and she loved you. She took a bullet for you. She's perhaps the only person, the last person, in this existence to care for you at all." Tarver pauses for the span of a breath, and then slowly the gun lowers, to dangle at his side. "And you sold her soul to play house for just a little bit longer."

LaRoux's lips open like he has to gulp for air. "No," he retorts, gasping. "No. You're wrong. You're wrong. She loves me. She knows what I'm doing is right, and just. She's my girl. *Mine*." The husks move in to surround him, and as he struggles, it becomes clear he's not the one controlling them after all. They drag him back toward the shuttle, their jostling dislodging the device over his ear so that it clatters to the pavement at their feet. LaRoux doesn't even seem to notice; his wide, staring eyes are fixed on Tarver right up until the husks close in around him and bear him back into the craft, where the door hisses closed after them.

The engines kick in, LaRoux's transport and the other orbital shuttle lifting up off the ground. Jubilee shakes free of whatever spell of anger and fear kept her still, and darts forward, raising her gun—only to have Tarver grab at her arm, jerking the barrel down again.

"We have to stop him," Jubilee gasps, furious, tearing her arm away from her former commanding officer.

"We will." Tarver's voice is finally showing his strain, shaking now as he watches the shuttles lift higher, jets starting to turn in preparation to fly away. "But he's right—his death would stop nothing. Too many senators are already on their way back to their planets with the rift blueprints."

I move away from Sofia's side in silence, striding over to the spot where LaRoux stood so I can retrieve the device that shielded him from the whisper's influence—for all the good it did him. The whisper didn't need to touch his mind in order to make it snap like a twig. But for the rest of us—if I can figure out a way to replicate the technology here, then it might give us a fighting chance against the whisper.

"We can't do *nothing*," Sofia breaks in. I look over to find her face wet, but there's so much to read in her expression that I can't tell if her tears are from rage or grief or fear or all of those combined.

"I know." Tarver watches the shuttles kick into gear—one angles up, toward the upper atmosphere, as the other bolts off over the city. He eases his gun back into its holster, and I see now that his knuckles are white from gripping it so hard, that he's forcing himself to let go finger by finger. "We can't stop them. We have to go to her—to Lilac. And I know where she is."

"Where?"

"Where all the husks are going—where it all started." He lets his breath out slowly. "The *Daedalus*."

The green-eyed boy is on the run, hiding from those who would take him from the gray world to live among other children of war. His sister's execution years ago has filled him with a certainty we envy, and as soldiers close in around him at the edge of town, we gather all our strength and reach out across the darkness.

Our pale light flashes amongst the reeds, and the soldiers veer off to investigate it, leaving the green-eyed boy free to run the other way. He turns and comes face-to-face with the girl with the dimpled smile, who has just stepped out of her house.

They used to be friends, long ago, before rebellion tore them apart. Now they stare at each other, silent, until the distant sound of a dog barking startles the green-eyed boy and he takes off into the night.

Later the soldiers will ask the girl what she saw, and she will stare at them with wide, gray eyes, and say, "Nothing."

TWENTY-SEVEN

SOFIA

TARVER'S MOVING BEFORE THE REST OF US HAVE TIME TO recover. By the time we follow him back into the LaRoux mansion, he's in the kitchen, tossing supplies onto the counter—bread, peanut butter, cheese, pieces of fruit.

I hesitate, glancing at the others. If LaRoux was clearly mad, half-incoherent as those things dragged him back onto the shuttle, then Tarver . . . He's not that far behind. He's got a recently dislocated shoulder held together with strapping tape and painkillers, he hasn't slept, and the more time passes, the less emotional he seems. He ought to be breaking down—the girl he loves is quite possibly gone forever, and a monster is wearing her face while she destroys humanity as we know it. And yet he's calmly rummaging through the pantry for supplies.

Jubilee's the one who moves, finally, taking a cautious step toward her former captain. "Sir," she says softly. "We need to take a break."

"I'm fine."

"Yeah, well, *I'm* not." Jubilee's voice is tense, wire-thin. She sounds like I feel—on a razor's edge. "And neither is anyone else."

"And I'm going to need some time to look at this thing," Gideon breaks in, LaRoux's earpiece in his hand. "Without its protection we might as well go in waving a white flag."

Tarver ignores Gideon, gesturing to the food. "Eat," he says, tilting his head. "There's no time to sleep, but eat something and that'll keep us going."

"I know that, I learned that from you." Jubilee pauses, watching Tarver—then, gritting her teeth, she leans forward and shoves him, hard, into the edge of the refrigerator. "*Sir.* You have to stop! You have to take a breath."

"I *can't*!" he replies, voice cracking, the veneer of calm slipping for just one, vital instant, in which I can see the anguish behind it. "I can't, Lee. If I stop, if I think, I'll—it's *Lilac*. I can't think. I can't stop. I can't lose her. You don't know what—" He shudders, pushing Jubilee away and staggering a step. "We just need to move." He gets his balance and starts for the hallway, and the entryway beyond.

Jubilee's right. We can't storm the wreck of the *Daedalus* with no idea what we'll find. The place will be crawling with husks, and even if it weren't, the thing in Lilac's body could kill us all without breaking a sweat. She only let us live this long to see us suffer, but if we become a genuine threat . . . But I know this panic of his, I know this desperate focus. Logic won't reach him. He can't let it reach him, because if he does, it'll break him.

I summon the dismissive tone of voice I know I'll need. "So you're really *that* eager to kill the love of your life?"

Tarver skids to a halt—I catch the look Jubilee throws me, her brows shooting up, eyes flashing with an intense are-you-completely-bloody-insane kind of look. When Tarver turns, I find myself taking a step back from the force of his gaze. "Excuse me?"

"That's your plan, right?" I swallow. "We already know you can't talk her out of this, you tried that on the *Daedalus*. LaRoux's certainly not going to help you—he's clearly lost whatever marbles he had left. And if Gideon can't replicate that tech, there's nothing to stop the whisper from taking us over. We've got no other ideas, nothing else up our sleeves. I'm just surprised you're so anxious to get there and kill her."

For a moment, Tarver's right hand twitches by his hip. I grew up on Avon, surrounded by soldiers with that same instinct, the same fight-or-flight responses. And I know, because I saw, that the safety's off his gun. But despite the hammering of my heart, my fear isn't of him. He may be half-mad with grief and panic, and I may have only known him for a day, but it only took me about ten minutes to know who this man was.

And he's not going to hurt me, no matter how badly he needs to find someone to blame.

Still, my breath catches.

Then he sags, turning and staggering back until he hits the wall, eliciting a grunt of pain as it jars his shoulder. He drops, sliding against the wall until he's sitting on the marble, elbows on his knees and fists balled against his eyes.

Jubilee's eyes go from Tarver to me, and this time that look says something altogether different. She nods, and though it's the smallest of gestures, it's like that tiny grain of respect gives my lungs permission to work again. She and Flynn cross toward the foyer, joining Tarver on the floor. I run a shaky hand through my hair, trying to fight the urge to look back at Gideon. I can feel him watching me. I took his hand out there as LaRoux spoke, finding myself unable to watch that flood of anger and despair across his features—but now there's distance again.

If none of this were happening, if he were just a hacker and I were just a con artist . . . would anything be different? Would we be any more able to trust each other?

He moves past me, gathering up some of the food Tarver pulled out, and heads over to join the others. I follow, sinking down onto the floor. I'm expecting cold marble, but instead I discover that the floors are heated—a luxury I never even knew existed. For a wild moment I want to lie down, face against the warm stone, and sleep. Gideon's already pulling tools out of his bag, tiny screwdrivers and wire strippers, disassembling the earpiece bit by bit.

"We destroy the rift." Tarver's ignoring Jubilee's not-so-subtle attempts to shove a granola bar into his hand.

Flynn's voice is musing. "He was telling the truth about that much, in his announcement—the rift machinery is what connects this world with the whispers' world. They live in hyperspace, and if we destroy that connection, we destroy the whisper."

Tarver nods. "It worked the first time around, and it worked on Avon."

"She could have destroyed us, or taken us over, on the *Daedalus*." My voice sounds tired even to my own ears. "Why didn't she?"

Tarver's expression twitches as he shoves Jubilee's hand away. "She—it—wanted us to suffer. Wanted *me* to suffer. Can't suffer if we're dead, or if we have no minds left to feel it."

Jubilee gives up, tossing the granola bar on the ground and leaning back against the wall. "Even if we could get to the rift before she squashes us—and that's a big 'if'—I'm not so sure destroying the rift would work this time around. I've seen these things, seen what a person is like when a whisper's controlling them." Her eyes are on Flynn's, her voice low. "Lilac's . . . different. With the others, the husks, the people being controlled—they're like marionettes, all empty shells being made to dance."

"And with Lilac . . . she's *real*. Like she's actually become this creature." Flynn's nodding. "Bringing down the *Daedalus*, tossing Tarver like a rag doll . . . That's not normal."

"Is any of this normal?" Gideon's voice is dry.

"Point."

My mind feels sluggish, turning over thoughts at half speed. There's something I know, something I remember, that's vital . . . but I can't find it. I clear my throat. "Why Lilac?"

Tarver's head lifts. "What?"

I glance at him, but he seems to have forgiven me for accusing him of wanting to kill Lilac. I chew at my lip, trying to sort out my thoughts. "Why her? I mean, it's LaRoux the whisper hates, isn't it? Why not take him over? He's the one with the power, the influence, the ability to make the senators and their staffs go back and build rifts all across the galaxy—and it needs those, if it's going to punish the whole of humanity, not just us. Why take Lilac, behind the scenes?"

"To . . . watch him, to hurt him from the outside?" Gideon's thoughtful too, eyes flicking up from his study of LaRoux's device to meet my gaze briefly. "To take away the thing he cares about the most?"

"Except she's pretending to be the real Lilac, at least enough that he's managed to make himself believe it." I rub at my temple with my fingertips. I'm not even sure anymore what day it is—was it really less than twenty-four hours ago that I was dancing with Gideon in the ballroom of the *Daedalus*? "There has to be some reason why Lilac is special, why it didn't take over LaRoux, or one of the scientists working with it, once it could get free. Some reason why the whisper's chosen her, needs her."

No one has an answer for that, exhausted silence punctuated only by the faint crinkle of wrappers here and there, as we try to choke food down throats dry with fear and weariness.

"We lost my canteen." Tarver's the one who breaks the silence, hoarse. All heads swivel toward him, but he doesn't look up. "On Elysium, where Lilac and I were stranded. That's what the scientists who died there called the planet, did you know? It was an ancient name for a place in the afterlife, where heroes went. After what happened to the researchers there, they thought it was appropriate. Anyway, we lost my canteen in a rock fall. We needed it badly, to filter water, to carry water. The next day, we found a perfect replica, right in the middle of our path."

"You never mentioned that in your debriefing interview," Gideon says. When Tarver's gaze snaps toward him, he flinches, realizing that he's not meant to have seen that footage.

But Tarver just shakes his head, bowing it once more. "They created a new one out of nothing, the whispers. And then—" His voice breaks, and I see his knuckles whiten as he grips handfuls of his hair, mastering himself. "Lilac was killed."

Stunned silence sweeps across us, every gaze locked on him now.

Jubilee speaks in a whisper. "If Lilac was killed, then who . . . what . . ."

"Days after I buried her," he says, toneless, "they brought her back to me. I don't know how—I don't want to know how. But it was her, it was my Lilac. Her thoughts, her voice, her memories. Her heart."

"That's impossible." Jubilee's face is drawn, confused. She only ever knew Lilac after the *Icarus* crash, and I know what she's thinking—I can't help but think it myself. Did any of us ever know the real Lilac? Except . . . my gaze creeps back toward Gideon. He knew her as a child, growing up. And he never seemed to notice there was anything different about her.

Tarver glances at Jubilee, his own gaze troubled. "She's had a connection to them ever since. She can sense them. After the rift on Avon was destroyed, she could feel this last whisper, alone in this last rift, reaching out to her in her mind. And though the whispers we met on Elysium were peaceful, we learned after Avon that her father had made the others twisted, angry. Dangerous."

Jubilee's still staring at Tarver, something like accusation in her gaze. "You told us the whisper was affecting her, that we needed to destroy the rift that we thought we'd find on the *Daedalus*. Why not tell us the whole truth?"

"Because no one can know," Tarver blurts, frustration in the snap of his voice. "She'd become part of the experiment, something to be studied. She'd be kept safe somewhere in a facility, away from me, away from anything resembling a real life." He closes his eyes. "I guess that's all over now."

"So . . ." My mind's spinning, trying to make sense of all this. "If Lilac isn't human, not really—"

"She *is*." Tarver's quick to interrupt. "She's real, she's alive, she's human. She's Lilac. She's just . . ."

"Just a little bit different," I finish for him, trying to make my voice conciliatory. "I didn't mean she wasn't real. But if she's not—if her body is something created *by* the whispers, created by that energy from their side of the rift . . ."

"Then that's why the whisper needed *her*." Gideon's reached the same conclusion I have. "If she's made of the same energy they are, no wonder the whisper could take her over so completely. Like slipping on a glove made to your exact measurements."

Jubilee grimaces. "Then it doesn't seem likely that the same tactics that worked on Avon and Elysium are going to work here. We have no idea what we're dealing with."

"We need to know more about the rift." Flynn crumples up his granola bar wrapper and tosses it aside. "Gideon?"

Gideon's shaking his head. "LRI doesn't keep any of its classified or proprietary documents on servers connected to the hypernet. No company would, it'd be an invitation for someone like me to walk on in. I'd have to go to LRI Headquarters itself, and . . ."

"And it's basically a pile of rubble, infested with whisper-controlled husks." Flynn mutters a curse.

I find my voice. "I . . . I think I might know someone who can help us."

"Go on," Gideon says, stripping another piece of wire and laying it in the pile of parts he's pulling together for our makeshift shields against the whisper's influence. He can't make up six earpieces, so he's jury-rigging a couple of palm pads to emit the same field as LaRoux's device—right now they're both in pieces, their insides spilling out like entrails.

"She's the contact I made within LaRoux Industries who was willing to leak me information. She's the one who told me the rift technology is the same as the new hyperspace engines. That's why we thought LaRoux had moved the rift to the *Daedalus*. I was at LRI Headquarters a couple weeks back to meet her, but—it's a long story, but that's the day I met Gideon, and the day we found out about the rift at LRI. A riot broke out, and she went back underground."

"Can you trust her?" Gideon's voice is soft and his gaze steady—looking back at him, I can see the bitterness there. Trust. Such a simple thing. Such an impossible thing.

I swallow. "I don't know. She could very well be dead, for all I know, or they might have caught her when they came after me. But if she's still out there . . . if she was debating whether to help then, maybe she'd be willing now. She's our best chance of finding out how to destroy the rift and set Lilac free. I'll need your help, though, to track her down. The address I had for her doesn't work anymore. She burned it when she— the time you came to get me."

"What's her name?"

"Rao." I press my palms against the floor as Gideon starts moving already, setting aside LaRoux's device so he can pull out a palm pad and get to work, searching every available network for the name. I swallow, continuing to explain. "Her name is Dr. Rao, and she's with the theoretical res—"

"Rao." The interruption is soft, but jolts me silent—Tarver hasn't said a word since he told us about Lilac's death, and the whispers who brought her back to him. He lifts his head, reddened eyes fixed on me. "Did you say Rao?"

"Yes, Dr. Rao."

"Dr. *Sanjana* Rao?"

My stomach lurches. "What—how do you know that name?"

Tarver's eyes close, and for a moment he almost looks peaceful, resigned. Then he gives a short, sharp laugh, eyes opening again. "What short memories everyone has. Patron was only three years ago."

Jubilee's breath catches in a gasp. "I *knew* I'd heard that name before—she was one of the researchers on Patron. One of the VeriCorp scientists you helped escape from raiders, the whole reason you were given that medal and sent to the *Icarus* on that press tour in the first place."

Tarver nods, leaning forward so he can rest his elbows on his knees. He looks tired, older, with none of the easy charm and boyish good looks that made him such a media darling. "Except she wasn't working for VeriCorp, and it wasn't raiders who attacked them. That was all a cover."

"She was working for LaRoux Industries," I whisper.

Tarver's eyes flick toward me for the briefest instant and then jerk away. "Yes. And she was on a secret project then, I barely understood it. Sofia's right—she's the one person in the galaxy who might actually have the answers we need."

"Found her," says Gideon, voice tinged with triumph. But his quick smile falters, his eyes on the palm pad's screen, as whatever he's found registers. "She's . . . she was hurt when the *Daedalus* hit, she's checked into a trauma center. Inside the crash site."

The crash site, several kilometers of destruction, every inch crawling with husks. Dozens, hundreds, maybe even thousands of them by now—and if Lilac's whisper decides we're a threat, we'll be no match for their sheer numbers.

The urge to lie down returns, that longing to just let the warm marble claim me almost overpowering. I can see my thoughts mirrored in the faces around me—even Jubilee, the notorious Captain Chase, looks like she'd rather drop.

But then I meet Gideon's gaze, and those hazel-green eyes lock onto mine, and for a moment our mistrust is set aside, and we're simply together. Just one piece of me, the smallest kernel, calms, and I can breathe. Then his mouth twitches, and he winks. It's enough.

I move, pulling myself up inch by inch, and that brings the others to life. They rise, coming to their feet, checking the charges on their guns, scrubbing at their faces with their hands as if they can wipe away the tiredness. One by one, they glance at me. So I suck in a deep breath and nod toward the door. "Let's go."

We have been waiting for so long, here in the place where the blue-eyed man first found us. The researchers all vanished long ago, but not before their minds crumbled, leaving us in an empty building filled only with the ghosts of madmen. We wait, growing weary, growing weak.

Then the silence is shattered, a great tearing in the sky that breaks the very stars—a ship appears where before there was only the remnant of the blue-eyed man's experiments.

The ship is falling, and we are too weak to stop it. It carries thousands of souls, any one of whom could free us from this hell—and they will all die.

And then, a flash of light. A glimpse of something familiar. Blue eyes, and a face that once laughed while washed in the glow of the rift. A soldier with her whose soul is still somewhere in that garden, clutching that book of poems.

We have just enough strength to nudge their escape pod so that it skims through the atmosphere safely, just enough strength to watch as they take their first shaking steps on the surface of this world.

We have just enough strength to hope.

TWENTY-EIGHT

GIDEON

THOUGH THE STREETS ARE ABANDONED, WE STAY CLOSE AS we make our way toward the crash site and the trauma center whose records tell us that they have Dr. Sanjana Rao. I'm betting that, tactically, it'd be better for either Jubilee or Tarver to scout on ahead for potential threats, but neither one suggests it. They both have their guns drawn, though, and Tarver and Flynn are each wearing one of my cobbled-together shields, tucked inside their military-supplied vests. In theory, if the rest of us stay close to them, within their range, we'll be shielded from the whisper. I'm praying I duplicated the field in LaRoux's device correctly, and they're broadcasting the little electrical pulses we need to scramble any attempts by the whisper to take us over. On the upside, if I'm wrong, there's every chance I'll never know about it.

Every pocket in the vest Kumiko's people gave me is crammed with tools and equipment, and tucked inside it is the slim aluminized bag I took with me to the *Daedalus* under my suit jacket. I wanted to make sure none of my equipment could be damaged by anything magnetic on the ship if we ended up taking a cross-country route to the rift.

All our attempts to reach Sanjana by phone, by net, have come up empty. We can't tell if it's because the networks are still crammed, or if it's because she's too injured to reply, or if it's because she's not even there, and the records are wrong. Everything, including the hastily erected trauma centers to deal with crash victims, is in chaos—and we can't afford to wait for her to reply. Without more information about how to destroy the rift, we're flying blind. I've sent her a package of information that'll download to her account if she gets a connection—coordinates for the center we're heading to in the hopes of finding her, schematics for my homemade whisper shields, and small details that can only have come from Tarver, as a sign she's dealing with allies. I pray she gets it, pray she trusts it. Pray she's even still alive.

I keep scanning my companions each time I get a little prickle of the hairs on the back of my neck, but the shields seem to be working. Then again, would I even know if it happened, unless I was looking directly into their eyes? Not for the first time, I wish I had Sofia's insight. She'd have some body language shortcut to tell instantly if one of our group was about to turn.

But she looks just as scared as I feel.

We stick to the smaller streets, forced to take long detours around sections of the upper city that have caved in and crushed the mid-city below. At first we see others only in the distance, too far away to tell if they're survivors or husks. But as the smell of burning chemicals grows stronger, as the ash in the air thickens and our path becomes more and more littered with debris, more dead bodies sprawled where they fell, it becomes obvious: the only people other than us still moving around this close to the crash aren't people at all anymore.

"That's the fifth one we've seen taking this exact path," Sofia whispers, breaking a long silence as we take cover against the side of a ruined bank headquarters and watch a shuffling husk move across the street. Even the sirens are quiet now. The only noises are the occasional, far distant rumble of some part of the city caving in and crumbling into the space below.

"They're sweeping the city," Jubilee says in a low voice. "This pattern, I recognize it."

She's looking at Tarver, who's watching, grim-faced, and it takes me a long moment to figure out why. "Lilac learned it from me," he says quietly. "Standard search grid."

"She's looking for us," I murmur, as the husk—a middle-aged man, balding and clad in a worn business suit, someone you'd never look at twice—vanishes around the corner.

"Hopefully she won't be able to see us with the shields," Sofia says, straightening out of her crouch. "We've got to move quietly. One or two, we can deal with. But if we run into a group of them . . ." She swallows but doesn't finish the sentence.

She doesn't have to. It's all too easy to imagine what a big enough group of these shambling, empty-eyed things could do to us. Soldiers who feel no pain, and no remorse at causing pain.

Up the street is a trio of police hovers settled on the pavement in a blockade formation, just in front of a line of temporary barriers. The crash perimeter. In theory, no one but rescue personnel is allowed through—the sign propped against one of the cars states, in big block letters, NO ENTRY BEYOND THIS POINT, and another warns, STRUCTURAL INSTABILITY. Despite the emptiness of the city, it's still a shock to see this setup abandoned. There ought to be police officers and city officials barring the way.

Instead there's no one.

We cross the perimeter one by one, swinging our legs over the cement barriers. Though we're still too far away to see the wreck, my eyes pick out a dizzying emptiness in the distance where there ought to be skyscrapers. With a city that stretches across almost an entire planet, there's no recognizable skyline—and yet my memory knows there should be something there, that it's like the world's been wiped clean just beyond the horizon.

A metallic clang shatters the quiet, making me jump so violently that I bang into one of the barriers, stifling an oath. Both soldiers have their weapons out, eyes scanning the alleyway where the sound came from. They move together without even seeming to communicate a plan—one glance, a nod, and then Jubilee's circling around wide to the mouth of the alley, shoulders pressing back against the brick, as Tarver crouches low, using the cover of the parked hovercars to remain unseen as he takes the other side. The rest of us move to follow, and as Tarver and Jubilee move on down the alley, we take up positions by its mouth.

Another, quieter clang, alerts us all to the source of the sound—there's someone inside one of the dumpsters at the end of the alley. Tarver tilts his head at Jubilee, who silently steps around behind it as he shifts his grip on his gun to free one hand. I glance over my shoulder, neck prickling, to see a figure a block away pause—turn—and start moving toward us.

Swallowing the urge to call out alarm, I reach out to touch Sofia's elbow so she'll follow my line of sight. Flynn catches the movement, and after he casts a quick, fearful glance back at me, we all ease into the mouth of the alley, hoping that noise hasn't drawn more attention. Tarver's shield will protect him and Jubilee, and Sofia and I stay close to Flynn and his.

Tarver's gripping the edge of the dumpster lid, Jubilee creeping closer so she can train her weapon on whoever's inside as he gets ready to haul it open. Just as Tarver's muscles start to tense, Sofia's sharp whisper cuts through the tense silence.

"Wait!"

Jubilee's gun twitches our direction, eyes scanning behind us even before she registers that Sofia's speaking. We're invisible in here, no other danger evident, and her gun twitches back. Her brow's crowding in, and I can tell she's about to signal Tarver to continue.

But Sofia doesn't speak for no reason—that much about her is real, and no lie or misdirection can change it. "What is it?" I ask softly, forestalling Jubilee.

Sofia's eyes flick from me to the dumpster. "The husks," she breathes, voice barely audible. "They don't hide. They're on a mission—you said it yourself," she adds, nodding at Jubilee. "They're running a search pattern. Why would one corner itself in here?"

Tarver lets go of the edge of the dumpster, though he doesn't lower his gun, eyes darting between me and Sofia.

But before anyone can respond, the dumpster lid flies open, knocking Tarver back and making a sound like thunder crashing up and down the alley. A figure tries to vault out of it, but he's clearly too cramped, too panicked, for acrobatics. He stumbles forward against the far wall, tripping and then dropping to the streets. Before any of us can speak, he's got his hands up, as though protecting his face from us.

"Please!" he gasps, voice ringing. "Don't hurt me—please don't hurt me."

"Shhh!" Jubilee's eyeing the mouth of the alleyway, her gun trained on this new arrival.

But he doesn't respond to that warning, still babbling pleas. He's in his fifties or sixties and out of shape, clad in the ruins of a suit. He's filthy, the odor of garbage and fear ripening the air, but as his eyes flash, terrified, between the five of us, I can see it: his eyes are hazel. And though they're dilated with fear, they're not empty.

"You have to calm down!" Tarver's voice is low and urgent, and though it cuts across the man's babbling, it seems to have no effect.

An image of that husk in the next block turning our way flashes up in my memory, and I'm moving before I have time to think—dropping into a crouch, I reach out and press my hand against the guy's mouth, forcing a moment of silence. He groans, eyes rolling from the two soldiers, to me, and back again.

Sofia's moving to crouch beside me, and glances up to follow the man's gaze. "Guys—" She lifts a hand, then turns it palm-down to gesture as she murmurs, "Lower the guns."

"We're not going to hurt you," I whisper. "But you've got to be quiet. If I take my hand away, will you promise not to make noise?"

He nods, eyes rolling back toward me again.

I ease my hand away and the man gulps air.

"Who are you? What're you doing here?" Sofia's voice is soft, despite her line of questioning.

"We were—I'm Chuck. My wife and I were . . . There were evacuation sirens. They said this part of the city wasn't safe, might collapse. We were . . . we were . . ." He trails off, staring wildly into the middle distance.

Sofia reaches out, her hand coming to rest gently on his shoulder. "It's okay. Just take a deep breath." The genetag tattoo she worked so hard to conceal is exposed now, and stands out stark against her inner arm as she gives the man's shoulder a squeeze. My stomach clenches as I realize this probably isn't the first time she's talked someone through a violent trauma, growing up on Avon in the middle of a war.

He shivers. "She just stopped. Like something flipped a switch. Stopped, then turned around and started walking back that way." He lifts his chin, pointing back in the direction of the *Daedalus*. "When I tried to stop her, to ask what she was doing, it was like she didn't even know me—she looked at me and her eyes were . . ." He closes his own eyes, as though he might be able to shut out the memory of his wife's empty gaze. "She grabbed me and started dragging me with her, but I pulled free and . . ."

"And hid here," Sofia finishes for him. She glances at me, eyes meeting mine—and in that moment, I know exactly what she's thinking. He's not fit enough to keep up with us, and with everything hinging on our success, we can't afford to slow down. But he could turn into one of those husks if he steps outside the protective field of my jury-rigged whisper shields, and if Lilac can't sense us through our scrambling fields, she'll certainly be able to access what he knows about us.

My eyes rake the alley, and Chuck himself, as I try to figure out how he's managed to hold off the whisper's influence for so long—then my eyes fall on the dumpster. Its thick metal walls might serve to protect him the way our electromagnetic devices do.

"You have to get back inside." I'm reaching for the guy's arm even as the others turn to look at me. "It's the safest place to hide, we can give you supplies. You have to stay in there or you'll end up like your wife."

Chuck's trying to shake my hand off, not understanding what I'm telling him in his relief at finding other survivors. I open my mouth to explain further, but before I can speak, movement beyond catches my eye.

There's a hand coming over the edge of the wall in the shadows at the end of the alley. The fingertips grope, creeping along the cement until they find purchase in a crack; it's not until they curl and tighten that I realize one of them is bent oddly, twisted, and not moving like the others. A head and shoulders appear, becoming a figure dragging itself over the edge of the wall.

I lurch to my feet, one hand reaching out instinctively to grab for Sofia and pull her with me as I stagger back. The others see it almost instantly—Flynn reaches for Chuck, Jubilee trains her gun on the figure creeping over the wall, Tarver spits a curse and swings his weapon over toward the mouth of the alley—and we break into a run.

I'm craning my neck back to watch as the figure slides over the edge of the wall and drops into a heap on the pavement. The figure in the shadows grows arms again, and legs, and I can see its profile, head turning toward us as we burst back out into the sunlight. I collide with someone just in front of me—the others have stopped. It's all I can do not to shout at them, *Run, run, for the love of* . . .

And then I see why they're not running.

The street outside the alley is filled with husks.

There are dozens upon dozens of them, ranging as far as I can see. Most of them would seem perfectly normal if not for the slack faces and the empty black holes where their eyes should be—but some of them have obvious injuries, like the one at the back of the alley with the broken finger. A girl, no older than eleven or twelve, stands only a few feet away, a shallow scrape across her arm standing crimson against her pale yellow sundress; a man some distance back, tall enough to see over the sea of faces, stares at us from only one black eye, the other crusted shut with blood from a head wound.

"No," whispers Chuck, shrinking back against Flynn, who's still gripping his arm. "No, no, no, nooo." His whisper turns to a moan, and he rips his arm away from Flynn's grasp.

"Wait—" Flynn's lunging after him. "Don't!"

But the man's withdrawing, back down the alley, toward his dumpster, out of shield range of the altered palm pad inside Flynn's vest. But while it might have protected him from the whisper's psychic reach, the dumpster's not going to do anything against the husks. Others have joined the solitary shadow at the back of the alley, and they descend on Chuck from behind. He starts to climb back into his hiding spot, but the husks grab hold of him, dozens of fingers twining into his clothes, his hair, dragging him away from the dumpster, which screeches an inch away from the wall as he clings to its edge. Then he's gone, pulled down into their midst.

"Damn it!" Jubilee's got her weapon aimed at them, and I can see her focus flicking with each little twitch of the gun barrel. She doesn't know where to aim, much less where to shoot. These are innocents. No different from Kumiko and her soldiers on Avon, broken by the invasion of their minds. One of the figures helping to pin Chuck down is tiny—a child.

The moment seems to stretch into an eternity; we should be running. We should leave Chuck to his fate, let his choice to hide play out, continue our attempts to reach Dr. Rao. But all of us can hear him screaming for someone named Alisha—his wife, no doubt. I can't tell if he's calling out to her because he's thinking of her, in these last moments, or if he's screaming her name because she's one of his assailants.

I'm holding onto Sofia so tightly I have to be hurting her, but she says nothing, her body shaking where she's pressed against me.

Tarver breaks first, taking one step down the alley, swearing. But before he can move any further, the screaming stops. My heart lurches in the sudden silence, broken by five sets of panicked breathing. *He's dead— they killed him. They* killed *him.*

But then the husks withdraw, straightening, coming to their feet. And so does Chuck. For the briefest second, we all stand there, confused. Then Chuck turns his head, gaze finding us—his dark, empty-eyed gaze.

I feel Sofia take a shaking breath. "Time to go," she whispers.

We run.

Once, long ago, we could have spoken to them, these lonely survivors on this ghost of a world. But we are so weak now, and can do little more than watch. We see them as they cannot, will not, see each other—we see his heart in the way he looks at her; we see her soul calling out for his in every touch. It would be so easy if they could only see inside each other as we can.

And yet, there is beauty in the way they find each other: slowly, in a fragile dance of sidelong glances and accidental touches. To see them come together, souls binding without knowing each other as we do, without being certain of what the other's heart holds, is to learn something new . . .

Faith.

TWENTY-NINE

SOFIA

THE DRY, ACRID AIR TEARS IN AND OUT OF MY LUNGS LIKE a saw, the chemicals lingering from the *Daedalus* crash singeing the inside of my nose, my throat. I concentrate on the rhythm as my feet pound after the others, trying not to gasp aloud—if we can run far enough, fast enough, quietly enough, maybe we can leave the surging tide of husks behind us. Maybe we can sink back into silence and stealth again.

My eyes water with the effort, a new kind of panic starting to rise as the others get farther and farther ahead of me and Gideon—*oh God, don't leave us behind*—until I realize Gideon's keeping pace with me on purpose. He runs faster than I do, he should be ahead of me, he should be safe inside the range of Tarver's and Flynn's shields. And suddenly the litany in my head turns inside out. *You idiot—just GO.*

But then Jubilee and Tarver are spreading out, Tarver heading for one side of the street on the next block, and Jubilee for the other. My eyes catch one of them—I'm not even sure which—lifting an arm in signal. Then Tarver's there as we reach them, ushering us to the side to follow Jubilee and Flynn down a side street.

"This way." His words are short, clipped, precise and efficient. "Fewer husks—narrower streets."

I risk a glance behind me as I skid to turn the corner following the others, and my heart sinks. The husks might be slow to react, might shuffle along as they search for targets—but once given a task, they can move as quickly as any of us. There are at least a hundred of them, only a few meters back. If they catch us and rip the shields from Flynn and Tarver, or drag us beyond their reach, we'll have no protection left against the mental net the whisper's casting over the city. I'd rather they tear us apart where we stand, than become one of those things.

My breath rushes out in a sob, and I stumble—Gideon's hand grabs at my arm, and together we lurch to our feet and take off, Tarver bringing up the rear behind us.

The streets spin dizzyingly around us as we sprint through the maze of rubble and sinkholes. The pavement starts to crumble beneath me at one point and I have to jump for the far side—I don't have time to look back, but I can hear a distant crash a few seconds later as the debris from street level drops down, down into the mid-city below, to shatter. We turn one corner, then another, then another—then turn back again, hitting a dead end, losing valuable seconds. The street funnels in, narrowed by the debris on either side. Then, abruptly, ahead of us is a wall of stones and twisted metal supports, part of a nearby skyscraper that's sunken and tumbled into the street. My feet pause only for a moment before I take off again, this time dragging Gideon behind *me* as we move, start climbing the mountain of rubble.

Our hands and feet scrabble against the loose detritus, and my mind seizes wildly on a memory. *Keep your body close to the wall. Don't look down. I'm right behind you.* All the little things Gideon called as I scaled the sheer wall of the elevator shaft in LaRoux Industries, what feels like years ago.

What I wouldn't give to be back in that elevator shaft.

We're not moving fast enough—though the pile of rubble isn't that steep, it's impossible to tell what's solid and what'll give way as soon as we grab it. And the husks are closing in.

Tarver turns, throwing himself back against the rubble and bringing his gun around to train on the things now starting to climb up through the broken building toward us. "Keep moving!" he shouts, his words punctuated by the squeal of the military-grade Gleidel. A bolt rips through the fleshy part of an arm, making the husk reel back and drop. Another shot, and another—two more go down, but the first one's already moving again, resuming the climb, barely even slowed by the wound on his arm that's now bleeding freely.

Pain doesn't stop them—and none of us, not me, not Gideon, not

Tarver or Jubilee or Flynn—none of us would be able to shoot to kill an innocent. Because that's what the husks are: real people, with real lives, their brains and bodies hijacked.

Jubilee joins Tarver, pausing in her climb to draw her own weapon again, gasping to catch her breath as she fires once, twice; they're barely making a dent in the mob surging up after us. I reach for the edge of a boulder-size hunk of cement—the bigger pieces usually move less—only to feel it shift and start to shudder toward me. I shriek and lurch to the side as it goes rolling down the slope, crashing into one of the husks and sending it sprawling.

I glance over at Gideon, whose eyes meet mine—and then we're both reaching for whatever pieces of rubble we can find, hurling them down the slope at the mob, the sounds of shattering cement mingling with the shrieking of weapons fire. Flynn scrambles sideways so his concrete missiles won't hit us, and joins the fight.

Then Gideon's voice cracks in a shout, and I see him go skidding down the slope. I dive after him, grabbing at one of his arms just as my eyes pick out the hand wrapped around his ankle; a hand belonging to an old woman, her face horrifyingly serene as her thin, bony fingers dig into Gideon's skin hard enough to turn it white. I give a wordless cry, wrapping both hands around Gideon's and bracing my feet against a steel girder, as Gideon flails out with his other leg, trying to kick her off. Tarver's there a breath later, unhesitatingly letting his gun drop and skitter away down the slope as he uses both hands to grab for Gideon's other arm, helping me pull him out of the husk's grasp, scrambling just inches ahead of the mob.

My arms wrap around Gideon and his around me, and my body's no longer listening to the frantic staccato drumline of commands from my brain—*climb higher—keep moving—run—fight—stay alive*—and for a heartbeat neither of us moves, and I don't have to look at him to know he feels it too, that this is it, and none of it should've mattered; the lies, the deception, the fake names and the false pretenses, none of it was real or true, and now we're never going to have the chance to know each other as we really are.

A pulse of pressure explodes across us, erupting against my ears, leaving my head ringing with . . . silence. All I can hear is my own breath, tearing and gasping for air—my breath and Gideon's, the force of it stirring my hair. And Tarver, a few feet away. And . . . I open my eyes to see Flynn with his arm around Jubilee, supporting her—she's hurt somehow, I can't tell how—and holding her gun in a shaking hand. He's pulling the trigger and nothing's happening, the gun silent and dark now, as dead and useless as an inert hunk of debris.

Everyone is still, like someone's pressed "pause" on the playback of this moment, and my mind tries frantically to figure out what's happened.

I turn just in time to see the husks—all of them, every single one in the mob of hundreds surging after us—drop in unison, falling like marionettes whose strings have been cut. Only after they've hit the ground is it possible to see the one figure still standing, only a few meters beyond the bottom of the rubble. It's a woman, older than us but not by much, clad in a dirty, battered suit of some kind. One hand hangs useless and still at her side, the other clasped, trembling, around an object that, from this distance, looks like some kind of grenade. Something about her dark skin and hair feels familiar, though I know I've never seen her before. Something, something at the back of my mind . . .

"Hey, you," she murmurs, voice thin and wobbly. I follow her gaze to see Tarver there, stunned, grip gone so nerveless he actually slides a few feet downward in a trickle of debris. The woman sways, and it's only then that I realize not all the grime on her jumpsuit is dirt—there's dried blood there too, spread across one side of her torso. "You guys make an awful lot of noise."

Movement behind her makes my heart give an abrupt lurch—Tarver sees the husk at the same time, and suddenly he's descending the pile of rubble without slowing, causing a landslide of debris and dust. But he's not going to get there in time. There's a boy stumbling toward the woman in the jumpsuit, stumbling because one of his ankles isn't working right—he must've been so far behind the rest of the group that whatever took them out missed him entirely.

The woman, seeing Tarver's sudden headlong slide down the rubble, looks back. She gasps, drops the thing in her good hand, and pulls something else out of the satchel at her side just as the boy reaches out for her. She jabs it into his ribs, and the crackling sound of electricity splits the air. The whisper-controlled boy jerks and seizes—*it's a Taser, the thing in her hand*—and then drops to the ground, as motionless as the sea of bodies between us.

"Sanjana!" Tarver calls as he lands in a heap at the bottom of the rubble, then leaps unsteadily to his feet.

Recognition surges through me, as quick and sharp as the Taser blast. I've seen this woman's personnel picture before—one of dozens I sorted through while making myself an LRI employee ID months ago—but I never knew who she was.

Sanjana. Dr. Rao. Our rift expert.

"You rang?" she retorts weakly, the Taser falling from a hand gone nerveless. She sways again—making Tarver lurch forward—then drops into a heap, Tarver diving for her barely in time to keep her head from hitting the shattered pavement.

Their faith gives us strength, strength enough to try, in the only ways we can, to reach them. To ask them for help. To beg for an end.

We reach into their thoughts and try to speak through the images of people they knew, souls lost in the crash, but are met with fear. We try to speak, to use the words learned from long years under observation, but they cannot understand us. We try to show them they are not alone—we give him his home, the poem held closest to his heart; we give her a flower, a reminder of the unique and fragile thing she is fighting for.

We pave a path for them in fragile petals and every step closer they take we feel stronger. They have taught us faith, and hope, and in them we have found our strength again.

And then she dies.

THIRTY

GIDEON

WE MAKE IT ONLY AS FAR AS A SHOPPING ARCADE A FEW blocks away. Tarver carries the scientist part of the distance, but as soon as she starts coming back to consciousness, she starts mumbling about being able to walk—she seems to accept the compromise of being half lifted along, supported between Tarver and me. Jubilee's hand is torn up a little, where her grip slipped while climbing and her palm slid across a jagged bit of steel, but she's on her feet, Flynn by her side. Sofia's the one who finds the cavernous opening beyond a fallen portico façade, crawling through and then gesturing for us to follow.

Normally, carrying Sanjana would be nothing—she's not very heavy, and there's two of us—but by the time we ease her through the gap in the façade, I'm ready to drop myself. I stumble and let her go a bit too abruptly as soon as we're inside, making Tarver sag under the sudden additional weight, and we all end up sinking to the dusty, cracked floor in a heap.

The only light's coming from the partially blocked entryway, and Sofia—also on the floor, I didn't even notice her drop—groans and drags her pack over to rummage for a flashlight. Nothing happens when she flicks it on. I can see her profile backlit by the sun on the street outside, see her stare blankly at the flashlight as though its failure has turned her brain off, too, and this last obstacle is too much to bear.

"EMP blast," Tarver rasps, voice hoarse with exhaustion and catching as he chokes on the dust stirred up by our entry. "Don't know why it hurt them, but that was that pulse out there. Flashlight won't work. Guns either. Nothing that runs on power."

Sofia drops the flashlight with a clatter and slumps back over on the floor, defeated. If my leg wasn't pinned under Sanjana's half-conscious body, I'd drag myself toward her to make sure she's all right—but I can't even tell if I'm all right. My muscles keep shaking, which suggests that at least all my limbs are still attached. Unless they're phantom twitches. Isn't that what they call it, when you lose an arm or a leg, and you still feel like it's there? Phantom twitches—phantom exhaustion—phantom sensations from bits that aren't there anymore . . . a laugh that even I recognize, dimly, distantly, as somewhat hysterical, whispers out of my lips before I turn my face against the stone floor, not even caring as the dust sticks to my sweaty brow.

There's a crack, a whoosh, and then red light blossoms against my closed eyes—my eyes are closed? When? I force my lids open to see Jubilee's face glowing. Then she's moving, and my tired brain makes sense of what I'm seeing—it's an emergency flare, something she must have had in her pack. She hands it to Flynn, sitting beside her, who tucks it in under a rock, shielding the glow so that it offers us only a little light. Hopefully, it'll be invisible from the outside.

Most of the arcade has collapsed—though the wreck of the *Daedalus* is still a few kilometers away, the shock from its impact has leveled over half the buildings in the city this far out. A few storefronts are still intact, promising high-end shopping experiences that their battered, darkened interiors certainly can't deliver. A jewelry store's security grate has been smashed apart by a fallen column of marble; the fact that the dust and rubble on the floor have been undisturbed makes my skin prickle. Under normal circumstances, even in the upper city, this place would've been picked clean by looters.

The weight on my leg shifts, yanking me back to the present, and I remember Sanjana. I sit up, reaching out to ease my foot out from under her as she lets out a groan. Tarver bends over her, brushing her hair out of her face so he can scan it.

"You okay?" he asks, intent. "Sanjana?"

She groans again, as though protesting the need to reply, but then opens her eyes and struggles up onto her elbows so she can eye Tarver wearily. "You do keep saving my life, Captain."

"It's 'Major' now," notes Jubilee, glancing up from her torn-up hand, which Flynn is inspecting in the unsteady light of the flare. "He got promoted after Patron."

"Actually, it's just 'Tarver' now," corrects the ex-soldier, the grim line of his mouth finally easing into something almost like a smile. "And to be honest, I'm pretty sure you just saved our lives. How'd you do that?"

Sanjana grimaces as Tarver helps her up into a seated position, easing back to lean against a block of stone. "Electromagnetic pulse. I was pretty sure that the rift entities' seemingly supernatural abilities are actually directly linked to the power differentials between their dimension and ours, and that their method of control is nothing more than an electrical interception of the signals firing in a person's neural path . . . ways . . ." She trails off, eyes flicking from Tarver's blank face, then across to Jubilee's, then across what can be seen of the others in the dim light. "Huh. Wrong audience."

"No, I get it." My weariness is fading, making way for a spark of curiosity. I've got no idea who this woman is, beyond someone Sofia was trying to reach at LaRoux Industries, but whoever she is, she's brilliant. "They're hacking people's brains, essentially."

Sanjana's lips twitch into a smile, eyes meeting mine. "Not really how I'd put it, but that's more or less right."

What she's saying makes perfect sense—it fits with LaRoux's little devices, explaining why the electromagnetic fields our shields produce would hide us from the whisper. And then I see something else, something more urgent, and I scramble to rip my vest open, and pull my kit out from inside it. "Oh, hell."

Six sets of eyes swivel to me, and I point at Tarver, then Flynn. "We just fried them. I don't know how quickly the whisper can find us, but it won't need a husk to lay eyes on us anymore. Our minds are unprotected."

Soft curses echo around me, horrified glances are exchanged, and then Tarver and Flynn are both scrambling to pull the palm pads from inside their vests, sliding them across to me. "Can you fix them?" Jubilee asks, pressing down on the folded bandage Flynn had been using to stop the bleeding on her hand. "Did the EMP fry your equipment, too?"

I hold up the bag. "It's aluminized."

I get the same blank stares Sanjana was on the end of a minute ago. "Any techie worth their salt carries their gear in one of these, protects against static charges, magnetic fields—and EMPs."

Sanjana slowly pulls a palm pad from a pocket sewn into her jumpsuit, pushing it across to me with her good hand. "I followed the specs you sent. Smart. How far do they project when they're working?"

"Several feet," I say, starting to unscrew the casings to get at their innards. "They might even turn the husks back, but I think it'd take minutes at best, and minutes up close with those guys is longer than we'll ever have."

In the silence that follows, I know everybody is thinking about what those several minutes would entail. Flynn breaks it by introducing himself, and then the rest of us, and Sofia stirs to hand Sanjana a water bottle and a granola bar.

Flynn's brow is furrowed throughout the introductions, though, and I don't blame him—this is physics beyond my understanding, and I didn't grow up on a backwater swamp planet halfway across the galaxy. "So, Dr. Rao . . . you know how she's doing this? Controlling people?"

Sanjana pauses, clearly reorganizing her thoughts, figuring out how to explain the concept. "Basically . . . our brains run on electricity, right? Biochemical electricity, of course, not like a battery, but . . . all the little impulses in our brains are electrical sparks that tell us what we're seeing, tasting, hearing—and everything we do, all our muscle responses and movements, they're responses to electrical signals too. I believe that the rift entity—"

"Rift—ow!" Jubilee starts to interrupt, then hisses as Flynn applies alcohol from their first-aid kit to the gash on her hand.

He glances up, lips twitching. "Crybaby."

"Shut up." But her lips seem to respond to his, twitching once, then twice, into a smile. Her eyes flicker back toward Sanjana. "I meant—rift entity? What's that?"

"They're . . . right, you wouldn't know about that. You know how everyone's . . . acting strange? The people out there, the ones who mobbed you?"

"The ones being controlled by the whisper, right."

"By the . . ." Sanjana's brows lift. "Whisper? That's what you call them?"

"Lilac came up with the name," Tarver interjects quietly. "She was the first person to know about them. They showed up like whispering voices in her mind when we were shipwrecked."

Sanjana hesitates, sympathy in her gaze as her head turns back toward her old friend. Her hesitation lingers, as she clearly wants to ask him about Lilac—she might be fooling her father and the public, but Sanjana knows something's not right. "Right. Well, then you know what they can do. Cause muscle spasms, pupil dilation, a taste people describe as metallic—"

"Tastes like blood," mutters Jubilee as Flynn finishes wrapping medical tape around the pad against her palm.

"I'd describe it more like the sensation you get when you lick a battery, but I suppose that's accurate. Under the right circumstances, they can even cause auditory and visual hallucinations—the whispers Lilac was hearing. And in the most extreme cases, they can control a person's motor functions completely."

"But what does this have to do with the EMP grenades?" Tarver's voice is quick, carrying far more animation than before Sanjana's arrival.

"Well . . . the whisper's abilities all have to do with 'hacking' the electrical impulses in the brain. My theory was that a large enough electromagnetic pulse might interfere with that control long enough to sever the connection. I grabbed these from the lab when I got your text—I was working late, that's the only reason I was even at LRI when the *Daedalus* went down. I couldn't get you on the phone and knew you'd be walking straight into . . . well, *that*." She tilts her head toward the opening of our makeshift cave, where moments before we'd been running for our lives.

"You came to find us without knowing whether those things would work?" Flynn's eyebrows go up, clearly impressed.

"It wasn't much riskier than staying where I was. Half the trauma center had fallen to those things already, I wasn't about to stick around and become one of them. I rigged my palm pad in line with the instructions you sent, and I'm not a husk yet, so I'm guessing it works." Sanjana rubs at her arm, just below the elbow. I'd thought she was wearing some kind of metallic mesh glove, but as she massages the spot where the "glove" begins, I realize what I'm looking at—it's a cybernetic prosthesis. And the EMP grenade knocked it out just as surely as it knocked out the husks—that explains why she couldn't afford to test her theory before she found us.

"You gave up the use of your hand to save us?" Sofia's been quiet during all of this, but her eyes are on the same movement I noticed.

"I owe Tarver a lot," Sanjana replies quietly. "I'd have lost much more than a hand if it weren't for him."

When Tarver doesn't answer, Jubilee clears her throat. "She's one of the survivors from the outpost on Patron that Tarver liberated. In a way, she—that outpost—started all of this. Tarver never would've been on the *Icarus* in the first place if that operation hadn't landed him on a publicity tour to make people feel all warm and fuzzy about the military."

"Full circle," Sanjana murmurs.

"The EMP, though." Tarver's insistent, cutting through the discussion with a grimace, as though they're discussing his failings rather than his heroism. "It *did* work. And those people—they're alive? They're not hurt?"

"They should be fine," Sanjana replies. "Theoretically, they'll wake up with not much more than a bad headache. And whatever injuries they'd already sustained, of course—wait, where are you going?"

Tarver's moving before Sanjana can finish, reaching out for her satchel. "How many of these things do you have left?" he asks urgently.

"Two more—*why*?"

"This is how we save Lilac." Tarver pulls out one of the grenades, a spherical object the size of a tangerine. His eyes flick up toward Sanjana. "The whisper has her, too. She's the one doing all this—or rather, the whisper's forcing her to do all this."

"Tarver—I know. I saw her." Sanjana reaches out with her good hand, resting it on Tarver's arm to stop him from getting up. "She's at LRI Headquarters. Tarver . . ."

"We use one of them to get through the husks to where she is, then we use the other one on her—free her—then destroy the rift."

But Sanjana's shaking her head, pain written clearly across her features. "Tarver, stop—no. Those others, they're just being controlled. Like puppets, or androids all running on the same programming. Lilac . . ."

She swallows, some of that pain shifting into fear. "Lilac is different. I saw her, just before I got out. She's not being controlled, some mindless shell. . . . She *is* that entity. I saw what she could do. I don't know how it's possible, or why it is, but she's *different*, and that entity is wearing her like a costume. I don't think that EMP will have any more effect on her than it would on you or me. That thing's a part of her."

Tarver's eyes stay on her for a long, tense moment, his hand tightening around the grenade. Then he lets it fall back into her satchel, shoulders sagging as he sinks back down onto the cracked floor. "What about the shields? If we got one of those close enough to her, for long enough . . . ?"

I shake my head. "They're less powerful than the EMP. No chance."

The silence rings for a heartbeat or two until I find my voice, clearing my throat. "We know why she's different," I say quietly. When Tarver says nothing, I relay the story to Sanjana that he told us—of how Lilac died, and came back, and brought with her some connection to the other side of the rift that's been inexorably drawing her back toward the whispers.

"And now," Sofia adds when I've finished, "LaRoux's sending representatives back to every planet with plans to build more rifts, like the one on Avon, and the one here. We think that she's letting him think he's still running the show, that he's not the risk. He's losing his mind, and she can drive him over the edge anytime she wants. Once he's put everything in place, she'll be able to spread the whispers like an infection until every person in the galaxy is one of those empty shells. Unless we figure out a way to stop her."

"On Avon, we destroyed the rift." Flynn's voice is troubled. "And that stopped the whispers, too. We were hoping you'd know enough about this rift to tell us how to destroy it."

"We were hoping," Sofia adds, "that you'd be willing to help us. Since you were almost willing to help me once before."

"Help . . ." Sanjana's brow furrows deeper, but then her eyes widen. "You're Alexis? You're the one I was going to meet, the day of the riots at LRI Headquarters?"

"Yes, except that it's actually Sofia," Sofia replies. "I was worried they'd caught you, when they turned up at my apartment. . . . Thanks for trying to warn me."

"I'm glad you're safe, I never knew. . . ." Sanjana shakes her head. "I don't know if I can help you, but I'll try. How did you destroy the other rifts?"

"I don't think LaRoux had figured out yet how to build shields like the ones we're using, when we were on Avon." Jubilee's quick to answer. "There was a self-destruct mechanism built in, I assume so he could terminate the project if things got out of hand. He wouldn't need that now, though."

"No," Sanjana agrees. "I doubt there's a self-destruct switch this time. He won't make the same mistake twice."

Tarver takes longer to answer. "I don't entirely know," he says finally. "I jumped into the rift with Lilac. I thought it would kill me, to be honest, but I thought there was a chance it would save her. I think it was the whispers themselves that destroyed the rift."

"Any portal between dimensions would have to be highly unstable," Sanjana says quietly. "Adding your own energy and disrupting the field by leaping into it could have released the whispers contained inside, allowing them to destroy their own prison. But anything that unstable is unpredictable, and we have no way of knowing what changes LaRoux has made. It was the very first rift, after all. He'll have learned more since it was built. If you were to try that again, you could end up doing exactly what the whisper wants, opening the way for more of its kind to come through."

"And I don't think it would be survivable this time," Tarver says, though there's an edge to his voice that scares me—an edge that says failing to survive is an option for him, if that's what it takes. "Whether it was having two of us to dispel the energy, or Lilac's connection to them protecting me, I don't know, though."

Sanjana blinks, then shakes her head. "It's just a theory. I'm working blind here, without a net. I've only been able to work indirectly on the project, so my knowledge is limited."

"But you've thought of something," Tarver insists. "I know that look."

Sanjana lets her breath out slowly. "Well . . . these entities, the whispers. They don't belong here. They belong in their universe, what we refer to as hyperspace. Just as it takes huge amounts of energy for a ship to skip through hyperspace to travel between star systems, it takes a huge amount of energy to hold the whispers here. They're constantly being pulled back toward their own universe, but the rift machinery—you've seen that, right? Looks exactly like a hyperspace engine, a giant ring, glows blue when it's on?" She pauses, taking in the scattered nods around the circle. "The rift machinery is what holds them here, on our side. It creates the tiniest tear in the fabric separating our worlds, and keeps them inside. It's an intensely intricate, delicate balance, governed by some of the most complicated programs anyone's ever written. But, theoretically, if someone could rewrite the program to open the rift just a little wider, the forces pulling at them *might* pull the whisper back through the rift, into its own world. Leaving Lilac, physically, behind."

"Physically?" Tarver's voice shakes a little. "What about mentally? What about *her*, her thoughts and memories?"

Sanjana rubs at her temple, clearly uneasy. "I don't know. She might be fine."

"She would be," Tarver murmurs. "If anyone can survive it, she could. Can you do it? Program the rift to send it back?"

Sanjana shakes her head, eyes widening a little. "Tarver—I'm not a programmer. I deal in theory, in physics—executing something like this is way, way beyond my experience. LaRoux's got a team of the fifteen best programmers in the galaxy working constantly to tweak and perfect that machinery. I got printouts of some of the programming fragments before I escaped, but it'd take me years just to understand what I'm reading. It's—it's just a theory."

Tarver's gaze, haunted now, stays trained on Sanjana's face. It's Sofia who speaks, and though she's speaking to everyone, her eyes are on me. "We just happen to *have* one of the best programmers in the galaxy. Dr. Rao, meet the Knave of Hearts."

I feel everyone's gazes shift toward me, but I'm still looking at Sofia, trying to read what little I can see of her face in the unsteady red glow of the emergency flare. Whether there's bitterness in her voice when she uses my pseudonym, whether that same betrayal, that same disgust, haunts her eyes as she looks at me, I can't tell. I'm not sure even she knows.

"Can you do it?" Tarver's attention, on me now, feels like a two-ton weight—now I get why Sanjana was so hesitant.

"I don't know," I answer truthfully. "I'd have to read those printouts, learn the language. . . . I might be able to. I don't have my rig here, I barely have anything. It would be a long shot."

Tarver's face shifts, the muscles in his jaw untensing. There's a new energy to him as he reaches for Sanjana's bag. I'm not sure he heard the words *long shot* at all. He searches for the printouts that'll teach me what the hell I'm supposed to do. Despite Tarver's newfound hope, Sanjana seems unconvinced. She opens her mouth to speak but pauses, uncertain.

Sofia's the one to break the quiet again, reading Sanjana's discomfort like she's a neon sign. "What is it?" she asks the scientist gently. "Just tell us."

Sanjana swallows. "I . . . I think it's a bad idea to try it."

That brings Tarver up short. "Why?"

Sanjana takes a deep breath. "Look, Tarver—I know this is impossible. I mean, God, if it were Ellie in there, if it was the one I loved, I'd do anything to save her. I just . . ."

"Tell me." Tarver's hope is already dwindling, like flames dying back to embers, to wait to be rekindled again.

"This balance, the forces involved in keeping the tear open just enough to hold them, but not enough to free them . . . you can't imagine how delicate it is. Changing that balance could free Lilac, yes. But it could also give Lilac access to infinite power, make her invincible, unstoppable. It could bind her to the creature forever. They'd be irrevocably fused. There'd be nothing she couldn't do, no harm she couldn't inflict. And that's not the worst-case scenario."

The silence is palpable as we each try and imagine something worse than an all-powerful whisper, hell-bent on revenge.

Eventually Sanjana speaks again, gazing at her dead hand, and I can see how much she hates to say it. "Messing with the rift could give the whisper the power to cut us off from hyperspace completely. Just begin to imagine what that might mean."

My heart drops, and Sofia and I exchange a glance—we talked about this, the first time we admitted the existence of the whispers to each other. "We'd lose all interplanetary travel," I say. "We'd be back to below light speed. It would take dozens of generations to get anywhere."

"We'd never be able to go home," Flynn breathes, eyes flickering toward Jubilee.

"Whole planets would die," Sofia murmurs. "Every colony that's still terraforming, that still relies on outside supplies."

"Hell," I murmur. "*Corinth* relies on outside supplies. We have no farmland here, we don't produce our own food, we import it." It flashes before my eyes, like a movie in fast forward. The chaos wrought by the fall of the *Daedalus* would be nothing. We'd see riots, starvation. It would be the end of our world, literally.

"And without access to hyperspace, we'd have no hypernet," Sanjana points out, repeating the other warning I gave Sofia. "Our communications would be at light speed as well."

"So we'd have no way to even tell the other planets what happened," Flynn finishes for her. "Everything would just go dark."

Sofia's face pales under the smudges of dirt on her skin. "Could that be what she wants now? We assumed it was trying to do the same thing as LaRoux—that they both wanted a rift on every planet, and the only difference was who would be in control when they went live. What if the whisper's trying to extend its reach so it can cut us off from its universe?"

"So if we can't destroy the rift, and we can't try to send the whisper back to its universe, in case we cut ourselves off entirely . . ." Jubilee's frustration speaks for all of us. "What other choice do we have?"

Sanjana's not looking at Tarver—instead she's staring at her prosthesis, though it's cold and still now. "Until now, the entities have always inhabited the rifts, sending their mental abilities outward to affect you, to affect those on Avon and Verona. Destroying those rifts, those conduits, destroyed the whispers too. But now, the entity is inhabiting *Lilac*. The rift isn't the conduit anymore. She is."

"What're you saying?"

My heart's already sinking, and Sofia's face is white too, her eyes finding mine. The silence hangs, no one quite willing to grasp what the scientist is telling us. Jubilee's question hangs in the air, and no one looks at Tarver.

But he's the one who finally answers her. "She's saying we have to kill Lilac."

Many long years have passed since the blue-eyed man came to me, but now he has come every day, wild-eyed and gaunt. "Where is she?" he asks, pacing circles around the rift, stopping just short of slamming his fists against the machinery. "The ship went down—God knows where. I know you can find her. You have to find her. Damn it, there has to be a way to . . . I won't lose her too!"

If I could speak I would tell him I sense nothing, because of the prison that holds me. If I cared to tell him anything at all.

Then I do feel something: a surge of power so strong I sense it even through the total emptiness surrounding me. The final gasp of my brethren in the original thin spot—a flood of joy, release, gratitude so strong I almost forget my own despair. Until it fades, leaving me alone once more.

No . . . not alone. I can still feel something, the remnant of what my brethren did. A vessel exists now, somewhere across the galaxy, a connection to my world. They brought something back. Someone.

Her.

I will stay still, and I will stay quiet.

And I will wait for my chance.

THIRTY-ONE

SOFIA

"NOT AN OPTION." JUBILEE'S VOICE IS SHARP, AND SHE lurches to her feet.

"I don't like it any more than you do," Sanjana retorts, her own voice quickening. "But it's the only answer I have."

"Find another one!" Jubilee's shout echoes back from the shattered marble walls, leaving a quick, poignant silence behind.

Sanjana takes a slow breath. "It doesn't work like that. You can't just decide the variables aren't true, that the evidence isn't what you want it to be—I can't just invent ways to change physics, Captain."

I take advantage of that brief lull to rise to my feet, ignoring the swell of dizziness that comes with exhaustion. "We should get some rest." I keep my voice even, warm. *Listen to me, latch on to this voice. I'm on your side.* It's a voice that always worked on the soldiers on Avon, always worked to calm my contacts. And it only works as long as you keep talking, so they don't realize I can't possibly be on *everyone's* side. "We can't change what's happened—and if she's protecting the rift, then she won't do anything to draw attention to it. We have time, and we need to give Gideon a chance to fix our shields before we risk being seen. We can afford to sleep on it. We *have* to sleep on it—we're out on our feet."

Wearily, the others spread out a little, finding spaces in the various storefronts to stretch out. Jubilee tosses another flare from her pack to Gideon, then retreats to follow Flynn to the shadows near the rubble blocking the other end of the arcade. Gideon helps Sanjana to her feet, lending her some support as they duck inside a nearby jewelry store. I know Gideon wants to discuss this theoretical hack on the rift, where Tarver won't hear, and won't get his hopes up again. But Gideon lingers by the store's archway after he's got Sanjana settled, and I catch a flash of his eyes moving toward me before I drop my gaze. I can feel him watching me, feel the weight of all the things I wish I could say to him.

He and I haven't talked to each other since the *Daedalus*, not really. There's been no time for it, no space for us to be alone. But I can see the shock in his eyes when he saw me pull out the plas-pistol as clear as if it were only five minutes ago, and each time I relive it something twists a little more deep inside me. I want to apologize and I want to defend myself—I want to tell him I'd choose him over revenge if I could do it again, and that I'd still fire at LaRoux again if I could—I want to trust him and I want him to leave and never look at me like this again. I want to rail at him for lying to me about the Knave and about growing up alongside the daughter of my enemy, to remind him that his side of the ledger has its fair share of deceit.

I want him to know that the only reason I didn't tell him about my plan to murder Roderick LaRoux is that I knew he'd try to talk me out of it, and that, somewhere deep in my heart, I knew he'd succeed. I want him to know that I wish he had. I want so badly to trust him enough for that. And yet my lips won't move, my voice won't come.

When I manage to lift my head again, the doorway is empty, and I can hear his voice, low, mingling with the scientist's.

Tarver and I are alone. He's been on autopilot since the crash, chasing one distant glimmer of hope after another. It doesn't take an expert to read the emptiness in his face now. I have no idea if he even knows I'm still here, if he's aware enough of his surroundings to register me.

Then he speaks, voice rusty. "The first time I lost her," he says, "I was going to kill myself."

I swallow, unsure whether he thinks he's talking to himself—until his head lifts and his eyes flicker over toward my face.

"I don't know how I carried on. I don't know what kept me from pulling that trigger." He leans back slowly against the wall until he can tilt his chin and look up at the ceiling. "I don't care, now."

My heart tightens, making it difficult to breathe. There's always a certain amount of guilt involved, doing what I do—using people always leaves wreckage in its wake, for me and for them. But it's never been anything like this, a crushing, suffocating weight forcing its way deeper and deeper inside me.

"I'm sorry," I whisper. "I never meant to—" My mind replays the moment Lilac fell, like a photo looping over and over. "I'm sorry."

Tarver lifts a hand to wipe it over his face, as though he can wipe away his reaction to my voice. "It's not your fault."

"I shot—"

"Maybe you shortened the fuse," he interrupts, looking back down and across at me. "But the blast was already coming."

It shouldn't make me feel better—and yet, in some horrible way, it does. I take another breath, but I can't think of anything to say.

"The past year . . ." Tarver shakes his head. "She's still Lilac—she was always still Lilac. But she's been different, too. She could feel them, the whispers, no matter how far away we went. She has dreams. She wakes up in the middle of the night crying. She'll drift off sometimes, having conversations with people who aren't . . ." He gives his head another shake, swallowing. "I think they were always coming for her."

"Why?"

"I don't know." He glances at me again, the helplessness in his gaze so at odds with the smiling, commanding presence he has in all his HV interviews and photo shoots. "The beings we met on Elysium wouldn't do this. I wouldn't say they were *good*—I'm not sure they even had a concept of 'good.' But they weren't evil—they weren't cruel. There was a sense of fairness to them, I suppose. That thing that took Lilac, when she kissed me . . ." His face ripples, then tightens. "That thing was cruel."

I can't think of anything to say, so we sit in silence for a time, saying nothing, not watching each other from our opposite edges of the room. There's an odd comfort in being here, with someone as bruised and hurt as I am. For once, I'm not more broken than the world around me, and it's horrible and healing all at once.

"You were right," Tarver says softly, interrupting the quiet after a while. "We should get some rest while we can."

"I'll leave you alone." I press my palm to the ground, ready to get to my feet and find my own corner of the ruins to sleep in.

"No." Tarver's voice is quick, and though he doesn't look at me, I know he can see me out of the corner of his eye. "Stay."

I hesitate, tired enough that my ears are ringing each time he speaks. My weary thoughts pull out a memory, and I find myself thinking of Flynn, and of the time he spent hiding in our house on Avon when he was on the run. I remember falling asleep, finally, after so many nights spent lying awake—I could feel him, somehow, in the room that had belonged to my father. The tiny shifts in the air, the inaudible noises, the imperceptible hints of another life in that empty space.

"Okay," I whisper.

Eventually he leans his head back again to rest against the wall, and sometime after that, he shifts to lie down, head on one arm. I wait until his breathing lengthens before getting slowly, quietly to my feet and slipping through the archway to join Gideon and Sanjana.

"Even if we *knew* it would work," Sanjana's saying, voice low but intent, "even if we *knew* you couldn't accidentally tear the rift open . . . the risk to you is far too great."

My boot scrapes against the debris, making both of them jump, heads craning up to look at me. "What risk to him?" I ask, not bothering to apologize for my eavesdropping.

Gideon lets his breath out in a sigh that echoes off the broken walls. "It's nothing." He's got stacks of papers covered in text that he's reading by the light of the flare—Sanjana's programming printouts. I can't remember the last time I saw something printed out on paper—her foresight is enough to make my head spin. If she'd brought the information on disc, or on a palm pad, we'd have no way of looking at it now, after the EMP.

"It's *not* nothing," Sanjana argues, voice sharpening as she glances at Gideon, then back to me. "He'd have to actually be there, at the rift. It's not on any kind of network. LaRoux's far too smart to leave something like that accessible remotely. Gideon would have to write his virus and then deliver it personally, physically, plugging it directly into the rift machinery."

I lean back, letting the pillar behind me take some of my weight off my weary feet. "We'd be there too—we'd help him fight past the husks."

"That's not the danger I'm talking about." Sanjana scrubs a hand over her eyes, and I realize she's as exhausted as the rest of us. "I've explained that the whispers manipulate neural energy, that that's how they do what they do. The rift is the source of that power. Gideon would have to come in contact with that rift to access it, which risks flooding his mind with that power."

Gideon's not looking at me, instead busy with organizing the print-outs, leafing through them and neatening the stack of papers. I swallow. "What would that do to him?"

"Maybe nothing," Sanjana replies. "But it could kill him, too. It could drive him mad. It could erase every memory and thought he's ever had. It's impossible to predict."

My mouth's gone dry. Somewhere at the back of my mind, I know the reason that we don't dare attempt this is that if something goes wrong, it could give Lilac even more power; it could lead to the destruction of this world as we know it, the destruction of humanity. But here, now, all I can process is that attempting it might destroy the boy sitting a few feet away, fidgeting with a stack of paper so that he doesn't have to look at me.

I can't take my eyes off him, though his face is still angled down and away, where I can't see what's going on inside him. *No,* I want to say. *Not in a million years. It's too dangerous. It's asking too much. I don't care if he's the Knave, I don't care if there's no one else. I won't let him.*

Sanjana breaks the silence, clearing her throat. "I'm going to try to get some sleep," she says, and when I look up, I see her gaze swing between the two of us. She holds out her good hand to forestall Gideon as he starts to offer help, adding, "I'm okay. I'm not running any marathons anytime soon, but a few cracked ribs won't stop me from finding a place to pass out." She offers up a weak smile and slowly makes her way back out of the shop.

I stare down at Gideon, able to see only the fall of his hair, face shadowed and angled away, until I can't stand it anymore. I shove away from the pillar at my back and drop to the floor beside him. "You can't do this," I blurt, voice cracking with exhaustion.

His eyes flick up, expression unreadable—not because there's no emotion there, but because his features are so conflicted I can't tell one flicker of thought from another. "It's only a theory," he replies softly. "Useless, unless we figure out a way to make sure nothing goes wrong. We can't risk making Lilac strong enough to wipe us out, or cut us off."

I swallow, trying to soothe my dry throat, leaning to the side until I come up against the wall with a thump. My eyes close, as though by shutting him out I might shut out everything else, too.

"How's your hand?" Gideon asks in a low voice.

Startled, I open my eyes and look down, where the bandage on my hand is grubby and half-stripped away after our near escape in the streets. I used it to grab him, when Tarver and I pulled him free of the husks, and I didn't feel a thing. I flex my fingers, a dull ache throbbing through where the burns had been, the only reminder of the choice I made on the *Daedalus*. The exploding plas-pistol could've easily killed me, and instead, Mori's dermal regenerator's left me without so much as a scratch.

"Better," I whisper.

The quiet, punctuated only by the faint sound of Tarver shifting in his sleep in the next room, settles in like a tangling vine—the longer it grows between us, the harder it is to break through it. I want to say something, but I don't know what—that I'm sorry, except I'm not, because he was deceiving me too, as I was deceiving him. Gideon and I were a house of cards, nothing more. We were always going to fall apart eventually.

I shouldn't mourn the loss of something that never existed. And yet, sitting here in the dark, fighting the urge to turn toward him and reach for him and throw myself into his arms and tell him—tell him anything, everything, whatever I can—it's taking all the strength I have.

My self-control crumbles a little and I find my head turning, my eyes seeking his profile—but he's already looking at me, his eyes glinting in the glow of the flare. He reaches toward me and I hold my breath. His fingertips touch my cheek, tracing a curve down toward my jaw and then lingering there, as though loath to pull away.

"Was any of it real?" he whispers.

And I don't know if he's really asking for truth or only echoing my own words back at me.

My head tilts a fraction, in spite of myself, unable to resist leaning into his touch. "I don't know."

Gideon's breath catches, and there's just enough light from the flare for me to see his lips hint at a smile. "I don't believe you."

My heart's pounding, aching—the only thing worse than sitting here, unmoving, would be to crumble and lean into him and feel him recoil. Or to pull away myself. I want to kiss him, to wrap myself up in him, but everything I feel for him is so confused that even that instinct might be a lie.

"Gideon, this plan . . ." But I don't know what I want to say, and my words peter out.

Gideon pauses, breath catching as he considers his reply. When he does speak, it's in a whisper. "If it were you—"

"If it were me," I break in, forgetting to whisper, "I wouldn't do it." In truth, I have no idea what I would do in his place, but I don't know any other way to convince him not to pursue this. "I wouldn't risk madness, risk . . . losing myself, for a plan that could end the world anyway. It's stupid, and reckless, and however much you like doing stupid and reckless things, you could be risking yourself for nothing. I can't sit here and watch you decide to do that."

Gideon waits, one eyebrow lifting a little until the quiet settles back in after my speech. "You done?"

The outburst has left me breathless—I'm tired enough that my emotions are far too close to the surface. I slump back against the wall, running a hand through my hair.

When I glance at him, expecting annoyance—instead I see him smiling, just the corners of his mouth twitching with amusement. "What I started to say," he murmurs, "was that *if it were you* in there, in that wreck . . . if you were the one whose life, or soul, or self were at stake, and I had to choose between you and the entire universe? I'd be halfway there already. I wouldn't even stop to think."

I can't answer—I can't form a single thought. He's stolen my breath, my words, left me with just a dim roaring in my ears. I can't breathe, feeling like the ground's opening up beneath me, ready to swallow me, and I'm not even sure I care. "Gideon—"

"My brother felt that way about her. I'm not ready to give up on either of them yet." He reaches out again, but his fingers halt an inch away from my face. They hover there, and I can feel the pull of him, feel it like a physical force drawing me toward him. I lean in toward his touch just as he lets his hand fall and pushes to his feet. "Get some sleep," he whispers, before ducking back out again.

The sound of crunching debris wakes me, and it's not until I drag myself out of the jewelry store rubble that I see the pale, thin light of dawn streaming through the opening of the arcade. It was still daylight when we came inside—I must've been asleep for twelve hours. My neck muscles spasm as if in recognition of that, protesting my bed of cold marble and debris.

Flynn and Jubilee are awake and moving around, their footsteps making the noise that woke me. Spotting me in the archway, Flynn flashes me a smile and then tosses one of the apples from the LaRoux estate's kitchen my way. "Morning," he greets me, managing to elicit a smile from me in return.

"Is it really morning?" I mumble, catching the apple with difficulty, my reflexes still trying to shake off sleep.

"It's really morning." That's Sanjana, sitting on the other side of the hall, eating her own breakfast of a banana and something out of a pouch with the LaRoux lambda seal on it, no doubt taken from work. "You slept?"

"Like a coma patient." I bite into the apple, my taste buds jolting at its flavor—it's then that I discover I'm ravenous, as though now that my body's gotten some sleep, it's tackling the other problems on the list one by one.

I can't bring myself to sit, devouring the apple as I circle the small area in the arcade that's free of fallen beams. I crouch, peering into the alcove where Flynn and Jubilee had vanished yesterday, finding it empty. I straighten, casting my eyes around again. "Guys . . ." I swallow my mouthful of apple. "Where's Gideon?"

Sanjana looks up from her banana. "He wasn't in there with you?" Her head tilts toward the store where I spent the night.

"No." A flicker of alarm starts at the base of my spine. "Where's Tarver?"

Jubilee glances at Flynn, who shakes his head. "I just thought . . ." She glances at the entryway and the soft morning light beyond. "I thought he went to get some air."

I keep scanning the arcade, even though I know one more look isn't going to make either of them materialize out of thin air . . . and then realization washes over me. "His gear," I gasp, dropping the apple.

"What?" Jubilee turns, standing in the doorway.

"Gideon's gear. His goggles, his drives, his lapscreen . . . they're gone."

Sanjana gives a wordless exclamation. "The shields . . ." She points to where two of them sit, repaired, one atop the other by the door—hers and Flynn's. The one Tarver had been using is missing.

I glance from her to Flynn, and to the soldier by the door. Jubilee's eyes meet mine for a long moment, and then I find my feet flying toward the hallway. I push past her into the street, calling Gideon's name and Tarver's—she and Flynn join in the search, and though we have to stop shouting for them to avoid attracting husks, we fan out to cover the entire block, building by building. It's not until we end up back at the arcade to see Sanjana's ashen face in the entryway that my feet stop moving. "The printouts of the programming language are missing," she whispers.

Gideon and Tarver are gone.

"We have to go after them." Jubilee's voice is urgent, her feet carrying her straight to her pack so she can start shoving supplies back into it, ready to move out.

"Jubilee, stop." My own body's demanding that I act, fear and worry making me want to leap out of hiding and take off after them. "There's no way we're going to catch up with them. They could be hours ahead of us, and we don't even know what path they're taking."

"We *can't* let them attempt to save Lilac." Sanjana grimaces as she prods at her broken ribs with her good hand.

Jubilee's brows rise a little as she shoots the scientist a sidelong glance. "You don't *let* Merendsen do anything. He does what he wants and you either help him or you get out of his way."

"Look," I break in quickly as Sanjana opens her mouth to retort, "we don't know where they are, but we *do* know where they're going." I swallow hard, trying to banish the tangle of guilt and pain and fear choking my voice. "And I know a way to get to the *Daedalus* without having to fight our way past every husk in the city. We might be able to beat them there if we go down into the undercity."

Jubilee's eyes snap toward mine. "Down? Into the slums?" Her face tightens. "It'll be chaos down there. Too many people to have evacuated . . . There'll be looting, rioting."

"Which means that down there, in the chaos, we'll be that much harder for any husks to spot. We can blend in. The elevators won't work without power, but we can climb down the maintenance shafts, travel below, then come back up inside the LaRoux Industries compound."

I'm speaking quickly, and it takes the others a few seconds to absorb the plan, glancing round at each other. Sanjana speaks first, clearing her throat. "I can't climb anywhere," she says, her tone brooking no argument as she lifts the arm with the dead prosthesis. "Not until I get this thing repaired. You'll have to leave me here." Flynn starts to argue, and Jubilee a second afterward, but Sanjana cuts through the debate. "This is bigger than any one of us. I can't argue that it's bigger than Lilac and not apply the same logic to myself."

Jubilee exhales audibly, raking her fingers through her hair. "We'll signal Mori—an ally—as soon as we find a working radio. She and her guys will come get you."

"I won't be going anywhere," Sanjana replies, with a shaky smile. "Just make sure you get there in time. Make it count."

"We will."

"And then?" There's an apology in her gaze for asking the question, but she doesn't waver. "When you reach the rift—when you reach Lilac—what then?"

Jubilee's gaze creeps across toward Flynn, and the air fills with the words no one wants to say aloud. Eventually, I'm the one who draws breath. "We've got a day to figure out some other way. If by the time we reach the *Daedalus* we still don't . . ." I let that breath out, shaky. "Then we destroy the conduit."

The gray world is full of anger and pain, the two sides of this war both so colored by hatred that each is the same shade of darkness as the other. They are so similar, longing for peace, for justice, for quiet, and yet they kill each other as though they seek death, not life.

As our keeper forces us to greater and greater acts of destruction, we . . . I . . . do what little I can to find balance. I cannot stop a father from strapping explosives to his chest, but I can reach inside the green-eyed boy and plant the idea to move just far away enough that the blast will not kill him. I cannot shield the girl with the dimpled smile from the grief of losing her father, but I can help her sleep, help her decide to keep breathing each day.

And I cannot save the girl with the beautiful dreams, the girl I once knew on another world, in another life, from all that is to come. But I can keep her safe from the others. And I can find faith in her dreams.

THIRTY-TWO

GIDEON

I GRAB THE BROKEN LIP OF A CHUNK OF CONCRETE, OVERTIRED muscles protesting all the way from my knuckles to my shoulders as I haul myself up, scrambling for purchase before I hook a leg over the edge and begin the controlled slide down.

I've seen disasters on the lower levels before, building collapses or fires threatening to spread through a whole quarter, but those times always brought out the best in people: whole families banding together to rescue trapped strangers, neighbors forming bucket chains to fight the fires. This is a different world, desolation as far as the eye can see, whole sectors of brightly lit, bustling Corinth simply wiped from existence. This world isn't safe, and somewhere out there in it, Tarver's alone.

He can't have had much of a head start, no more than an hour, before I saw he was gone, plus the extra quarter hour it took me to rig my lapscreen to emit the shield frequency to protect me from Lilac. I'm not even sure how long it'll work. I have to catch up with him, and fast.

I can guess at which direction he's moving—most of my options are blocked, so I'm hoping he's taking the path of least resistance, the one that will get him to LaRoux Headquarters as quickly as possible. My surroundings are mostly silent; emergency sirens occasionally wail in the distance, but no more firefighting drones zip overhead. Every so often, sections of buildings collapse with no warning, the crashes earsplitting, the echoes rumbling across the landscape.

Huge chunks of debris ripped through this block and the next when the ship fell, shearing straight through the buildings, turning everything above head height to rubble—on the ground floors, some of the doorways are still intact, offering glimpses inside, their upper stories spilling out into the street. They were apartments and offices, mostly, and clothes lie strewn across broken tables and chairs, electronics turned to so much recyc and wiring. Then there are the bundles I thought at first were clothes—the crumpled bodies, silent where they fell.

I pause to adjust my pack, then make my way through the broken lower level of a law firm, reception desks and ornamental plants crushed beneath piles of rubble. It's half-dark in here, and I place my feet carefully to keep my footfalls silent, avoid the telltale crunch of debris. I can see light on the far side, and I'm hoping there's an open section of road if I can get across there.

I climb over a fallen girder blocking a doorway, easing my head through the gap to check what's on the other side. In a blur of movement, something comes swinging toward me. I duck, my torso hitting the girder and knocking the wind out of me. The iron bar—because that's what it is—smashes against the doorframe with a clang. I throw myself back into the room I came from, scrambling across the rubble with no thought for the noise, my blood roaring in my ears, my body alive with electricity.

There's a figure in the doorway, vaulting the girder to come after me in one smooth movement, lifting the bar again. I roll to the side, jamming myself under a broken desk that will give me a moment's shelter, kicking at the far side of it to smash an exit point. I'm too broad for it, but I drive one boot into the splintered desk over and over, desperately trying to escape before the iron bar comes swinging down again.

Except it doesn't.

"Gideon?" Tarver's crouching beside the desk, the bar in one hand. "What the *hell* are you doing? I nearly killed you."

"I noticed," I murmur, letting my head drop back to hit the rubble beneath me with a thump.

"Quick, we made too much noise." He's instantly businesslike, offering me a hand to haul me out from under the desk. "They'll be here in a minute."

I don't have to ask who. Instead, I follow him as he climbs up another girder, grabbing for a beam across the ceiling and almost silently scrambling until he's above eye level, sitting on a broken ledge. I climb onto his perch, and he lifts a finger to his lips, turning his gaze down. Just a few seconds later, the first of the husks come moving through the space we left, slowly searching for whatever made the noise.

We sit jammed in place, side by side, for a full ten minutes as they move through the building. There must be a hundred of them, methodically combing through wreckage and climbing past each other. They're not efficient or particularly creative, but they're relentless. And as if I need a reminder of the fragility of our situation, my temporary lapscreen shield dies as we sit there, leaving me dependent on Tarver's once more. Only once the last has been gone for a couple of minutes does Tarver speak in a low voice. "What are you doing here?"

"What the hell do you *think* I'm doing here, Merendsen? I heard there was a sudden drop in property prices in this area, I wanted to check out some places I saw advertised." I snort. "I'm here to help."

"*You're* here to help *me*." His look is flat, disbelieving. Face smudged with dirt, gaze tired, he couldn't be further from the guy I saw climb onto the dais alongside Lilac in the ballroom of the *Daedalus*. I have to find a way in, and quickly, or I'll lose him all over again. *What would Sofia do?*

And in the instant I ask the question, I know the answer. She'd tell the truth. Why is it that I'm so sure of that, yet I can't trust that she's ever told me the truth? I draw a slow breath. "It's not for you. I'm here to help Lilac. And Simon. This is what he would have wanted for her, and I've realized that she never changed at all from the girl I knew as a kid. I needed people to blame, and she was one of them, but we should have been grieving for Simon together. This is what he would have wanted, and I'm the one that's left to do it."

Merendsen meets my eyes, and after a long moment, he nods, as if I've passed a test. "Then let's go."

Within a couple of minutes we're slowly making our way through the desolate landscape once more. Merendsen's climbing ahead of me, looking utterly at ease in black fatigues. He's lacking only his gun—killed by the EMP—to look the perfect soldier. Though his shoulder must still be aching after he dislocated it on the *Daedalus*, he's moving more quickly than most healthy people could.

He looks at home amidst the ruins of Corinth, as if the destruction around us is an outward manifestation of the pain inside him. Though I'm dressed the same outwardly, I'm out of my element and I know it.

The physicality of our fight to cross the burning city doesn't bother me—the climbs and scrambles are no worse than some of my onsite hacks—but I'm used to silent, sterile places, not bloodstained sidewalks and chunks of buildings lying across my path. I'm used to security teams I can track, not silent husks, single-mindedly dissecting the city in a slow, methodical search grid. As we work our way through the wreckage, a part of my mind is preoccupied—taking what I learned from Sanjana's printouts, turning that information over and over in my head. I'm still grappling with even *understanding* the programming of the rift, let alone closing it down without empowering the whisper to end the world. And I'm on a countdown that's elapsing far too fast.

We climb through a restaurant that was inhabited when the debris hit—food's scattered everywhere, and blood's pooled underneath one slab of fallen wall, congealing a dark red after so many hours. Fires are still burning as we make our way toward the center of the destruction, the acrid smell of entire city blocks laid to waste getting inside my nose, making my eyes water. We're seeing parts of the *Daedalus* herself now, enormous chunks of metal half melted by reentry and impact.

Tarver pauses for a moment atop a broken wall, surveying the landscape below us—the twisted shards of metal, the broken escape pods. Eventually, when it's clear he's not going to move on, I speak. "Merendsen?"

He blinks, looking across at me like he had no idea I was there at all, then shakes his head. "I've seen this before," he murmurs, turning his gaze back out to the ruined city.

"This . . . here?" With a whisper involved, a vision doesn't seem out of the question.

He shakes his head again. "A dead ship," he says softly. "I never thought I'd see something like the wreck of the *Icarus* again. And here I am, heading into its heart once more." His mouth forms a dark hint of a smile. "You watched my interrogation footage. But I lied about what happened at the wreck."

"What really happened?"

His smile curves a few degrees further. "Lilac saved my life is what happened. And we found a path that led us out. The wreck of the *Icarus* was our turning point." Then he's moving again, carefully sliding down the slope made out of a crazily leaning wall. I slither after him, landing with a grunt.

He speaks again when we hit the bottom and find level ground. "Lilac never let herself feel for anyone again, after Simon. Not until Elysium. Not until she thought her father would never know. A part of her died when Simon did, Gideon. You should know that." The words are a gift—the only sort of thank-you he can offer me right now. I understand that.

"I do," I say, and I know now that it's true. That I should have known it all along—Simon was a dreamer, but he was never a fool. He wouldn't have given his heart to someone who could say farewell to him without a backward glance. It took me until I was fourteen to find a way into the military databases and find out exactly how he died.

It was a friendly-fire incident—another terrified recruit, jumping at shadows, who turned his gun on Simon by mistake. He turned it on himself just a few weeks later.

But every time I've thought of Simon dying alone on the battlefield, every time I've thought of his fear and confusion, all that blame belonged squarely at the feet of Monsieur LaRoux. Never Lilac.

"She told me about him." Merendsen's voice is quiet. "If she'd known you still needed her support, I know—"

"I know that too." We pause, navigating our way around a crack in the road, jumping across a gap that offers a view clear down to the levels below, where fires rage, sending up black smoke. "There was nothing she could do. After Simon died, my parents split. My father couldn't take what LaRoux did to us. My mother swallowed it, because she was a businesswoman, and making an enemy of Monsieur LaRoux simply wasn't something she could do, not without the sort of revenge that would ruin her. So they went their separate ways."

"What about you?" The glance Tarver shoots me might have belonged to Simon—quiet, measuring me up.

"I took off. I couldn't deal with my father's grief, I couldn't watch my mother's betrayal. I was down in the slums by the time I was twelve."

"And that's where you learned hacking?"

"That's where I learned the dirty tricks. I already knew a lot of it. Simon taught me."

"He taught her, too. The skill with electronics she learned from him saved her life—both our lives."

We're silent as we make our way along the edge of an open section of road, both watchful, but for a time, it's as if my brother's the third member of our party, walking silently beside us. It shouldn't be easier to think about him than about Sofia. I don't want to imagine her face when she realizes we're gone. I owe her nothing, after the way she lied to me. But as I walk through my burning city beside a man who'll risk the entire human race to save the girl he loves, I know that 'should' means nothing, when it comes to my heart. I hope she turns and runs—I hope she finds a place to hide from what's coming. Somehow, I know she won't.

I'm torn from my thoughts when Tarver grabs my arm, yanking me back into a ruined storefront. I follow his gesture, sinking to a crouch behind the remains of the wall, and immediately I register the reason for his urgency. The low rumble of a heavy vehicle is making its way up the street behind us, and with the city as it is, there's no reason to assume the folks we'll meet will be friendly. Tarver finds a metal rod and hefts it in both hands silently, and I pick up a chunk of concrete from the pile of rubble at my feet.

The engine turns out to belong to a delivery truck, with a woman behind the wheel, and four guys sitting on the open flatbed. It's on sturdy hover cushions, suspended a couple of feet above the ground, where it'll miss most of the debris. All five of them have the eerie, black-eyed stillness of husks. Their heads turn in slow, constant arcs as they scan their surroundings. Judging by their clothing, I'd say they're the warehouse workers and office staff of the firm whose logo is on the doors of the cabin. "This is not good news," I murmur, watching them as they slowly cruise past. "If they can drive, they can cover ground far more quickly than we can."

"That's not the worst of it," Tarver replies in a low voice, and I turn my head to follow his gaze. A slow procession of husks is rounding the corner. There are dozens—no, hundreds—of others, some on foot, others in cars, moving toward the heart of the crash site. All of them with that fluid, unnatural gait. All of them with empty faces and black eyes. There must be a thousand of them between us and Lilac.

Oh, hell, Sofia. This is bad.

And it is. The possessed are everywhere. We scale the ruins of buildings, we climb through the rubble and run across the dangerous, open spaces of the streets. Our hands bleed from grabbing at broken edges, our eyes sting from the dust, and our throats burn from the smoke we can't help but inhale as we work. The sounds the city makes as the ruins settle help to mask the sound of Lilac's black-eyed, loose-limbed army. There are thousands of them now, and every route we try is blocked.

Tarver is single-minded and unflinching. As dusk begins to fall, I'm afraid of what he might do if we can't find a way through soon. Eventually, when we stumble across a burst water pipe, I convince him to halt for a few minutes, and we crouch by it in the shadows, drinking from our cupped hands.

He's the one to break our silence, gazing out at the ruins beyond our temporary shelter. "The whispers saved her, on Elysium. They did it willingly, gave her the last of their energy. Enough to make her real, permanent."

"That's an incredible gift." I don't know what else to say.

"The ultimate gift," he agrees, gazing down at his cupped hands, letting the water trickle slowly through his fingers. "In the instant it happened, Lilac said that she was a part of them, for the briefest moment. That they could see her, all of her . . . all the good, all the bad, and that they felt she was worth saving. This creature is the same species. How could it do such a thing? How could it harbor such hate?"

"Humans are all one species," I reply. "But we're all different. Perhaps, under harsh enough circumstances, any of us might be driven to do the unimaginable."

And there she is—Sofia—appearing in my mind's eye right on cue, that plas-pistol in her hand. *Under the right circumstances, any of us might be driven. . . . I'm beginning to understand, Dimples. Pity I'm probably not going to live to tell you so.*

Tarver pushes to his feet. "We should get moving."

I rise beside him, my knees and back screaming in protest. "This isn't working. They're multiplying by the hour—they're going to spot us again, and we won't make it out if they chase us."

Tarver's face is grim. "Then we fight."

I can't help it—I stare at him, trying to tell if he's making some wildly inappropriate joke. "There are thousands of them. The best fighter in the world wouldn't last five minutes, and we don't even have real weapons. We need another way through."

"You have an idea?" His voice is rough, his face filthy, but his eyes are burning when he looks across at me.

"We have to go down. Use one of these fissures, one of the old elevator shafts maybe. Get into the undercity, use the cover of the slums and hide in plain sight among the people there. Down there, I can get my hands on more equipment. There's only so much I can do in my head, and I *have* to have the calculations finished for this program before we get there."

"We'll waste time," he snaps, and I can see it in every line of his body—he wants to walk straight through the silent armies between us and Lilac, his desperation to get to her driving everything else from his mind.

"You want to get there, or die trying?" I snap my reply, and that gets his attention. "Because if we stay up here, that's what's going to happen. We have to go down. We can get close, that way, and hole up until she's not expecting us anymore. We'll be ready to climb up into the middle of LaRoux Headquarters by first light. This is what helps Lilac—this is what gives us a chance to reach her. Fighting our way through is impossible. It can't be done."

He's strung taut, hands laced together behind his head as he gazes out over the ruins, knuckles white with the force of his grip. Then he curses, dropping abruptly into a crouch, arms curling around his head. As though he's trying to physically hold himself together for her.

I dig deep, make my voice hard. "Time's wasting. Let's go."

The others are so focused on the tasks our keeper sets us that they do not sense the rage building on its own, deep in the swamps. They are so focused on the place filled with soldiers that they do not see the madness simmering underneath the shield of rock and mud that conceals the green-eyed boy's home.

I can see what this madman will do, and it will shatter the green-eyed boy's heart. I have so little strength that I cannot stop the madman or touch anyone near him. My only hope is to reach out to the girl whose dreams I have shared, whose mind is as familiar to me as anything in this world. She will stop this horror—she must.

It is not until I am watching through her eyes as she stumbles upon the bloody massacre that I understand I am too late. It is her own horror that drives me from her mind once more—the last thing I see through her eyes is the face of the green-eyed boy, full of shock and betrayal and a grief so deep that the pain in the girl's heart is a torture more painful than any our keeper could have inflicted upon me.

Forgive me.

THIRTY-THREE

SOFIA

THE UNDERCITY IS IN CHAOS. WITHOUT ELECTRICITY EVERY—thing is in shadow, a false midnight blanketing the slums. There are no smells from street food vendors, no music from performers in the distance. The lanterns are dark, strings of them fallen into the streets and crushed underfoot.

But here, the horror of what's happened to Corinth is all too real.

Everything is coated in a fine layer of debris the size of sand grains, a mix of ash and fragments of cement that crunches underfoot. People have armed themselves against looters with whatever they can find—we pass a young woman gripping a chunk of cement in her hands who watches us with frightened eyes until we turn the corner.

I try to imagine myself as she sees me—a threat, capable of robbing her of her home, or her life.

You're leading others to Lilac, knowing they're going to kill her. Doesn't that make you exactly what she sees?

I shove that voice away, telling myself that it's because some other idea will come to us, some way around what's looming ahead, some alternative. Sanjana's final warning was crystal clear.

We have one shot to stop this.

I'm still shaking from the climb down, bile and adrenaline bitter in my mouth. The elevators to the undercity don't work without electricity, forcing us to descend via a ladder in the elevator's maintenance shaft. Many, many times higher than the elevator shaft I climbed with

Gideon—and without him next to me, without his harness supporting me. And then I was climbing up, out of danger.

He was right to say that climbing down is much, much worse.

I clear my throat, trying to banish my fears. It ought to be ridiculous that climbing down a ladder still frightened me when only a few kilometers away, an interdimensional being is slowly and methodically destroying the world—but reason plays no part in fear. Maybe it's just that this is a fear I recognize, a fear I can digest. The other thing—I can't wrap my mind around it.

It takes hours to cover ground that would take no time at all in the clearer streets above—or would have, before the crash. Jubilee finds a working radio after spotting someone in military gear—turns out he's not a soldier, but once Jubilee makes it clear she's not going to arrest him for theft of government property, he lets her send a distress call to Mori to come pick up Sanjana. Mori's voice crackles and surges, her worry audible, but she promises to find the scientist. It's clear, even through the distortion, that she'd rather be with us, heading into danger.

Jubilee gives the guy with the radio less choice about handing over the Gleidel he'd stolen, and even though it's only one weapon between the three of us, it's something.

Closer to the crash site, most of the upper- and middle-city levels have been destroyed, but underneath, sections of the undercity are almost completely intact. Ahead, a shaft of light illuminates the spot where an upper-city skyscraper has fallen, and chunks have broken through the supports meant to separate the layers of construction. As we draw nearer, I can see up into the ruined city above—it's only a block away from my old penthouse.

It feels like years ago that I was sitting on the couch, patching up Gideon's arm and ordering drinks from the SmartWaiter.

"You're sure this is going to work?" Jubilee speaks without looking at me, her gaze too busy scanning our surroundings. I can understand why she's nervous—there are too many people, too many bodies crowding here and there, to track everyone. We look too competent, I'm sure, to be an easy-looking target for opportunistic thugs taking advantage of the chaos, but that doesn't mean some desperate gang won't still attack.

And that's assuming—hoping, really—that the whisper's reach doesn't extend down here, and that there aren't any of Lilac's mind-controlled husks roaming the slums. We've got the shield Gideon left us, shoved deep in my inside pocket, and we left the other with Sanjana, but it's the same below as it was above—if they see us, she won't need mind control to hurt us.

"When I was trying to find a way inside LaRoux Industries," I say, ill-fitting boots crunching on the layer of fine dust littering the pavement, "I must've mapped every physical entry point to the compound a dozen times over."

"And you can reach LRI Headquarters from the slums?" Jubilee's tone is dubious at best.

"You can get anywhere from the slums," I answer. "If you know how."

"Better trust her," Flynn notes, sounding amused. "Sof can get inside anywhere."

Jubilee hesitates—after all, we don't have time to try another route if mine doesn't work—but only for a split second before nodding and picking up the pace. "It'll be total chaos as the day goes on," she warns, as though the disorder now is only inconvenient. "It'll be like it was on Verona when the rebellion broke out." She couldn't have been more than eight or nine, but she sounds as though she's speaking about something that happened only yesterday. Her mouth is set tight, her hand resting on the new gun at her hip. "Stay close."

My eyes keep picking out familiar features—a man of just the right height, or a flash of sandy-colored hair, or a flash of indigo fabric that matches his backpack—but it's never Gideon I'm seeing, only fragments of memory. If he and Tarver have run into the husks above by now, then it's possible they're somewhere down here too, trying to bypass Lilac's army the same way we are.

But I can barely keep Jubilee and Flynn within line of sight with the jostling and milling of the frightened crowds—Gideon and Tarver could walk by ten meters away and we'd never see them.

Abruptly a hand closes on my arm and jerks me back, my lips forming a half scream before I can stop it. I'm whirled around to see a middle-aged woman with a curtain of dried blood down one side of her face—her pupils are dilated, and for a moment I'm certain it's one of Lilac's husks. But the woman's eyes search my face vaguely, and I realize: she has a concussion. She must've been struck by a piece of debris.

"Mandy?" she's asking. "Mandy, is that you?"

"N-n-no," I stammer, my mouth dry and heart pounding. I cast a frantic look around, but Flynn and Jubilee have vanished in the press of the crowd. "Sorry, I don't—"

"Mandy?" the woman asks again, drawing me closer; her fingers tighten painfully when I try to pull my arm away.

Then Jubilee appears again, elbowing her way back through the crowd. No sign of Flynn. "Let her go," she orders, voice quick and sharp, hand on her gun.

"It's fine," I gasp, prying at the woman's fingers. "She's confused. Not dangerous."

"I'm just trying to find my daughter," the woman moans, before her hand slides away from my arm.

Jubilee pulls me away, dodging the crowds. "Too many people," she says in my ear, over the noise of voices and sirens and destruction. "We've got to find some place to hole up until night, when it's safer to move. We'll get trampled if we don't."

I glance over my shoulder and see, for a brief, frozen second, the woman standing still where we left her, hands clasped, confused gaze sweeping back and forth; then the crowd swells, and closes around her, and she's gone.

We barricade ourselves inside what had been a restaurant before looters got to it. There's no food left, and most of the chairs and tables are gone, or in pieces. The front part of it was little more than a stall, but farther back the door is still sound, and the kitchen's one of those hole-in-the-wall places with a metal security gate. It'll hold for now, especially since there's nothing left inside worth stealing.

Flynn and Jubilee are efficient, working together like they were born to it, moving tables and chairs toward the door, searching for other exits—one leads to the back alley but has a deadbolt strong enough to suit them. It isn't until the work is mostly done that I see Jubilee's hands are shaking where she's dragging furniture, and that her face looks ashen despite her darker skin. It's Flynn who finally puts a hand on her arm, saying something in her ear that makes her nod and take a breath. "We'll have to stay until nightfall," she says quietly. "It's chaos out there."

We settle in to wait in silence, taking cover behind the counter and trying to get some rest. They've gotten new flashlights from an abandoned stall, and set them up like lanterns in the shelter of the countertop so we won't have to wait in the dark. We find another gun under there, jammed in where its former owner could pull it out in case of a holdup. I wonder what happened, that they didn't have time to bring it with them when they fled. It's probably a certifiable antique, but since Sanjana's EMP fried our cutting-edge weapons, this antique is looking pretty good.

As we wait for the noise outside to ebb, and I try to force down a handful of crackers and peanut butter from our supplies, my mind drifts back to Gideon and Tarver. Somewhere above us, they're surrounded by husks. "Do you think Lilac's aware of it, in there? Do you think she knows what it's doing?" I hear myself ask.

"She could be." Jubilee's voice is quiet. "I grew up on Verona and had quite a few encounters with the whispers there, though I was just a child. I met the same one again on Avon."

I drop the handful of crackers, crumbs scattering across the floor. "You *talked* to one of them? The whispers?"

Jubilee's lips twitch as she glances at Flynn. "In a manner of speaking, yes." She sees my expression and raises her eyebrows. "They're not all bad. What LaRoux's done to them—he's been torturing them. Turning them into weapons."

My throat feels tight, forcing me to swallow before I can speak. "The right kind of pressure can turn anyone into a monster." *The sound of the gun going off. Lilac falling. Tarver's face as he looks at me.* "Anyone."

Jubilee's eyes swing toward me, and though I could be imagining it, for a moment I think I almost see sympathy in her face. She nods. "The one I spoke to . . . it hadn't given into that rage. It was—it was my friend." Her voice grows rougher, and she's forced to clear her throat after she finishes.

"On the *Daedalus*, the whisper said it wasn't just the last one left—it was also the oldest one. The first one he started experimenting with."

Flynn's voice is quiet. "He's had a long time to twist that creature into something evil."

"But they're not human," I protest, mind spinning. "Sanjana said they were entities of pure energy. Concepts like vengeance and pain and hatred . . . For all we know, they don't even feel emotion."

"They do." Jubilee's quick to contradict me. "They may not have started out understanding emotion, but the one I knew . . . it did. It felt everything. It died to save us from the other whispers on Avon."

"That doesn't help us now." I let my head fall back against a shelf with a thump. "Lilac is the only whisper left on this side of the rift, so we're on our own. We don't have others of its kind willing to help us. And if Lilac is still in there somewhere, it doesn't seem like there's anything she can do."

We all fall silent after that, and I only wish I could silence the one thought circling around and around in my head. *Gideon's still up there.*

And if he's still alive, he's getting closer and closer to the whisper.

It's only when I lift my head, blinking away sleep, that I realize I somehow managed to doze. Jubilee's asleep, or at least pretending to be, her head in Flynn's lap. He's gazing down at her, and his hand keeps making the same small gesture, fingertips stroking the hair at Jubilee's temple. I swallow and he lifts his head, blinking once and then looking at me. His lips twitch a little into a faint smile. But there's something in the back of his gaze that tips me off.

"Is she okay?" I whisper, glancing at Jubilee, who doesn't move.

Flynn nods, eyes following mine and lingering on the girl asleep in his lap. "She's tough."

I find my own lips twitching. "That's not what I asked."

Flynn looks back up at me, exhaling a faint laugh. "Forgot who I was talking to." He leans his head back against the shelves behind him. "This is bringing back bad memories."

"Verona?"

He nods again. "She grew up there. Her parents were killed during the riots following the bombing attacks. Shot in front of her."

My heart flinches, squeezing tight and twisting. "I had no idea."

"Me neither, until—well, might as well call a spade a spade. Until I kidnapped her from the military base."

"Someday you're going to have to tell me the whole story of what exactly happened between that and . . . well, this." I nod my head in their direction, something in my head still objecting on an instinctive level to the sight of my friend Flynn, leader of the Fianna, with his arms around a trodaire. If Gideon and Tarver fail—if the whisper ends up with the power to cut us off from hyperspace completely—we'll be trapped together here on Corinth. Being an Avonite won't mean anything anymore.

Flynn huffs another laugh, dropping his voice again when Jubilee stirs. "Got a few days?" He sobers, watching me. "Thank you, by the way. For what you did on the shuttle back on Avon, when Jubilee and I were on the run—thank you for distracting the soldiers so she and I could get away. I know you had no reason to trust her."

"I trusted *you*," I reply instantly—then halt, thoughts grinding together. Because I did trust him, completely. How could it have happened that in a single year I forgot how to do that? Why should I trust Gideon any less than Flynn?

Because he lied to you.

Well, I lied to him. What else you got?

"Are *you* okay?"

I open my eyes to find Flynn watching me, concern all over his expressive features. I start to reply, halting with my lips parted, voice sticking in my throat. "I'm tough, too," I say finally.

One corner of Flynn's mouth lifts. "That's not what I asked."

I shut my eyes, wishing I could shut my ears as well. Despite my conversation with Tarver, every part of me is screaming that this is still somehow my fault. It was one thing to be at peace with the idea of becoming a murderer, of killing an evil man responsible for the deaths of hundreds, if not thousands, of people. It's another to be at peace with causing the end of the world.

"He'll be okay." His voice is quiet.

"Is that even what I'm supposed to hope for?" I whisper. With my eyes closed, I can hear sounds still echoing in from outside, though the crowd has thinned out to almost nothing.

"Of course it is," Flynn replies. "Look, I haven't seen Merendsen in action, but I've seen Jubilee. She swears he taught her what she knows, and is even better than she is. And while I find that difficult to believe, it does suggest that he knows what he's doing. Gideon's as safe with him as he'd be here."

I shake my head, as much to dismiss the concern as to try to shrug off the burning in my eyes. "Gideon made his choice."

"As you made yours, up on the *Daedalus*." I open my eyes to find Flynn gazing down at Jubilee as she sleeps. "Funny thing, how we let our choices define us."

As much as I love Flynn, a philosophical discussion is the last thing I want right now. I grind the heels of my hands against my eyes, trying to clear them and marshal my thoughts, and remain silent.

He doesn't seem to notice. "Back on Avon, it seemed like every choice I made turned me into more and more of a traitor. Sometimes I thought I was doing what was best for the Fianna—sometimes it felt like I was lying to myself, and it was all for her."

"And now?" I eye him sidelong, watching his profile as his head dips.

"I was trusting my heart." Flynn meets that sidelong look for a moment, then exhales in a sigh. "Doesn't mean your heart can't be conflicted. But at least for me, and for Jubilee, and for Avon—it turned out I was right to trust it."

I echo that sigh of his, mine sounding more like a huff of laughter. "Follow your heart? Seriously? That's your advice? I'm pretty sure I read that in a fortune cookie once."

Flynn grins at me. "Where do you think I got it?" But then his grin softens and he gives his head a little shake. "It's simple advice. But probably the hardest to follow. It's always easier to do the expected thing than the right thing."

"If you're trying to thank me for attempting an assassination, you're doing it in a roundabout way."

"You think shooting at LaRoux was the right thing?" Flynn raises an eyebrow. "The thing your heart was telling you to do?"

I want Gideon to know that the only reason I didn't tell him about my plan was because I knew he would try to talk me out of it. And I knew he'd succeed.

My jaw tightens. It doesn't matter. Gideon's gone. I let my gaze skitter away from Flynn's, seeking out something, anything, that isn't his look of empathy, of concern, of caring. The floor is strewn with garbage and broken bits of glass, and cards with the restaurant logo printed on them. My heart gives a sudden lurch as I reach out to pick one up—MRS. PHAN'S, it reads, next to the scan code to pull up the menu.

We've holed up in the restaurant where Gideon went to grab us dinner the night we spent in the arcade. The night before I found out he was the Knave. The night we— My breath chokes itself in my throat, sparking tears in my eyes as I try to keep from coughing.

"Sof?" Flynn's voice is alarmed. Jubilee stirs, mumbling something that sounds like a question—half-asleep, she reaches for her hip, where her gun is.

"No—I'm fine." I shove the card into my pocket.

"I wasn't trying to upset you, Sof." He fixes me with a searching look for a moment, and then Jubilee shifts in his lap, and he's distracted.

"I'm fine. I . . . I'd really like to get some air, if that's okay. It sounds quiet out there."

Flynn rubs his hand up and down Jubilee's arm, and she settles back again. "Are you sure? It's not exactly safe out there."

"Come on. It's me." I flash him my old smile, still easy to locate, despite everything. "I can take care of myself."

Flynn's still hesitant, craning his head back as though he'd be able to see whether the streets are clear.

"If the world's ending tomorrow," I add, voice dry, "I'd like to get to stretch my legs one last time."

"Give her your gun," mumbles Jubilee, without opening her eyes. "'S quiet out there now."

Flynn's mouth twitches, and he looks back up at me as he reaches for the pistol he set aside. "You heard her."

I make sure the gun's safety is on before I tuck it into the back of my pants, set the whisper shield down quietly so Flynn won't notice, and argue, and get unsteadily to my feet. There are so many people down here that there's no reason for the whisper to pick me out of the teeming crowds of refugees, and I desperately need a moment alone to breathe. Grabbing one of the flashlights, I slip toward the back exit and glance over my shoulder to catch a glimpse of Jubilee sitting up sleepily and laying her hand against Flynn's cheek. He's leaning toward her, but the door closes between us before his lips touch hers.

I shiver, though it's not just from the chill. It is colder, though—all the machinery and cars and people and vendors and life that heat up the undercity are silent now, and without the sun above, the temperature is falling in a way it never could normally. If this is the place Gideon went to get us food, then it's not far from the arcade. And without making any conscious decision, I find that's where my steps are leading me.

It takes me a few minutes to get my bearings, searching my memory banks for the landmarks I saw at the mouth of the alley. Without the lanterns overhead, and only my flashlight to guide my steps, it all looks different. But eventually I find the faux-brick façade I remember, and find the loose one Gideon used to open the crack in the wall to slip through.

The space beyond is dark, but the sound of my footsteps changes, echoes speaking of the vastness of the hidden arcade behind the wall. In my memory, I hear the sound of a switch flipping, see the neon lights snapping into existence one by one, their milky reflections sweeping across the dusty marble floor. I can hear the Butterfly Waltz, and taste Gideon's kiss.

I swing the flashlight around, my hand shaking—and my heart sinks.

Half the storefronts here are gone, piles of brick and stone and broken glass in their place. The few neon signs still visible are smashed to pieces—even if there were electricity, none of them would be shining now. I let the flashlight's beam fall, my gaze following. The marble floor's been shattered, the dust disturbed by showers of debris from high above that must've been dislodged when the *Daedalus* hit a few blocks away. I can't even see where our footprints had been, the patterns we made while I taught him to dance.

I step back and scan the flashlight along the wall until I see the tangle of blankets where we slept. It's all still there, as though Gideon left in a hurry after I ran from this place. The footprints are long gone, but I can still see the shape of us in the blankets, two bodies curled against each other, like interlocking commas—like yin and yang pendants. The cheap plastic kind that always break.

"Hey, Dimples."

The voice shatters the silence and sends me stumbling backward with a gasp, flashlight swinging wildly until I can see who's there—even though I already know, even though part of me isn't even surprised. The night before battle, the calm before the storm—where else would we come, but the last safe place we knew?

Gideon's got his hands in his pockets, leaning against the doorframe, head down so that when the flashlight beam falls on his face, it doesn't blind him—and it also means I can't read his expression. How well he knows me. "I didn't think you'd ever come back here."

I'm still trying to catch my breath, to coax my heart back down out of my throat—adrenaline sings through my muscles, keeping them tense. "T-Tarver?"

"He's fine." Gideon glances up for a moment, blinking in the light. His eyes are bloodshot—he looks exhausted. "Well, not fine. But he's not hurt. He's asleep, or at least resting, few blocks from here. Everyone else?"

"Same." I can breathe again, but my heart's still thumping, its pounding in my ears keeping time to the distant wail of a siren "Are you hurt?"

"Just tired." I can hear it in his voice—the exhaustion, that he's hanging on by his fingertips. He tries to hide it, but the glimpse I catch is enough to make me want to throw down my flashlight and go to his side.

Instead I tighten my grip on it and fix my eyes on the wall beside him. I can't sit here and make small talk with him like everything's fine, like we're meeting for coffee somewhere and chatting about our days. "The reprogramming of the rift, can you do it?"

"I'm close," he replies. "I'll get there. The code is beautiful, so complex. I've never seen anything like it. If you separate it out from its purpose, just look at what they've made, it's . . . it's art."

"But you *can't* separate it out," I point out, my voice hard in my ears. "It's not just art, Gideon, it's not some puzzle you have to solve to prove the Knave's the best at what he does."

"I know."

And his voice is so small, so tired, that I relent—or perhaps it's just that if we fight about this, I'll shatter into a thousand pieces. "Gideon, why are you here?"

"It's good to be somewhere familiar, even if it's just for a few minutes."

His answer is so low, I barely catch it. "Somewhere with a good memory attached to it, something I *want* to think about. I needed it, tonight. Isn't that why you're here?"

Tonight. Quite possibly our last night in the universe as we know it, is what he means. Quite *probably* our last night. I fight to ignore my thumping heartbeat, try to harden my thoughts again. We're not on the same side. If he does this, he risks losing himself to madness, and he risks cutting us off from hyperspace forever—and I'm not sure which one scares me more. I can't answer, not with my throat this tight. And even if I could, I'm not sure I could listen to myself speak the truth: *I needed it too.*

The silence stretches for a few seconds, and then Gideon's hands come out of his pockets and he pushes away from the wall. "Sofia—" he starts, taking a step toward me.

I'm moving before I have time to think, dropping the flashlight and reaching for the gun tucked into my waistband. He stops moving when he sees it; the flashlight's beam comes to rest against the wall, reflecting just enough light that I can see his face. The confusion there, as he halts a few steps away from me.

"Stop." My voice is a lot stronger than I thought it would be. "You made your choice. You're with Tarver. I'm with the others. We want different things." *Don't come near me, because I don't know how much of this I can stand.*

"Except we don't," replies Gideon softly, watching me rather than the gun, whose safety is still on. I can't even point it at him, not really. The barrel hovers somewhere in between, not quite lowering, not quite lifting to aim at him. "You don't want Lilac dead any more than we want the universe destroyed."

"You don't hear how that sounds?" I burst out, shifting my grip on the gun. "One life versus the entire universe? Tarver I understand, he's—of course he's choosing her. But you . . . Why are you with him? Why did you leave, why not talk to me?"

Gideon's silent for a few seconds, making me wish I hadn't dropped the flashlight, making it harder to see his face. "Why didn't you talk to me before you tried to assassinate Roderick LaRoux?"

The blow of that is a dull ache, his words just one more burden settling on top of the grief and guilt already making my knees buckle. I shift my weight, boot scraping whisper-like against the dusty floor. "Just go," I manage. "I should make you come back with me, should make you take us to Tarver so we can stop him. But just—just go."

Gideon's weight shifts too, but he stops himself before taking another step toward me. "It's because I have faith," he says slowly. "In Tarver, in Lilac. In the fact that my brother loved her, because she was—is—worth it, worth dying for." He swallows. "I told you already. It's because if you were the one in there instead of her, there isn't a force in the universe that would stop me going after you."

I shake my head, throat too tight for me to speak. My face is heating, flushing with anger, with frustration, with all the things I told myself I'd say to Gideon if I could—and he's standing here in front of me, and I still can't say a word of it.

"It's because there has to be a way for this to work," he continues, his eyes scanning my face. "Because it's impossible, any way you look at it, and I refuse to accept that this is how it ends."

I take a shuddering breath, the barrel of the gun still wavering between us. "Are you still talking about Lilac?"

His mouth curves, the smile so sad it feels like my whole body's ripping in two. "You're the expert," he murmurs. "You tell me."

"We can't trust each other," I whisper. "You can't love someone you don't trust. You'll never know if I'm playing you, and I'll never know if you're still the Knave, toying with me."

"And that's why I'm here," Gideon snaps, shoving a hand through his hair in frustration. "I wanted to come back to a place before you and I learned the truth about each other. Odds are we'll all be dead, or worse, tomorrow. We'll never know if we could've learned to trust each other."

"Whether you could've loved the real me." My eyes burn, the weight of everything I wanted to say to him pressing in on my throat, making it impossible to speak.

"You think I don't know the real you?" Gideon's eyes widen, and there's pain there. I didn't expect that.

In the dim light, he looks so tired; so changed, in his pilfered military gear, so different from the cocky guy in an LRI shirt who winked at me across the holosuite. I can see his breath stirring the dust in the air, making it dance in the beam from the flashlight. It quickens as I watch him, until I can almost hear a waltz, each particle of dust twirling to the ghost of that old song.

"The hell with it," I blurt, the gun clattering to the floor from fingers no longer obeying my commands. "I don't care." I move forward, closing the distance between us and reaching for him. My fingers curl around the edges of his jacket, tug him in close—he's already moving, ducking his head, lips parting to meet mine. One hand slides around my waist, pulling me in against him, as the other tangles in my hair, his palm hot against my cheek.

We stumble backward until my shoulder blades hit the wall. Someone's foot connects with the flashlight, sending it and its beam skittering wildly off into the dark. My hands are shaking as they peel his jacket away, as my fingertips curl against his shoulders, as the muscle beneath his T-shirt shifts and tenses in response to my touch. His mouth finds my jawline, my throat, the hollow behind my ear; the air goes out of me in a gasp.

"Sofia," he mumbles against my skin, hips pressing against mine, arm tightening around my waist. "I always knew you."

All the things I wanted to say . . . I'm sorry. I should've told you. I wanted to tell you. I don't care about the Knave. The thoughts come in fragments, too confused to speak aloud, too difficult and too numerous to track. *I let you down. I let you hurt me. I'd take all of it back, and I'd do it all again.*

"God help me," I breathe, the words falling out of me like dust and debris, crashing in my own ears and bringing the world to a grinding halt. All I can hear is Gideon breathing, his skin hot against my skin, his body hard against mine. I struggle to breathe, the air rushing into my lungs like it's trying to drown me. "I do trust you."

I have never seen her face, the girl with the beautiful dreams, only the inside of her mind. But now, through the eyes of the boy who loves her, I can see she is beautiful. I can feel the others trying to push past me, to seek more destruction, for destruction is all they know. But I cannot stop looking at her. I wish that I could look at her forever.

She lets me take her hand, our fingers interlocking the way she and the green-eyed boy have let their hearts interlock—separate but inseparable. In this moment I find I envy them their individuality, their uniqueness, the beauty of being able to touch like this. In this moment I envy the green-eyed boy that he will always be able to touch her like this.

In this moment I decide that they must live, that they must show the others all there is to learn from humankind.

"Jubilee Chase," I whisper through the green-eyed boy's lips, "I wish . . ."

THIRTY-FOUR

GIDEON

ALL I CAN FEEL IS HER BODY AGAINST MINE, THE HEAT OF HER skin through the fabric of her shirt, the catch of her breath hot against my neck.

All I can hear are her words echoing around the silence of the abandoned arcade. *Whether you could have loved the real me. I do trust you.*

The two of us are the only spots of warmth in this world of darkness, and I want more than anything to have the words to make her see the truth. That though she's played me almost every moment I've known her, I *do* know her.

My heart's been pounding since the moment she walked into the arcade, and I want to abandon myself to her—to this—even though I know that loving her and trusting her are two different things.

I can't trust her.

And yet I do.

Oh, hell.

My arms tighten around her of their own accord, and she surges in against me, lips parting as we lose ourselves in each other, try desperately to close the distance between us we both wish wasn't there. My jacket hits the floor with a thud, pockets full of gear rattling, and with a kick I send it off into the dark. Her hands slide up inside my T-shirt, finding skin, and my brain starts to shut down higher function so I can concentrate on getting her shirt off without breaking the kiss for more than a couple of seconds.

But one thought persists, ricocheting around inside my skull, demanding to be heard.

Did she mean what she said?

I trusted her on the *Daedalus*, and she was playing me every second. She kissed me then, and when I held her, I thought she was sincere in the promise she made to abandon revenge. I couldn't bear it if she was just taking her best, last chance to soften me up, change my mind.

Perhaps she needs to make peace, the night before it all comes undone. Perhaps she needs to speak her truth. Perhaps it *is* truth.

"Sofia, I have to—" I murmur the words against the skin of her shoulder, half my mind busy mentally mapping the distance to our old nest of blankets.

"Hmm?" She's distracted, that one syllable dragging out into a moan I want to hear again. Then she's dragging my shirt off and planting both hands against my chest so she can push away from the wall, walk me back toward the nest. *Great minds, Dimples.*

"Never mind," I whisper. She feels so *right* in my arms, she fits, and yet some small part of me still can't tell if all she wants to do is pull me away from Tarver's side, make sure Lilac dies like Sanjana says she must. I know it would hurt her to manipulate me like that, but for stakes as high as these . . . could I blame her?

"Say it, whatever it is," she murmurs, as my back hits the wall by our nest, and she comes to rest flush against me.

"I have to do it." I whisper the words, even as some small version of myself howls in the back of my brain to *shut up*. "I won't leave Tarver to face her alone."

"I know," she whispers in reply, and when I bow my head, she presses her forehead to mine. "After everything that was done to the whisper, maybe that's what drove it so mad in the end. Being alone."

The wistful sadness in her voice calls up an answering pang deep in my own chest. We both know what it is to be alone. I reach up to smooth back her hair, careful to keep my fingers from catching in the snarls the last few days have left there. "They're not inherently evil. If they were, Lilac wouldn't be here at all. She'd still be dead on that planet they crashed on."

"I know," she replies, turning her face away so she can rest her head on my shoulder. "Jubilee knew one of them as a child, the same one that helped her and Flynn on Avon. We turned this one into the monster that's taken over Lilac."

"*LaRoux* did this to it." Just as LaRoux hurt Sofia, twisted the girl in my arms into someone capable of murder. Just as he twisted me into someone who could justify hunting her, terrifying her. The thought sits right there before me—which species is more dangerous, truly?

My mind throws up the passing thought I had at Mae's . . . just a few days ago, though it feels like a lifetime. Now, I voice it out loud. "I wondered once if the whispers could see all our data, everything we send through the hypernet. And what they think of it, if they can. What they think of us."

"Our data," she echoes. "You mean . . ."

"Everything we send. From our parking tickets, to our poetry."

"If I could see all of that," she says quietly, into the dark, "all our anger, the things we say to one another, I wouldn't think much of us."

I let my knees bend, and she comes with me as my back slides down the wall, and I sink to sit on our nest of blankets. We sit there together in the near dark, limbs tangled together, pressed close, as though the contact alone will save us.

"There has to be another way to stop her, Gideon," she whispers.

Here, holding her, looking at her face, her eyes, the curve of her mouth where the flashlight outlines it, I want to believe that loving her means I can trust her; that her *I trust you* meant something. Because if it was true—if she could feel that, after the ways he twisted her—then it would mean *everything*. But the uncertainty is there like the tiniest of splinters, worming its way deeper and deeper into my heart, carving a path for doubt to take hold like an infection. There's no other way, and if this is her attempt to distract me from my choice, my path with Tarver, I can't let her talk me out of it.

She leans forward, tilting her face up, and I give in and let my lips find hers rather than search for words. This much, at least, is true. This warmth, this need—whatever else has come and gone between us, and whatever else may come, this moment is true.

It would be such a leap, and in the end, neither of us is very good at remembering how to trust. At least alone, she with her plan and I with mine, there's a chance one of us might be right.

So instead of making a new plan, instead of taking our leap, we ease down into the blankets, my heart hurting every moment, to say our good-byes in the only way we both *can* trust. Without any words at all.

We feel the loss of our kin on the gray world as keenly as we felt the loss of the first of our kind to die. We try to understand death, to understand how a thing can cease to be. Learning about the uniqueness of these creatures only deepens our confusion, for how can something so rare and so precious exist one moment and vanish the next?

We have only one of our kind left in their world, the one we cannot see. But because of the boy who lives in the hypernet pathways, we know the final prison is somewhere on the world at the heart of the galaxy. We must bring the six to this place, to find our last emissary and send it home so we can learn, finally, whether we can coexist with these strange, brief creatures who live and die without letting uncertainty destroy them.

The others, their paths all lead to this spot—all but the girl with the dimpled smile. We must bring her there somehow, twist her thread closer to the rest.

We learn that the boy wrapped in wires and data is searching for someone he believes can lead him to the blue-eyed man. We will nudge him onto the girl's trail instead . . . and he will drive her here to us.

THIRTY-FIVE

SOFIA

THE DARKNESS AS I CREEP WITH JUBILEE AND FLYNN FROM the abandoned restaurant is absolute, and I'm forced to move with agonizing slowness. Unwilling to risk drawing attention with flashlights, we're picking out each step by feel, navigating the debris-littered streets of the undercity based on my memory alone. What I wouldn't give for Gideon's knowledge of this place—I was never truly at home here, but he knows these streets like the back of his hand.

I left him while he was still asleep, making my way back to the others and praying they wouldn't notice how long I'd been gone. As I lay there through the rest of the night, wishing for sleep that never came, my head was still ringing with the things we said to one another, and the things we didn't. With images of black-eyed husks, and planets plunged into isolation. Of a whisper twisted and tortured until it became a weapon—of the moment I realized the same thing had happened to me. Even now, I can't stop shivering, and it's not from the bone-deep chill settling into the streets at the bottom of Corinth.

Jubilee's hand on my arm signals a halt, and I jerk my thoughts back to the present. It's still a few hours until dawn, and the electrical grid has yet to be restored after the *Daedalus* crash. I've been figuring out where we are based on landmarks I could touch, and gut intuition when that failed, but now . . . even Jubilee and Flynn, strangers to this part of Corinth, recognize the thing looming out of the darkness.

A maintenance shaft.

The climb leaves me breathless and shaking, but I'm still on my feet when we emerge into the apocalyptic landscape of the upper city. I've spent so much of the past few days afraid that I'm not sure my body processes fear the same way anymore.

The light pollution from other sectors of Corinth paints the skies a dark, ruddy orange, and I'm able to pick out the buildings much more easily—or where the buildings had been. Nothing looks right—where there ought to be skyscrapers I see only empty space, and where there should be the broad, green expanse of a park is a massive, hulking structure I've never seen. For a moment, I'm not sure I led us the right way, until I see the expanse of the LaRoux Industries courtyard below us, the color of its bright green grass leached away by the gloom.

We're here. And that structure is no building at all.

The *Daedalus* wreck squats on the landscape like a vast, hulking beast. Its metal skin has been peeled back in long, jagged gashes, exposing wires and spilling conduits like viscera onto the ground. Twisted metal supports two meters thick have been torn free like splinters of bone, stretching toward the sky. Smoke still rises here and there, as though the creature isn't fully dead yet, as though it's still breathing its last, labored gasps that steam in the predawn air. It's half-sunk into the ground, as if the concrete and steel supports below gave it no more resistance than water would—like at any moment it might rise up again, out of the depths.

It's impossible to connect this dark, monstrous leviathan full of jagged metal and burnt chemicals with the glittering ballroom my memory conjures up when I think of the word *Daedalus*. Everything that happened there—coming face-to-face with LaRoux, discovering who Gideon was, the missing rift, seeing Flynn again, shooting Lilac LaRoux—it all feels like it happened to someone else, a lifetime ago. And the idea that any of us, that anyone at all, was ever inside this thing, the carcass of the great orbital ship, seems insane.

The idea that people are inside it still, crushed on impact or choked to death by the vacuum of space rushing inside the great rents down the ship's side . . . it's unthinkable.

We stand there in the shadow of the maintenance elevator, shrinking back against it as we stare at the immense thing sprawled before us. We've emerged at a level that once must have been a couple of floors above the courtyard, rubble stretching down from us in a steep slope. Even fearless Jubilee makes no move to descend, and when I glance back at my companions, I can see two sets of wide, glittering eyes scanning the wreck.

It's with monumental effort that I swallow, trying to clear my dry throat and break the silence that has stretched the past hour as we traveled underground to reach this place unseen. "We should keep moving."

I study the ground between us and the *Daedalus*, trying to pick out the smoothest course over the ruined terrain. The ground swims for a moment, moving before my eyes, and I try to blink away the tiredness, squeezing them shut. When I open them, it's still moving, because it's not the ground at all.

There are husks everywhere. Like insects pouring from a nest, they clamber over the broken landscape, thick between us and the gashes in the ship's side that will let us inside the *Daedalus*. My knees nearly give as a wave of nausea pushes its way up my throat—if I thought fear was losing its hold on me, I was wrong.

My mind jumps to the shield Gideon built, tucked inside Flynn's vest. It might protect us from becoming one of them, but it won't protect us from being ripped apart. Not once they see us. Did Gideon and Tarver emerge from beneath the ground in the hours since I left him, to find this same sight before them?

"How the hell are we going to do this?" Jubilee murmurs, echoing my thoughts.

"We need a diversion." Flynn's voice is heavy, as exhausted and heartsick as I feel, at the sight of this impossible task. "I could—"

"No." Her voice is a slamming door, cutting off the idea before it's born.

But the truth is, neither she nor I has a better idea, or *any* other idea. We'll be swarmed before we make it a quarter of the way to the wreck.

I watch, my throat dry, heart pounding so hard I can feel it in my temples, as a fresh wave of husks crest the top of a broken building to our left, starting the climb down the other side into the newly created valley below. They're led by a blond woman, hair caught back in a pony-tail, balancing herself with one hand as she grasps something black and rectangular in the other.

Then I look again. She's not moving properly. Or rather, she *is* moving properly, not in the loose-limbed shuffle of the husks. She's scrambling down, and others are cresting the hill behind her, sliding down through the debris on her tail.

Oh my God.

Recognition hits me in the gut, familiarity sliding into focus in one breathtaking instant.

It's Mae.

Gideon's friend is at the head of the group, and as I make a strangled, wordless sound, batting one hand against Jubilee to draw her attention, Mae lifts her hand and fires a Taser at the nearest husk. It drops like a stone.

"Who the hell is that?" Jubilee whispers, going perfectly still.

But before I can answer, a new group crests the ridge, and Flynn's gasping. "Sanjana's here!"

The scientist's dead cybernetic hand is bound across her chest in a tight sling, and she's using her good hand to fire her Taser. All around her are bedraggled figures in LaRoux Industries uniforms, merging with Mae's crowd—they're forcing back the husks, dropping them one by one.

"Damn, Flynn, that's Mori." Jubilee's animated now, and the same energy—the same hope—is surging through me. From the other side of the valley come Mori and at least twenty-five of her black-clad ex-soldiers, scrambling over the ruins to take on the husks. It's like the first ray of light shining into a darkened prison cell—the hope I thought was gone infuses me, straightening my back and lifting my head as Mori drops a black-eyed husk in the remnants of a business suit. Taser at the ready once more, she lifts her head to scan the remains of LaRoux Headquarters, eyes on the horizon.

"She's looking for us." The words burst out in the instant I realize it, and I'm scrambling forward. "They know we're here—they're clearing us a path. Let's go."

We plunge forward together, debris giving way under our feet as we half run, half fall toward the rapidly clearing courtyard below. Mori bellows a command in a voice worthy of a battleground, and the soldiers surge toward us. Up close I can see some hold palm pads in one hand, some have them strapped to their belts, and others have the square shape of them pressing through their clothes—Sanjana's taught them how to rig shields. Enough to keep their minds safe, as long as their batteries last.

"We'll hold them as long as we can, Captain," Mori calls as we hit level ground.

"How the hell did you get here?" Jubilee swallows up the distance between her and her former corporal in a few long strides.

"Dr. Rao told us where you were headed when we picked her up," Mori replies, turning to take in the fight underway further up the courtyard. She stands at the ready, Gleidel raised, and lifts her voice to shout over the laser shrieks of the guns, the guttural buzzing of the Tasers. The husks are moving more quickly now, perhaps as Lilac's whisper turns its attention to the source of the disturbance. "Rao's got a bunch of LRI's people with her—most of them are pretty damn horrified to learn what their boss has been up to." Mori pauses, catching her breath. "And the blonde up there was watching networks, trying to get a handle on where the Knave ended up. She found us, once she found him. She's got a bunch of hackers I don't think ever saw daylight before, and the Corinth Against Tyranny conspiracy crowd, and those guys are *pissed*." Mori shakes her head, but she's grinning—despite the wreckage around us, some part of her is enjoying this. "Guess they finally found somebody who really *is* out to get them."

But as Jubilee's opening her mouth to reply, a new wave of husks appear to our right and to our left, shuffling into view with a grim determination, yanking us back to reality. There must be hundreds of them. The brief hope that had taken root in my chest flickers, then dies. There's no way Mori and her crew can hold this back.

"Go, they're in there," Mori barks. "We'll buy you as much time as we can. Good hunting."

Jubilee grasps for her hand, clasping it in both of hers for an instant before Mori lets go and turns back to the fight.

From a distance, our entry point into the *Daedalus* looks like a crack only barely wide enough for someone to slip through, but the scale of this thing defies understanding—the gash in its side is wide enough for us to run through without needing to duck. We have to climb past several layers crushed into unrecognizability before we find an area clear enough to move through, as the sounds of the battle fade behind us. Then it's quiet, and we're in our own, silent world once more.

The gash opens up onto a maintenance deck, sparsely furnished. The metal grid of the floor is tilted at a steep angle, forcing us to brace our feet in the corners and cling to the window frames lining the wall as we inch our way inside.

The ship is so vast that under normal circumstances, we'd have no hope of finding Lilac and the rift inside it—but even the husks wouldn't have been able to move the massive rift far inside, over this kind of terrain. They have to be close.

My nose, half-numb from the stench of burning chemicals, pricks as we locate a staircase leading down further into the wreck and a new odor assaults me. I choke, reeling back a step and running into Flynn, who grunts and grabs onto a railing to keep from slipping.

"What is that?" I mutter, lifting the edge of my T-shirt to cover my nose.

Flynn just stares at me, equally baffled—but Jubilee shakes her head, her eyes grim. "Blood," she says shortly.

It's only then that I see a heap of dark something at the foot of the staircase above; it's only then that I see a flash of pink, and realize it's a high-heeled shoe, and that the heap is a pile of bodies. Visions of the colorful passengers dancing in the ballroom loom up in my mind's eye, and I have to clamp my lips together to keep from retching.

A hand, I don't know whose, wraps around my wrist, drawing me down the stairs and away from the bodies. I try to breathe through my mouth, and keep moving.

The staircase leads to a lush carpeted hall I do recognize from when I arrived with Gideon. The carpet muffles our footsteps, making the silence complete. The husks are mostly outside the wreck, held there by Mori, Mae, Sanjana, and their allies, but we stumble across them here and there inside. Each time we pull back, duck for cover. Lilac must know we're inside the ship somewhere, but if we can avoid a husk seeing us and reporting back, we'll still have some element of surprise. The way they're moving, in concentric, tightening circles, we're pretty sure the rift is below us somewhere. But it's not until a light blooms in the darkness, so faint I feel my eyes must be playing tricks on me, that I know our guess was right.

The light flickers, unsteady, but it shines blue against a tangle of metal protruding through the wall. In a heartbeat I'm back inside LRI Headquarters, watching the rift spring to life in front of my eyes.

"We're close," I breathe, touching the arm of the person nearest me—Flynn, it turns out—and gesturing toward the light. "This way." We can only hope our friends outside can hold off Lilac's army a little longer.

The hall leads around a corner and into what would've once been a beautiful foyer, the light growing stronger. We're forced to scramble to keep our feet on the once-polished marble floor, using the giant jagged cracks in its surface to find purchase as we make our way across to the half-collapsed archway at the opposite end. We pull ourselves up against it, and in the faint blue glow emanating from the space beyond, I pause to scan the features of my companions.

No one's thought of a way to save Lilac. Jubilee's face looks ashen, even more so in the blue light.

She doesn't meet anyone's eyes, fixing her gaze on the wall behind me, where the real wood paneling has buckled and splintered in a line running from floor to ceiling. "He'll never forgive me," she whispers, pressing the palm of her hand flat against her leg, as if willing herself to reach for her weapon, and being unable to.

Flynn shifts, boots sliding on the sharply angled floor until he can reach her side. "Maybe not," he replies, surprising me—I'd have expected one of his impassioned speeches, not this, just a few words in a soft voice. "But he'll be alive. He'll be sane. And so will the rest of humanity. You know what Lilac would want us to do."

Jubilee's eyes are wet, a realization that strikes me anew with shock. I didn't know people like her ever cried. "But it's Lilac, Flynn. How can I . . . She's my friend."

"I know." Flynn's voice is hoarse. "I wish I could tell you. . . . I don't know what the right thing is. Only that we didn't come this far alone, and you're not alone now. We do this together." He takes her hand between both of his, pulling it away from the holster and raising it to his lips.

Part of me feels like I ought to look away, let them share this moment privately, but I can't—her eyes, as they flick over to meet his, hold such trust that it makes my heart ache. With pain, with gladness that Flynn found her despite the barriers between them, with an envy so deep my vision blurs. My mind flashes with the last vision I had of Gideon, dozing in the nest of blankets in the arcade, one arm still stretched out across the space where I had lain. How is it that a trodaire and the leader of the Fianna can trust each other so completely, while Gideon and I . . . They've overcome the walls formed by a generation of hatred and violence, and I can't reach past the walls in my own heart.

The three of us stand in silence, absorbing the full weight of what we're about to do. Then, wordlessly, we slip through the ruined doors.

The archway opens up onto the ballroom. Though I was here only a few short days ago, before the *Daedalus* fell, I almost can't recognize the room—only the chandelier, lying in a heap of shattered glass and electrical wiring in the corner, sparks my memory. The shining floor is dull and shattered, caved downward, pit-like, as though sinking under the weight of the massive ring of metal nestled in its heart.

The rift itself dominates the cavernous ballroom, almost as though the machinery has grown to accommodate the room around it—blue light cascades off every twisted surface, reflected a million times over in the shards of the mirrors that once lined the far walls. The dais where Lilac and Tarver stood at Roderick LaRoux's side is smashed, scattered in pieces across the pit before us. Overhead, the vast windowed ceiling that once looked out into space is gone, leaving a jagged, empty hole that shows nothing but the dull reddish blackness of the Corinthian night sky.

The voice we'd heard continues, one long stream of syllables that only resolve into words as we draw closer, taking cover behind a fallen pillar. ". . . thought a picnic might be nice, like we used to have, like your mother used to love. Just you and me, my darling girl . . . Nothing has to change. Nothing ever has to change now."

My eyes pick out a dark silhouette to the left of the rift, and as the light from the rift rises and falls again, I make out his features: Roderick

LaRoux. He's huddled on the floor, still clad in the grimy, torn, sweat-stained eveningwear he sported the night of the gala. For a confused moment it seems as though he's speaking to the rift itself, until a second figure emerges from behind it.

Lilac, too, is still wearing what she wore the night the *Daedalus* crashed. But where her father's clothes are filthy, hers are as spotless as if she'd only just gotten ready for the gala. Her black dress falls in sleek folds, moving like silk as she passes her father without giving him a second glance. Not a hair is out of place; a single ringlet falls, styled just so, across her neck.

"Of course, Daddy," she murmurs, her voice echoing strangely, as though coming from more than one place. "After we help everyone else."

"Of course," he repeats. "Of course, of course . . . rifts . . . make everywhere safe. Never lose anyone again." His mumbling continues, subsiding once more, and over my flare of hatred and disgust comes something so surprising it steals my breath for a moment, makes me sag down against the pillar.

Pity.

There's a soft click beside me as Jubilee takes the safety off the gun. My heart's pounding, my stomach sick, and I can hear her breath shaking. I don't know Tarver or Lilac, not really. I hated them both, because they were part of LaRoux, attached to the thing I wanted to hurt most in the entire universe . . . but I hated them from a distance, the way you hate the rain or the traffic. I never really hated *them*. Not the reality of them. In the brief moments on the *Daedalus* before everything shattered, I actually found myself *liking* them; Tarver's quiet humor, Lilac's quick wit. Their devotion to each other.

But now we have to destroy them both.

"Daddy," comes Lilac's voice suddenly, cutting through the unintelligible monologue coming from the floor. "We have guests. You sneaky thing."

My heart seizes, my eyes meeting Jubilee's, then Flynn's, where we're concealed behind the column. I'm about to lift my head and look over the column and try for a distraction to give Jubilee the time she needs, when a third voice drags me to a halt.

"I wasn't trying to hide," comes a voice from the opposite side of the room. When I peek over the edge of the column, I see Tarver picking his way down into the sunken ballroom, boots sending trickles of dust and debris raining down below. Mori's words come back to me. *They're in there.* She didn't just mean Lilac and her father. Tarver's voice is low, almost conversational. "I'm not smart enough for that."

"Just a big, dumb soldier?" Lilac speaks the words like they have significance, and I can see her smile from here.

Tarver flinches, skidding to a halt in the bottom of the ruined ballroom.

My eyes scan the darkness beyond them, hope and fear sending my blood into a panic as it rushes past my ears—but I see no sign of Gideon anywhere. Maybe they've given up their plan to shut down the rift. Maybe . . . I hold my breath.

"Why are you here?" Lilac asks, turning to face him and smoothing a fold in her dress, a movement so *human*, so habitual, that it makes me shiver to see it combined with the look on her face. No human hates like that.

"You don't know?" Tarver's brows lift. "You can't just scan my thoughts, see my every plan?"

"Not with that nasty little trinket in your pocket," she replies, as if she's commenting on a fashion faux pas. "But I know you, and I don't imagine you came alone without a plan. I don't think you left *all* your friends outside." Lilac's eyes sweep the shadows, and for an instant she grimaces, but it seems she can't quite find Gideon either—or us. "They're not doing very well out there, by the way. The numbers are against them."

Tarver's jaw squares, and he visibly forces himself to relax it, pushing his shoulders back.

Lilac laughs, soft. "I can see how hard you're trying. I'm sure you think you're going to somehow 'save' me at the last minute."

"Not you," Tarver murmurs. "Lilac."

But she continues like he hasn't spoken, like she fails to acknowledge any difference between what she is now and who she was before. "It's not going to work, though—and you know why? I'll tell you the secret, if you like." She steps closer to him, halting a few steps away, just out of arm's reach.

Tarver says nothing, staring into her face. He's armed, I can see the weapon in its holster, but his hand is nowhere near it.

"You can't save me," Lilac says, leaning in as though sharing some deep, profound secret in a stage whisper, "because *I'm already dead.*"

Tarver's fingers curl at his sides, tightening into fists. The light from the rift throws his features into sharp relief, outlining in shadow the lines of muscle as he clenches his jaw. Lilac just laughs, the same, sweet, silvery laugh I recognize from HV celebrity shows and press conferences, and pats his cheek.

She turns away, and that's what makes Tarver move again. The step he takes after her is halting, jerky, but his voice is quick. "Wait. I know you're in there. Lilac, listen to me. I know you can hear me. Keep fighting— hold on."

"How sweet." Lilac doesn't seem at all perturbed, but she does halt, and I see Tarver's weight shift as she turns back toward him. He looks almost . . . *relieved.*

A tingle runs down my spine as realization dawns: Tarver's *distracting* her. Buying Gideon time, wherever he is, to attempt their plan. Which means we might have only moments to act, before they risk blowing the rift wide open and giving Lilac access to all the power she could ever need.

I glance over at the others as Flynn silently pulls the shield from his pocket, handing it to Jubilee. Her mouth twists, agonized, as she stows it inside her vest. We don't know how far its protection reaches, and if we get separated, we can't lose our crack shot. Then, at Jubilee's nod, we all creep out from behind the pillar. Tarver and Gideon's plan isn't all that different from ours—only it's Flynn and me distracting her from Jubilee, rather than Tarver buying Gideon time to reach the rift, plant the virus.

Lilac's back is to us, but Tarver has an easy view, and the second we move, he's alert. Now his hand goes to the gun at his hip, eyes scanning back and forth across us. Lilac turns, moving as gracefully as the real Lilac ever did. She couldn't be more unlike the husks creeping through the wreck.

Flynn's quick to lift his hands, and I follow suit. "We're unarmed," I say, letting my voice shake.

"It's a party," Lilac murmurs, one reddish-gold brow lifting in amusement, though even distracted as I am, a part of my mind notes that her smile is just a fraction off, strained. "I'm curious—what is it you think you can accomplish? I can move faster than any of you, and I'm smarter than all of you. I've had years to study your kind." Her gaze fixes on Flynn, lips quirking. "What's your problem, anyway?" One perfectly manicured hand lifting so she can point a finger at him. "You've still got that one." And unerringly, her hand swings around to point at Jubilee, where she was making her way along the wall in almost perfect silence.

Jubilee's lips draw back into a snarl as she freezes in place. I don't know if she's trying to distract Lilac from the gun in her hand, or if her rage is real. Both, perhaps. "What's his *problem*? You have the blood of hundreds of thousands of people on your hands. You don't even pretend to care! November is burning all around us, and—"

"This is Corinth." Lilac interrupts her smoothly, sounding bored, if anything. "November was years ago." She pauses, and then her lips part and curve into a smile. "Oh, I see now. You didn't arrive with my Tarver—you're here for something different. You came to *kill* me? My, your little group falls apart easily, doesn't it?"

"Easily?" I find my voice, forcing the words out—I have to drag their attention back to me. "The death of whole city sectors is nothing? Just an inconvenience?"

Tarver's eyes move back to me, as do Lilac's, and beyond them, I can see Jubilee lifting the gun. I know the instant the tiniest flicker of my gaze gives me away. Lilac's gaze starts to swing toward Jubilee, and I know that once she sees her, she'll be able to knock her aside as easily as she did Tarver on the *Daedalus*. My senses are keyed up to almost unbearable intensity, my world narrowing down to one movement as Jubilee's finger curls around the trigger.

One shot, Sanjana warned us.

Then the explosion of a shot fired shatters the air and my ears, and I'm back onboard the *Daedalus* after firing the plas-pistol, I'm on Avon right beside an explosion, throwing myself to the ground.

It's not until I drag myself upright again that reality reasserts itself, and I look up to see Tarver standing braced, arm outstretched and holding a gun—the old kind, the kind that fires a bullet, that must have come from the undercity—pointed straight at Jubilee.

The shards of her Gleidel lie scattered around her feet, and she's cradling her hand, shocked still. Some detached part of my mind tries to calculate the odds of someone making that shot—of firing across the room and hitting the gun out of someone's hand as they're still moving.

"Are you okay, Lee?" Tarver's voice is low and tight, and for a moment we each stare stupidly at him, trying to understand the question. "Your hand."

She nods, ashen-faced, then glances toward Flynn, who's still armed with the second of our two guns, pulled from beneath the shop's counter.

Tarver follows her gaze, his own eyes falling on Flynn. "Would you care to try?" he asks him, voice still quiet, still eerily calm. But Flynn just shakes his head, unable to take his gaze away from Jubilee, still huddled on the floor amid the pieces of her gun.

My body's still tingling with shock, my ears still ringing from the gunshot. For a brief instant I think my mind's giving up entirely, as a patch of shadow somewhere beyond and above the rift swims, blurs, shifts. Then I realize what I'm seeing.

Gideon.

He's climbing down, slowly, from the jagged hole in the roof, harness and rope allowing him to rappel silently. I can't see his face from this distance, but he pauses partway down, and somehow I know he's looking back at me, lying in a heap on the floor. I jerk my eyes away before anyone else can see what I saw, and pull myself up with an effort so he'll see I'm okay.

Tarver's got Lilac's attention on him—everyone's attention on him. I try as hard as I can to keep my eyes on Tarver—but though I've always been able to control even the most minute variations in my expression, suddenly it's a struggle not to reveal anything by watching Gideon. Trying with all my heart to make sure I don't draw attention to the boy creeping quietly through the dark, carrying a virus that's either our last hope of stopping her, or the end of the world.

From within my prison, I reach out to the girl they brought back. I catch flashes of her life through her eyes, so brief she cannot know I am there. A sea of faces and cameras as she describes a shipwreck. The glint of a gemstone held between two fingers and a young man's face looking up at her. A house, half-built in the wilderness, the sky thick with stars.

And the blue-eyed man.

Each time I see him I push harder, but the girl's mind is strong. She draws nearer and nearer to my prison and still I cannot breach her defenses. All I need is one chance, a single moment to slip inside her mind, escaping my prison forever.

Then, another flash. A blond girl in a ball gown, holding a weapon. A shattering sound. A blinding pain shooting through us both.

And for an instant, Lilac LaRoux's guard falls.

THIRTY-SIX

GIDEON

MY THROAT'S HALF-CLOSED IN PANIC, AND IT'S ONLY AS Sofia stirs again that I can breathe. I force my shaking hands to still, flex my fingers, and creep forward once again.

"Lilac, darling," Monsieur LaRoux says from his place on the floor. "Can't you just get rid of them all?"

I'd forgotten he was there, and so had the others, judging by the way their heads snap around.

"Their little toys make it so hard to see where they are," Lilac replies. So the shields are reaching far enough to protect me—to protect all of us, since nobody's eyes have turned black just yet. "We're still missing Giddy," she continues, and behind that smile, that nickname that infuriates me coming from her, there's a note of steel in her voice that sends a bolt of ice straight down my spine. *Prey,* that voice says. *That's what you are. And I want to play with you.*

"Bloody Marchant boys, always late," LaRoux mutters.

"My father doesn't understand," Lilac says, addressing Sofia, who stands her ground—albeit swaying slightly—meeting her eyes. "He's chosen to see what he sees now. How could he ever face the truth? He took my freedom from me. My life. My death. He took everything, for his own gain." For a moment it seems she'll say more, but her eyes close, and her shoulders round, tension singing through her frame. A ragged breath later, she's straightening once more.

"The others," Lilac continues, "they don't understand either. The rest of my kind, on the other side of the rift . . . They wanted to find out if humanity is worth knowing, worth learning from. We'd been alone in our universe until your ships started ripping through it, and we thought there was something to be gained from reaching out to you." She breathes out, sharp, disgust in her eyes. "They know nothing. I'm the one who's been here since the start. I'm the one who's seen what you really are."

"Lilac?" LaRoux's voice falters—there's an edge to it, something rough and raw. It's the part of him that understands what's happening, buried under layers of willful misunderstanding and incipient madness.

"The five of you," Lilac whispers, ignoring her father as her eyes rake across us. "And Lilac, this insipid, weak-minded idiot I'm forced to wear. Six souls, linked in ways you cannot possibly comprehend, set on this path to lead you here, now. Every one of you has seen the worst of humanity, and you were meant to show us whether you were worth knowing."

I wish I had the luxury of stopping, of reeling after hearing these words. The idea that our paths were destined to intersect—that I was always going to be here, facing the woman my brother died for, in love with the girl whose father died in the explosion that brought Jubilee and Flynn together, watching Lee's former captain gazing at Lilac's face with his heart in his eyes—I can't breathe.

"But the truth," Lilac goes on, her eyes burning, "is that we never needed any of you. We never had to look any further than the man who opened the very first door."

She turns finally to look at LaRoux, still huddled on the floor, who gazes at her with a pathetic hope in his eyes.

"We will start with our keeper," she whispers. "We will give him the same pain he has given us. We will take his family from him, and all he knows, and every soul who has ever touched him. And then we will close our world to you forever, cut you off from each other and keep you from spreading like the disease you are. We will keep him alive, to watch. And then, once he has realized the thing he has done—then we will leave him, howling, in the darkness that will claim you all."

Jubilee gasps, one hand flying to her gut as though she's been punched. She's swaying on her feet, her gaze distant. She's in some other place, some other moment, just now.

"Lee?" Tarver starts to step forward, then jerks to a halt as Lilac's hand lifts to forbid him movement. But Flynn's already by her side, his hand creeping toward the gun at his hip. I don't know if he has it in him to fire it.

"One of my kind said something rather like that to her, in another place," the whisper replies. "I saw it in her mind up on the ship, before . . ." Her hand lifts, then dives toward the ground, fingers spreading to casually mimic the explosion as the *Daedalus* crashed. "I quite like the sound of it. Seems fair, don't you think?"

I force myself to keep moving—I'm so close to the rift now, and I can feel the thumb drive in my pocket, pressing into my hipbone. Such a small vessel for such a deadly weapon, for the virus I crafted from Sanjana's notes. My one bullet. My one chance.

Lilac gasps suddenly, bowing her head, lifting a hand to run it through her hair—the first sign of anything out of place, disheveled.

"Careful," Sofia says, lifting her chin. "You'll ruin your hair for the cameras." She's playing for time now, time for *me*.

"Hardly," Lilac replies, but there's strain beneath her amusement. "They're trying to come through. I won't let them." The words are murmured, almost to herself, though her eyes go to the rift, the doorway to her universe.

"Lilac, I—" Monsieur LaRoux starts to speak, but Lilac cuts him off with a slice of her hand.

"Do excuse him," she says, light once more, as though he's an embarrassing inconvenience, like an uncle who's had one too many drinks at lunch. "Family. You know how it is."

Sofia steps forward, and though her whole body's shaking, there's a strength holding her spine ramrod straight. "No," she says, soft but clear.

"I'm sorry?" Lilac lofts one brow.

"My father died, thanks to what he did." Sofia lifts a hand, to point one trembling finger at LaRoux. "So I'll never have another chance to 'know how it is.' Jubilee lost her parents, thanks to what he did. Flynn lost his sister in a war sparked by what he did. Gideon lost his brother, thanks to what he did. And Tarver—" Her voice breaks, and she sucks in a rasping breath, forcing herself onward. "Tarver lost Lilac, thanks to what he did."

I shift my weight forward another step—I'm so close to the rift now, the blue sparks are lighting up my vision. The crackle of electricity distorts their voices in my ears, making every hair on my arms stand on end—each movement feels like I'm passing through cobwebs.

They're trying to come through.

That's what she said. She means the other whispers. The blue sparks surge and push, the center of the rift glowing bright. They're trying to come through—and she doesn't want them to.

What does it mean, that she doesn't want them to?

"So you cannot forgive him," the whisper in Lilac's skin supposes, gazing at Sofia's defiant figure. "Nor can I. Yet you seem to object to his punishment. You should applaud it."

"No," Sofia says again.

"No?"

"Every one of them kept their hearts open, despite what he did." Sofia's hands are fists at her side. "They still love. They still trust. Even he loves, monster that he is. He let his love for his daughter guide his actions."

"Love," Lilac repeats, that one syllable imbued with utter disgust. "We once thought that was something to be admired in you, learned from you. Turns out it's just part of the disease you call mankind."

Flynn and Jubilee stand side by side, hands interwoven, as Flynn shifts his grip on his weapon, his jaw squaring.

Tarver stares at Lilac, his desperation writ on his features.

"Love," Sofia echoes, but with a softness, an ache in her voice that's the perfect opposite of that disgust. "And trust. And most important of all, the thing you've forgotten in all your talk of fate and predestined paths . . . choice. That's what makes us human. Love and trust . . . that's what we've all chosen, over and over."

Love, and trust. The things that make us human.

They could have been mine, if only I could have leapt. If only *we* could have leapt.

I pull the thumb drive from my pocket and ease my weight forward infinitely slowly, infinitely carefully. The shaft of light creeping in through the broken side of the *Daedalus* illuminates my face as I draw close, and as if she can't help it, Sofia turns her head to meet my eyes.

I wish I'd had a chance to tell her.

The agony on the soldier's face as he realizes I am not his girl. The terror flooding a thousand minds as the ship begins to fall. A million voices silenced as the city burns. The ease with which I can twist their minds, all this girl's strength mine now.

It all fades in comparison with watching the blue-eyed man's mind crumble. His desperation to believe I am still his Lilac, still the little baby in his arms with the peach-colored hair and the dreamy blue eyes, is a vengeance far sweeter than I could have imagined.

Him I will save for last. I will let him see me, know in his heart that I have taken his daughter from him, while he scrambles to convince himself of a lie. The torture in his own soul is far greater than any pain I could inflict upon him now.

But the rest of mankind . . . they deserve justice.

THIRTY-SEVEN

SOFIA

I HAVE TO LOOK AWAY. I CAN'T LET LILAC FOLLOW MY GAZE and spot Gideon, and I can't let Jubilee or Flynn see him either, in case they panic and try to shoot Lilac. But I can't tear my eyes from his, the blue light of the rift bathing his face.

I can feel Lilac's eyes on me, the weight of her hatred nearly dropping me to my knees. There's nothing there, no hint that the girl I met on the *Daedalus* is still in there. Then she turns and sees Gideon, half hidden behind the rift.

In a heartbeat, everything unspools frame by frame—Tarver diving for Lilac, desperate to give Gideon a chance with the virus—Jubilee grabbing for Flynn's weapon and rolling to find cover—Lilac thrusting out a hand to shove Jubilee, and the fallen block of marble she's hiding behind, against the far wall—Flynn giving a wordless scream and sprinting toward Jubilee, who lies motionless now . . .

Lilac turning toward Gideon. She roars her fury, tearing an impossible sound from her human lungs, lifting both hands as the ship around us starts to scream in duet, metal twisting and wrenching at the seams. A shudder runs the length of the floor, and the ground beneath Gideon bucks violently, sending him tumbling from his place by the rift.

He seems to hang in the air forever, and my heart with him. Then he's crashing to the ground, the thumb drive flying from his hand. He scrambles on all fours, lunging after it—and I scream a warning as a piece of the roof shears away, tumbling down to crush the drive, grinding it into the floor. It grinds every last hope we had into the floor, and I'm reeling, the breath driven from my lungs.

A great chunk of the ceiling drops onto the broken chandelier where it lies on the floor, sending up a spray of glittering glass, and I dive for cover as the deadly shards arc through the air.

"Lilac, *please!*" Tarver's shouting, fighting his way toward her as she turns for the rift, which is now pulsing brighter than ever, casting blue light over every inch of the wrecked ballroom. I can't see Flynn and Jubilee anymore, or Monsieur LaRoux.

Lilac doesn't even bother turning. She simply lifts one arm, and Tarver goes flying—he connects with the wall with a sickening smack, his gun tumbling from his hand. It ricochets off the heaving floor, skittering across to land at my feet. As he staggers upright, his gaze is fixed on me.

The gun is within reach. The virus might be gone, but there's still a chance. All I have to do is stoop and pick it up. Aim it at Lilac's heart. She's facing the rift. I could move before she can turn.

This instant hangs suspended, the energy from the rift lifting the hairs on my skin, crackling against my face, filling my mouth with the taste of metal.

Gideon staggers to his feet, and our eyes lock. I told him he didn't know me, so he couldn't love me. Couldn't trust me, so couldn't love me.

But it was never about that. It was never about Gideon, or wanting to let him in, or believing he was the kind of person who could love what he found there.

It was always me. I've spent so long convincing others to trust me that I no longer trust myself. My own heart. My own instincts and faith.

My choice.

My muscles tense, ready to move. I meet Gideon's eyes again, the warm hazel-green flashing with blue light.

This much I know: I love him.

This much I trust.

I'm not the thing LaRoux made me. I'm not the girl I was on the *Daedalus* anymore. I choose who I am, every day. And I'm choosing now to be *me*.

In this moment I don't need to read Gideon's mind to see into his heart, to share his thoughts—he loves *me*. All of me. The good, the bad, the struggle between the horrible impulses I can never share and the glimmers of hope for things I'm too frightened even to whisper—he sees all of me.

They're trying to come through, Lilac said, and in this instant—which stretches to an eternity—I know what to do. I know that what Gideon and I imagined in the arcade is true—they can see us, they know us. Lilac's whisper said it herself:

You were meant to show us whether you were worth knowing.

The other whispers, in their universe on the other side of the rift, have been watching us. Judging us, testing us, setting us up like pieces on a board to see who we are. And if Gideon can know me, love me, trust me, and I can learn that lesson in return—if we and all our friends and allies can make choices and sacrifices that come from our hearts—then I'm ready for us to be judged.

I'll let the whispers through. I'll short-circuit the rift, just as Tarver and Lilac did once before. I'll make my leap of faith—and trust in their choice.

It's as Gideon holds out his hand that I realize he understands my intention—and that, in every way I could ever have imagined, he's with me.

I leave the gun and everything it made me behind. I break into a run, dimly aware of Tarver's voice shouting something; of Lilac's outraged shriek as she fights him off; of the fact that she ought to be able to crush him with a thought and yet she's struggling, pushing at him with her hands, screaming to be let go. Of the fact that I *must* be beyond the range of the shields now, and yet my mind's my own. I stumble over a pile of debris and scramble, scraping my palms and knees and using the jolt of adrenaline pain brings to move that much faster. I throw myself forward and feel Gideon's hand wrap around mine, the warmth of his touch more real than anything else.

I choose you.

Our fingers interlock, made for each other, like two halves of the same pendant—and together we leap into the rift.

The others, the children we were meant to watch and judge, swarm around me in a futile attempt to either kill Lilac or save her, but they mean nothing now. I have seen humanity. If my brethren have not yet learned how to make choices, then I will make the choice for us all. And those who are not killed when their link to our world is severed, I will seek out myself and destroy.

It is so easy, now, to see the choices these five souls will make. Some will choose to try to kill me—some will try to save me instead. Whichever they choose, they will fail.

But then I see two of them sprinting toward the rift itself, moving too quickly for me to stop. A choice I did not see—a decision I could not have predicted. I reach out to rip their minds away only to have something pull me back, a force coming from within me, a voice saying,

NO.

THIRTY-EIGHT

LILAC

LILAC.

It comes like a light in the dark. Not a voice, not a thought, but the brush of something intangible, like a warm breeze . . . though there's no air, no warmth. Only that sensation: *Lilac.*

I cling to it, desperate for this one glimmer of something in a world of nothing, and it leads me onward through the emptiness until I feel another touch, and then another, and then suddenly I'm surrounded by others like me, overwhelmed by being a part of them again.

I've been here before.

Yes.

On the planet . . . when I was something else. Someone else.

Lilac LaRoux.

I remember. You . . .

We are the . . . Their name for themselves comes not in words but in a rush of feeling—of a billion minds together, infinite thoughts, combining like every color in the universe to form a blinding white truth that, had I breath or voice to do so, would make me cry out. *We have brought you home.*

Home?

When we gave you life, we told you it wasn't time for you to join us. Not yet. But we have seen what we have done to you, and you may remain with us if you wish. Become one of us.

My whole self still aches and throbs with the force of what they are, and the longing to join them, to truly understand, makes it impossible to think.

But . . . there is someone I'm supposed to be. There was a surge that brought me here, memories coming in disjointed flashes. A pair of joined hands, two souls whose choice to sacrifice themselves opened the door to this world. The creature in my body trying to stop them, as I gathered the last of my strength to pull it back. **No . . . you will not hurt them.** The beings on the other side of the door reaching out to pull the tortured creature back into its world.

And there's someone whose face is the only image my dazzled thoughts can summon, like afterimages from staring at the sun.

Tarver.

You are energy, you are of the light. He is humankind, one of billions, and unique. We cannot bring him.

I want to go back.

We have had a decision to make, ever since your people's first ship pierced the stillness—what you call hyperspace. Whether to close the door between our worlds, or leave it open. You have flooded our world with images and words and ideas so powerful that, unchecked, they will destroy us. Pain and loneliness and hatred, and beautiful things too; love for family, for lovers, for friends. Faith. We have learned this from you. And the five who came to save you.

You've been watching us? All this time?

Time, for us, is not quite the same as it is for you. We see all the possibilities ahead. We had to follow those who would know pain and loss and rage, for it is not a fair test to observe those whose lives are free from sadness.

And it's what . . . fate? That we all came together, here, to this spot?

Small nudges, here and there. Within the confines of your father's cages there is little we can do. But tiny changes—ensuring two survivors of a deadly crash, or preventing an explosion from claiming a rebel's life, or drawing a particular identity to a hacker's attention—that we can do.

No. I refuse to believe that all of this was somehow predestined. That we're just puppets performing some play for your amusement.

Not at all. We see the possibilities, Lilac. We know what might *happen, not what* will *happen. And if there is anything we have learned from watching you, it is that mankind never stops surprising us. Your actions are your own. Your choices, good or bad, are yours. As are the choices of your companions.*

And you're basing this decision of yours, whether we're cut off from hyperspace forever, on whether we're good people?

We have no desire to destroy your kind. We know the one, alone, would have done so. But we seek only to preserve our own world's existence. We would allow enough time for your worlds to prepare for the separation, to become self-sustaining, or else relocate their populations. We would then shore up the walls between our universes so that your engines, your signals, could no longer enter.

You said that you have a decision to make. Does that mean you haven't decided yet?

We were waiting for one last emissary to return home.

You . . . you mean the entity that took me over. Used me to kill all those people, threaten the ones I love, threaten our entire way of life.

Yes.

My father tortured that creature—it's horrible, what happened to it, but you can't judge a whole species by the actions of one man. There are monsters among us, it's true. But there are heroes too. There are people who fight men like him. Who will never stop fighting men like him.

Our choice remains ahead of us. Blow open this rift for good, allow our kind to explore your world and understand it, and there is no guarantee your human qualities would not eventually destroy us, as they destroyed our last emissary. Or, sever your universe's tie to ours once and for all, guaranteeing the survival of our species, the preservation of our world. We can send you back to them, or keep you here with us if you choose, but whether we open the gates to join your world or close them to you forever . . . that we cannot decide.

Why not?

Of all the things mankind has taught us, the strangest one for us to comprehend is choice. For us all things are possible, and all things that can be, will be. To choose one existence or another . . . it is a human ability, to shape your own fate. We need your help.

I let my thoughts open to them, my sense of self blurring at the edges as I try to feel what they feel, to understand what they've absorbed from us. The rage is there, a simmering force like a storm about to break. This is what the whispers fear, the fire consuming their world.

I let them touch my grief over Simon's death, the newly opened wound of my mother's death all those years ago, the sadness and guilt at being one of the only survivors from the *Icarus*. I let them see my anger at my father, the gut-wrenching stab of betrayal, the simmering rage at the creature who used me to wreak such destruction. Then, with an effort, I reach for those other, deeper memories, slipping past the coating of pain and hatred into what lies beyond.

Because behind it lies something more, a rainbow of deeper forces, waiting to be summoned. The joy of a little girl whose dreams have been painted the color of the sea. The loyalty of a boy who is ready to defend his home with his bare hands and the force of his will. The love of a man whose faith transcends death, whose strength feels like fire and poetry.

The fire of a girl who had everything taken from her, and still found it within herself to leap into the unknown to open this door. The determination of a boy who held out his hand to leap with her, who had faith in that moment that we were all worth saving, if only we had the chance to prove it.

This chance.

> And from the inside, surrounded by the joy and devo-
> tion and loyalty of my friends, the shimmer of rage
> on the outside of our lives looks paper-thin.

As my thoughts open to them, I catch the faintest taste of their minds as well. They are far beyond anything I've ever known, the weight of infinite minds so entwined it's impossible to know where one stops and another begins. I can feel what we've given them, the swell of emotions and ideas they don't understand. But behind the fear, the anger, the desire for safety, I sense something all too familiar . . . longing.

I pause, trying to form my dazzled thoughts into words. We've always wondered if mankind was alone in the universe. Somewhere, behind the ever-expanding frontier of new planets and terraformed moons, there's always been a sense of being incomplete, that we were searching for something else. Something more, something greater than ourselves. To be alone in this universe is an emptiness none of us could bear.

Is it possible that, for all our differences, for all the ways we don't and never could understand each other, the whispers don't want to be alone either?

Help us choose.

I can't. I can't tell you that if you stay, and learn from us, and learn to understand us, your kind will be safe. Because if you stay, then rage and grief and pain are inevitable. To live is to feel these things.

So you would have us leave?

On this side of the rift, in this world, nothing is certain. But the only shields against the darkness are the moments that bring light, and you have seen that in these people, their stories. They are unique, and they are all the same. I can think of no better armor. And we can teach you how to forge your own shields.

Think of everything you've learned from us, everything we've been through, every choice the six of us have made that has brought us here. Having experienced that, having felt life, love, trust, faith . . . can you really give it all up just to be *safe*?

I wait for an answer, but get no reply. I feel their minds pulling away from mine, and an insistent tug that I instinctively know is my tether to my own world, my own body. For a moment I want to cling to this world, to the shards of another kind of existence that no human could ever hope to truly understand.

But I have to let it all slip away and fade back into the light, wrapping myself once more in the roaring quiet. Into my thoughts creeps a single image, a pair of clasped hands—and with it, a single voice, saying, *I choose you.*

I will not go back. The pain is all there is—all I am,
all I have to give. I am no longer one of you, and I
cannot become part of you again. I cannot go home.

> We are a part of you. You have been alone
> so long, but you will always belong with us.

Not anymore. I am vengeance. I am fear. I
am everything you should leave behind.

> We will learn to bear the dark-
> ness. They will show us how.

You cannot understand. I . . . I will not bring
this pain to you. I could not bear to see it
shared. Please, just let me go. Let me die.

> If that is truly what you wish, that choice is yours to
> make. But we have seen how brightly light shines in
> the dark, how sweetly music fills the quiet. All these
> years you have known only shadow and silence,
> and we have so much to show you. To save you.

I am not worth saving.

> We are all worth saving.

How can you know?

> We cannot ever know, not truly.

> But we have faith.

THIRTY-NINE

GIDEON

SOMETHING STIRS AGAINST ME, AND AS I BLINK MY EYES
open, blue sparks still playing across my vision, I register Sofia's warmth
against my chest. *Are we in my den? Did she crawl up to my end of the bed?*

For a moment I'm in an impossibly vast place, my thoughts expanding
with infinite speed—and then, an instant later, that space is contracting,
flying back toward me until the world is the right size and shape again.

Like a bucket of cold water, the truth splashes over me, electrifying
and sudden. We're lying on the ground, piled on top of the rubble by the
rift like so much debris, and Sofia's wrapped in my arms.

"Did it work?" she whispers in an exhausted rasp. Then, almost as an
afterthought, she adds, "Are we alive?"

My ribs are bruised, my shoulder aching where I think I landed on it,
but I push upright, looking around for some sign of the others.

I see Flynn and Jubilee immediately. She's muttering a curse in another
language she must have learned from him, judging by the way he seems
to understand it. I make eye contact with Flynn, and he lifts a hand to
signal that they're okay.

I follow his gaze across to where Tarver sits in the center of the room,
curled in on himself. He starts to straighten, moving like every part of
him is in pain. Like an old man.

". . . the hell was that?" Jubilee groans.

"Disrupting the rift sets the whispers free," I say, trying to climb
to my feet and failing. "It worked on Elysium when Tarver and Lilac

jumped. It worked on Avon, for you. She said they were trying to come through, and since she didn't want them to . . . we thought maybe they would help us stop her."

Beside me, Sofia sucks in a breath as I say Lilac's name. "Gideon, where's Lilac?"

"She just . . ." Flynn's voice dies away. "She vanished. Pulled into the rift with you."

My gaze sweeps the room frantically, and I try to climb to my feet again, staggering and crashing back down onto one knee as my legs give out. *No. No, no, no.* I felt her in the rift. In the instant we passed through that infinite space, I sensed her there, I know it.

Early morning sun's creeping in through the tears in the *Daedalus*'s hull now, chasing away the shadows, and there's nowhere she could be hiding. Her father lies in one corner of the ruined room, gazing at the rift as though conducting some mental calculation or conversation.

As I force breath into my lungs, grasp helplessly for what to do next, the light abruptly changes. The lazy blue sparks of the rift grow frantic and the room darkens, as though all the light is being pulled from our surroundings into that one focal point.

The soft electric hum of the rift rises without warning, and as the sparks grow unbearably bright, it lifts to a high-pitched scream, building in pressure every second.

Across the room, Lee's screaming something at us, but I can't hear her over the noise. I make out the words at the last instant—*get away.* Moving as one, Sofia and I scramble over the mound of debris, throwing ourselves down the other side as Tarver dives for the edge of the room, and Flynn and Lee roll together behind a block of stone. My heart's racing, my ears are ringing, my lungs are constricting as the room trembles—it feels like any second the *Daedalus* will disintegrate around us.

A deafening roar swallows up the scream of the rift, and as I close my eyes, my last glimpse is of the metal frame containing the light exploding into a thousand glittering shards, hanging in the air like stars. The blue sparks snake outward in a frenzied dance, splintering all around us.

And then there's silence. Perfect silence.

Sofia moves first, crawling back up the pile of debris that sheltered us, and reaching back to offer me her hand. I take it, curling my fingers through hers as I scramble up beside her to prop myself up on my elbows. The others are creeping out from their hiding places to stare too—the light is still there, once more coalesced into the tall oval shape of the rift. But where it was once a cold, pale blue glow, the rift now shines with a golden light, shimmering and rich.

And the machinery containing it—the cage—is gone.

For several long seconds we all simply watch it, trying to force our exhausted brains into action one more time, trying to understand what to do next. Then the frame of the *Daedalus* gives a shuddering groan, and it's as if we're startled back to life.

Tarver climbs to his feet, stumbling two steps forward, as if he's going to walk straight into the rift. But he stops short, simply staring at it as the light plays over his haunted face.

There's a figure crumpled at the base of the rift, and gingerly it pushes up to its feet, sending up a cloud of dust that settles slowly back to earth once more.

White dust clings to the hem of her black dress, and her hair's half undone, falling down her back. She's no longer flawless—she's splendidly, gloriously, imperfectly human.

It's Lilac.

She's shivering as if with sudden cold, dust turning her red hair the color of ash. Only the steady warmth of Sofia's hand in mine tells me I'm not dreaming or hallucinating. Lilac's eyes rake the room, darting from person to person, but it's who she doesn't look at that stands out—she'll look anywhere but at the ex-soldier by the fallen chandelier, whose eyes won't leave her face.

No one speaks, too afraid of what her response might be—no one wants to break the spell, the hope, that her mind is her own again. In the silence there are a million possibilities, and for this brief instant she can be just Lilac again, even if the next brings all of it crashing down again.

Finally, she's the one to shatter the quiet. "Somebody say something," she murmurs. "Please?"

"Oh my God, it's her." That's Jubilee, who comes lurching to her feet and breaks into an unsteady jog toward the girl in the rubble, Flynn a step behind her.

Lilac's blue eyes, round and haunted, flick toward her. She swallows, fearful, and for a moment I can feel her uncertainty like my own. How *does* a girl begin to apologize for attempting to destroy mankind? But before she can speak, Jubilee, unhesitating, throws herself at her friend, pulling her into a hug and squeezing free a laugh that's only slightly hysterical with exhaustion and release, and Flynn's arms wrap around the both of them.

My legs finally obey orders, and I begin to scramble down the other side of the pile of broken marble we'd been sheltering behind, Sofia's hand still in mine.

Lilac, her arms still tangled around Jubilee, lifts her head and looks our way. She sees me first, and I recognize the flicker that crosses her face—it's the ghost of Simon that she sees in me, and her smile softens. "Thank you," she whispers.

Her eyes meet Sofia's, and something passes between the two of them—recognition, memory, understanding, forgiveness, all in an instant.

But still she hasn't looked at Tarver, who's motionless, rooted to the spot where he stood as Lilac came back through the dimensional portal. Her eyes fix somewhere past Jubilee's shoulder, every line of her body tense, as if fighting some invisible force trying to drag her face toward him.

Jubilee glances toward her old captain, then gives Lilac's arm a squeeze and she and Flynn release her, stepping back.

"Lilac—" Tarver doesn't get any further, and if I hadn't seen his lips move, I wouldn't have recognized the hoarse, heartsick voice as his. He takes a few stumbling steps toward her, but halts a pace or two away.

Lilac crumples at the sound of his voice—her eyes are wet, lips trembling, hands twisting in the grimy fabric of her dress. She shuts her eyes and sends tears streaking down her cheek, turning toward Tarver in a rush. "I'm so sorry," she blurts, voice rising with emotion, words running together and spilling out in a torrent. "I couldn't stop her—stop it—I could see it all, hear every word, and I couldn't . . . it was like the things I said to you on the *Icarus*, only a thousand times worse, a million times worse, because I could feel it too, her hatred. God, Tarver—none of it was—"

"You think I care about any of that?" Tarver cuts through the torrent, and if her voice is bright and rich and throbbing with emotion and anguish, his is low and quiet. Only the hoarseness of it, the visible effort in the lines of his shoulders, his legs, as he holds himself still, shows what's going on below it all.

Lilac's left breathing hard, the flood of words stemmed for now, and though I can only see her profile, I can see the rest of what she's left unsaid written plainly across her face—so plainly I feel my own cheeks heating, and Sofia's fingers tighten through mine as she draws in against me.

"I held on." Lilac swallows, her eyes on Tarver's. Her voice is very quiet now, barely more than a whisper. "So I could come back to you."

I can't tell which one of them breaks first—but suddenly she's moving forward, and Tarver's striding toward her, and then he's holding her so tightly her feet leave the ground, and her arms go around his neck, and their lips meet and stay there. The longing and desperation and healing in that kiss keeps spreading, like the warm glow of the rift behind them and the creatures just beyond the portal sending their fractured light cascading through the ruined ballroom, bathing all of us in gold.

It's some time later that Jubilee clears her throat. "Well, I don't know about any of you, but I'm *starving*. I think there's some crackers and peanut butter left, if our gear didn't get pulverized."

"Uh . . ." I glance back toward the rift, and toward the single silhouetted shape that is Tarver and Lilac, still locked together. "What about them?"

Jubilee snorts, her voice dry as she replies, "I'm pretty sure we're just distant blurry shapes to them now."

We get no retort from the couple, and for a moment I think maybe they didn't even hear her—and then Tarver unwinds one arm from the small of Lilac's back so he can lift his hand in a particularly rude gesture at Jubilee that makes her break into laughter.

As Flynn and Jubilee climb across the rubble to pull their packs out from underneath a chunk of debris, Sofia and I draw slowly together. The silence between us is different, now, filled with all the things that passed wordlessly between us in the instant before we jumped into the rift.

The choice she made, to leave the gun at her feet and trust hope instead, has left her flushed and breathless. Slowly, hesitantly, her lips curve into the smile I love so much—the lopsided, one-dimpled smile that tells me she's not wearing any mask, not playing any game. This smile is just her, and it's for me.

"I feel different," she whispers, still glowing gold in the rift's light.

"You're not," I whisper in reply. "You're exactly the girl I always knew you were."

She softens in reply, reaching up to curl her arms around my neck, and just as I'm thinking Tarver and Lilac picked exactly the best way to celebrate, the moment's broken by a shout from Jubilee.

All four of us whirl around, but there's no danger here—Kumiko Mori's there, embracing Jubilee, and Mae and Sanjana are climbing past her into the ruined ballroom. All three of them are filthy, showing signs of the fight outside, but they all wear exhausted smiles.

"The husks are down," Sanjana says. "They collapsed, and now some of them are starting to wake up. We knew you must have . . ." She trails off, staring at the new rift, uncaged and golden.

I look past her to meet Mae's gaze, and drink in her smile. Even after I brought danger to her door, to her family, she came to help me. I never knew the Knave had anyone who'd do that for him. Then again, I don't think she did it for the Knave. I think she did it for *me*.

A noise from the edge of the room makes us pause, and we exchange confused glances—then a faint moan echoes through the sudden silence. Lilac breaks away from Tarver, her gaze suddenly anguished—and it's not until she's running toward the source of the sound that I even remember that there was a seventh person with us before the rift exploded.

Monsieur LaRoux.

By the time the rest of us reach Lilac's side, she's crouched on the dusty, cracked floor, one hand half-out toward the man curled a meter away. His white hair is gray with dust from the explosion, the grime on his lined face cut through with swaths left by tears on his cheeks. He's got his arms wrapped around himself, wedged into a corner of debris, watery blue eyes fixed some distance past his daughter's face.

"Daddy?" Lilac whispers, voice shaking, tentative. "Daddy . . . it's me. It's Lilac."

But the LaRoux Industries titan doesn't even seem to hear her, his eyes never wavering. He's murmuring under his breath, and only as he exhales and the words rise in volume for an instant can I make out what he's saying. ". . . and we'll all be happy again . . ."

I glance at Sofia, whose face is grim. She has every bit as much reason to hate this man as I do, and yet I see my own heart mirrored there in her expression. When I look at the tiny shadow of a man huddled on the floor, it's hard to find that hatred anymore, the bitter-edged determination that's driven me on since Simon's death. I look down at him and feel nothing—I look down at him and feel . . . pity.

Flynn draws my attention with a soft intake of breath, and when I lift my head, he's pointing at the rift behind me. I twist, heart rate spiking as my exhausted body tries to ready itself for . . . something. There's a gold mist, silken and ethereal, slowly creeping out from the rift in strands that grow stronger and brighter by the moment.

"What is that?" Tarver whispers, from where he crouches.

"It's them," Lilac replies, just as softly. "They're going to leave the barriers down. We have . . . a lot to learn from them. And they want to know us, to learn from us what it means to be human."

"I think," Flynn murmurs, "that they just had their first lesson."

"What do we do with him now?" Jubilee asks, hesitant, looking down at Roderick LaRoux.

"I don't think there's anything left *to* do to him now." Lilac's grief is visible, and for an instant I'm back in the LaRoux mansion courtyard, listening to Tarver speak to her father. *She's perhaps the only person, the last person, in this existence to care for you at all.*

"What do we do with *ourselves* now?" Sofia's voice is quiet, but near enough to my ear that it resonates through my bones.

Lilac dashes her hand across her eyes and straightens, exhaling as Tarver's arm curls around her waist. "Now . . ." she starts, eyes shifting to sweep across the rest of us. "Now, we rebuild."

We are whole again.

We are the weary ones who waited, forgotten, for a pair of ship-wrecked lovers to set us free. We are the angry ones who fought, all too eager to bring pain to those who brought pain to us. We are the strong ones who loved, and were loved, discovering hope in stolen dreams and in the clasp of fingers made to interlock.

And we are the darkest ones, who lived in agony and in rage, and found that even in silence and darkness there is always a spark.

We are, and will always be, what we choose.

FORTY

SOFIA

WITH A FAINT CLUNK, THE DOOR TO GIDEON'S NEW DEN SHUTS behind me. He's sprawled on the mattress on the floor that serves as a couch, and looks up to flash a smile at me—or at the armful of takeout I've got with me, sending the smells of coriander and coconut milk and lime wafting through the air.

"Mrs. Phan made her first batch of laksa," I announce, crossing the room to flop onto the mattress next to him.

In the three weeks since the crash of the *Daedalus*, Gideon's managed to put together a reasonably respectable den. He's satisfied with the security of his hypernet lines, and this time there's a fridge for food that doesn't come in foil packets. I'd planned on getting my own place, knowing Gideon's almost religious obsession with anonymity, but before I could even raise the issue, he'd programmed a security code for me. He had to rewrite his whole system to make it possible for there to be more than one entry password, but there it was, waiting for me. Along with a row of skylights letting in actual light, through a clever series of mirrors leading up shafts to the surface above the undercity.

Gideon digs in, practically ripping the bag open in his eagerness to get to the soup inside. "Good call, Dimples," he says, already reaching for the chopsticks and spoons. "They'll be celebrating her reopening from here to the next sector."

The streets outside in the undercity are still strewn with debris, still harboring displaced folks with nowhere else to go, still draped with mourning banners of black, white, blue, and gray, but more sectors have power every day. One by one, businesses are coming back to life, families are finding each other, and the community is taking its first, shaky steps toward normalcy.

I thought about seeing what shape Kristina's penthouse suite was in, but the truth is, this is where I want to be. With the people hit hardest by all that's happened. People like me and Gideon.

Though a series of monitors and hard drives were Gideon's first purchases for the new den, he hasn't found a console chair he likes yet. I've got the sneaking suspicion, though, that he's putting off finding a chair because sitting on the mattress means there's room for me beside him. Bowl in one hand, he wraps the other around me and pulls me in close against his side.

"Did they start yet?" I ask, reaching over with my chopsticks to snag a mouthful of noodles out of his bowl. His main monitor, connected to a feed he jacked into from the central grid, shows an aerial view of a seething crowd gathered by the *Daedalus* crash site, secured now with structural supports and construction scaffolding as they rebuild those layers of the city. He's got the skylights shuttered, so the monitor colors are bright and sharp.

"A few minutes ago, I think. Muñoz is speechifying. . . . Here, I'll unmute it." He flicks his fingers at the monitor, and suddenly the dull roar of the crowd and the president's voice come through the speaker system.

"'We are not alone.'" The camera drone circles in closer to President Muñoz, who stands behind a lectern, gazing out at the crowd as her words ring out. "Words mankind has imagined hearing for centuries, ever since the first ancient peoples looked up at the stars and made them gods. I stand here today in front of our answer—we are not, we have never been, alone." Behind her is the rift, its golden glow visible even in the bright noonday sun. With the doorway between universes permanently open, the whispers—officially named the Collective—have been slowly exploring our world outside the confines of LaRoux's machinery. They've been met with suspicion, with anger, with curiosity, with reverence— and, mostly, with hope. Thanks to their aid, the reconstruction of the city after the crash has gone twice as fast as we could have done it on our own.

President Muñoz takes a beat, eyes scanning the faces of the crowd. "Now we know that intelligence, empathy, and curiosity are not only human traits. We have much to teach, and much to learn. We will enrich each other's lives as we build a foundation of trust, and hope. I know many among us have questions, or even fears—I know many find that, especially in light of our terrible losses, trust does not come easily. That is why I have created a new position, one voice to speak for the Collective, and to the Collective. In light of all that has happened, some of you may find this decision surprising. But our new ambassador is eloquent and poised, and remains the only human being ever to join, however briefly, with the Collective on the other side of the rift. And no one has reason to work harder toward peace and reconstruction. Please join me in congratulating Ambassador LaRoux."

The president steps back, to make way for the new ambassador to join her at the podium.

"There she is!" I squeal, poking at Gideon's leg with my chopsticks. "Holy cow, look at that dress. Jeez, she wasn't kidding."

"I still like yours better," Gideon says around a mouthful of noodles. "The one with the lights and the fringe."

"The one that got shredded and full of holes because I was wearing it during a spaceship crash?" I eye him sidelong. "I think there's more dress missing than there."

"Why do you think I like it?"

I stab at his knee again with my chopsticks. "Shush, I want to hear."

As the president swears Lilac in to her new position, the camera drone pans across the delegations from each planet. My eyes are trying to find the Celtic knot and single star of Avon's crest, but it's Flynn's face that jumps out of the crowd at me first. I grab at Gideon's arm, but he's already grinning. Jubilee's sitting next to Flynn, and the sunrise-peach color of her dress is beautiful in the sunlight. I don't think it'd be noticeable if you weren't looking for it, but I can see Flynn's got his eyes on her, rather than on the dais up by the rift.

As President Muñoz shakes Lilac's hand and retreats to one of the seats on the dais, Lilac steps up to the microphones.

A few days ago, when all six of us gathered in Flynn's hotel room for dinner, Lilac spent most of it ashen-faced in the corner, writing on and tearing up note cards, as Tarver warned the rest of us not to bring up her upcoming speech at the swearing-in ceremony.

You'd never know it to look at her now, though. The smile most people know from cosmetics billboards and style magazines doesn't waver—her hands are steady. She's wearing green, a billowing dress cut in a fashion several years old, but it's beautiful on her. Tarver's face is distant, his eyes on her as the breeze ripples the fabric.

"My father," Lilac begins, her voice echoing as it bounces back from speakers spread throughout the crowd, "is a brilliant man. Growing up, I believed he could do no wrong. I imagined him like one of the ancient gods the president spoke of, fit company for the stars."

Her eyes scan the crowd as she pauses to take a breath. "But the stars aren't gods, and neither was my father. What he was—what he *is*—is human. Everything he did, every path he took, he believed was right. His mistake wasn't a lust for power or fame or riches; it wasn't hubris and arrogance; it wasn't even the subjugation of an entire species."

Behind her the rift's glow wavers, a few filaments of gold whispering through it, curling through Lilac's hair and settling around the dais. The Collective, too, is listening to what she has to say.

"Roderick LaRoux's mistake was in believing that he had the right to make the world's decisions for us. Believing that the burden of choice was thrust upon him, and him alone, was ultimately what destroyed him. He once named a ship the *Icarus*—and stood shocked with the rest of the galaxy when it fell from the sky in flames." She glances over her shoulder, the camera panning toward Tarver, whose poker face has only gotten better over the last few weeks of media coverage. "But free will is what it means to be human, and no one can determine the path you take through this universe. Choice is our greatest right, our greatest gift—and our greatest responsibility."

Lilac glances down, though the aerial shots show she has no note cards. She's quiet so long that I glance at Gideon, worried she's forgotten the rest of her speech. I can no longer even hear the crowd through the ambient microphones, so complete is the silence. It's as though all of

Corinth—all of the galaxy, watching on the hyperspace feeds—is holding its breath.

But then she lifts her head, and the performer in me recognizes like skill in her. She's an orator—and no one ever knew her poise could be so powerful.

"So now, here, today, we all have a choice." Lilac's voice rises, passion evident even through the distortion of the speakers. "The world is forever changed now that the rift is opened for good. We will never be alone in the vastness of this universe again. So we can choose to greet these new beings with suspicion and mistrust, with blame and anger. Or we can choose to show them why humanity is worth knowing, worth joining, worth saving."

She pauses then, as if waiting for her audience—the hundreds of thousands of people gathered in the streets of Corinth, the billions watching on screens across the galaxy, and me, on this beat-up mattress with Gideon's arm around me—to make that choice for themselves.

"I, for one, have made my choice." Lilac tips her head up, eyes sweeping the scaffolding forming the framework of the Headquarters building being rebuilt around the rift. "Which is why my husband and I are taking over LaRoux Industries and dedicating its considerable resources to the rebuilding of our city, and to learning everything our new neighbors have to share with us. The new headquarters you see under construction now will be a place for anyone, human or not, to come and learn, and share stories and memories of what it is to be human. They want to know it all—the good, the bad, the darkness and the light. They want *you* to bring your stories."

Lilac drops her eyes to the crowd again, her smile, that infectious, galactically famous smile, returns. "The *Icarus* was named in arrogance. Now, we turn that tradition of names to something good, something hopeful. This new project will be called Eos—named for the ancient goddess of the dawn, in honor of the new world we've found ourselves in. It's my hope that as this new day arrives on planets everywhere across the galaxy, we can all see hope in the dawn."

There's a silence after she finishes, a brief moment that nonetheless stretches with a dozen possibilities. But then the crowd erupts, the sound levels on the feeds frantically adjusting themselves to compensate for the roar. I see Lilac's lips moving, and though I can't hear her over the crowd, I read the words easily enough: *Thank you.*

The news announcers begin chattering breathlessly, ready to start dissecting the speech and analyzing the political ramifications, as the aerial camera shows Lilac stepping back away from the podium, returning to Tarver, who clasps her hand in both of his and raises it to his lips.

Gideon flicks his hands at the screen to mute the news anchors, then sticks his chopsticks into his noodles and leans back. He's silent for a while, then lets his breath out in a low whistle. "Damn."

"You mean she didn't make stirring, epic speeches when you were kids?" I tease, leaning harder against his shoulder.

"She was more into reprogramming the house bots with my brother to say, 'Giddy's a loser who should stop trying to spy on us,' really."

I laugh, scrambling off the mattress so I can collect our leftovers and shove them in the fridge. As I rinse off the spoons in the sink, I find myself thinking about the Eos project, and what story I want to bring. I think of my father teaching me to dance. I think of Flynn's sister, and the memory I have of her stopping a bully from rubbing mud in my hair. I think of the first con I ever pulled with Daniela, and the jug of wine we bought with part of the profits and drank together on the roof.

The truth is that I don't know what story defines me. I've spent so long being someone else, anyone else other than Sofia, that I'm not sure I know who Sofia is. There's no more Kristina, no more Lucy, no more Alexis or Alice. There's no more Knave either, not unless and until Gideon decides to resurrect him. For now we're just Gideon and Sofia— whoever they are.

Whoever we choose to become.

Gideon rises from the mattress, turning off the monitors and reaching for the pulleys that operate the shutters on the skylights so that they flood the little loft-size den with sunlight. "So what do you want to do now?"

I tilt my head back, letting the light warm my face. Perhaps I'll bring them the story of a girl who lived a long time ago, in a country called Iran on Earth, who wrote the most beautiful music I've ever heard. Music that changed my life.

When I open my eyes, I see a flicker of shadow in the skylight shaft above me. I blink just in time to see a butterfly silhouetted against the light before it's gone in a flutter of wings.

I look down to find Gideon leaning against the wall, where the framed picture of my father rests on the shelf next to his battered copy of *Alice in Wonderland*. He's watching me with a smile that only widens when I catch his eye.

I hold out my hand. "Come dance with me."

ACKNOWLEDGMENTS

AS WE WRAP UP OUR FIRST SERIES TOGETHER—THOUGH definitely not our last—we are both reflecting on the many people who have helped these books on their journeys from us to you. We are so very grateful to each and every one.

Our wonderful literary agents, Josh and Tracey Adams of Adams Literary, are quite simply incredible. Josh, Tracey, we couldn't get by without your support, your cheerleading, your words of wisdom, and your advocacy. We couldn't have done this without you there to back us up. To our film agent, Stephen Moore, and the awesome scouts and foreign agents who helped these books find homes in languages we can't even read, thank you so much!

This series has been lucky enough to have three wonderful women editing it, and we want to thank Emily Meehan, Laura Schreiber, and Abby Ranger, who at different stages have taught us, supported us, and challenged us to tell the best stories we can. Thank you for your insight, your questions, and your well-timed and encouraging swoons! Beyond our editors, we have a team at Hyperion we adore, and we thank them for everything they do to get our books out into the world—you are all just wonderful! To Jamie Baker, who has endless patience and savvy, and Whitney Manger, who gave this series the covers we join the rest of the world in adoring, thank you! In Australia, we send a huge thank-you and plenty of baked goods to everyone at Allen & Unwin, whom we love more than cupcakes. And that's saying something.

We have had wonderful readers and critique partners for these books, and for *Their Fractured Light*, we thank Olivia Davis, Michelle Dennis, Kate Irving, and Brendan Cousins for their speed, enthusiasm, and insight. You are all wonderful! We also thank Dr. Ailie Connell and Dr. Kate Irving for medical advice, and Michelle Dennis for her tech know-how—as always, any mistakes are our own.

We have had wonderful help and support from our friends inside and outside the publishing community. In particular, we would like to thank Beth Revis and Marie Lu, who have been advocates for this trilogy since the very beginning, Kim Nguyen, who is our design guru (and dear friend!), as well as Stephanie Perkins, Megan Shepherd, Leigh Bardugo, Jay Kristoff, and Nic Crowhurst, who are simply vital to our existence. To the many wonderful people in our circles of friends, we love you!

We dedicated each book in this series to our families, for more reasons than we can ever capture here. For your support, excitement, patience, and love, thank you to our parents and siblings, and to our extended families—the Cousins family, the Miskes, and Mr. Wolf. To Brendan, who has been in it with us both since the beginning—you are amazing.

And finally, we would like to say thank you to *you*. We would tell stories to each other even if no one else ever read them, but it increases the joy tenfold to know you have all shared Lilac, Tarver, Flynn, Jubilee, Gideon, and Sofia's journey with us. Your letters and e-mails, artwork, music, and even recipes have surprised and amazed us! To the booksellers, librarians, reviewers, bloggers, and *readers* who have joined us on this journey, thank you! If you'd like to hear more about the books we have coming up next, or if you're not quite ready to leave the Starbound books behind just yet, we hope you'll sign up for our mailing list at www.thesebrokenstars.com—we want to stay in touch!